Low-Life Deeps: An Account of the Strange Fish to Be Found There

James Greenwood

LOW-LIFE DEEPS AN ACCOUNT OF THE
STRANGE FISH TO BE FOUND THERE BY JAMES GREENWOOD
AUTHOR OF "THE WILDS OF LONDON" *A NEW EDITION* London
CHATTO AND WINDUS, PICCADILLY
1881

Preface

THE best excuse I have to offer for so soon again venturing to set before the public yet another book composed of selections from my contributions to the Daily Press, is the favour with which the last - "The Wilds of London," was generally received. Moreover, it may be claimed for the present volume that it is not entirely re-print. Included in it are several hitherto unpublished articles - "Sunday in the City," "A Fallen Star," "Down Ratcliff Way," and "A Night with old Tom." There is also another trifle of "original matter," for which I would respectfully bespeak the kind reader's attention. It refers to a subject which has occasioned me more anxiety and disquiet than any other that in my long experience it has been my lot to deal with. I allude to the Dog and Man Fight, witnessed by me last year, in Hanley, Staffordshire, and described at the time in the columns of the Daily Telegraph. I sincerely hope that the "further particulars" herein and for the first time made known, although not so absolutely conclusive as I could desire, will, at all events, go far towards convincing the most incredulous that the "Man and Dog Fight" was a Fact.

JAMES GREENWOOD
Upper Holloway
October, 1875

Contents

Chapter 1: In the Potteries
Chapter 2: A Fallen Star
Chapter 3: A Night on Waterloo Bridge
Chapter 4: A Moonlight Excursion to Rosherville
Chapter 5: Sunday in the City
Chapter 6: "Bummarees"
Chapter 7: Bendigo's Conversion
Chapter 8: Charles Orton's Confession
Chapter 9: The Italy of Leather Lane
Chapter 10: "Down Ratcliff Way"
Chapter 11: Curiosities of "Alley" Life
Chapter 12: London Factory Girls
Chapter 13: The Ice Harvest
Chapter 14: The London 'Busman
Chapter 15: Cellar Life in St. Giles
Chapter 16: A Cockney Holiday
Chapter 17: A Night with "Old Tom"
Chapter 18: London's Bane

Chapter 19: A Coal "Marriage"
Chapter 20: Some Secrets of Gipsy Life
Chapter 21: The Last Day in the Old Country
Chapter 22: Baby Greybeards
Chapter 23: The Betting Baker
Chapter 24: Master Jonathan Maxsey
Chapter 25: A "Round" with a Tally-man
Chapter 26: The Day's Work of a London "Cadger"
Chapter 27: A Queer Christmas Party
Chapter 28: "To All in Debt and Difficulty"
Chapter 29: Barnet Fair
Chapter 30: A Londoner's Sunday Outing

ALMOST every day of the week, in the summer season, there appear in the newspapers urgent and touching appeals directed to the benevolent for the promotion of philanthropic schemes to enable the multitude of court and alley dwellers of London, especially the little children, to enjoy just one day out in the green country or by the sea side. It is a fact, however, despite all that has been said and written respecting the unparalleled disadvantages of the unfortunates in question, that, in the matter of opportunity for inhaling fresh air and enjoying rural sights and sounds, there are other cities and places the inhabitants of which are worse off twenty times than they are. There is not a back-street resident in any part of the metropolis who has not, within thirty minutes' walk of his own door - supposing him not to be a cripple, and to be able to step out briskly as does a man eager for the distant feast which is already spread for him - a broad and handsome, well-wooded, green-sloped, flower-bedecked park, where he may roam about to his heart's content.

Such blessings are not vouchsafed to all townsfolk. Take the people of one of the largest towns - Manchester, for instance. Recently I happened to be in that vast and prosperous city, and walked out in the morning, under the fiercely hot June sun, to see what the suburbs were like, and presently I came to Ardwick Park. We Londoners have a queer sort of park, so called, Whetstone by name, situated somewhere behind the houses in Lincoln's Inn Fields; but Whetstone Park is merely a little joke with us on account of its diminutive size, and the fact that no green thing grows there. Ardwick Park, Manchester, is larger than Whetstone, but not vastly so. It is a wedge-shaped bit of ground, and, as regards size, bears about the same relation to our Regent's and Victoria Parks as a pound and a half piece cut out of a Cheshire cheese does to the half-hundredweight of which it formed part. It is a regular park though, and has its lodge at the gate, and the customary notice-board of pains and penalties against flower-pickers, gamblers, and trespassers on paths which are sacred; but for all that, and regarding it as a pleasure-ground, it is but a sad-looking enclosure. It is paved evenly with pepper and salt-coloured asphalt, with here and there an edging of grass, as wide in comparison as is the list to the broad-cloth, with here and there a few flowers of the hardier kinds languishing in beds of sickness and unmistakably dying of consumption.

But the gem of the Ardwick Park is a fountain in the middle of a good-sized basin, in which are rockwork and gold and silver fish, and all round the basin are fixed seats, that at a pinch might accommodate a hundred and fifty sitters. On that bright Sunday morning, every form was as completely occupied as are the seats in the pit of a theatre when a popular piece is being played, and all by working folk, while scores of other work-people, too late for the front rows, sauntered over the hot asphalt, patiently waiting for a chance to sit down and enjoy at their ease the beauties of nature, and listen to the refreshing trickling of the plashing fountain. Many of them must have thought it worth while to trudge a long way to participate in the treat, for their shoes were white with dust, and the lodge-keeper was doing a brisk trade in ginger beer. But it was for fresh air that these mill hands, all the week pent up, thirsted chiefly, and there they sat in solemn silence, inhaling mouthful of it, as though it were physic of a flavour foreign and strange to their taste, but in the efficacy of which they had learnt to place perfect faith.

There are people, however, who are worse off than the mill hands, whose abiding places are the slums of Manchester. I should not have thought it possible, but so it is. There are toilers and sweaters for daily bread whose condition in life is worse even than that of the miner who delves in the bowels of the earth or the smelter of iron who works naked to the waist. A creature of goblin aspect, who wears a leather mask to keep his eyes from being melted in his head, as is the red ore in the melting-pot it is his business to feed and keep at a molten simmer. I have visited the Potteries and passed half a day in Longton, which is the centre of the murky region where half the crockery that is used in the world is produced; and I am afraid to say how many times dirtier, smokier, and to the unaccustomed, more stifling than any other pottery parish round about. As it happened, it was a wet morning when I first approached Longton, and allowance should perhaps be made for that unfavourable circumstance; but I think I never in my life was more amazed. Amazed is exactly the word. As I approached the place from Fenton, the choking smoke that blew from Longton in my direction forced me to cover ray mouth and nostrils with my pocket-handkerchief; but, advancing towards the main street, I discovered the utter futility of the precaution. It was as idle as shutting one's mouth with the head held under water as a safeguard against getting drowned. There was not the least use in sneezing and coughing; there was literally nothing for it but to breathe chimney smoke, or to turn and flee to purer air before it was too late.

    I have not the faintest hope of doing justice, by any description of which I am capable, to the smoke of Longton. I might do better with a fairer chance; but the moment it beset me I became a victim to its obfuscating influence, and, filled with smoke in every crevice and cavity, had for the time barely sense remaining to gasp and grope my way. The nearest approach to it that I had ever previously experienced was a very foggy day in London. But London fog is a mild and pleasant mixture compared with the subtle concoction that comes pouring out of the pottery kilns. There is much more sulphur in the latter, and a sharpness which is refreshing as far as a single whiff goes, like the odour of vinegar sprinkled on a red-hot fire shovel. But the great difference between a stout and substantial London fog and the daylight darkness of Longton consists in the fact that fogs, as a rule, come in winter time, when keen winds blow and the air is frosty; whereas, in the other case, we have a fog of equal density, with the thermometer registering eighty in the shade.

    Nor, when a man grew somewhat used to the smarting mist, and could look about him a little, was there the least reason for wondering that Longton should be so afflicted. From one end to the other, it is chockfull of manufactories where pots and pans and plates and dishes are turned out every day by the hundred thousand, and kilns may be counted ten and a dozen in a single street. And let it be understood a pottery kiln is no mere chimney shaft. It is an oddly shaped thing, the sight of which, especially when the imagination is assisted by the unearthly fumes that rise on every side, is vividly suggestive of that bottle which the fisherman in the "Arabian Nights" found on the beach and uncorked, and out of which, in the midst of evil-smelling and blinding smoke, the escaped genii appeared. The kilns of Longton are brick-built, squat-bellied bottles, with wide gaping mouths, out of which issues, as though by necromantic art, a constant out-rolling of vapour that looks as substantial as wool, and a little of which must go a long way towards poisoning any current of pure air it may happen to fall in with. On a very fine day it is not unlikely that a great part of this ascends and is dispersed by the winds, but on such a day as that when I was there-a still and sultry day with close rain falling steadily - the before-mentioned "wool," as soon as it was vomited. Forth, seemingly became saturated with water, and after staggering with its load a few feet above the housetops, sank down into the streets.

    But nobody seemed to recognise in the existing state of things anything particularly uncommon. I went into a shop to buy a newspaper, and as I opened the shop door, the heavy smoke came tumbling after me as though it had been waiting on the threshold, and was glad of the chance of getting in. But the shopkeeper seemed quite unaware of it. "Nice day, sir," he cheerfully remarked. "But just a little cloudy, I think," I ventured. "Well, perhaps it is," said he, as he swept some soot off the newspaper before he handed it to me. "Perhaps it is, but the rain cools the air and makes it pleasant." If this was pleasant weather at Longton, what must it be in November or December, when, in the brightest of places, rain and fog, and mire combine to make the short day appear even too long, and every one is eager for evening, when the shutters may be closed, and the cheerful lamp set to illumine the cosy room? It is no exaggeration to imagine that at such times Longton, and Fenton, and Burslem, but especially the first, must be so dark as to make it difficult to see from one side of the street to the other, even at noon; while, as for the plague of "blacks," which, even with us, is at certain seasons of the year so sharp .a thorn in the side of the decent housewife, they must fall as thickly as snow. Perhaps snow at Longton *is* black - it is quite impossible that the fleecy particles could penetrate the tangle of thick chimney stuff overhead and descend white - and that the roads, and paths, and the people, and the cabbage of the greengrocers, and the meat in the butchers' shops, are one and all, thickly covered with feathery grime; and that the children play at soot-balls.

And how fares it with the population of such a gruesome place? Neither worse nor better than might be expected. 1 had a good opportunity of observing this, for by the time I had walked once through Longton, the bells began to ring for "knocking off" for the day; and out from the scores of "yards," at the head of which a swag-bellied, black-muzzled kiln so snugly nestles, came swarming the pottery hands - men, women, and children - until the gloomy street was alive with them, if any place could be made livelier by the presence of such a sickly-looking company. In a purely mining district the crowd one encounters in the streets, when the day's or the night's labour is over, is certainly not a prepossessing one; but the "pit lad," be he old or young, with his face and all that is visible of his body as black and as polished as jet, and his coarse and patched frock and trousers of heavy flannels, is, at least, an individual capable of enjoying that state of life to which it has been his destiny to be called; and he is ever ready to go in heart and soul, when he is free to do so, for those sports and pastimes in which he takes delight.

But, if he may be judged from his appearance, the pale-faced potter is a man of quite another kind. It is by no mean; a cheerful spectacle this turning out of pottery hands in the dusk of evening. One and all - and there seem to be as many women as men, and as many children as either - they are as white as bakers, as the most careless of journeymen, who recklessly splash their shabby clothes with flour slop, and are not at all particular as to how much flour finds lodgement in their hair and whiskers, and in the folds of their neckerchiefs. They are like bakers - toilers in the most dingy and unwholesome of our London underground bread-making places - in their haggard aspect, in their shambling gait, in the wearied and utterly "knocked-up" expression of their countenances. Males and females, grown-up and children, they are all of the same type. "All work and no play" has made the dullest of "boys" of them, and their white figures stalk through the smoke which fills the streets in a manner that suggests but one idea - that they are hurrying home to get to bed as soon as possible to rest their weary limbs, and fortify themselves against the drudgery of tomorrow.

And the worst of it is, as I am informed, matters are fully as bad as they seem with the unhappy potter and his wife and family. Their work is sadly against their health. They are, in the majority of cases, dangerously exposed to alternate heat and cold, and the dust of the baked clay goods it is their business to scrape and plane and polish, finds its way to their lungs and breeds fatal disease there. This would be bad enough if, on being released from his hurtful work, the potter were blessed with pure air to breathe; but, with the seeds of consumption thriving within him, with a bad cough, he is doomed, poor fellow to pass his nights as well as his days in the kind of atmosphere I have already attempted to describe.

It occurred to me, as I contemplated the potter children, as well as the potter fathers and mothers, creeping home in so melancholy a manner, what a splendid thing it would be if a great committee of kind-hearted ladies and gentlemen were to take in hand the task of treating the inhabitants of each district to say, three days at some seaside place. It would be an experiment that would require careful management, however. In all probability there ate at sonic of the worst of these localities - at Longton, for example - scores of young men and women whose belief is that the sun is ray less and lemon-coloured, and that the world at large is shrouded constantly in chimney-smoke. What their first sensations would be on making acquaintance with perfect light, and pure air, and dazzling sunshine, is doubtful. It would be embarrassing if, like bats and owls routed out of their gloomy abodes at noontide, they were dazed with the strange glare of real day, and on their arrival at Brighton terminus they went blinking and blundering about, and knocking their confused heads together, and against all manner of hard projections, and, taking fright at the mere threshold of enlightenment, scuttled back to the comparative dinginess of the railway carriages, obstinately refusing to budge from them until they were conveyed home again. Equally awkward for the projectors of the scheme and those who were responsible for its propriety, if the brisk and light quality of the Brighton air had an intoxicating effect on the white-faced host, causing it, with delirious yells, and leaps, and hand-clapping, to overrun the town and swarm the beach.

The most serious result, however, and one that would be almost inevitable, would be the immediate revolution that would ensue in the pottery trade. It is only reasonable to assume that least half the enlightened excursionists would never return to Longton. A very few hours' acquaintance with the new life with which the sweet and bracing air of the sea and the downs would endow them would effectually settle the question of staying where they were, and picking up a living somehow - anyhow - or going back to be once more enshrouded in the black smoke from the Pottery kilns; and as to those who found the courage to return, they would no doubt insist on such measures being adopted by the master potters as should insure for them a longer life and a merrier one.

In the potteries coal-pits abound, and while exploring the delectable locality I availed myself of the privilege of peeping into a pitman's pothouse.

When at full blast, as miners say, it is an awful spectacle, and one that would possibly daunt the courage of even doughty Sir Wilfrid himself, supposing him to have conceived the idea of bearding the lion of beer in its den, and of commencing the campaign in the neighbourhood of Brierly or Hanley. The pitman fresh from home, and taking his accustomed "last pipe" and his evening wet before he is lowered into the black bowels of the earth, is not a very remarkable-looking individual. To be sure the brand of carbon is indelibly set on his brow. He may, and in all probability has, within the last six hours, had his sousing in the big wooden tub that in a pitman's home is as indispensable an article of domestic convenience as a chair to sit on or a bed to lie on; but nothing short of a scientific process can free the lines and wrinkles of his hard face from the ingrain of coal dust. Besides, leave alone his visage and his eyes, that blink at the glare of gaslight, and his horny hands dotted with dull blue scars, and with the finger nails as blunt as though they had been filed, however a pitman may be attired and wherever he may be met, he can at once be known to be the man he is the moment he opens his mouth-not by the style of language that issues there from, but by the dazzling whiteness of his teeth, scrubbed constantly by the ebon grit, and by his gums, which from the same cause, are ruddier than coral.

But this is not the individual regarding whom I have suggested that Sir Wilfrid would probably hesitate ere he attacked him with the virtuous intention of dispossessing him of his beer at the moment when lie is at the point of indulging in it - it is the pitman who has recently come up. A score of these honest delvers of coal, roistering in a dingy room by firelight - the miner can see almost as well in the dark as by aid of gas or candle - is an appalling sight. There is no creature in existence that is as black as a pitman. A negro is merely slate-coloured beside him, a chimney-sweep a person of dusky complexion; coal is black, but the pitman is blacker than coal, a shinier black; he has jetty grit in his hair and in his eyebrows, and it glistens in the very lashes of his eyes, heightening the contrast to his eyeballs, which roll in their orbits like marbles of white china. He is dressed in his "flannels," which are as thick as ordinary blanketing, and his frock is all open at his hairy chest, which is laden with so much pounded coal as to suggest the possibility of kindling a fire there by the aid of a stick of wood and a Lucifer match. He is not a tall man, but he is immensely broad, his shoulders are rounded, and he carries his shaggy head as a man who does not often enjoy the luxury of standing upright. When he sits, as be almost invariably does, with his great black hands spread out on his knees, he has the appearance of a creature that is about to spring at you. There are miners rough and miners smooth, and I am now speaking of the former; and I say that a man must possess a fine spirit who while a score of such jolly fellows were clinking cans, and using towards each other - quite in a friendly kind of way - such language as to suggest the notion that the pit from which they had recently emerged must have been the bottomless one, would go in amongst them and snatch away their beer.

One who is less virtuous, however, and who is so debased as not to feel shame in making confession that there are many flavours more repugnant to his taste than those of malt and hops, may sit for half an hour in such company, with nothing to fear and perhaps something to gain. To some extent I discovered the truth of the latter statement. There was, in the bar room in which the men sat, a newspaper which reported the speech of the farmer who found that his men, after a few weeks of roughing it in the world, had yearned for the peace and pure air of the distant Suffolk village, and finally fairly ran back to those blessings as a truant child runs back to its mother. I could make out from a grizzled old pitman's reading of the newspaper by the firelight, that Hodge had extended his explorations in search of better wages (it was at the time of the agricultural strike) even into the Black Country, and that, tempted by seven shillings a day, he had made a desperate plunge six hundred feet under the earth, of which his previous knowledge had gone no deeper than a beetroot.

I had no opportunity of discovering how Hodge acquitted himself as a miner; but there could be no doubt - judging, that is, from the tone of the comment which followed the grizzled one's reading - that the pitmen present very strongly resented the pretensions of the innocent countryman to "come a-pokun his nose" into their field of industry. So far as I could understand, certain agricultural lock-outs had sought and get employment in some neighbouring pit, and had taken a sudden departure there from; and my friends of the glistening teeth and the gritty eyelashes had settled it in their minds that the penitent "hands" spoken of by the Suffolk farmer were these identical fellows. No pity was expressed for them. As regards the revolt of the men generally, the pitmen were unanimous in their expressions of approval; and one gentleman who had brought up out of the pit his coal-pick, and who drove its blade deep between the floor bricks by way of illustrating what should be done, if he had his way, with every pig-headed old farmer in England, so pleased the rest that, upstanding, every pitman present emptied his quart of the much or little it contained in the speaker's honour. It was on all sides declared that the contributions towards the men's keep should be kept up by all other trades, even though the lock-out lasted for a whole year. Had a gang of locked-out labourers been coming that way at that time, and by chance looked in at the Baker's Rest - they have the queerest signs for these pitmen's drinking shops - they would have been joyously received and generously treated; but I verily believe if the gang had expressed its intention of seeking a job of pit-work there would have been a row and broken heads on the spot.

I can imagine my young man from the country advancing so far into the town as Black horse-lane, but not going a single step further. Black Horse-lane is not at the outskirts of the town. It is within three minutes of the market-place, and the town hail, and the bank, and the post-office. That the more immediate associations of Black Horse-lane are not entirely barbarous is sufficiently proved by the fact that at one corner of it there is a cosy-looking beer shop bearing the alluring sign of the Old House at Home, and at the opposite corner there still appeared, when I was there, sticking to the wall a placard referring to a Christmas pudding club held in the vicinity; but two hundred yards distant is a spectacle appalling enough to make the hay-coloured hair under Hodge's billycock, adorned with a sprig of green wheat, rise in horror. The entrance to Black Horse-lane is rising ground, and standing there with the back to the street, one looks down into a hollow, and at first sight, especially at dusk of evening, it appears as though nothing less than a dreadful earthquake had just commenced, and that presently the towering black chimney shafts, marked by the ragged caps of flame, must come toppling down with a crash.

Amidst such distracting din and such stifling murk it is not easy to give a correct estimate of space, but I should think that the scene in question occupies not more than three acres - but such a three acres! Hodge, the aghast beholder, is aware of a rustic ditty in which a tender swain, addressing his lady-love, says, "More lover-ly art thou than an evenun in June!" and, in face of his ferocious outlook, he shudders as he reflects on the fire-and-brimstone order of young woman that might be truthfully likened to the kind of June evening he has now encountered. A hideous sunken patch, hedged all about with mountains of jagged slag and pit refuse seething, boiling, and bubbling in the midst of dense smoke and steam, spurting up sudden and fierce in unexpected gusts like the jets from the touchholes of great cannon; while below all manner of fire seems to peep up out of the ground or leap a-tiptoe high up into the air as our flame-headed London monument. With a roaring and rattling noise, with a body big as a tun, and with outstretched arms and forked fingers, the flames leap from the squat chimneys of the iron smelters, or the fires are smouldering, winking, and blinking in various colours - green, yellow, and crimson - and everywhere seemingly striving to tear a way through the heavy black pall that is stifling them. And then the noise, or rather the blending of a thousand noises that are so appropriate an accompaniment to the hissing steam-jets and the leaping flames. The engine that heavily groans, the engine that shrilly shrieks, the engine that is spasmodic in its ejaculations and utters intermittent yells and roars as though some of the fiery demons in attendance were torturing it by pulling out its teeth; squealing engines - engines chiefly used there for sucking mighty lifts of water out of mines that otherwise would be speedily drowned - engines that gasp and snort and whistle and scream; while through all and over all are heard the puny and piping voices of the swarms of men whose half-naked forms may be dimly seen flitting hither and thither, in the midst, as it seems, of the fires and the steam and the choking smoke.

Everywhere fires; and, as the evening becomes night, spellbound Hodge perceives that they burn with a merrier blaze, and that they exist in spots hitherto unsuspected. Before it grew dark he had observed notice-boards stuck on the vast hillocks of slag and cinders, that trespassers would be prosecuted. It would have been more candid if the words had been " Trespassers will probably be burnt to death;" for, as though taking advantage of the darkness, here, there, everywhere in these pit-heaps, fiery forms, that all through the daylight had lurked under the rubbish and ashes, now wriggle out like glow-worms of boa-constrictor size, play about the black surface, and making towards each other, join heads and tails, and writhe into a quivering heap, to make a blazing night of it. And it is to this singeing, scorching, pestilent place that jog-trot Hodge, with the clay of the quiet fields still adhering to his boots, and with the scent of growing clover still in his nostrils, has come to better himself! I think I see that scared-visage young fellow lingering, long after dark, on the great furnace-clinker he has utilised as a seat at the mouth of Black Horse-lane, contemplating the life that coal-miners and iron smelters and casters and forgers lead, and weighing in his sobered mind whether the inconveniences of the agricultural frying-pan are not probably more endurable than a sweating, toiling, grimy existence in this ugly district of smoke and fire, despite the advantage of increased wages; whether fifteen shillings and the old wholesome work, and the healthful Newmarket breezes, and the easy old manners and customs are not on the whole to be preferred by such a slow-moving, calm-loving creature as he is, to thirty shillings and all the dirt and hurry and uproar that are inseparable from bread-winning in the Black Country.

What will be his share of domestic comfort if he stays here? For the probably not model, but still homely, cottage, with the bit of flower garden in front and the few rods of vegetable ground at back, he will have - provided it is his intention to "rough it," as thousand of pitmen do - to lodge in a brick-floored hovel in an ill-drained back street; his food will be coarse and inferior, his companions such as have been described partaking of the social glass at the Baker's Rest. If he be a bachelor these are the maidens he must in future consort with - these shock-headed, bare-armed, ankle-jack-wearing damsels, of whom a sample three pause on their way to chaff him and chuck him under the chin to the great amusement of a bevy of middle-aged married women who are engaged in friendly gossip on the other side of the way, lounging on the doorsteps and window-sills, and each one smoking her pipe-not a short pipe, but a regular full-length "churchwarden" that was brought in with the last half-gallon of beer from the public-house. Hodge ponders on all these things, and if, a week afterwards, he is found whistling amongst the ripening corn a more contented man I for one see no great reason for wondering at it.

In a certain district in this land of crocks and clinkers, I recently made acquaintance and had some conversation with a collector of dog tax. I should rather have said a would-be collector of the canine impost, but one whose fidelity to his trust was most provokingly and harassingly baulked by the unscrupulous devices of those who regarded him as their common enemy.

He had - as almost with tears in his eyes he informed me - formerly filled the office of collector of arrears of poor-rates, but had resigned that situation and accepted his present one in the hope that, while it would be less distressful to his sensitive feelings, it would be a lighter job. But he was grievously mistaken. It was utterly impossible, he informed me, for him to perform his duties properly and conscientiously. Through all the working days of the week his district was comparatively clear of dogs. This, during his first week of office, was the more remarkable, because personal observation and diligent inquiry convinced him that the brisk trade driven at the various dog's-meat shops indicated the existence of at least five times the number of pups to he discovered at large or tied up at home. But come Sunday, when my informant's official functions were suspended, the riddle was unmistakably solved. When the pitmen emerged from the mines on Saturday evening they brought up with them any number of "tykes" that had been disporting below since the previous Monday, and now were released so that they might enjoy themselves and minister to their masters' innocent pleasure on the Sabbath Day; and, as at that time no steps could be taken towards frustrating the fraud, the dog-keepers were enabled to laugh at the collector and defy him.

But I remarked, "You have proof that these dogs whose masters avoid the tax are really down in the mine."

"I am certain of it."

"And does not your jurisdiction extend to where the animals are confined?"

"Of course it does."

"Why, then, do you not descend the shafts and do your duty? Since you have a right to go down, why don't you?"

The unhappy collector regarded me with a melancholy and meaning wag of his head.

"My friend," he replied, "it is not my authority to get down into a pit that I for a moment doubt; it is the improbability that I should ever come up again that troubles me. Heaven forbid I should be driven to try it! Fancy, my dear sir, having all those confounded animals set at you in the dark, and you don't know by whom! No, sir, the revenue may suffer, but I have a large family, and my office does not provide a pension for my widow."

I am of course unable to say whether the same influences prevail with the collectors of dog tax at Hanley, but it must he patent to the most ordinary observer that, if it does, the amount returned must represent a very inconsiderable sum. Of the dogs that exist under the earth in this region of smoke and fire I cannot pretend to any knowledge, but on the earth's surface they literally swarm. It does not appear that any particular breed of dogs find favour at Hanley to the exclusion of all others. Of bull pups, and bull terriers, and other fighting varieties, there is a fair sprinkling; but the homely maxim respecting the loaf seems here to apply to the animals in question, and a half-bred dog is regarded as better than one of no breed at all. Anything in dog's hide, with teeth to bite and a tail to wag, is acceptable to those who cannot afford better. One discovers, especially in the slums, whole streets, the inhabitants of which are, apparently, incapable of indulging in canine or any other luxury, bitten to a man with the dog-keeping mania. Tykes of all ages, sizes, and complexions sprawl over the pavements, and lounge at the thresholds of doors, and sit at the windows, quite at their ease, with their heads reposing on the window-sill, hob-and-nob with their biped "pal," who cuddles his four-footed friend lovingly round the neck with one arm, while his as yet unwashed mining face, black and white in patches as the dog's is, beams with that satisfaction which content and pleasant companionship alone can give. And it must be allowed, to the credit of the pitman, that, however hard it may fare with the wife or the child of his bosom, the dog of his bosom is nurtured with the tenderest care, and has as comfortable a time of it as though the transmigration of souls were a thing the worthy toiler steadfastly believed in, and therefore thought it prudent to pave a way to the time when he might be actually, as well as figuratively, on all fours, with his darling "under hung, tulip-eared" Brindle.

A home for starving dogs would be almost as much out of place at Hanley as an asylum for indigent bees on a common, where the yellow gorse is in flower. I believe that the town in question would hold itself in lasting disgrace if a starving or even a lean or ill-conditioned cur were seen prowling about its streets. Neglected children maybe found in plenty; but there is no lack of fatness or sleekness amongst the dogs. The fact is, the hard-working pitman of these parts is not a child-fancier - he is a dog-fancier. This, to be sure, makes it somewhat hard for the small, two-legged creature; but it is difficult to see how it can be helped. It is a nice question whether it would be justifiable to risk shaking the pitman's faith in the burden of "Rule Britannia," by endeavouring to control any of his little predilections. At the same time let it be distinctly understood that, while I write in this spirit concerning the Hanley pitmen, I allude exclusively to the "roughs" of the class, who have not yet succumbed to the indefatigable exertions which are being made by his friends for his conversion. It is only just to state that at the present time in

Hanley and elsewhere there are tens of thousands of pit hands who are as sober and industrious and well-behaved as any class of workmen in the three kingdoms.

But, as it happened, it was amongst the inferior kind that my unguided feet led me, and coming down a bye-street I saw a sight that I could not exactly understand. There was a man black as ink, and evidently a pitman, and two deplorably thin and ragged little girls, who appeared to have been to meet father returning from his works - not, however, because of his loving impatience to behold them as soon as his day's toil was over, but to gladden his eyes with the sight of a female dog, of the retriever breed, and two fine pups. The pups the pitman carried, one under each arm, as tenderly as though they were babies born to him, while their mother, walking sedately by his side, bore in her mouth about two pounds of prime looking and perfectly fresh shin of beef. My first idea was that the man had been drinking, and that it was a tipsy freak of his to insist on the dog carrying home the meat that was for the family supper; and I could not, seeing the shoeless, hungry little girls, but reflect on what a sore disaster it would be if the dog were to take it into its head to run away with the joint. I suppose that the pitman read something of this in my face, for when I got up with them, he remarked good-humouredly,

"Never fear, mun; she wull na' droop it."

"It would be safer, I think, if one of the little girls carried it," I ventured.

"Na, she's old enow," rejoined the pitman; "it's danged hard if the dawg can't carry home her own meat" - a joke which made the two squalid-looking girls laugh as they caressed the retriever and stroked its silken ears.

"She's a lucky dog, I should say," said I. "Does she always live on this kind of food?"

The twinkle at once faded out of the pitman's eyes, and he looked serious. "Mun," said he, "she dew."I canna' help it, but she dew. I've a family iv 'em" - here he jerked his thumb resentfully in the direction of the hungry-looking mites of girls - "and eight pence the pound is the best I can afford for her!" and, his hands being both engaged, he paused a moment to administer a kind caress with the toe of his boot to the retriever's back.

It was not a difficult task to lead him on to talk about dogs and their habits and customs; nor did it require any tremendous effort to induce him, when he reached his home, to adjourn to the nearest alehouse, where he might at his leisure continue his narrative of the last dog-fight he had been witness to.

At the alehouse we met with doggy company, and the conversation turned on the lamentable decline of that particular British sport in which two of the canine tribe are the chief actors. It was, I was assured, as difficult in these degenerate times to "pull off a dog-fight all right and regular, and without any hole-and-corner business and fear of the police," as it was to bring about a man-fight under the same open conditions.

"Ah! It was a pretty sport," remarked my friend, with a sigh; "and the more lively-like, because, in fighting young dogs, you could never be sure, however tip-top their breeding, that when they were brought to the scratch, they would not 'turn felon.'"

"Very much depends, perhaps," I remarked, in quest of further information concerning the "pretty sport," "on the way in which a young dog is trained." At which he laughed, and said there could not be any mistake about that, as there was only one way, and at once he good-naturedly proceeded to explain which way that was.

I was given to understand that the first practice a fighting pup had was with "a good old gummer " - that is to say, with a dog which had been a good one in his day, but now was old and toothless and incapable of doing more than "mumble" the juvenile antagonist that was set against him, the one great advantage being that the young dog gained practical experience in the making of "points." The next stage, as I was informed, in training the young aspirant for pit honours, was to treat him to a "real mouthful," or, in other words, "to let him taste dog."

It is a villainous process, and I never felt so grateful to the laws of my country, which have decreed that dog-fighting is an offence punishable with severe imprisonment, as when my informant enlightened me thereon.

"You look about," said he, "for a likely-looking street cur of fit size, and if with a bit of blood in it why all the better, and you take it home and tie it up and spice it up with good grub. Then, just before it's wanted, you clip off its hair at those points that you know your young 'un will want to get at, and you lather and shave em down to the skin. Then you put your young 'un and the cur in a pit together. Most likely the cur, not knowing his customer, will show fight at once, and there'll be quite a lively set-to between 'em for a few minutes; but breed will tell presently, and then the cur knocks under, and your young 'un has it all his own way, and, being now warm to his work, he doesn't shirk it. If he is slow you set him on. You set him on to the shaved parts, which are the vital parts behind the shoulders and that, and you worry him into letting the cur have it hot. There'll be a awful row, of course, for the cur, now he finds his master, will do nothing but slink and crawl along the floor and into the corners, and kick up such a caterwauling' as may be heard half a mile off. But your young 'un, if he's got the right stuff in him, won't mind that; it'll give him an appetite, and he'll go at the cur, and make a regular meal of him."

I have not given a quarter of the sickening details that attended the operation of giving the "young 'un" a "mouthful" with which the knowing Old Hand favoured me, mistaking for apt attention what was in reality on my part the fascination of horror. Had the individual in question confided to me that he was a descendant of a celebrated ogre family who devoured babies, I don't think I should have experienced such a sense of fear and shrinking towards him as I did. As for the dirty white bull-dog he had with him, who during the recital was engaged in chewing one of his master's hoot laces, as though it were a quid of tobacco, all the while blinking and winking with his red rimmed eyes as though he perfectly well understood every word that was said, and highly enjoyed it as recalling to his memory one of the happy episodes of his puppy hood, it would have afforded me much satisfaction to have administered to him a dose of strychnine on the spot. Observing what the dog was at, he jerked the hanging boot-lace out of its mouth, and gave it a sounding kick in the ribs.

"Ah, that's right!" remarked another miner, approvingly, "he'll take all the edge off his teeth, biting that thing. You re a old hand, and know he'll want all the teeth he's got, I'll wager."

The Old Hand gave him a quick, reproachful look, but it was too late. "He's in training, I suppose," said I, with as much indifference as I could assume. "No, he ain't," replied the Old Hand; "don't I tell you that there ain't no dog-fighting done now in these parts? You get under there" - this to the bull-dog, its master at the same time expediting its retreat under the seat with the heel of his boot. But at that moment the door swung open and a man's head appeared - a head with the nose almost flat to the face, and squinting eyes, and an enormously wide mouth. It was fortunate that the bull-dog's chain was made fast to the leg of the seat, for no sooner did the ugly face appear than the dog made a spring out, its bloodshot eyes starting with fury, its teeth exposed, and straining madly against its tether in its frantic desire to reach its enemy. "Ha, my beauty! You're there then?" spoke the head, with a grin which if possible increased its ugliness. The Old Hand was almost as furious as his dog. With a terrible string of oaths, and addressing the owner of the ugly head as "Brummy," he bade him be off; and tauntingly demanded to know why, if Brummy funked on the match he had made, he did not cry off like a man, instead of coming there to aggravate the dog in the hope that he might have a fit and break a blood-vessel. "You'll have enough of him quite soon enough, and I'll put another sovereign on it if you like," exclaimed the exasperated Old Hand, whose ire, however, cooled when the grinning head vanished.

By the time a half-pint brandy measure had been filled at my expense, and emptied by the Old Hand and his friend, his good temper was quite restored, and - may Sir Wilfrid forgive me - a little drop more made him quite kind and confidential. With a friendly slap on the shoulder he swore that I was the right sort, and that if I liked to meet him to-morrow night, although he couldn't promise me "all a dog-fight," I should be treated to a bit of sport it would do any man's heart good to see.

"And that chap who looked in at the door, will he be there?" I asked.

"Well, there won't be no fight if he ain't," replied the friendly Old Hand with a laugh, and so, with my promise to meet him next night, we parted.

"You had better not meet us at the alehouse," whispered the Old Hand, as we parted on the previous night;

"after what has happened somebody might smell a rat, and be on the watch. Stand at the corner of Mill Lane, and when you see us, follow without taking notice."

The Old Hand and his friend, the owner of the brown retriever, were as faithful to the appointment as I myself; and when they strolled up Mill-lane, innocently smoking their pipes, a figure whose appearance was somewhat questionable, I fear, in point of attire, happened to be going in the same direction, and kept in their wake, up one street and down another, until the chase began to grow somewhat wearisome. At last, however, a halt was called near a dirty row of houses, at the door of one of which stood a man in miner garb, who, as soon as he perceived us, knocked the ashes out of his pipe against the doorpost, and this evidently was a preconcerted sign that nothing was amiss, for my companions made straight for the house in question without further delay, and speedily the outer door was bolted from within, and further secured with a stout chain. It was quite dark inside, and a woman came out of a back room to us with a candle to light the way down to the cellar or kitchen, whichever it might be called.

Whatever the nature of the coming performance, the company who were privileged to witness it were already assembled. The scene was a place, about sixteen feet square, with bare walls and a brick floor, and at the four sides a rope was already extended, leaving a space of about a yard between it and the wall, and here, railed off from the centre, three deep, were the sightseers. Pit-lads most of them, some black as when they came up out of the pit, with a sprinkling of individuals of the "rough" and costermonger order, the most prominent of the gathering being half a dozen "swells" of the country "fancy," with snuff-coloured trousers and cutaway coats, and waistcoats and caps of sealskin.

A paraffin lamp hung from the ceiling, and as the window was quite covered with a shutter, and the only means of ventilation was afforded by the chimney, while the "swells" had their cigars alight, and the commonalty their short pipes, no wonder that the place was evil-smelling, hot, and stifling. There was, happily, a wide chimney-place, and the stove had been moved. A bit of board based on brick-bats made out of this quite a commodious and airy recess and I was glad to share it with two promising young pit-lads, who, with a view to thoroughly enjoying the festivities of the evening, had brought a bottle of rum with them.

But the personage who chiefly attracted my attention was a dwarf - a man of at least middle age, judging from his grizzled grey hair, and the enormous size of his head and ears, but certainly not more than four feet and a half in height, yet with tremendous hands and feet and bandy legs. This was "Brummy," the person whose head and face I had once before seen under circumstances which the reader may possibly remember. Brummy was evidently a person of consideration. He was honoured with much notice on the part of the sporting "swells," which shook hands with him, ill-looking and repulsive as he appeared to be, even favouring him with their whispered confidence. The grizzled dwarf critically examined the saw dusted space in the centre of the kitchen, especially at one particular part; there he went down on his knee and felt the bricks all over with the flat of his hand, and, discovering an inequality in them, called for a hammer and remedied the defect.

"He's a careful old codger," remarked one of my fellow-occupants of the chimney: "he knows what a slip and a stumble might cost him - it was that wot lost him the match last time." "What rot!" growled his companion; "he didn't make no slip at all; and it's all lies to say he did. He was licked on his merits, like he will be this time, I hope, and win me my quid. What do you say, chap?" This last query was addressed to me, and it seemed like an opportunity for gaining the enlightenment I was longing for almost as much as for fresh air.

"He'll win, I suppose, if he's better than the other one," I ventured; at which both the young pitmen laughed as at a good joke.

T'other one, indeed!" remarked the elder of them; " ----- his old carcase, - he's as artful as a two-legger, anyhow."

And then they began to talk about something else. It was still uncertainty with me, though I had an uncomfortable idea of the truth. Whose was the "old carcase" against which Brummy, the dwarf, was about to exercise himself? It would never do to inquire. Being there, I was, of course, supposed to know all about it.

Then one of the sporting "gents" took out his timekeeper, and called "five minutes to time," whereon there was a clapping of hands, and the bandy-legged Dwarf proceeded further to mystify me. He divested himself of his coat and his waistcoat, his blue-checked shirt, and his boots, leaving himself with nothing on but his trousers and a dirty under-flannel, cut off high at the shoulders. Stripped, he appeared an extraordinarily muscular fellow, and his arms, which were nearly covered with hair, were scarred, each of them from the wrists to the elbows, as though at some time or other he had been badly burnt. The creature likewise had a scar, ugly and jagged, within an inch of his collar-bone, and another - now one came to examine him for wounds - at the right side of his chin, which looked like a piece bitten out of a dirty apple and put back again. He now produced a strap, to which was attached a bright iron ring, and this he proceeded to buckle round his waist, at the same time dispensing with his braces. Then he took from a pocket of his coat a phial filled with what looked like oil, which he handed to the sporting "gent" with the watch, who took out the cork and smelt at it. After which all the sporting "gents" smelt at it in succession, and pronouncing it "all right, gave it back to Brummy, who, amidst almost breathless silence, commenced to anoint his arms and fists with it, rubbing it well in.

"Dan'l won't bring in Physic till the last minnit," remarked one of the young pitmen.

I still managed to refrain at that moment from demanding of my companions in the chimney who was Dan'l, who the physic was for, and what it all meant, but it is to this hour a wonder to me how I resisted.

Yet it would have been a pity if I had shown rash ignorance, for within a minute my curiosity was only too well satisfied. "All ready?" asked the sporting swell with the watch.

"Ay, mun, bring him as sune as ye like," grinned the dwarf; and then there was heard the pattering of a four-footed animal, and an anxious whining, and, the kitchen door opening, in came Dan'l, with Physic. It was my friend the elderly miner of the evening before, and Physic was the hideous-jowled dirty white bull-dog. For a few moments the scene of last night at the alehouse was repeated. The instant that Physic caught sight of "Brummy" he gave a furious gasp, as though he had not for a moment ceased to brood over the insult he had been subjected to when last they met, and though it might cost him his life, was now determined to bring the quarrel to an issue. But Dan'l had him fast by the great leather collar, and, with both hands, hauled him to the wall, where another man hitched a stout chain to a holdfast, while one performed the same office for the dwarf, except that in his case it was a substantial strap which was used. Like the dog, however, he had his measured length of tether, one end of which was attached to the ring at the back of his waist strap and the other to a staple in the wall opposite. I dislike rum, and especially is it to me unpalatable to gulp it out of a bottle; yet, on account of the sudden sensation of sickness which at this moment overcame me, I felt positively grateful when the sociable young pitman by my side pressed a "flip" on my acceptance. There could no longer be any misunderstanding as to the horrible encounter which was about to happen. This dreadful dwarf had backed himself, or had been backed by his friends, to engage in combat with Dan'l's bull-dog. "It's their third go in," said my friendly young pitman as he drank "T'ord's you" out of the rum bottle; "it's one and one with 'em as yet; this time it's who shall."

    Perhaps at this juncture I should have escaped, if I could, from the hideous lists; but flight was out of the question, and it was necessary to appear interested. As well as I could make out from the arrangements, and the wrangling and disagreement respecting them, the terms of the fight were that both dog and man were to be allowed length of rope enough, as it was called, to get at each, other, but there was not so much of it that either could fail to get out of the other's reach should he deem it prudent to do so. The biped brute was to kneel down or go on all-fours, which he pleased, and was to use no other weapons than his clenched fists. He was by no means to take hold of the quadruped's collar, or to attempt to grapple with the dog unless it "made fast" to him, when he would be at liberty to use his hands in order to extricate himself. In case the bull-dog should be lucky enough to pin his enemy, the man had only to cry out "I'm done," and means would be promptly taken to compel the victor to loosen his grip. On "Brummy's" part, to win the fight, he was to knock the bulldog "out of time" - in other words, either to stun it or so punishes it that, despite all it's master's urging, it would refuse to face the dwarf again after a full minute's notice. Dan'l set out a bowl with vinegar and water, and a sponge on his side, while the dog's antagonist received from the hands of a kind patron a pint flask of brandy, at which he took a pull, and then stood "convenient" in a corner, together with a towel. Then he tucked down his flannel shirt at the neck, spat in his enormous hands, made them into fists, each almost as big as a stonemason's mallet, and knelt, smiling. Meanwhile Dan'l was giving the finishing touches to Physic's fighting toilette, and man and dog were ready at almost time same moment. There was no need to encourage the red-eyed Physic; he was too eager for the fray. He did not bark, but he was frenzied with passion to that degree that tears trickled down his blunt nose, and his gasping became each moment more shrill and hysterical. He needed no urging on for the first "round," at all events. As soon as the umpire called "Let go," the dirty, glaring, furious brute sprang forward with an impetuosity that caused the last link of its chain to click with a ringing sound against the staple which held it.

    The dwarf, however, was not to be stormed and defeated all in a moment. Once the ghastly fight began, there was a dire fascination in it; and I now noted closely the combat. The man was on all fours when the words "Let go" were uttered, and, making accurate allowance for the length of the dog's chain, he arched his back, cat wise, so as just to escape its fangs, and fetched it a blow on the crown of its head that brought it almost to its knees. The dog's recovery, however, was instantaneous; and before the dwarf could draw back, Physic made a second dart forward, and this time its teeth grazed, the biped's arm, causing a slight red trickling. He grinned scornfully, and sucked the place; but there was tremendous excitement among the bull-dog's backers, who clapped their hands with delight, rejoicing in the honour of first blood. The hairy dwarf was still smiling, however, and while Dan'l held his dog, preparatory to letting it go for "Round 2," he was actually provoking it as much as he could, "hissing" at it, and presenting towards it the bleeding arm. The animal, flushed possibly with his first success, made for its opponent in a sudden leap, but the dwarf leapt forward too, and smote the bull-dog such a tremendous blow under the ear as to roll it completely over, evidently bewildering it for a moment, and causing it to bleed freely, to the frantic joy of the friends of the man-beast. But they, in turn, were made to look serious, for, with astonishing energy, Physic turned about, and with a dash, was again at the dwarf, and this time contrived to fix its teeth in one of his hairy arms, a terrible gash appearing as the man snatched the limb out of his ravenous jaws. The bull-dog was licking his lips, and had fewer tears in his eyes as his master drew him back. As for the dwarf, he retired to his corner for a whet of brandy and a moment's comforting with the towel. He was ready and smiling again, however, for "Round 3," and this time it was a fight in earnest - the dog worrying the man, and the man dealing it terrific blows on the ribs and on the head with those sledge-hammer fists, till in the end both the man's arms were bleeding, and a horribly cheerful business was going on behind the ropes at 2 to 1 on Physic. But let me make short work of the ensuing seven "rounds," which in some of their details were so shocking that more than once I would have left the place if I could. The company generally, however, were made of far less sensitive stuff. The more furious the ghastly fight, the keener was their relish for it; and in their excitement they leant over each other's shoulders, and over the rope, and mouthed and snarled, and uttered guttural noises when a good hit or snap was made, just as the dog and the dwarf were doing. By the time Round 10 was concluded the bull-dog's head was swelled much beyond its accustomed size; it had lost two teeth, and one of its eyes was entirely shut up; while as for the dwarf, his fists, as well as his arms, were reeking, and his hideous face was ghastly pale with rage and despair of victory. Fate was kind to him, however. In Round 11 the bull-dog came on fresh and foaming, with awful persistence of fury, but, with desperate strength, the dwarf dealt him a tremendous blow under the chin, and with such effect that the dog was dashed against the wall, where, despite all its master could do to revive it continued to lie, and being unable to respond when "time" was called, Brummy was declared to be victorious.

* * * * * *

In venturing to give publicity to some "further particulars" of an affair which by this time, probably, has passed well nigh out of recollection, I cannot but be aware that some explanation is due from me. It may be reasonably asked "why have these said particulars been so long withheld?" To this I can only reply, that circumstances over which I had no control forbade it. As long ago as September, '74, the proprietors of the *Daily Telegraph* were in possession of all the additional facts here following - indeed, it is from the newspaper printer's proof of the article sent to me for revision, with a view, as I imagined, to its immediate publication, that this account is written. That it was not published in the *Daily Telegraph* at the time was, I still must think, scarcely just to me.

I regret to make known that my "further particulars" do not include the discovery of "Brummy," and the more so, because I am aware that there are folks so sceptical that nothing short of the actual production of the dog-fighting dwarf will convince them. As the reader will find in the following statement, the individual in question on more than one occasion ventured, as it were, within arm's length of those who were anxious to make his closer acquaintance; but he evidently has peculiar and private reasons for refraining from declaring himself. If however, the testimony of many witnesses - including several of the dog-fighter's intimate friends and boon companions bears the value claimed for it, then there can no longer be a question as to the happening of the man and dog-fight at the time and place as stated by me in the narrative printed in the *Daily Telegraph* on the 6th of July of last year.

About six weeks after the appearance in the *Daily Telegraph*, of my account of the man and dog-fight, and while the matter still occupied a considerable amount of public attention, a remarkable letter was received by the editor. The writer described himself as holding a responsible position on the medical staff of the Manchester Infirmary. The purport of his communication was that he had strong reasons for believing that he might be able to furnish the long-desired clue to the whereabouts of the individual who fought with the bull-dog at Hanley, on the 24th of June. His statement, in effect, was that a few days previously he was going a railway journey from Manchester to Bolton, and that on the way he fell in with a man named Tapley, and whose acquaintance he had made at a time when he - the medical gentleman in question, and who may be here spoken of as Mr. Blank - took an interest in exploring the mysteries of Manchester back-street life. Tapley was going to Bolton, and arrived there with Mr. Blank, they went into a public-house for some refreshment. Tapley knew the manager of the public-house, who, addressing him, remarked, "Why, Tom, an old friend of yours was here and asked after you yesterday."

"Who was that?" Tapley asked.

"Why the chap who fought the dog at Hanley," was the reply. This naturally excited the curiosity of Mr. Blank, to whom the public-house manager was a stranger, and a conversation ensued, from which it appeared that the individual called "Brummy" was tolerably well known there, and that Tapley, about two years before, had fought with him in a street brawl, and that Brummy, in throwing Tapley, had broken the leg of the latter. Further discussion of the subject of the man and dog-fight convinced Mr. Blank that there could be no doubt that the "Brummy" there spoken of and the individual who was the chief performer in my narrative were identical, and after revolving the matter in his mind, he addressed the editor of the *Daily Telegraph*, as already stated, at the same time expressing his willingness - provided his name was kept out of the affair - to assist all he could in any inquiries it might be thought fit to institute. Steps were promptly taken towards acting on this welcome information. The main thing was to entrust the business to a man on whose tact and judgment the proprietors of the *Telegraph* had perfect reliance, and it was finally resolved that Mr. J. M. Le Sage, who holds the responsible position of manager of an important department of the paper, should at once proceed to Manchester, with power to act in every way as seemed best to him.

By appointment, Mr. Le Sage met Mr. Blank of the Manchester Infirmary, and the two straightway proceeded to where Mr. Tapley lived and questioned him. Tapley was nothing loth to assist. No money was given to him, and none was promised. All that he stipulated for was that his railway fare should be paid. It was reward enough for him, he said, to pay off an old grudge he had against his enemy by compelling him to come forward. "I knew at once," said Mr. Tapley, at this first interview, "I knew at once, when I read the account in the *Telegraph* who it was that fought the dog, although Mr. Greenwood made a queer mistake in the names. It isn't the dog that's named Physic, it's the man. Richard Physic is his name, though he's commonly known as Brummy." From which it would appear, that without being aware of it, I must have heard, during the progress of the combat, the name "Physic," mentioned, and that it came back to my mind when, while writing, I paused for a moment to find a fanciful name for the dog. I may mention that Mr. Le Sage did not fail to make an immediate entry in his note book of this odd, but not insignificant item of evidence.

The three, Mr. Blank, Mr. Le Sage and the man Tapley, then proceeded to Bolton and to the public house where Mr. Blank had first heard of the affair.

It is a drinking bar, in some way connected with a place of public entertainment known as Weston's Music Hall, and the manager's name is John Bayley. The person last mentioned made no mystery of what he knew of the matter. It was quite true, he admitted to Mr. Le Sage and the others, that the man who was called "Brummy," but whose real name was Physic, occasionally "looked in" there, and was well known by him (the manager), as well as by many of the frequenters of the smoke room. Bayley described Mr. Physic, and, excepting that he fixed his height as being at least three inches more than I should have thought it possible the bull-necked "Brummy" could be, the description tallied, with curious exactness, with that of the man it would afford me so much pleasure to identify. Bayley even mentioned that Mr. Physic had a small bald place on the crown of his head, and so had Brummy, as I distinctly remember, although I did not mention it in my description of him. Questioned as to Mr. Physic's means of livelihood, Bayley only knew that he "went about the country," and had heard that he dealt in gas-burners. Asked was Physic proud of his notoriety, and whether he bragged of the Hanley affair, he replied that for fear of the law he said very little about it, but that when he did it was to express his wonder that such a trifling business should cause such a lasting fuss. Could he furnish Mr. Physic's present address? No. All he knew about that was that he did not live at Bolton.

Finally, Mr. Bayley was commissioned to communicate as speedily as possible with Physic, *alias* Brummy, and to inform him that, if he would consent to come forward and enable me to identify him, he should be guaranteed against all legal consequences, and receive for his trouble a handsome present. Two days afterwards Mr. Le Sage called on Mr. Bayley, whom he found in a mood much less communicative than formerly. Had he seen Brummy? Yes, he had. He had seen him the day before, and had delivered the gentleman's message and promise; and Brummy had replied that he would "see about it." Where was Brummy now? Oh! He had gone off - gone away to Newcastle, Mr. Bayley believed, and he couldn't take it upon himself to say when it was likely he would return.

Mr. Le Sage forwarded to London this discouraging information, upon which it was represented to me by the editor that he might get on better with my assistance, and I at once adopted the suggestion, and went to Manchester, and joined Mr. Le Sage at the White Bear Hotel. Mr. Tapley was again applied to, and we went in company to Bolton and to the public house where Mr. Bayley, the public house manager, was to be found.

That person professed to have heard nothing further of Physic, *alias* Brummy; but, on proceeding to the smoke-room, Mr. Tapley there recognized several of his acquaintances and amongst them a man named Bernard Mullany. In reply to questions put by Tapley, Mr. Mullany frankly admitted in our presence that he knew all about the Hanley dog fight; that Brummy, otherwise Physic, was the man who had fought the animal; that Brummy had found two pounds towards the stake that was fought for; and that there were not more than thirty persons present at the fight. Mr. Mullany, however, when pressed on the point, stoutly denied being one of the thirty. His intimacy with Mr. Physic, however, appeared to be almost brotherly. He described his friend as being almost like a gentleman when quite sober, but as being more like a devil than a man when he was drunk. He related one or two stories of his friend's tipsy eccentricities and habits, which certainly went far to establish the accusation of his being devilish when in his cups.

"Of what size is he?" was asked.

"Oh! A little fellow as regards height, but wonderfully deceiving as regards bulk," Mr. Mullany replied. "It is a dodge of his, when in a smoke-room where there is company, to turn the talk to measurement of chests and that, and then to wager his chest measurement against that of somebody else; and, though he stands only five feet one or two, he measures fair three feet four round the naked chest, and as for his fists, they are bigger than mine," said Mr. Mullany, who is a stout-built young man of five feet nine or ten in height, and not altogether innocent of pugilistic practices.

Mr. Mullany was shy of replying to a question as to when he had last seen his friend Physic. It was a little bit ago; he wasn't sure how long. Asked as to his opinion why it was that his friend had not taken kindly to the offer made to him through Mr. Bayley a few days ago, he replied that Brummy wasn't a man who was hard up for a pound, and that he was afraid, because of the law, to "come forward and face it." Further, Mr. Mullany intimated that, for his part, he did not blame him for keeping back; "It's all very well you saying that the law can't ketch hold of him now," said Mullany; "but, in my opinion, it's a second Tichborne business, and penal servitude for anybody proved to be mixed up in it."

Some conversation with Mullany seemed to convince him of the absurdity of this belief, and though he more than once expressed his reluctance to being "mixed up" in the affair, finally he agreed to go next day to Hanley, and confer with a "party" who was present at the fight, and afterwards to come to Manchester to our hotel and tell us the result. I have forgotten to mention Mullany informed us that Physic, or Brummy, had fought several dogs to his knowledge - one at a public-house, the name of which he mentioned, at Manchester, and another at "Evans's" in Liverpool. Before we left him, said he, "The man you ought to get hold of is Frank. He's Brummy's bosom friend, and could get at him better than anybody." But he either could not or would not tell us where this Frank might be found.

Whether Mr. Mullany paid his promised visit to Hanley it is impossible to say, but he neither came nor sent to us at Manchester. We had a visitor, however, at eleven o'clock the night following - Saturday night. Within a few minutes of the time for closing the hotel doors, word was brought to Mr. Le Sage, whose name was known at Bolton - mine was not - informing him that a man outside wished to speak with him. Going outside, Mr. Le Sage found three men, but two stood aside, and took no part in the conversation which ensued. It was brief, but promising.

"Is your name Sage?"

"It is. What is your name?"

"My name is Frank - Frank Ward. You've been down to Bolton, I hear."

"Yes."

"Well, I know what you want. You want to know about the dog-fight at Hanley. You want it to be proved that what Mr. Greenwood told about was true."

"Yes."

"Well, what about the money - is that square?"

I should have mentioned that in his increasing anxiety to bring matters to an issue, Mr. Le Sage had step by step increased his offered reward for Brummy's production from ten pounds to a hundred - meanwhile, and in order to avoid the danger of tempting persons of such questionable morality to concoct a hoax, steadily refraining from parting with any sum whatever. Indeed, too much stress cannot be laid on the fact that every one concerned was in turn frankly informed at starting, that, whatever sum might afterwards be distributed, nobody would get a penny until Brummy was induced to declare himself. In reply to Mr. Frank Ward's inquiry, he was assured by Mr. Le Sage that the hundred pounds promised would be paid the moment the conditions imposed were fulfilled.

"Can you prove that he was the man who fought the dog?" he was asked.

"I can," replied Mr. Ward.

"And will you?"

"Not while you stay down here. We won't deal with you here. If you want to know all about it, you get back to London, and then we'll deal with you."

"But how will you do so?"

"By telegraph, we'd rather."

"And when will you telegraph?"

"Can't say - in a day or two. There's two or three others to see and talk to about it. But you get back. I tell you nothing will be done while you stay here at Manchester."

"Did you come from Bolton to-day?"

"Yes."

"Are you going back to-night?"

"No; the last train has gone. We shall stay here tonight, and go back tomorrow." And so saying, abruptly as he had made his appearance, the man calling himself Frank Ward and his two companions - who had stood aloof during the brief conference, taking no part in it - took their departure. To suit their own, and, it may be presumed, the ends of their friend Brummy, these three men had paid their railway fare from Bolton, were put to the expense of staying at Manchester all night, and would, next morning, have to pay a further sum to get home again; *and they never asked for or received from Mr. Le Sage a single penny*. In order to make sure of remembering the whole of his conversation with Ward, Mr. Le Sage returned immediately to the hotel, and proceeded to detail it to me, taking down as he did so, a strict account of it in shorthand in his notebook. I need not say how high were our expectations that, at last, the matter which had caused me so many weeks of pain and anxiety was about to be satisfactorily cleared up. But, alas! The bond of brotherhood which is said to exist amongst thieves would appear to be equally efficacious in attaching dog-fighters one to the other.

We did not return to London immediately. Perhaps it would have been better had we done so; but we were unwilling to quit a neighbourhood somewhere about which it appeared so likely that the man we sought was lurking. But a few days afterwards we did return, and ever since Mr. Physic, *alias* Brummy, *or* his comrades, have made no sign.

By the bye, it may not be out of place here for me to make known the particulars of another business transacted by the gentleman who was my companion and me during our residence at Manchester.

It may possibly be borne in mind that some time after the occurrence of the fight the Mayor of Longton - which adjoins Hanley - created some sensation by the public announcement that a gentleman, for whose integrity he could vouch, had made known to him the fact that on the morning following the night on which the combat took place, and while in a railway carriage, he had overheard two men talking about a man and dog fight which had taken place at Hanley the night previous, and at which one of the men was present. The gentleman questioned the man last mentioned, and was by him informed that it was all true; that the fight was between a dog and "a little stout-built fellow, as ugly as sin," and that he had never seen such a sickening sight before, and hoped to never again. Mr. Smith, woollen merchant and wholesale clothier, of Manchester and of High Street, Ashton-under-Lyne, was the gentleman in question, and the conversation he had with the man in the railway carriage took place on the 25th of June, whereas it was the 6th of

July before any account of the fight appeared in the *Daily Telegraph*. On Mr. Smith's statement appearing in print, my ingenious enemies, the editors of certain Black Country newspapers, openly declared their belief that it was I who was the man who talked with the woollen merchant in the railway carriage - being, I suppose, so brimful of my splendid invention that I could scarce contain it until I found opportunity to commit it to paper. In order to set this unjust suspicion at rest, in company with Mr. Le Sage, before mentioned, I went to Ashton-under-Lyne and waited on Mr. Smith. On making our business known to him, that gentleman declared his willingness to give evidence of what he had heard in any way that might be thought desirable. He repeated the conversation he had had with the man he met in the train the morning after the fight, at the same time describing his informant as a tall, brawny-built fellow of about five feet ten in height, and as looking like a market-gardener. My height, I may mention, is a trifle under five feet six. After this, for the first time, I made myself known to the woollen merchant, and he expressed the satisfaction it afforded him to be able to render such convincing proof of the happening of the man-and-dog fight at the time and place stated by me.

ALTHOUGH in and about the great city, things, marvellous and previously unheard of, are continually happening, it cannot be regarded but as an uncommon circumstance when a viscountess is discovered seated on a beer barrel before the bar of a low pothouse in Leather Lane, partaking of a baked potato, hot from the can of a peripatetic vendor of that nourishing vegetable.

If, however, one may credit the evidence of his own eyes, and rely on the testimony of witnesses who could have no object in imposture, I myself can vouch for this strange happening. It was not altogether an unexpected discovery. A gentleman with whom I am acquainted, and whose charitable mission it is to look after the spiritual welfare of the heathen court and alley dwellers of one of the worst parts of the metropolis, so long ago as four or five years, imparted to me the interesting fact that he reckoned, amongst his flock of black sheep, one whose fleece, in bygone times, was, at least from a worldly aspect, the finest and snowiest imaginable. Just as an ancient silver spoon, blackened and battered out of all shape, might be discovered amongst the coarse dross and dregs of a marine-store shop, so was the individual in question revealed to my friend during his explorations in slums and out-of-the-way places. She was the associate of drovers, sweeps, and costermongers, male and female, and lived and lodged with them, "And yet," said my friend, "from her own statements, as well as from such inquiries as I have had opportunities of making, she was once in the enjoyment of a title of rank, and moved in the most fashionable society; her beauty being no less notorious than its baneful influence on the large number of high-bred nobles who, dazzled and betrayed by it, had fallen wing-singed and crippled for life."

This, however, was a very long time ago; so long, indeed, that George the Fourth was then king. Since, however, it is not impossible that there may be certain persons who would be rendered uneasy were they made aware that this one brilliant star, now fallen so low, is still in the land of the living, it may be as well to call her Lady Blank. She is a stickler still for the old title. She is proud of it. When she is getting drunk - a habit to which I am sorry to have to state she is by no means uncommonly addicted - she is frequently seen to raise her gin glass, and to mutter something about "dear old times;" and when, with perseverance worthy of a better cause, she has succeeded in reducing herself to a condition of perfect intoxication, she imperiously resents all undue familiarity on the part of the squalid crew ordinarily her bosom friends and cronies, and will reply to no question unless she is addressed as "your ladyship." As I was informed before I had the felicity of being introduced to her ladyship in person, her intimates, indeed all who know her, have the most perfect belief in her pretensions, and drink good luck to Lady Blank in simple sincerity. When her funds are gone they will lend their aristocratic acquaintance a few halfpence to "keep the game alive," relying on the sufficient security of her word of honour for repayment. Occasionally, at extremely hard-up times, they oblige her ladyship by carrying her boots or her shawl to the pawnbroker's; and probably when that obliging tradesman, in faithful pursuit of his profession inquiries "What name?" that of Lady Blank is given and duly inscribed on the ticket.

This much, and more that need not be repeated, I knew beforehand. Likewise that her ladyship's passion for strong waters had been the cause of her face being as well known almost, to more than one metropolitan magistrate, as that of his own clerk. It was only recently, however, that fortune favoured me with an opportunity of contemplating this poor old mud-foundered wreck of ancient gentility. As before mentioned, it was in Leather Lane, High Holborn; and the first intimation I received of the presence of her ladyship was as follows. A man at the drinking bar was in conversation with a vendor of baked potatoes, which he carried in a can, slung on his arm:-

"I want a halfpenny off you, governor," remarked the baked potato man civilly.

"Wot for?" was the response; "I ain't had no tater."

"No; but she has." And the potato man jerked his thumb over his shoulder to indicate whom he meant.

"Oh, that's it! Now I tell you what it is, my fine feller," returned the other man with a scowl; "for 'arf a pin I'd let you go on wantin' that a'penny. Who are you calling 'she?' Hain't she got a handle to her name?"

"Well, well; you know who I mean. Her ladyship; will *that* do for you?"

"That's better," replied the man at once mollified. "Did you pick her out a mealy one?"

"She picked it out for herself;" said the potato dealer; "let her ladyship alone for that *She* ain't to be put off with a waxy 'un, or a watery one either, I can tell you."

"I shouldn't think you'd try it on with her - a woman who used to ride in her own carriage, with flunkies behind her; and the fat o' the land to be had for the asking." And as he spoke he glanced in my direction in a manner which betokened that his observation was intended for my ears rather than for those of the baked potato merchant. I comprehended the position of affairs instantly. "Her ladyship" alluded to could be no other than the celebrated Lady Blank, concerning whom my friend the missionary had long ago spoken with me. It was an opportunity not to be neglected. In ten minutes afterwards the man and myself were on conversational terms, and had drunk to each other's health, and to that of her ladyship.

"No; I don't in the least wonder at your doubting it," he remarked, wagging his head with admiration, if not with tenderness, as he regarded the remarkable looking old female of whom we were speaking. "You wouldn't think it to look at her - nobody would. Certainly, I am bound to admit that there isn't much of it shining on the surface of her now; but there *was* a time - it's a precious long while ago - but there was a time, sir, when that old party was a dasher of the first water. None of your French paste and cheap plated goods, but solid gold and diamonds. It isn't easy to believe it, sir, as you say, but it's true, for all that."

Certainly it was not easy to believe the man's assertion, although it was evident from his earnest manner that to the best of his knowledge he was speaking only what was true. As she sat there on a beer barrel in front of that dirty gin shop bar, it was difficult to associate her present or any previous portion of her existence with water of the first, or, indeed, of any other quality. She wore no bonnet or any other kind of head covering, excepting a few spare wisps of iron-grey hair which had escaped from the almost toothless comb perched all aslant on the summit of her cranium, as though the liquor that the woman was imbibing had got not only into her head but into the comb as well. Her dark eyes were bleared and bloodshot, and blinked with tipsy satisfaction on the partly empty measure of rum which stood on the metal counter before her.

She must have been a tall woman before age had bowed her shoulders, the broad bones of which were painfully indicated through the ragged flimsy shawl pinned tightly across her chest, as though to conceal some deficiency of bodice or stays beneath. She appeared to be little else besides bones and rags. In the intervals of sipping her rum she was engaged in making her supper off the baked potato; and as she screwed up her old mouth to blow the smoking vegetable, it really seemed as though her jaws must fall asunder. Her hands were of the colour of the baked potato skin, and were fleshless almost as those of an Egyptian mummy. She sat on the tub with a squareness which suggested that her legs were attached to her body as are the legs of a cheap wooden doll; and the scantiness of her bedraggled skirts betrayed the bagginess of the stockings which hung about her shrunk old shins.

It was by no means easy to guess her age. She must have been at least sixty-five. Probably she was seventy-five: probably eighty-five. I put the question to my friend, who exhibited great gratification at the interest with which I regarded his *protégé*.

"How old is she, governor?" he repeated. "Lord only knows. I never trouble myself about that. It's the quality I look at."

"And you think that the quality for which you admire her does not diminish with age?"

"Well, if you ask my private opinion," he replied, buttonholing me, that he might convey it in the lowest of whispers, "I shouldn't like her to hear it, because it might make her vain, and lead her to take advantage. But *I* think that the older one of her kind gets she gets the more preciouser."

"Becomes a greater novelty, eh?"

"No, I don't mean that; new things is novel. I mean to say that she gets rarer - better worth keeping by you. Like a old guinea or a painted picter. Lord bless you, it wouldn't make no difference in my treatment of her if she was as old as Methusalem."

"She's your wife, I suppose?"

"My what?"

"Your wife."

My friend was incautiously drinking at the moment, and he was taken with so violent a fit of suppressed laughter that his liquor went "the wrong way;" and for a time he appeared to be in danger of death from suffocation.

"Not she," he replied at length. "You don't know her, or you wouldn't ask such a question. She's miles too stuck up, even if I wished it, which I don't. No, she's a fancy of mine - a kind o' curiosity; and I looks after her, that's all."

I was unable to make out with entire satisfaction who and what was the gentleman who, at this stage of her decline from former greatness, Lady Blank deigned to honour with her particular acquaintance. My hints on this head elicited the shy rejoinder that he was a "dealer;" and certainly there was an air about him which savoured of old furniture, house clearings, and other things brokerish; which symptoms, however, were directly at variance with the tight-fitting corduroy trousers and red ochre stained jacket, which bespoke him a drover. But again, to this last view there was contradiction in his cap, which was a close-fitting, smooth-napped article, such as is seldom seen on any human head excepting that of the British costermonger.

Lady Blank's tastes must certainly have deteriorated along with her falling away from her ancient tip-top associations. The individual who at present honoured her with his protection was not what would generally be regarded as a prepossessing person. His hair was cropped close, his nose much flatter on his face than noses usually are, while his massive chin and lower jaw were blue with a rare strength of bristly growth lurking beneath the skin. His only redeeming features were his eyes, which were merry and twinkling, especially when he turned them in Lady B.'s direction; there could be no doubt that his admiration for the old woman was sincere. It was he who had replenished her measure of rum. It was he who had paid for her baked potato. He did not appear anxious to press either his company or his conversation on her; and as the degraded old creature munched and mowed, and soaked a piece of her potato which was underdone, in the rum glass, Mr. Dealer evinced the unspeakable satisfaction the spectacle afforded him by the blandest of smiles; at the same time tenderly caressing with the tip of his forefinger a bald expanse behind his ear.

"Pon my soul," remarked the dealer, after a prolonged fit of contemplation, "when I think about it, it takes me all my time to believe in the realness of it all."

"You have no doubt of it, however?"

"How can I have? If she was always drunk, as she is now, it might be that I was took in; but it's very different from that. I've heard her pedigree over and over again, as I've been a sittin' peaceful, blowing my bacca with her by the fire side."

"And when she has been quite sober?"

"When there hasn't been so much as a half-quartern amiss with her, sir. I've heard her tell that same story twenty times if once, and she never deviates so much as a single sinnable in telling it. She's as much Lady B., wot's left of her, as she was when out-and-out swells ruined themselves a buying diamonds for her; and she thought no more of being waited on by lords and dukes than I do of a game at skittles. Why, dools have been fought about her!"

"Duels?"

"I've had it from her own lips. At least, there was one dool fought, and all because one chap trod on her broidered skirt at a ball, and sort of sneered when he was asked to 'pologize; so the nobleman she was a dancing along with called out the other, and they went and settled it on Wormwood Scrubbs. That's the party, sir - she what's now a sitting on that beer barrel, that Lord T. once gave four hundred guineas for a saddle-horse for. Them there old fingers of hers, which are glad now to hold on to a baked tatur, one time o' day blazed with diamond rings that cost over a thousand."

"They were whiter then than they are at the present time," I ventured to remark.

"White as milk, sir; I'll go bail for it," replied Mr. Dealer, enthusiastically. "Lord, what a beauty she must ha' been! And a lady, too - a real harristocracy lady, you must understand. Opera box, whacking great mansion up steps, and flunkies to hold her umbrella over her when it was raining, and she was stepping from her mansion to her carriage. That's her on the tub. I drove her down to Barnet last fair time in a donkey barrow belonging to a friend of mine."

"And how do you agree together?"

"Oh, we rubs along pretty well, mostly," he replied, gallantly kissing his hand to Lady Blank, who at that moment was holding up the upturned rum measure as a sign that she would regard it as a favour if he would yet once again pay for its refilling. "Sometimes she cuts up rough, though," he continued in a lower voice; "its nat'rally to be expected, considering her breed, that she should; but I ain't always in the humour to make that allowance. When she gets audacious drunk and rides the high horse, why then, of course, I have to put on the kicking strap."

"Of course," I remarked, "you merely take it for granted that she was at one time the beauty you would make her out to be."

"How d'ye mean?"

"You have no proof of it; it is only what she tells you."

"There you're wrong, governor," replied Mr. Dealer, his confidence warming. "I've seen what she was in them days with my own eyes."

"You? Why you are not more than fifty, while she -"

"I don't mean to say that I've seen her living figure when she was a splendid swell, but I have seen her likeness painted on a egg-shaped bit of ivory. It's no more like her now than a golden necklace is like a halter."

"I should like to see it."

"Werry likely; so should I," replied Mr. Dealer, laconically.

"What has become of it, then?"

"It's a deuce of a time since I saw it, but I recollect it well enough," he continued, not heeding my question. "The pictur of quite a young girl, with a low-neck frock, and a regler all a-blowin' and a-growin' kind of bust, plump as cauliflowers, and with a heart-shaped thing hanging round her neck, made out of precious stones, and fastened by a gold chain. It was no wonder the degree to which the nobs and swells of them times courted her. Such ringletty hair, such eyes, and the white teeth a showing between the lips, just open a little, and looking as temptin' as - as a hiester (by which I suppose he meant oyster). It must ha' cost a heap of money. It's as cracked and yellow as a old pie-dish now. It used to have a gold rim, but she didn't set any store by that, and so she took it off and sold it. But she wouldn't part with the painted pictur: there, I don't believe," continued Mr. Dealer, solemnly, "that she would make away with that cracked old portrait if she was dying for a drop of rum, and what she could get for it would save her."

"But what has become of it? Does she wear it?"

"She used to," he replied, whispering, lest the dreadful old creature on the tub might overhear him, "but she don't now. She's too much afeard of losing it."

The tipsy comb that up to this time had been holding on by a single tooth atop of her head had now fallen down; and with her thin grey hair all loose and dabbling in the spilt rum on the counter, Lady Blank, despairing of more rum at Mr. Dealer's expense, just at present, was indulging in a refreshing nap with her head resting on her folded arms.

"Yes; she used to wear it always," the man continued, "with a hole bored in the edge of it, and a bit of string round her neck, and hid down her bosom; but since I accidentally biled it she hides it away somewheres at home."

"Since you did what with it?"

"Biled it, sir. It was quite a accident, though at the time she didn't believe it was. I'll tell you how it happened. We had a old iron kettle what was only fit to keep odds and ends in, because the spout was knocked off. We didn't have no other kettle, so we used to bile the water for breakfast and tea in a saucepan. Well, one day when she had been sent to quod for her old game, I thought that I'd surprise her when she came home by having a bit of a treat ready for her. She is werry partial to a stewed cow's heel, on account of her teeth being bad; and that's what I got her. Well, the saucepan being engaged in cooking it, and water being wanted for a cup of tea, I thought that I'd make shift with the old iron kettle with the spout off, that I told you about just now. So I took, as I thought, all the rubbish out of it, and put some water in it and set it on the fire to bile, and laid the plates and the cups and saucers all ready, when in she came, sniffin' what was cooking and breaking into words of gratitude, because I hadn't forgot her. But all on a sudden she spies the old kettle steamin' away on the hob, and then she alters her tune in a manner that surprised me, I can tell you. She squeals out and makes a sudden dash at the fireplace, like a scalded cat. Next minute, in a manner of speaking, she *was* a scalded cat; for before you could count six she had whipped off the lid, and, bilin' hot as the water was, she plunges her hand into it, and after scraping about for a time she fishes up the blessed portrait. It had laid flat at the bottom, d'ye see, when I hooked out the other bits of rubbish, and I had overlooked it. 'Course, there was a end to the 'armony," said Mr. Dealer, bringing his narrative to an abrupt conclusion.

"What did she say about it?" I asked.

"What didn't she say?" grinned Mr. Dealer. "She carried on at me at such an orful rate that anybody would have thought that it was a young un' of hers I had biled by accident, instead of that ivory thing. It isn't often that I wallops her ladyship, but I certinly did on that occasion; I couldn't help it."

"And the miniature?"

"That was the last time I ever saw it. She's took better care of it ever since. She's got it safe enough, I'll bet - up the chimney, or in a crack under the floor boards, or somewheres."

"But what makes you think that she still has it hoarded away?"

Mr. Dealer directed a cautious glance towards Lady Blank, and, finding that she was still asleep, he turned, with an air of relief, to continue the conversation.

"Do I look like a superstitious kind of a man?" he asked, mysteriously.

I readily answered that he certainly did not.

"I'm glad of that," said he, "because if I did, I should look like what I ain't; which isn't pleasant. No; I ain't superstitious, but I've got my ideas; and what d'ye think they are?"

I assured him that I had not the remotest notion.

"I've got the idea," said he, bringing his mouth so close to my ear that he might easily have bitten it, "that there's dollartery in that there likeness business."

"What's dollartery?" I was fain to inquire, after a few moments of vain surmise.

"Dear, oh dear! fancy you being so ignorant!" returned Mr. Dealer, pityingly. "Dollartery is worshipping hidols. It's my belief that the Duchess makes a hidol of that little ivory painting. I shouldn't be a bit surprised," he continued, "to find out that when she's all alone in that room, she locks the door and forrages out that blessed pictur, and reglar worships it, just like them foreign heathens do to idols; there ain't nothing in the world she thinks so much of. I don't believe that, put all together, the scores and scores of times she's been run in for the two D's" (drunk and disorderly, as he afterwards was kind enough to interpret) "that she has suffered half as much as she would if any one was to take that little pictur away from her."

"You are sure that it is a likeness of her?" I remarked.

"Quite," returned Mr. Dealer, confidently.

"Why so?"

"Because she says so, and she never tells lies. That's the beauty of her," he continued, in tones of admiration. "It's the only beauty she's got left, you'll say; but I'll answer for her having that one, at all events - that and being game."

"How do you mean?"

"Plucky; ready; show her breed and spirit: that's what takes my fancy. It don't matter what it is - birds, animals, anything what's been cultiwated and got their best p'ints brought out. It's blood, you know, that's what it is."

"Then you think that if it wasn't for superior breeding, Lady Blank would never have been the remarkable old person she is now?"

"If she hadn't been real lady bred, sir," returned Mr. Dealer, speaking in the tone of an authority, "if she hadn't ha' started with the real stuff in her veins, she'd have knocked under years ago. She'd have gone 'slommicking,' as we say, and she wouldn't have been any curiosity at all. Now she is a curiosity, and I'm proud of her."

"I hope that she appreciates your high opinion."

"That don't matter a button; it's what I think of her. Her opinion of me! You should hear it sometimes!" said Mr. Dealer, good-humouredly. "Why, if ever a woman - of the common sort, you understand - was to call me only half the names she calls me, I should turn rusty; but I admire it in her. You see, mister, it's no small thing for a humble, and in a manner of speakin' a common cove like me, to have one of your high-bred 'uns all to himself; like he might have a tip-top strain of goldfinch or canary, or something not easy to match in the way of a tarrier or a spannel. A man naturally takes a pride in such things, especially when he's got a fancy that way. I have. There's nothing like blood, in my opinion. You get it in horses, and it lasts 'em until they come down to a night cab, and haven't got a leg to stand on or an eye to see out of; and you gets it in dogs, and it lasts 'em while they've got a tooth in their head; and you get it in women. She - Lady Blank, I mean - hasn't got a tooth in her head; but you should see her sometimes when I stir her up, by way of amusement, and chaff her about them old times. My eyes! she's as fierce as a kangaroo then."

At this point of our conversation, Mr. Dealer's quick ear informed him that Lady Blank was roused from her slumber; and, looking in that direction, there she was, off the barrel and on her feet, beckoning him to come to her.

"She's making signs that she wants to speak to me," said he; "come along, and we'll have a chat with her."

But he was mistaken in supposing that Lady Blank was sociably inclined. As we approached her, she was evidently endeavouring to conceal something under a corner of her shawl from the keen eyes of Mr. Dealer, as she fixed her eyes on him in a half-frightened, half-defiant manner.

"What's the mischief now, duchess?" said he cheerfully:

"Nothing that concerns a low beast such as you are," her ladyship replied, hugging the corner of her shawl and shrinking away from him.

Mr. Dealer, however, was not at all offended by the ungracious rejoinder to his civil observation. On the contrary, he winked at me an unmistakable injunction to remember what he had said about pluck, and blood, and breeding.

"Draw it mild, my beauty," he remarked; "if there isn't anything the matter with you, your safest place will be on that tub you've just got off of. Allow me, Lady Blank."

By "allowing him" he meant permitting him to lift her up on to the beer barrel again, and as he did so, he discovered the cause of her ladyship's embarrassment. She was without her shoes.

"Oh, that's what's the matter," said he, with no abatement of his good humour; "you know we can't allow that, duchess, we've got too much respect for your precious health. Drop 'em now, that's a good creature, and put 'em on this minnit, or I shall be obliged to make it warm for you."

And as he spoke he gave the corner of the shawl a tug, and down dropped her ladyship's muddy boots, which were there concealed.

"She wanted to leave 'em over the bar for a quartern of rum, but I wouldn't take 'em of her," remarked the spruce barmaid coming forward, her ire excited less, I am afraid, by the proffered pawn than by the fact of her ladyship having by accident left some of the skin of her baked potato in the rum measure. "She's a disgrace to her sex! she's worse than the pigs in the street!" said the barmaid.

It was evident that Mr. Dealer had spoken only the truth when he asserted that this wretched old wreck of a fine lady was still game. Hearing the barmaid's uncomplimentary insinuation, she straightened her back with such suddenness, that one might almost have imagined that he heard the bones click in their sockets, and her bleared eyes blazed up fiercely as she turned on her defamer. It was a fortunate thing for the young lady that Mr. Dealer had disarmed the "duchess" of her boots; had he not done so, of a certainty they would have been launched at the barmaid's head. He nudged in; and whispered rapidly:-

"Now you can see her breed. That's blood, that is! Only look at her! Why she looks the gal behind the bar down as mere trash, old as she is. It's something, you know, for a chap like me to own a woman like that!"

He, nevertheless, deemed it prudent to interpose, with a view to mitigating her ladyship's wrath; and this was easily effected by his volunteering once more to replenish the rum measure.

Having done which, he commenced to put her boots on as she sat. Unfortunately, however, he could not resist the opportunity the act afforded of saying a smart thing at her ladyship's expense.

"Here's a pair of trotter cases for feet that once upon a time would turn up their toes at anything but white satin shoes," he remarked, exhibiting one of the muddy old boots with a grin. "That's right enough old lady, isn't it?"

But the old lady was still smarting under the barmaid's unkind remarks, and fired up once more as Mr. Dealer addressed her.

"I wish," said she, passionately, as she clenched both her bony fists and shook them at him, "I wish that I had worn out my feet with the last pair of satin shoes I ever cast off. I wish I had worn my soul and heart out rather than have lived to sink to the level of a coarse, low-lived cur like you!"

But Mr. Dealer took it all in good part; he was not at all offended. On the contrary, as her ladyship continued to launch at him the most bitter invective, his countenance assumed quite a gratified and delighted expression.

"What did I tell you," he whispered to me behind his hand. "Ain't she a star? I've never before had women of this sort to deal with; but I've had game fowl, and I've had dawgs, and it's the same with 'em all, if they comes of the right stock. Why I recollect, a bit ago, having a tarrier dog what got old and disagreeable, and was turned out on that account from a swell house in Belgravy. Well, he come into my hands, and nat'rally I put him on paunch, like the rest. Would he eat it? Not he. He had been used to his chicken, and his mutton chops, and his 'ashes: and he turned up his nose at anything commoner. It was no use coaxing him; the more we persewered, the more he showed his teeth; till one day, having severely bit the boy what was trying to tempt him to pick a bit off the skewer, he curled hisself up in a fur corner of the kennel, and that was the last that was ever seen of him alive. I had him stuffed though."

And as with these words he brought the touching narrative to a conclusion, he pensively regarded her draggle-tailed ladyship on the tub, as though strange speculations were flitting through his mind. Finally, however, he shook his head with a regretful sigh. Suddenly, altering his mind respecting her ladyship's boots, he cast off the one he had already adjusted, and put them both in the pocket of his jacket.

"When once she sets her mind on doing a thing, she'll do it, if she can anyhow manage it, especially when she's put out, as she is now," he remarked to me confidentially. "If I was to turn my back on her for only ten minutes she'd conwert 'em into rum, so I think I'd better see her safe home."

Then, turning to the shameful old person on the beer barrel, he said cheerfully:-

"Drink up your liquor and hop down, old beauty; you've had as much for one night as is good for your health."

And, understanding from his tone of voice, or, which is more probable, the peculiar glance that accompanied the observation, that Mr. Dealer was no longer in a mood to be trifled with, the "old beauty" got down as requested, and followed him out of the door, her stockinged feet squelching in the mire, with much more docility than would have been displayed by the high-bred "tarrier" dog, with the story of whose. heroic demise Mr. Dealer had just before made me acquainted.

IT was not in furtherance of any preconceived plan that midnight found me on Waterloo Bridge, or that I might set at rest any speculations previously formed on the subject of suicide by drowning from this the scene of so many terrible leaps in the dark. It was not that it had occurred to me that the Bridge of Sighs offered a fair post of observation to any one who felt curious in the matter, for gaining information as to the growth and development of self-murder madness when it took this direction - to learn how many "unfortunates" there were who came to the centre parapet of the grey bridge to brood on the terrible intent, perhaps in the hope that opportunity for its consummation would suffice to dispel the lingering love of life and the horror of death that hitherto had held them back. I had, I say, no inclination to speculate on how many had repented of their rash design as soon as they had paid the halfpenny, and the click of the turnstile intimated that now the way was clear; how many came hurrying in the dark and in frantic haste to find wholesome sedatives for their disordered brain in a contemplation of the black and awful depth, and in the bleak wind that blew off the icy water. I had not sought the bridge of Waterloo for any such study. Had such been my intent, I should probably have selected a finer night; for, even in early summer, the arches of granite that span the river Thames do not present the most desirable promenade after the churches have chimed twelve, and there is a north-east wind blowing, with a rain which is none the less spiteful because it is small.

I was a passenger on the bridge in question, and at the time stated, simply because, in the course of common events, it happened so, and I don't suppose that I should have paused between the boundary turnstiles, only that I came on a policeman in altercation with a woman, who, it appeared, had made herself as comfortable as circumstances would permit, and with the intention of passing the night huddled up in a corner of one of the stone recess seats. She was an elderly female, and very drunk, which may have accounted for the unreasonableness of her argument. In the first place, she fiercely resented the officer's interference at all, and, with an outburst of virtuous indignation that rendered her almost unintelligible, wished to be informed what that functionary took her for? Perhaps it was too bad of the policeman to hazard the opinion that she was "what he called a 'nonderscrip,'" and fortunate for him that the appalling imputation reduced her to a condition of speechlessness, from which she emerged several seconds afterwards in a flood of tears.

She would not move off the wet stones, in which her skirts were dabbling. She "had paid her ha'penny," and that, she maintained, entitled her to the use of Waterloo Bridge during her pleasure. But the policeman, who was good-natured and forbearing, could not be brought to take this view of the matter.

"That's a stale story," said he; "if I was to let it pass with everybody who pitches it to me, the seats would be like a common lodging-house. You're a foot passenger, not a lodger, don't you know? and your ha'porth is to go over, not to lie down; and if you don't go over one side or the t'other, I shall be obliged to walk with you a little further than may be agreeable." After which unmistakable hint, in the most friendly manner, he threw the light of his "bull's-eye" on her, stood her upright, put straight her bonnet, which was flat as a pancake in consequence of her having made a pillow of it, and turned her face to the Surrey side, towards which she went staggering, still bewailing that she should have lived all these years, and reared eleven children, the ugliest one of which was a beauty compared with the policeman, and after all to be compared to a "nonderscrip."

"You are not troubled with many such customers as that, I hope, policeman?" I remarked.

"A dozen of 'em in a night, sometimes," he replied; and immediately added, "but they are of a mild sort compared with some we have to deal with. No fear of a man going to sleep on this beat, I can assure you, sir."

"Of what sort are the very bad?" I asked.

"Oh, all manner, chiefly the women going home to the Blackfriars side after it has got too late for them to stay out any longer. There's a lot of trouble with them poor devils very often."

"Tipsy, I suppose?"

"No, not so much that, as down on their luck as a rule," replied the friendly policeman, with a shrug of his broad shoulders; "and when it's that way with 'em, they somehow seemed to find the bridge an awkward bit to get over."

"How an awkward bit?"

"Well; I ain't equal to explainin' it; but it's a dark and solitary bit after the gas of the public-houses and that, and it strikes 'em as such, I suppose, and sets 'em thinking of the lots that have made a jump of it when they got as far as the middle arch, and then they get the 'blues,' and there's no doing anything with 'em. It would do good to some of them fast young fellows who go in for 'seeing life,' as they call it, if they could see some of them miserable gals shivering home over the bridge here, in the dark and rain, sometimes at one or two in the morning."

I expressed to the worthy constable my opinion that there could be no doubt of it; at the same time resolving that I would wait a little on the bridge in order to see for myself what were the kind of customers that passed the toll-man's wicket at the small hours of morning.

It was then nearly one o'clock, and nothing particularly worth mentioning occurred for nearly an hour, except the amazing number of wretched girls and women who came hurrying from the Strand side of the bridge, and, with an aspect exactly as opposite to "gay" as black is to white, making haste, through the rain which had saturated their flimsy skirts and covered the pavement with a thick paste of mud, cruelly cold to ill-shod feet, towards the miserable "lodgings" in the poorer neighbourhoods of Lambeth and Blackfriars which were dignified with the name of home. The only ones of the shocking sisterhood who evinced any signs even of cheerfulness were those - and they were the majority - who were the worse for drink; and they might always be known from the rest, though their step was steady as the best, by their singing, which, perhaps, was by way of keeping their courage up, as small boys in dark places take to whistling. But there were many, and amongst them the youngest, who looked so wretchedly wet, cold, and utterly comfortless, that it would have been a mercy rather than a sin to have conferred a glass of brandy on them.

"Give me a penny, the Lord will be good to you," said one of these poor little mortals, whose thin shawl clung wet to her narrow shoulders. "You wouldn't think twice about it if you knew how perishing cold I was."

"But what can you buy for a penny, and at this time, that will warm you?"

"I can get a penn'orth of coffee at the stall on the other side, and a warm at the fire; that'll be better than nothing, before I go home."

"And is it true that you can get a cup of coffee and a seat by the fire for a penny?"

"It would be a bad job for a good many like me if they couldn't. He's as good as a father to us, that old coffee man," and the wretched child - for really she was little better - laughed at her small joke, till she set herself coughing in a manner that would have been unbearably painful to hear, but that there might be heard in it a grim promise that the downward steep on which she had set her young feet would be but a brief one.

Having furnished her with the price of the coffee, I thought it might be worth the few minutes' walk to see if the fatherly stallkeeper had any but an imaginary existence. She was truthful in this instance, however. There was the stall - a snug little cabin of a place, of boards and canvas, with the cheerful glow of a charcoal fire within, and there, too, was the individual who had been so gratefully alluded to, dispensing the smoking beverage and bread and butter to seven or eight female outcast wretches who huddled together in the friendly shelter, two or three being seated on a form dozing by the fire, at the heat of which their drenched clothes steamed, and by the light of which might be observed the ghastly contrast between their pinched and haggard faces - pale except for the paint patches that glared like plague spots and their wretched finery, the drooping feathers and festoons of rainbow ribbon with which their hats were trimmed.

By the time I again reached Waterloo Bridge it was past two, and either the policeman had gone off duty or had given up as hopeless the endeavour to convince certain people that payment of a halfpenny did not confer on them the right to use any one of the stone seats as a couch. They must have some such notion, or why do they pay their money when they must be so deplorably short of it, and when there are "free seats" on all the other bridges excepting Vauxhall? Of course, it cannot be that the stones of the Waterloo recesses are softer than other stones. It must be done purely for the sake of the seclusion and quiet that, as a lodging, are afforded by Waterloo Bridge as compared with London and Blackfriars - though, indeed, it is hard to understand how a human being reduced to such a deplorable strait can for a moment hesitate between the open air and the cold stones, and a refuge in a. workhouse.

Here they were, however - in one recess a woman and a child of five or six years huddled up in a shapeless bundle or rags, the only sign of humanity about it being two small feet. In the next recess there was a drunken man, a drover I think, fast asleep on his back, and with his mouth open, while his hat, which had rolled off was in the safe keeping of his dog, who lay with his body curled about it. In another recess, however, there was life that was not of the still kind. There sat two women, one young and well but flashily dressed, the other a miserable shabby woman of middle age, with an old black stuff cloak on; and with the two was an individual of the male sex, whose appearance it is not easy to describe. If the reader can imagine a man whose visage was a blending of the characteristics that distinguish the dog-stealer, the area sneak, and the fighting man, he may form some idea of the cadaverous, vicious-looking individual in question. The place was so still that there was no necessity to cross the road to hear what was going on.

"It's all nonsense what she says about not going back, you know," said the shabby woman; "she'll have to do it. I ain't going to get into a row on her account."

"Lor! you needn't fret about that," growled the cadaverous gentleman, with a growl that sounded like a preliminary to a bite, "she'll come to her senses when she's had her temper out a bit, and had a cooler. She'll find it hot for herself if she doesn't. She's a pretty one to cut the high caper - without a rag to call her own."

This last sneer at her poverty stung the showily-dressed young woman over whose fine mantle and bonnet the shabby woman had solicitously cast a corner of her frowzy old cloak to protect them from the rain, and provoked her to immediate and fierce reply.

"Curse you both!" she exclaimed, starting up from the shabby woman's protecting wing. (" Dear me! she'll get her clothes drenched!" cried this worthy person, wringing her dirty hands in despair.) "Curse you both!" exclaimed the girl, "and who was it that robbed me of my good clothes? Who cheated and plundered me but you, you thief" - (this to the cadaverous gentleman) - "and the set over there, till I hadn't a skirt to call my own."

"Never mind who cheated you; that's nothing to do with them clothes what's only lent you," growled the bully. "If yer don't know how to behave in 'em, come on home and get out of 'em. It isn't likely that this woman who is sent with you to look after you is going back to tell 'em that you're slipped off;" and then, for the first time perceiving me, the villain nudged the shabby woman, and again addressing the girl, in a softer voice, remarked that it was no good her sitting there "ketchin cold," and that they might just as well walk as they talked; on which the trio moved off towards the Surrey side; the young woman still persisting that she wouldn't go back - she would sooner be dead and buried.

"That's the way with them marms; they gets a silk gownd on, and then a Duchess ain't good enough to be their sister. Serve her right, whatever she gets." It was a female voice that gave utterance to these generous sentiments - a ragged wretch, starved-looking, and with the bones showing sharp under her white skin, but who somehow had contrived to get so intoxicated that she had to hold on by the stone-work for support.

"Do you know her?" I asked.

"Not her, I don't; but I know the set," returned the scarecrow, spitefully. "She's a dress-woman, that's what she is."

"A dress-woman?"

"Ah! one of them that they tog out so that they may show off at their best and make the most of their faces. But they can't trust 'em," pursued the awful creature, venturing to take the steadying grasp from the stone coping that she might clap both her skinny hands in gleeful malice, "they can't trust em, you heard that. They never trust 'em further than they can see 'em. You might tell that by the shadder."

"By the what?"

"The shadder. That was the shadder, that woman that was with her. They call 'em that because they sticks so close to 'em, and never leave the track of 'em, not for a minute. They're no more their own mistresses than galley-slaves are; and serve 'em right."

"And who was the man?" I asked. But, however much the creature of rags and gin lacked sympathy for the wretched victim of the "shadder," she had no good word for the male ruffian.

"He! he hasn't got a name," she replied scornfully. "That has "- and she spurned some mud before her with her broken old shoe - "but he hasn't. He's worse than a dog, for dogs don't eat each other. He'd steal his mother's crutches if she was a cripple, and get drunk with the money he sold them for, and go home and beat her."

So saying, the shameful creature staggered away, and as by this time morning was breaking, and it seemed to me unlikely that the toll-gate man would have many customers more interesting than those I had already made acquaintance with, I too passed out at the turnstile.

IT was a "happy thought" which inspired those who guide the destinies of our river steamers to promote a moonlight voyage on the Thames. The idea, had it been started ten years ago, might have appeared absurd. In that dark age the stream was banked throughout its whole length by pestilent mud accumulations and odious wharfs and factories, and the water itself was of a kind unpalatable to any fish more fastidious than the eel. But we have mended our water ways since then, and with a flowering Thames Embankment, and a tidal flow so pellucid that the finny tribe have been tempted back to it, there seemed no reason why the river's refinement should not progress yet a step further. Its chastened bosom was surely as susceptible to romance as those puny puddles in Italy about which pictorial art is so fond of fussing, and, "weather permitting," it would be easy enough to travel by moonlight, and in a manner worthy of the greatest commercial city in the world.

It would, of course, be ridiculous to attempt the gondola style of thing, with a picturesque waterman, and grapes, and wine, and a guitar on board. It would not pay in the first place, and in the second it would hardly be effective at certain points of the voyage - in the Pool, for instance, where the coal lighters lie thick, and the surface of the stream is so thickly mantled with inky dust, that if the lady ventured, as they do in those Venetian pictures, to toy with the water over the boat's side, her lily hand would immediately become as though it had been coated with the finest liquid blacking. But why not charter a steam vessel, and do the thing as it should be done? So it came about that on a certain Saturday night, the moon being at that time near the full, and therefore eminently favourable, a steamer left Greenwich Pier at half-past six for Rosherville, to return therefrom when the sun had sunk to rest in the west, and Luna, Queen of Night, perambulated the starry heavens in her silver car.

Punctual to the moment, the Zephyr steamed gallantly up to the starting-point at Greenwich. It was a brave sight. At the fore part of the vessel a hundred tiny bannerets streamed gaily in the evening breeze, while neatly furled from funnel to fore-peak was the friendly tarpaulin which would unfold its sheltering wings in the event of rain. At the after-part of the vessel there was not so much festive display; but then there was this advantage - the brass band faced in that direction. Discarding lutes and flutes and twanging guitars, the projectors of the trip had provided seven performers on brazen instruments and a drummer, and these sat in a row on the bridge which spans the gulf between the paddle-boxes. It was an experiment, possibly a delicate one, but at a glance, and even before the Zephyr touched the pier, it was evidently worth trying.

Moonlight trippers, to the number of a hundred and fifty at least, were there ready to embark, and very curious, and, for that matter, touching as well, was it to observe how, if you can only get at it, there is romance in even the commonest natures. Of course, it was no more than one expected to find Augustus and Angeljna there - Augustus, the pale and poetic, with his hair brushed back from his noble brow, and with his slim throat severely socketed in a spotless turnover collar, and Angelina in muslin, with *his* likeness in her brooch and a white rose in her dress, a zephyr shawl over her arm, and in her hand a volume of the sweetest poems. Such a pair there was in at least dozen places; but the individuals one would not, on such an occasion, have missed had they been absent, but who were there too and in considerable force, included lovers of a humbler sphere of life. The lithe-limbed young costermonger from the "Brill" and from Bethnal-green had somehow got wind of the excursion, and here he was with his young woman. He came in a new hairy cap, and a waistcoat as flowerily sprigged as though he was on the way to be married, and the poetry newly kindled in his breast found expression in the pensive manner in which he drew on the store of winkles with which his pocket was filled, wriggling them out of their shells with a pin, and thoughtfully swallowing them as though with the vague idea that somehow or other there was a similarity in the fate of thw winkle and that of the young man who meditated matrimony His companion, though probably not less sentimental than he was too shrewd and sensible to believe that her affianced could exist on romance and winkles from six in the evening until midnight, and had prudently brought with her a convenient hand-basket full of provisions; while in her own behalf, and to mark her respectful appreciation of the event, she came with her honest red hands encased in lavender-coloured cotton gloves, and with a market pottle of strawberries for her refreshment.

There were youths and their sweethearts of a much less respectable type than the love smitten couple last mentioned, and, oddly enough, any number of middle-aged pairs - hard-working, cosy and comfortable looking Darbies and Joans - who came linked together as lovingly as the rest, except that occasionally there was a sheepishness about Darby that was not natural to him. It is not unlikely, however, that Darby's sheepishness, inasmuch as it invested his countenance with a certain amount of bashfulness and lover-like bewilderment, rather heightened than detracted from the romantic effect. As we started, the brass band on the bridge played some selections from "Madame Angot;" while the sun was shining, and the river merrily rippling, the little flags gaily flying, in defiance of melancholy, and all the dull world and its drudgery, and altogether things looked promising. At Blackwall we took in at least a hundred more moonlight trippers, amongst whom were a score or so whose room would have been preferable to their company, for we were getting uncomfortably crowded; and at Woolwich we made a final call and took in some sixty or seventy more. By this time we were chokeful from stem to stern, with both cabins below packed as closely almost as herrings in a barrel.

By the time we reached Greenhithe I am afraid that many of the company began to suspect that the affair was a mistake. It did not seem to have occurred to any one before that there is all the difference between going out to greet the moon and making a voyage on the chance of meeting her on the way. Likewise, it is one thing to pull along at one's ease on the surface of a pleasant tide, with luxurious lounging and gossip and pipe-smoking to beguile the time, and quite another to be rammed and jammed on the deck of a crowded steamboat, with not room even to turn round without vigorously exercising one's elbows. I was considerably incommoded in this way myself but, if I felt it, how must it have been with Angelina and Augustus! Just imagine the mental condition of those twin souls of poetry, in such a crowd that it was impossible to count its number; but on board the Zephyr there must have been a least a dozen such unhappy pairs who were being "scrouged" and hustled about in the most deplorable manner; and if ever the human countenance wore an expression of hatred and disgust for all, except one, of humankind, that expression was visible in every agonized Augustus on the boat. Tender looks, tender words - stuff and nonsense! Never mind your heart and its throbbings; be careful that that gentleman who is struggling over your beloved's shoulder to borrow a corkscrew of a friend half a dozen yards away, does not poke her eye out with the sharp-pointed instrument. Angelina's face is flushed and her hair is coming down: she regards Augustus with tearful eyes which convey a well's depth of reproach; but what can that unhappy young man do? Were he in a train he could ,et out at the next station; were he in an omnibus it would merely be a question of alighting and hailing another vehicle; but on board the Zephyr he is for the time as much a prisoner as though he were on board a transport ship, and bound for penal settlement. He is pledged for the "moonlight trip" and there is no release for him or for his affianced until the trip is consummated. Perhaps when the moon rises he tourists will settle down, or stand quiet, at all events.

By half-past eight Rosherville is gained, but we do not land The captain, seeing that some of his party have become a little too lively to be trusted on shore, will not entertain the idea for a moment, so we turn homeward. It is a disappointment, but there is at least this consolation: it is growing more and more dark, and the moon may be expected at any moment. We do our best to invite her, for in half a dozen different spots there are as many parties singing " Rise, gentle moon," "When the moon is on the waters," "Meet me by moonlight alone," and so forth. Then, all the songs in which the word moon is mentioned having been sung, those who are still in a sentimental mood, continue to serenade her coy ladyship with many melancholy ballads of the " Poor old Jeff" and "Mary Blane" order; but whether the moon is sulky or frightened, she certainly declines to illumine the heavens. It is a pity, and the moon herself can hardly be aware how much she has to answer for in consequence of not shining out that Saturday night. There were those on board that boat who, I feel convinced, were "open to conversion." There was that young winkle-devouring costermonger and the many bosom friends and acquaintances he discovered on the steamer. The "moonlight trip" was to them the dawn of tenderness and sentimentality. Had the orb of night fulfilled the share assigned to her in the programme, there is no knowing but that the contemplation of her full splendour would have acted on his corrugated nature as a hot flat-iron acts on rough linen, and that he would have appeared a smooth and glossy character ever after; but since the moon saw fit to flout that impetuous young fellow, and declined to respond to his shy advances, why, "the moon be blowed!" says the young costermonger to his sweetheart; "wot's the use of stopping up here to ketch cold?" As the night grows darker sentiment is thrown overboard altogether, and, as they sit and stand, young men and maidens, fast boys and their female acquaintances, respectable middle-aged women and their husbands, all huddled together in the dark, go in for music-hall ditties of the fullest strength and flavour, and other melodies of the same classical character. There is an attempt at dancing, but it ends in an inevitable trampling on the feet of the innocent, and a fight that is promptly suppressed by the policeman in attendance. There is finally drinking and smoking everywhere, and downstairs more, I think, than anywhere else, judging from the steady cloud of tobacco smoke that ascends from thence, and the mutual tenderness for each other evinced by couples whose affection does not seem diminished by their discovery of the moon's faithlessness. On the whole, the return to Greenwich was not nearly so dignified as the outsetting; and perhaps it was, after all, a kindness on the part of the luminary we had been voyaging in search of that she did not peep out at this last moment, and show to all assembled there what a very unromantic crew it was that had sought to bask in her smiles.

ONE of the most common of popular errors, and strangely enough, especially amongst folk who all their lives have resided within omnibus ride of the Mansion House and the Monument, is that on Sunday London is a deserted city; that its streets both wide and narrow, and which from Monday morning until Saturday night are as busily thronged as a bee-hive at swarming time, are all through the intervening four and twenty hours utterly empty and forsaken. It is generally accepted that the reason why the goodly sprinkling of churches to be found within the city's limits fall so uncommonly short as regards Sabbath day congregations, is to be found in the fact that there are people to speak of left within earshot of the ringing of the church bells, and that if on a Sunday the whole community to be discovered within the various gates which indicate the jurisdiction of the Lord Mayor were compelled to go to church, St. Paul's Cathedral would afford ample accommodation for the purpose, with room to spare.

It is not a little singular that such a bare-faced affectation of fact should so long have existed without challenge in an inquiring age such as the present. Is Aldgate with its world-renowned pump included in the city of London? Is Houndditch and the half-score of streets in the last-mentioned thoroughfare, and which have outlet in the Whitechapel Road? Why, the truth is, - and in order that there may be no mistake the evidence is renewed every Sabbath Day throughout the year, - there is no place in England so crowded, so densely mobbed and close packed, as during certain hours of the forenoon is this, the very heart and centre of the city, on a Sunday morning. Goodness knows it is not because their tongues are not loud enough to reach the ears of those whom they would summon that the chimes in the belfries fail to cause the various churches in the city to be full to overflowing. It is exactly at that time when the ringers, fresh to their work, are setting the bells clanging their loudest that the streets below swarm thickest with the hundreds who, with their faces turned all in one direction, and who have come from south, and north and east and west by twopenny 'bus and tram and penny steamboat, and who though as yet a full quarter of a mile from the place whither they are bound, find the pavements so full that rapid headway is not to be made without elbowing, and elbow they do vigorously, lest all the bargains be sold before they are there to bid.

They are rough customers, nine out of ten of them, and the fact that the urgency of the mission on which they are bound did not admit of their staying to denude their hands and faces of any of yesterday's work-a-day grime, or to pass the teeth of a comb through their uproarious shocks of hair, does not do much towards redeeming the unfavourable impression created by their untidy aspect, and the prevailing greasiness and raggedness of their habiliments, from the crown of their battered hats or caps to where should be the sole of their, in most cases, dilapidated old boots. So they go trooping, quick march, down Leadenhall Street and Houndsditch and Aldgate towards the Old Clothes Market.

It is like no other market in England. It has covered ways and spacious "exchanges," which on week-days are guarded by toll-takers, who exact a certain sum from all corners ere they may enter to engage in their daily business of buying and bartering. From Monday until Saturday these places are resorted to by dealers only - those who collect old wearing apparel - the "bagmen" who are of the lingering race of London street criers, and those who purchase wholesale the said collections. But on Sundays, exchanges, squares, bazaars lanes and alleys, all are thrown open free to all corners and the amount of business transacted during Sunday morning church time can only be judged by personal observation of the immense concourse or patrons that flock to and block up every passage and avenue and outlet and inlet. Round about the exchanges and covered ways are streets innumerable, Cutler-street, Harrow-street, White-street, all long and narrow thoroughfares, and one and all literally crammed full, road and pavement.

Such an amazing spectacle is to be found nowhere else. There used to be something which bore a faint resemblance to its general aspect in those good old times when murderers were publicly strangled in the Old Bailey; but that is an affair of the past. Occasionally such a mob is seen in modern times at some great conflagration; but that is only for a little while, and before the police have time to arrive and disperse it, while here the enormous mass of people is permitted to roll sluggishly through the over-gorged streets for hours together.

There is no opportunity for retreat when once the adventurer is fairly launched. There is no choice but to abide in the thick of the unsavoury stream, moving as it moves, until some fat distant outlet is attained. It must be said in its favour, however, that it is a perfectly good-humoured mob. Considering the perpetual crushing of unprotected toes by hobnailed heels, and the bending of ribs under the crushing pressure of uncompromising elbows there is heard on all sides an astonishingly small amount of cursing and swearing; but the most marvellous part of the business is the various things the people contrive to do in the very heart and thick of the crush. There are shops for the sale of second-hand clothes on either side of all the narrow thoroughfares, but the bulk of the business is done by those dealers who bear their goods about with them, slung over their shoulders or hugged in their arms, and who push and drive through the mob with the rest, screeching out with all the strength of their lungs what it is they have got to dispose of, and what the price of it is. The vendor's of second-hand hats cannot, under such circumstances, go about with their's hugged in their arms, so they mount them sometimes on the dome of an expanded umbrella, and holding the latter aloft pass through the crowd, crying out, "A hat for a shillin'! A hat for a shilhin'!" until they are well nigh breathless and red in the face. "Here's a weskit! Who'll have a weskit for a tanner? Who's the buyer of coat? Here's a stunner for three-and-six - half-a-crown - two-bob - anything!" "Who wants a shirt? Who'll buy a pair of trousers? Who ses a pair of hard working trousers for nine-pence?" And while five hundred voices are blending to advertise these and a score of other amazing bargains, dealers in another line of business wriggle their ware through the close-jammed multitude with bright tin kettles balanced on their heads containing hot green peas, sheep's trotters and pickled cucumbers for sale.

Everything goes on in a wonderfully peaceable manner, though to the uninitiated it would seem that pugilistic encounters were going on in twenty different spots at one and the same time; for there may be seen able-bodied men and strapping lads stripping themselves of their outer garments, and that with an earnestness of purpose that can apparently only indicate impending fisticuffs, especially as in each case there us something of a "ring" formed, and the individual reduced to his shirt and trousers is sedulously "attended to" by a friend who holds his jacket and waistcoat. But there is no battle, nor is one intended, and all this stripping portends nothing more alarming than the trying on of some garment offered for sale.

Boots and shoes are "tried on" in the same unceremonious fashion, the persons who contemplate becoming purchasers squatting down on the pavement or in the muddy roadway. A rare trade in old boots is done in this place, the great attraction being that a pair of some sort may be bought for almost any price, and it is no uncommon thing to see some poor wretch negotiating for a pair so deplorably dilapidated, that it seems no boots can be worse until you direct your attention to those he has on. And to be sure, the pair coveted cannot be so vastly superior, since all that is asked for them is fourpence and his old ones in the bargain.

And are all these thousands of people who patiently move with the crowd, or violently elbow their way through the evil-smelling, almost overwhelming crush, in search of bargains in the shape of more than half-worn-out coats and waistcoats, and threadbare trousers, and boots and shoes, the vamped-up defects of which grin perceptibly through the polish with which they are so bountifully coated; are all these hunters after something worth more than the price required for it of the tag-rag and unwashed order? Undoubtedly.

Surely you cannot for a moment suspect that the very considerable number of black-coated, semi-genteel individuals who mingle with the mob, and evidently take such deep interest in what is going on, even to the handling and close inspection of the goods offered for sale; surely you cannot imagine but that these grave and decently dressed men, elderly as a rule, have come to pick up bargains in such a place? Oh, dear no. They are simply persons of an inquisitive turn of mind, and who have somehow heard or read concerning this wonderful market, and who have slipped away from home, and - just for once - from church-going, that they may satisfy themselves that it is a reality, and not a fiction. If you are still sceptical as to this being their real intention, you may be quite convinced by overhearing - and when one is so closely wedged in a crowd how is it possible to avoid overhearing what your next neighbours are talking about?

Listen to the dialogue which takes place between two of the decently attired clerkly-looking personages alluded to. They are acquainted evidently, for they address each other respectively as Jones and Robinson, and shake hands as cordially as their pent-up condition will permit.

The unexpected encounter has a striking effect on both. Robinson's countenance changes to a sickly hue, and he visibly breaks out in cold beads of perspiration; while, as for Jones, his face glows hotly, and there is an embarrassment, not to say a wildness, in his eye, that certainly did not exist there a few moments since. In a breath, as it were, they ask of each other, "Why, who on earth would have thought to find *you* here!"

But the matter is easily explained. It is curiosity, pure and simple, that has taken them both to the Old Clothes Market. Ha, ha! How confoundedly strange that the same inclination should have seized on both at the same time, - on a Sunday too, of all days of the week!

"Well, it's a queer place, isn't it? Never could have supposed that such a place existed. Couldn't have supposed that the old clo' trade played such an important part in the domestic economy of the people. But, there, you know the old saying, my boy," remarks Jones, at the same time taking his friend by a disengaged button-hole at the breast of his coat, "you know the old saying, that one half the world has no idea how the other half contrives to jog on and eke out an existence."

The two friends are so close together that it is nearly in at Robinson's ear that Jones whispers the sage observation above recorded; and had Jones's breath been the wind of a powerful pair of bellows, and the face of his acquaintance a flagging fire, it could not have blazed up more suddenly under the operation.

"Ah, indeed! Well you may say that, Jones!" gasps the guilty man, and at the same moment gently disengages his friend's finger from his button-hole, and, with a ghastly affectation of thinking of anything in the world but of what he is doing, applies it to the button on the opposite side, and there secures it. But with the most disastrous effect. The increased tightness suddenly develops an extraordinary bulginess of Robinson's breast pocket, which assumes the strange shape of the heel and sole of a small boot.

Jones has a quick eye, and acute indeed are Robinson's sufferings as he fancies that they are fixed on the identical spot.

"Phew! it's awfully hot here," exclaims the poor fellow; "I shall try and get out of it. Perhaps you would like to have another turn round!"

"Well, the fact is I've only just come," replies Jones lightly, and so the friends part, mightily glad to be rid of each other.

Well, and what of all this? What has it do with the remarkable fact that mixing with this motley gathering of dirty corduroy and greasy fustian is to be found a tolerably thick sprinkling of threadbare broadcloth and seedy gentility? What of the shoe-shaped thing in Mr. Robinson's pocket? This of it, - it provides a perfect key and explanation to very much that otherwise might have remained mysterious and inexplicable. The shoe-shaped thing was a veritable shoe, one of a small pair, and suitable for a child of ten years or so old, and which the sorely pinched Robinson had been so fortunate as to secure a few minutes before at a cobbler's stall, at the ridiculously low price of fifteen-pence.

And Robinson is a very decent and respectable fellow, highly esteemed by the firm he has served for at least fifteen years,- an assertion incontrovertible in the face of the fact that when he first entered the office of his present employers, it was at the insignificant salary of fifteen shillings a week, and that now, thanks to a succession of "rises," he is in receipt of the handsome emolument of seventy-five pounds per annum. Out of this sum, however, he has to maintain a genteel appearance for himself, his wife, and the large circle of small Robinsons who form such a compact, hungry selvage to the family dining-table. For the trifling sum of one shilling and threepence, papa has purchased a pair of shoes with tolerably sound soles, and a neat and imperceptible patch on one of the upper leathers; and Miss Louisa Robinson, who since Wednesday last has been excused from attendance at school on account of being rather poorly, will be able to-morrow morning to resume her academical studies.

There now, the cat is out - Robinson's cat that is; the creature he tried so desperately hard, poor fellow, to conceal beneath the breast-lappet of his coat; and the truth is that almost every one of the decently attired individuals conspicuous amongst the Rag Fair mob carries about with him, jealously concealed from inquisitive eyes, a creature of the feline species. Jones's cat very nearly escaped at the same time as Robinson's. An extra hard poke of an elbow, or a sudden push from behind, would certainly have released the animal; for all the while that make-believe gentleman, taking-a-walk and peripatetic philosopher, was discoursing to his friend of the mysteries of human existence, he carried, concealed in his hat, a diminutive second-hand waistcoat and four small collars, in excellent condition, excepting that they were slightly frayed at the edges and bore the name of their original owner in full length in indelible marking ink-a "lot which Jones had picked up in the course of his Old Clothes Market ramblings for the small sum of one-and-six.

And it is no exaggeration to say that there were scores on scores of unfortunate Joneses and Robinsons - worthy, real good fellows every one of them - abroad that Sunday morning, and all bent on the same errand. That they find it worth while may be safely assumed; they wouldn't be there else. At the same time, there can be no question but they are awfully swindled by the unscrupulous persons with whom they are brought in contact. They are ignorant of the art of haggling, and even were it otherwise, they dare not practise it. The reproachful ghost of respectability is ever at their elbow, whispering "there's somebody looking", and urging them to get the shameful business done as soon as possible. Their dealings are extremely rapid. The movement of the crowd with which they are progressing is so slow that ample time is afforded for the unobtrusive contemplation of the goods exposed for sale, and whenever the article sought for - a boy's jacket or a waistcoat, or a pair of mended shoes - is identified, out comes the bit of tape, with knots in it betokening the requisite length and breadth, a hasty investigation for lurking stains and artfully concealed rents and bare places, and then the price asked is paid; and as soon as may be the shy purchaser makes his way out of the crush, so that he may retire to some secluded gateway, and make a neat parcel of what he has bought with the sheet of brown paper and the piece of twine he has brought with him from home for the purpose.

THE title of this paper will, doubtless, be more or less an enigma to the vast majority of readers. The origin of the name is involved in deep mystery. Who the first Bummaree was I am not in a position to state; but he has left a goodly progeny behind, not one of whom, however, so far as I am aware, is able to throw any light on the circumstances from which his peculiar name is derived. We are left, therefore, simply to accept the Bummaree as an established fact, and, antiquarian research on the subject of his appellation failing us, to look at him as he is - a link in the chain through which London is supplied with an all-important article of consumption.

The Bummaree is not widely and casually diffused over the metropolis. Indeed, the fraternity are all concentrated in one locality, and that locality is not one affected from special choice by any great proportion of the reading population of London. Nor is he, even there, visible to the naked eye at any hour of the day we may choose to go in search of him In fact, he has left the scene of his labours before many of us have finished our matutinal tea and toast, and long before noon he has vanished for the day and left not a trace behind. If we want to see him in all his glory, a task of no ordinary magnitude is before us-a task only to be accomplished by a stern resolve.

Four o'clock in the morning must see us out of bed, and on the way to study this variety of the human species. One word of caution is necessary before leaving home. It will be prudent in more than one sense that we put on the very worst garments our wardrobe can furnish. Special precaution is needful in the article of head covering. The conventional tall hat must be abjured peremptorily, for various cogent reasons which will appear hereafter, and a cap of the most tight-fitting type will be found the most correct and comfortable wear under the circumstances. Thin boots, too, are to be repudiated. A pair of long thigh boots, if we have them, will stand us in excellent stead, in default whereof our thickest pair of ankle boots, surmounted by a pair of leather knickerbockers, will tend materially to comfort and cleanliness.

Billingsgate is the theatre of our observation of the Bummaree. Arriving here about half-past four o'clock, we find the market just awakening into full life. The approaches to it are blocked half a mile each way by railway vans piled high with fish hampers and salmon boxes. Two or three smacks, countless lighters, and a screw steamer are fast to the jetty, and the market porters busily engaged in conveying into the market the fish with which they are laden. They deposit their burdens on and around the various stands of the fish auctioneers, who have not yet commenced business, but whose men are in attendance seeing to the correct disposal of the various consignments. Strange, amphibious-looking individuals are, without much apparent aim, dodging about in the open unoccupied space of the market; but soon we find them doff their coats, and having seized on a coign of vantage, proceed to erect a rampart of baskets round the position they have taken up.

Suddenly a discordant bell rings out with a harsh "cling, clang," the market is opened, and everybody starts into activity, and becomes preternaturally wide awake. Porters rush about frantically with huge loads on their heads, and now you bless your stars that your chimney-pot hat is safe at home. You are hustled on one side by a Colossus with a salmon-box on his head, who imagines that the magic words "By your leave!" give him full license to butt you out of his path. Getting out of his way rather precipitately, you are brought up by an attack of fish-baskets on the stomach; an urchin with a wicker stack on his head is running a muck, and you are the victim.

In much discomfiture you take refuge in a comparatively quiet corner by one of the pillars, and are congratulating your self that you are out of harm's way when a sudden slam on the sloppy pavement about an inch in front of you of a ponderous box, accompanied with the warning shout of "Toes," rudely dispels this belief, and sends you backward with an impetus which probably procures you a volley of oaths both loud and deep from the lips of some unfortunate you have cannoned against. The auctioneers are by this time in their rostrums, selling away with desperate rapidity and wonderful power of lung. "Turbot! turbot! turbot!" is shouted in stentorian tones from one pulpit; loud roars of "Salmon! salmon! salmon!" emanate from the opposite one; the shouts of the auctioneer mingle with the responsive yells of the buyers; the din becomes tremendous, and you feel you would give anything for peace. The leathern-throated auctioneers bellow louder, their men vie with them in the din, the buyers get excited and "bid out" vociferously; the rush of porters gets more bewildering, the general turmoil and burly-burly more wildly confusing.

It is not unlikely that after having been jostled, trodden on, plentifully besprinkled with fishy water, sworn at, chaffed, and utterly deafened, you will be sorely tempted to spurn the mud of Billingsgate from off your feet and rush impetuously from the scene of your tribulation up one of the many narrow lanes which lead out of it. But if you lose courage at this stage, and suffer yourself to be disheartened thus on the threshold, you will lose your golden opportunity of making acquaintance with and studying the idiosyncracies of the very men you are in search of - the Bummarees. Wherefore, buffeted one, take heart and keep your eyes open, and see what manner of men they are who are thronging round the auctioneers' stands. The contrast between the auctioneers and those who surround them, you will observe, is very strongly marked. The former are sprightly, well-dressed, gentlemanly-looking fellows, most of them gifted with brazen throats, and with a volubility which would almost put Mr. Charles Mathews in the shade, but evidently the patrons of fashionable tailors of a sort, and not insensible to a weakness for well-fitting kid-gloves, and the latest pattern in shirt collars and the newest thing in neckties.

The latter are of a different stamp altogether. They may be classed under three heads : Rough, rougher-roughest. Great burly fellows the majority, with bluff faces, deep chests, and still deeper voices, with a smack of the waterman about them, a lingering suspicion of the costermonger, and a faculty for mental arithmetic which is perfectly surprising. These, good reader, are Bummarees and Bummarees' men. They fill an important niche in the economy of the fish market. The leading fishmongers, who have a large demand for the different kinds of fish, no doubt come in person or by deputy to the auctioneer's stand, and are purchasers at first hand of the large quantities they require to meet their extensive custom. But they are the exception. The great bulk of fishmongers and the whole fraternity of costermongers do not require fish in parcels so large as those sold by the auctioneers, and here the Bummaree steps in and makes his livelihood by acting as middleman between the large salesman and the retailer. He buys in the bulk from the auctioneer, and removing to his own "pitch" the fish so bought he sorts it into convenient parcels such as his experience tells him will meet the requirements of the class of customers he cares to attract. Of course he does not do this for nothing. Let us take the case of salmon, for instance. The Bummaree buys half a dozen boxes from the auctioneer, sends them to his own pitch, and lots them out into various qualities and sizes, according to the contents of each box.

The market price for salmon is fixed early in the morning by a sort of committee of the leading salesmen, and this the Bummaree pays to the auctioneer for his wholesale purchase. He puts a price on his assorted goods sufficient to recoup him and leave a fair profit besides. The profit in the case of salmon is a penny to three-halfpence per pound, or as high as twopence if the customer make but a small investment. This increase in the cost the fishmongers find it their interest to submit to, and in preference deal with the Bummaree rather than with the auctioneer, because the latter sells in the pile and with all faults, so that the purchaser from him, in addition to having to make a large investment, has to take his purchase as it comes, good, bad, and indifferent all together, when perhaps he has a market for only one quality. The Bummaree, with one or another customer, has the means of disposing of all kinds; therefore, it suits his purpose to sort the large parcels, and he is accordingly patronized in preference by the retailer, whether he is a swell suburban fishmonger or a Whitechapel costermonger. I say in preference; but the truth is that a dealing with him in many cases is without choice, as when, from whatever cause - whether it be a limited requirement or a slender purse - a smaller purchase is desired than one of the large lots put up by the auctioneers.

A Bummaree's judgment of fish in the bulk must be not only accurate, but has to be arrived at with a promptitude which in the midst of the hurry-skurry of the market, and formed, as it apparently is, at little more than a simple glance, is something perfectly wonderful to the uninitiated. Besides, he is, from the nature of his business, an habitual speculator. Fish is one of the few articles in which supply and demand do not bear a reliable relation to each other, and the Bummaree who buys incautiously may find himself at the close of the morning's transaction in danger of being left with a large unsaleable stock of a very perishable nature on his hands. Rather than do this, towards the close of the market he takes for his motto "No reasonable offer refused," and then is the time for the wary and astute costermonger, who has studied the signs of the times, to make a cent. per cent. bargain, long after his more impetuous fellows have supplied themselves at much higher rates or with other varieties, and are off on their rounds.

There are grades in this profession of the curious name. There is the swell Bummaree, whom you can hardly tell from the auctioneer (the aristocrat of the market), and who "bids out" freely for the choicest consignment of turbot and the highest-priced parcels of Tweed and Severn salmon, knowing that he will make his money out of West-End fishmongers, who *must* buy the pick of the market, no matter what the price may be. He doesn't trouble himself with the lower and cheaper classes of fish, but confines himself to the higher qualities, and the fishmongers mostly clear him out by eight or half-past. The second-rate Bummaree, again, leaves alone sturgeon and turbot, and mullet, and salmon, and goes in for soles, whitings, haddocks, and herrings. His harvest is not over so early. About eight o'clock there comes a fresh incursion into the market in the shape of small vendors, stall keepers, and costermongers, rough of speech and gesture, frill of strange oaths and practical jokes, "hail fellow, well met" with every one in a good-humoured way; and these are the chief customers of the second-rate Bummaree. He doesn't do badly with them, although they have not so much money as the West-End fishmongers; but they are ready, eager buyers, and the class of fish they deal in is always in demand.

There is a casual Bummaree lower still in the scale. He is a "coster" who has made a little money, or perhaps he is a broken-down fishmonger who is turning his experience to account. Knowing the sort of fish likely to be most in demand, he "throws in" for a single lot (all he can afford) at the auctioneer's rostrum, and then removes his purchase to some pitch he has previously fixed on-perhaps had to fight for; and having sorted it into the quantities he knows will suit the twopenny-halfpenny customers who are all he can hope for, takes his chance of making a profit out of them. These casual Bummarees are principally found about the pillars supporting the water-front of the market, and are objects of the special vigilance of the market constable, who often finds it a matter of some difficulty to extract from them the market fee of sixpence, to which every one makes himself liable who takes up a pitch within the market boundaries.

THAT William Thompson, for a quarter of a century renowned in the P.R., the vanquisher of Deaf Burke, the giant Caunt, formidable Paddock - the bold "Bendy," who until the past year or two was notorious as the foremost "bully boy" amongst the "lambs" of Nottingham - that such a terrible fellow, after squandering through threescore chapters - counting each year a chapter - of his book of life should, after all, resolve on turning over a new leaf, seemed of all things the most improbable. But when it transpired that William Thompson evinced a determination to go far beyond even this - to go as far, indeed, as the public platform, and there, in the face of all corners, courageously offer himself as a living example of the truth that, no matter how far advanced in sinful conflagration a man is, he may still, if he has a mind so to do, be a brand plucked from the burning. It was scarcely to be wondered at, if those who heard the strange news were incredulous, and shook their heads, and regarded a relapse as a foregone conclusion. Under these circumstances, it appeared to me not an improper, if a possible, thing to get from Bendigo's own lips the story of his conversion.

There were no difficulties to overcome. I found him in the peaceful enjoyment of the hospitality of the superintendent of the Cabmen's Mission Hall, at Kings Cross, and within ten minutes of my introduction we were sitting a cheerful company about the parlour fire; and the comfortable-looking elderly gentleman with his legs crossed in his easy chair, and with a manner which unmistakably betokened how kindly he had taken to his amended career, proceeded with as much modesty as good nature to give me the information I required.

It may not be out of place, before I endeavour to reproduce for the reader's edification Bendigo's narrative pretty much as he confided it to me, to render some idea of the sort of man, as regards personal appearance, the renowned champion, now in his 63rd year, is. Aged and used-up prizefighters are not invariably pleasant objects to contemplate, but Bendigo is a shining exception to the rule. He has the cheery aspect of an English country squire who has lived a life of unbroken serenity, and who, barring accident, may have a score of enjoyable years before him. His shoulders are immensely broad, and still as square as a plank, and the calves of his legs are hard almost as wood, and a fair sixteen inches about. He is light on his feet, and as active with his arms as a school-boy, and he has the laugh and certainly the bright eyes of one, all evidences of great physical power, and which are the more remarkable taken in connection with the tact that he has, in one sense, had "everything against him" all through his life. In the first place he was one of three children of one birth, his mother having presented his father with eighteen boys and girls besides. His boyhood was for the most part a scramble for the necessaries of existence, and at the early age of sixteen he stepped out of the streets, where his prowess as a bruiser had already made him famous, and entered the prize ring to fight for money.

"That was my first set-to," said Bendigo; "it was for a purse, a collection made amongst the crowd on Silston-common and offered, for the sport of the thing, to any two lads who would fight for it. I fought and won it, and from that time, till in my fortieth year I fought Tom Paddock, I was engaged in twenty-one matched fights, and never was beaten in one. What is more, I never in my life had a hit on the nose hard enough to make it bleed, and in all my battles I never got a black eye. I've got a broken thumb, as you see, and a broken finger, and I've got the bridge of my nose rather flattened, and one of my teeth knocked out, but that was through a kick in the face I got at football many years ago. I've got part of my ear knocked off - Deaf Burke did that when I was six-and-twenty; and I've got a damaged big toe - that Caunt did with the spike in his shoe. There's nothing else the matter with me that I know of 'cepting a broken knee-cap, which lamed me for seven years. I don't know that I took to fighting because I liked it. It came natural to me, and I was always at it as far hack as I can recollect. Besides, I did it to get a living.

I could do it better than I could do anything else, and I had my mother to keep. She didn't mind me doing it - not she; she encouraged me to it. If anybody came to her in a fright and said, 'Lor, Mrs. Thompson, your boy's being half killed,' she would say, 'Ah, you leave him alone; he'll come off all right.' If ever I came home when I was a youngster, and she found out that another boy had licked me, she would say, 'Now just you go back and lick him, or I'll lick you.' She would, too.

"She was a wonderful old woman. She was mainly the cause of my last fight - that with Tom Paddock. I held the belt then, and hadn't fought for some time. Well, I went to see her; she was eighty-two years old then, and I found her at her lodgings smoking her pipe and reading *Bell's Life*. 'There you are then, mother,' I says. 'Yes,' she says, answering me sharp, 'here I am. Have you seen this?' It was the paper she meant. 'No,' I says, 'I ain't.' She says, 'Have you seen this Tom Paddock?' 'No,' I says. 'I have,' says she, 'a needle-pointer at Redditch; a fellow with no more breadth to his shoulders than there is between the eyes of a mouse, and he challenges you to fight. And I tell you this, Bendy, if you don't take the challenge you are a coward. And I tell you more, if you won't fight him I'll send and take up his challenge myself.' Eighty-two she was at that time. So of course I fought him, and beat him under the hour. But I'm a getting away from the beginning.

"Did I in my young days ever have any religious thoughts? Well, not to speak of. When we were little un's at home together, mother used to make us say the Lord's prayer, and that, but I didn't think anything about it. Bat here was a strange thing. I used to pray before I knew anything about religion. It's a fact, sir, though it mayn't sound such, that I never fought a fight yet for money that I didn't go on my knees over-night and say, 'Let me win this fight, so that I may keep my old mother out of the workhouse' It wasn't religion; not a bit of it. I didn't know what religion was.

"Now I'll tell you how I think it happened. My father, though a cabinetmaker by trade, had a bit of a turn for science, and he had a big telescope. He used sometimes to let me look through it, and I liked it. He used to talk about the starry heavens to me, and pint out Wenus and the Great Bear and Jupiter, and tell me a lot about 'em, and who it was that made em and looked after em. Well, they looked so beautiful through the telescope that I used to think a lot about this at times, and what a wonderful power it must be who ruled over 'em and kept 'em going; and when I was going to fight I used to think if He can do all that, He can help me, and so I used to ask Him. Did I used to say I'd try and do better if He would let me win the fight? No, I didn't; I did not want to do any better than win, but I put it in that way, 'to keep mother out of the workhouse.' And she was kept out of the workhouse. When my uncle died - a optician he was, and left us his stock-in-trade and his tools - I says to my brother, You take the lot, and allow mother six shillings a week on my account like, and so he did. And I used to buy the old lady her winter clothes, and he bought her her summer clothes, and so she did pretty well until she died at eighty-three.

"And now I'll tell you how I came to leave off my old goings on, and to be converted to the right way. You won't care to hear of my queer ways from the time I turned up fighting until I found grace; besides, I am going to get a kind friend to write my life, and I mean to get it published shortly.

"So I'll skip over the time that I was knocking about Nottingham, and when the most common line in the newspapers was 'Bendigo in trouble again,' and which led to my seeing the inside of Nottingham Gaol seven-and-twenty times. I will skip over all that till we come to the twenty-eighth time. What was it for? Not for thieving. No; it was never as bad as that. When I was a boy, and up to the time when I was a young fellow, my life was a rough 'un, and if I saw any chap eating, and I was hungry, I'd take his grub away from him, Oh, yes, I'd do that; or if I was dry, and had no money for a drink, I'd think nothing of making free with somebody else's beer; but, d'ye understand me, I never would what you might call steal anything.

"Well, this twenty-eighth time was for the old game. It was at one of the public-houses where they were set against me, and wouldn't serve me with any strong drink, even though I had the money to pay for it. So somebody got a pint of ale for me, and just as I was going to drink it, the landlord come along and knocks the jug clean out of my hand. Well, no sooner was he knocked down himself than in comes the policeman, and there was a row, and it was, 'Bendigo in trouble once more.' And I had to make the best of it before the bench of magistrates. Of course I knew em, well enough, and they knew me. There was one of em, a hearty, John Bull kind of man, that I took a likin' to, and I used always try and get round, and generally managed it, putting the matter to him in a man to man kind of way, d'ye see; but there was another, a vinegar-looking, narrow-jawed cove, who was always hard on me.

"Well, I made my story out pretty well, and made 'em laugh a bit, and, thought I, I shall get off this time; but I didn't. Said my friend on the bench, 'Bendigo, when you're sober you are one of the nicest men in Nottingham, but when you're drunk you ain't; therefore you will go to prison for two months, and afterwards give bail to keep the peace for three months longer.'

"Well, somehow that sentence seemed to knock me over more than any of the twenty-seven I had served before, and I took to thinking what a fool I was not to live quiet and comfortable on my pound a week like another man. Yes, a pound a week-that's what I've got to live on. Did I save it up? Not I; I couldn't save. No; what I did when I was making a heap of money in the ring was to hand it over to my brother on condition that he always gives me a pound a week, and that's how it comes. And I've got a nice little country house, for which I pay two shillings a week, and I never was happier in my life, though I ain't very rich, you'll say. But I'm better off now than ever I was. I've got my belts - three of em the champion's, which was never took from me, and two others, and a lot of silver cups and things; they're all out of pawn now, and I've got em all at home in the cupboard.

"Well, I was going to tell you about the conversion. Twice a day on Sunday we had to go to chapel - to hear the parson. I didn't care much for listening to such things in general, but, somehow, this Sunday I did. When I say somehow, I mean to say I couldn't but do it. It was just in my line. It was about the set-to between David and Goliath. And when the parson began to talk about the big un-how tall he was, and how broad and strong - I was all the time picturing him as being a man after the style of the big on I had fought three times - Ben Caunt that was - and wondering how I should have got on in a stand-up with Goliath. Well, the parson went on and told us about the little 'un - about David, and about his pluck in facing the giant, though he had only a sling and a stone to tackle him with.

"When he came to describe the fight, I listened with all my might, quite lost myself listening, and when it came to the wind-up, and David floored the giant and killed him, without thinking that I was in chapel and that it was against the rules to say a word, I bawls out 'Brayvo! I'm glad the little 'un won.' It was very wrong, and what made it worse for me, all the prisoners and the warders burst out laughing. The parson he turned away, but I could tell by the move of his shoulders that he was laughing too; which, perhaps, made it a little better. They thought it was a joke of mine; but it wasn't. I took to it too serious for joking, and when I got to my cell and was quiet, I kep' thinking about it, and about how somebody must have helped little David to lick the giant with his sword and armour, and about them old times when I used to ask that I might win the fight, that I might keep my old mother out of the workhouse.

"Well, it was as sing'lar as though it was done on purpose. The very next Sunday the parson preached another sermon which seemed hitting at me harder than the one the week before. It was all about the three men, Shadrack, Mesheck, and Bendigo, who was cast into the fiery furnace, and who was saved by the Lord from being burnt. Oh, yes, I've heard about that since; it wasn't exactly Bendigo who was third man; but the name sounded like it to me, and I took it as such, though I didn't say anything to anybody. If one Bendigo can be saved, why not another? I said to myself; and I thought about it a great deal more than anybody there thought, I'll wager. If I'd have told em I might have thought that the sermons was got up for me. It really seemed so. Sunday after Sunday I looked out for something about me in the sermon, and there it always was. After the one about the fiery furnace came one about the twelve fishermen. Now, I'm a fisherman myself. Bless you! I should rather think I was; one of the best in England. I've won lots of prizes, and got a fishing-rod that Mr. Walter, of the *Times*, give me. Well, after that come another sermon about the seven hundred left-handed men in the Book of Judges; and I am a left-handed man. Of course I am. It was that what took in the knowing ones I have had to stand up against.

"Well, it was this always going on that made me make up my mind to turn as soon as ever I got out. It was on a Thursday, and in the winter, and when I was let out at the gaol door there was my old friends kindly come to meet me. 'Come along, Bendy, old boy,' they said, 'we've got something to eat and something to drink for you all ready. Come along.' But I had made up my mind, and wasn't to be shook; so I turned round, and I ses, 'Look here, I never will eat or drink along with you, or along with any man in a public-house again as long as I live. I've done with it.' They looked at each other, I can tell you. They couldn't make it out. But there was one man amongst em named Waters, and he said, 'Bendy, will you come along with me? I'm going to Beeston.' And I knew if I went with him I should be all right; and I went. And there I met another friend who wished me well, and said he, 'Bendy, what do you say to coming to the hall to-night to hear Undaunted Dick?' 'Who's he?' says I; 'I never heard of him.' 'It's Dick Weaver,' says he, 'a collier chap that was once in a bad way, but who is now converted and turned preacher.' 'Ay,' said I, I'll go and hear him; 'he's one of my own sort;' and I went, and I set on the platform, and there I could hear ' em: 'Why, how's this? there's Bendigo up there;' 'Look, look, there's old Bendy.' But I took no notice; only sat quiet and listened.

Well, next night I was there again, and heard what did me good more than ever. It was bad weather and snowing hard, and I had to make my way home late at night across a park; and when I was half way across I couldn't hold out any longer. So in the dark, and with the snow coming down, I went on my knees and prayed as well as I knowed how; and when I got up I felt a new man. I didn't quite go without ale; I had one half-pint between then and Sunday, and then I went to the chapel again and on to the platform, and, in the face of everybody who was there, I knelt down and told em how I was changed, and how that nothing should tempt me to go wrong again, and I've kept my word, and I mean to go on keeping it. Ever since that time not a drop of beer or spirits has passed my lips, and I never felt healthier, or stronger, or more lively, than I do now. I've tried the right road now for two years, but I ain't much of a hand at preaching as yet, because I can't read; but I'm learning as fast as I can, and then I shall get on better."

And so Bendigo brought to a conclusion his singular story, to which may well be added that it would be difficult to conceive anything more convincing of the renowned old prizefighter's perfect sincerity than the spectacle of him holding in his formidable fists a limp child's first spelling book, and doing his desperate utmost to master the mysteries of A B C, as the first necessary step towards attaining the summit of his present ambition, which is to be able to read the Bible.

THE extraordinary endurance of popular interest in the "Orton imposture," after the lapse of more than a year, since the bulky "first robber" of that memorable melodrama has been satisfactorily disposed, will perhaps be regarded as sufficient justification for here reproducing what was perhaps the most conclusive evidence of the man's guilt at the time, or since brought to light. I am glad to acknowledge that the confession of "brother Charles" was obtained by me, the more so when I reflect on the vast amount of patience and perseverance it was found necessary to exercise in order to bring the individual in question to book. Indeed, it is doubtful if I should ever have succeeded had it not been for the kind offices of a good friend, whose official connection with the Tichborne case though not prominent, was deep, and whose influence over the elder brother of the "claimant" was very remarkable. The confession was made at my friend's house, and in that gentleman's presence. Said the aged Charles:-

"What I wish to do is to make a plain statement of all that I know, or ever did know, of the bad business which has just ended so unhappily for my brother Arthur. I don't hope, nor I don't want, to make myself out to be a martyr, and I don't pretend that I shall be able to give a good reason for all my actions in the affair; but I do hope to make it appear that I am not, by a great many shades, as black as I have been painted, and that although I am very much to blame, I was made to do a great deal - firstly, on account of my being so poor; and secondly, on account of being drawn, a little at a. time as I may say, into a mess which it wasn't easy to escape out of. That, however, if you will be so kind as to print my account, will be for the public to judge of when they have read it. I will only add, at starting, that it is a true account, and one which I defy any one mixed up in the Tichborne trial to contradict.

"First of all, perhaps, it may be as well, after the many wrong statements which have appeared in the newspapers, to say a few words concerning my brothers and the family generally. I may mention that my father was a journeyman butcher, in the service of Mrs. Hoad, who kept a shop just about opposite to where our old shop was afterwards, and that Mrs. Road had a niece, and that she and my father got married, and set up for themselves at 69, Wapping, in the year 1818. Thomas was the first boy, and when he grew old enough he went to help in the shop, and also looked after the Shetland ponies which father dealt in. Thomas was just the build of what Arthur grew to be, a very big man, and just like Arthur in the face. Thomas died about ten years ago.

That was something over a year before father died when this happened, and mother being dead six years before that, my sister Margaret (Mrs. Tredgett) took the business, and I was her foreman. This lasted until things went wrong, and Mrs. Tredgett sold the business in 1866 to Mr. Pitt. I was the next son to Thomas; and then came George. George began his seagoing career in i842, and kept steadily at it, voyaging to and from England until 1856. Then he sailed for Hong Kong. He settled at Singapore, and became master of the steampacket that carries the mail between Singapore and Bankok. That, I believe, is his occupation at the present time. George has for a good many years behaved very handsomely by his two sisters who were left widows - Mrs. Tredgett and Mrs. Mary Ann Jury. He allowed them five pounds a month between them, beside sending money to keep the children at school. He may be doing it still for all I know; but, not being friendly with my sisters, I can't say for certain. William was my next brother, and he was apprenticed to a grocer. It was William who was known about Wapping as 'Gentleman Orton.' He was a smart-built young chap. He got into difficulties about betting, and in 1854 went away to New York, From there he went to California. From there he shipped for Panama, but cholera broke out in the vessel, and he and a great many others on board died of it.

"Then there was my brother Robert. Like all the rest, he helped as a boy in the butcher's business, and when he was old enough, being inclined for the sea, as they all were, he was bound to a Mr. Lisle, a shipowner. His first voyage was in the Mayday, Captain May, bound with a batch of convicts for Norfolk Island, in the year 1843, The Mayday was never heard of afterwards. Then there was my brother Alfred. He was apprenticed to the sea, but, while still a boy, died of fever out in Calcutta. Of all the eight brothers there are only four now alive - George, Edmund, Arthur, and myself.

"Edmund is the only brother I have not told you about, and it is more particular that I should speak about him than the rest, because his name has been very often mentioned in the course of the trial. Edmund was born in 1829, and would, therefore, be five years older than Arthur. Edmund stayed at the butcher's shop until he was fifteen, and then, like all the rest, having a taste for roving and adventures, he took to the sea. He was apprenticed to Captain John Hall, of Sunderland, in 1847. In August, 1849, he sailed from Liverpool, in the Niagara, on a voyage for Valparaiso; but before he went this voyage, and having been away from home a long while, he got a fortnight's holiday, and came home. He had grown a great deal since he was last there, and had took to wearing gold wires in his ears. Edmund at this time was quite a maj and between five feet nine and ten in height.

"This is how the mistake might have come about with the witnesses who said they recollected that when my brother Arthur came home just about that time he had earrings in his ears; and it isn't much of a wonder that they made the blunder for a very short time after Edmund had set off for Valparais Arthur came home, and remained at home for two yean Arthur wasn't expected home at that time. It was thought thought by his friends that he was in the neighbourhood of Valparaiso. They were anxious about him, because the last they at that time had heard concerning him was by means of a letter that was sent to father by a naval officer. It stated that being a Valparaiso, he had there met with a destitute English boy, who told him that his name was Arthur Orton, and that he had run away from his ship, being unable any longer to put up with the ill-usage of the captain. Thc letter further said that the naval officer had asked the boy what he meant to do, and he replied that it was his intention to make his way up the country. It was agreed that when Edmund got to Valparaiso he should make inquiries about Arthur.

"After a few months there came a letter from Edmund, to say that he could hear nothing about his brother, and that he himself had deserted his ship at Valparaiso, as Arthur had done, and was going up the country too. As we afterwards heard he made his way to New Mexico, where he found adventures enough; for there he was taken prisoner by a hostile tribe, and kept so for nine months, when they began to trust him a little and let him have a gun to go out shooting game for their living. Edmund took the opportunity of making his escape in company with a native woman, and finally made his way to a place called Guymas, where he married a native, and settled there with his family.

"As for my brother Arthur, I can tell you nothing more concerning his boyhood than has already been made known in the newspapers. It is quite correct all that they say about him being a healthy boy before that fire at St. Andrew's Wharf, when he was six years old, which was just by our place at Wapping, and when he was so frightened at being woke out of his sleep to see the flames that he was at once took with St. Vitus's dance, and for a long time seemed to have no control over his features or his limbs. But he never grew thin with it all. He was a wonderfully thick set boy, like Thomas was when he was a lad, and the nickname he had amongst us was the Fat Boy in 'Pickwick.' He was nearly well, however, when at the age of fourteen he was apprenticed to Captain Brooks, of the 'Ocean.' I will not go over the story of his voyage and his running away and getting to Melipilla, only that I may mention that at that time, when Edmund absconded from his ship at Valparaiso, and was so anxious to find Arthur, Arthur was probably all the time only seventy miles away, comfortable at Melipilla.

"Perhaps I may as well state here, that if my brother was ever severely bitten by a pony while he was a lad at home with us, I, who was always at home too, never heard of it. It was equally news to me when I heard that he had been thrown from a pony, and received a deep cut on the face; likewise that he ever wore earrings. I may also say, that as regards the tattoo marks of A. O., that were said to have once been on his arm, and afterwards got rid of, I never saw them nor heard of them. But then they might have been there without my knowledge, for I was married when Arthur was a lad at home, and slept away, and only saw him about in the business. As for the brown mark on his side, I never saw that either but it was commonly known in the family that he had a birth mark. There are a good many other things that have been said about my brother at that time; but it will be better perhaps for me to get on with what I at first promised to do.

"At about Christmas time of 1866 I was keeping a small butcher's shop in Hermitage Street. Another man and myself had the business between us, though it wasn't such a big business but that one of us might have managed it easily. Three or four days after that Christmas-Day, my sister, Mrs. Robert Jury, came to the shop and brought a letter for me to read. It was the letter signed in the name of Stevens, that had been left a day or two before with Mrs. Pardon, to be handed to Mrs. Tredgett. My sister Mary Ann had married Mr. Pardon's brother, so that there was a sort of relationship. My sister told me when she brought the letter, that from what she had been told by one and the other who had seen the strange gentleman in disguise, that she verily believed that it must be Arthur himself. I didn't know what to think about it myself, but I at once recognized the letter as being in the handwriting of my brother Arthur. I heard no more about the matter for a week or two, and then I thought I would go and see my sisters, Mrs. Tredgett and Mrs. Robert Jury, and ascertain whether they had heard anything more about the matter.

"I found that they had. They had received two letters, which when I saw I knew at once to be in the handwriting of my brother Arthur, who had remained so many years unheard of. They, too, declared that they knew the handwriting, although there was no signature to the letters. I don't recollect all the writing, but I know that one of the letters asked my sister Mary Ann to be good enough to go and see a person who lived at Victoria Cottage, Victoria Park, and find out who the man that lived there was. This, I may say, was the house where Mr. Pittendreigh and his wife lived. From what I could make out, Mr. Pittendreigh was a lawyer's clerk, and in an office belonging to some of the big lawyers engaged in a lawsuit that Arthur had got mixed up in, and that somebody had writ from Victoria Cottage to give Arthur a hint of telling him something to his advantage if it could be done quietly, and that my brother, not feeling sure but that it might be a trap, wanted to know who and what the person at Victoria Cottage was.

"As well as I remember, my sister told me that she had been able to manage the affair very well. There was, it seems, in the window of the house, a bill of apartments to let at Victoria Cottage, and my sister made it her business to inquire respecting them, and that then, in quite a natural way, came up the question of references, &c., and so she found out where Mr. Pittendreigh was employed. I ought to have told you that this letter was addressed from Essex-road, Croydon. And when we had talked about this letter my sister told me that Arthur had sent her another with a five pound note in it, together with word that so long as she was careful and kept her own counsel he would send the like sum every month, to help keep the two sisters who were living together.

"Well, I waited, thinking perhaps, that I might hear from my brother Arthur. Business at the butcher's shop was very bad, and I thought if five-pound notes was so plentiful he might send me one or two. So, finding that he didn't take any notice of me, I wrote to him, getting his address at Croydon from Mrs. Tredgett. I addressed him as Sir Roger Tichbomne and put it to him in this way. Says I, 'I hear that you know where my brother Arthur is, and that you know him to be a rich man. Will you kindly send me his address, as I should like to write to him asking him if he can give me a little assistance?' Well, no answer came to this. I was very hard up at the time, and, after thinking about it, and of what I had by this time heard as to what it was my brother was doing, I took advice of my partner as to why I shouldn't make a move towards getting a little money out of the matter. I didn't like to go about it, for fear I might injure my sisters, who, I knew, were receiving their five pounds in a regular manner. But my partner and me talked it over, and I made up my mind that I would go and offer myself to the side my brother was wrongfully setting up against.

"But I didn't know quite how to set about it. I recollected about Victoria Cottage, where the lawyer's clerk lived, that my sister Mary Ann went to find out about, but I didn't know which side the lawyers he worked for were on. So I thought that I would go and see if I could find out. I went to Victoria Cottage, and saw the clerk's wife; but she was as sharp, if not sharper, than I was, and wouldn't answer straight out any question I put to her. When she got out of me that it was something about Tichborne I had come about, then she asked me in, and then we talked, and I told her that I thought about giving evidence in favour of the infant heir, provided it was made worth my while to do so. I didn't say more than that, nor how much I wanted, or anything. I only said that I bad some information to give which that side might be glad to get. Mrs. Pittendreigh persuaded me not to be too hasty in the matter. 'You leave me your address,' said she, and 'I think it very likely that to-morrow you will be wrote to.' I didn't care at first about doing this; but at last I did. I gave her the address right, but not the name. I put the name backwards - Mr. C. Notro, butcher, Hermitage-street, Wapping.

"Nothing came of it all next day, but on the following day there came a letter with the Croydon postmark. My partner, who knew all about it, opened it, and brought it over to the house where I was living. It was not a letter exactly, but an odd scrap of white paper, on which was wrote these words: '*Why should you injure one that never did harm to you? I shall send you in a day or two what you require. Desist.*' The last word, 'Desist,' was wrote where the signature should have been, but it didn't want any signature for me to be able to identify it as my brother Arthur's writing. Of course, I can't be sure that my going to Victoria Cottage had anything to do with him writing to me, though I think it must have, because he wrote to me as Mr. C. Notro. Well, the very next morning there came another letter, likewise with the Croydon postmark, and with a five pound note in it, and a scrap of paper, written on these words: '*I shall allow you this sum every month at present.*' This was wrote in the same writing as the one that said 'Desist,' and like that which came to my sister Mary Ann at first to ask her to go and find out about the people at Victoria Cottage. It was my brother Arthur's writing. Amongst ourselves - my sisters and myself, I mean - there was never the shadow of a doubt who it was who was sending us the money. When we talked about it and about how he was getting on- quite by ourselves, of course- we never spoke of him but as Arthur, though so many at that time where beginning to call him Sir Roger Tichborne.

"Well, I received my five pounds a month - a five-pound note in an envelope - regular, from the commencement until the beginning of August in the same year. Then I got a letter in the same old handwriting, but without any name at the end. It was to request me to leave Wapping and its neighbourhood as soon as I possibly could. It didn't explain why. All that the letter said was that I was to get out of Wapping immediately, and at the same time it was mentioned that the money I was receiving was quite enough for me to live on at present, and that, if I was careful as to what I was about, when the 'case was over there would be no lack of money, and if I wanted a thousand or two, why I should have it.' At the time I only thought that my brother was afraid that people might find me out, and make inquiries that mightn't be good for him: but now I can see that there was something more in it. While I had the butcher's shop in Hermitage-street, although it mightn't be much, there was something to be made by it, which would give me a little independence, but if I was took away from it and made to depend on the five pound a month for my living, I should be all the more afraid of doing anything that might give offence. However, I thought it best to do as I was asked, and the next day I left my house at Wapping, and took lodgings in the Keaton-road, Bermondsey. As regards the notes I received from my brother, I took them all, endorsed with my name or with that I was going by to the Bank of England, and afterwards several of them were traced by Inspector Whicher as having been issued from the Alresford or Croydon Bank a day or two before they came in my possession.

"I still got my five pounds regularly, seeing my sisters sometimes, but not so often as I used, for Mrs. Tredgett seemed to think that I had no right to put in my claim for assistance. Near the end of the year, Mrs. Tredgett came to our place and said that the plaintiff's solicitor wished to see me. By-the-by, I should have mentioned that some time before I had received from my brother Arthur one of the usual unsigned scraps of paper, telling me to have nothing to say to a person named Holmes if he came to me. So I thought it best to write and ask him if I was to act according to Mrs. Tredgett's message, addressing my letter to Sir Roger Tichborne, as usual, at Croydon. He wrote back, 'Yes; go,' and so I went to the solicitor's office in Clement's-lane, Lombard-street. There was nothing done that day except the making of an appointment for me to come next day.

"When I went next day Mr. Holmes was there, and he brought out a very large photographic likeness, which I saw at once was my brother's likeness, although, when asked, I denied it, he had so much altered. Perhaps I ought to say that I had seen Arthur some time before. I felt curious as I had not seen him for so many years, and so one day when I went to Croydon to cash a five pound cheque on the Croydon Bank he had sent me, I took the trouble to find out where he lived, and as I was passing the house I saw Arthur looking out at the door. I knew him at once, and I nodded. I believe that he knew me, for I think he nodded back again, but of that I cannot be sure. I wasn't the only one of his relations that went to Croydon uninvited. His sister, Mrs. Captain Jury, did so just after he went to live there, and the door was opened by the nursemaid, who had one of the Claimant's children in her arms; on which Mrs. Captain Jury exclaimed, 'Lor! what a regular little Orton.' Arthur refused to see her. He said he was ill; but he sent a letter to Elizabeth, begging that it might not happen again.

"Well, when I saw the photograph that the solicitor showed me I knew it in an instant, but I also knew that it wasn't expected of me to say so; so when the solicitor said to me, 'Do you see any resemblance between this gentleman and your brother Arthur?' I said, 'No.' There was writing on the margin of the photograph, saying that the undersigned had seen it, and saw no likeness in it to Arthur Orton. Mrs. Tredgett's name was signed there and I signed mine.

"I did not hear anything more of him for a matter of two months, and then I got a message that he wanted to see me again, and I was made to understand that this time I was to meet the 'Claimant' himself. I went, knowing of course what was expected of me, and having made up my mind what I should do. When I got to plaintiff's solicitor's office there were two gentlemen there-Captain Angell and Colonel Lushington. Sitting in another chair was my brother

Arthur, but he did not move when I went in. He just raised his eyes to my face once, and then he looked away, and never looked at me again, and never said a word. 'Do you know this gentleman?' I was asked, and I said 'No,' just as I had said concerning the portrait. Then I came out, and I was asked this time to swear an affidavit, but I said I would rather not, but that I had no objection to sign a statement. And I did sign a statement, making it seem that, for all I knew different, the gentleman I had seen might be Sir Roger Tichborne or anybody else. For all that, I recognized him.

"I did not hear any more, but went on living on the five pound a month, which came pretty regular, until I had been receiving it about a year. Then the money didn't come so regular. One day while I was out Mrs. Tredgett came in a hurry, bringing with her a letter, which she read to my wife, and which she had received from Arthur, and which desired her to come as soon as she could to our house, and tell me that things were getting dangerous; that it had come to his knowledge that our house was watched by detectives and that, for fear of accidents, if I had by me any of the letters he had sent me they had better be burnt immediately. As it happened, I had kept by me every bit of writing he had sent me, ever since he sent that first letter, asking me why I should wish to injure one who had never hurt me, and signed 'Desist.' I had all the scraps of writing in a box, and I did not want to burn them; but Mrs. Tredgett said that they must be burnt for the sake of everybody. Mrs. Tredgett told my wife that Arthur would have written to me himself, but that he was afraid to, because he knew that the house was watched. She also said that Arthur had sent her five pounds, and that if we burnt the letters she would leave us one pound out of it. On my wife promising that the letters should be burnt she left a sovereign.

"When I came home my wife told me what had happened, and she was so frightened that, against my will, I agreed to what Mrs. Tredgett had asked, and the box was brought out, and the letters were burnt, every one of them. Before Mrs. Tredgett went she told my wife that Arthur began to be doubtful about me. Next day I wrote a letter, addressed to Sir Roger Tichborne, saying that he need not be at all doubtful of me while he acted by me as he promised, and that if he was afraid to send the usual money in the usual way, for fear of the name of Orton being on the envelope, that I would change my name and call myself Mr. Brand, which was my wife's maiden name. I asked him to send me some money as soon as he possibly could. I thought that I should have got a letter by return, with the usual five-pound note, but instead of that, in a day or two a railway porter came with a little parcel, and asked for Mrs. Brand. My landlord opened the door, and said no such person was living there, but I overheard it, and said it was for me. It was two sovereigns and a half wrapt in blotting paper, in a sort of a pill-box.

"Well after this the money got more and more uncertain. I didn't have anything else to live on, and very often I didn't know what to do for a few shillings. What was sent was in small sums-very often in French money. Many times he would send me a twenty-franc piece in a letter, which was to last me for the week; and as he seldom paid for the registering, I had to pay double when it came - eightpence out of sixteen shillings. I never made a calculation, but I think I may safely say that what I all along received from Arthur didn't amount to more than eighteen shillings a week. But I should have kept my word with him if he had kept it up regular. I didn't know what was the reason of his treating me so, and thought that it might be better if I moved, and so I left Keaton-road and went to live at Melon Ground, Peckham; but the money did not come any better. Then I heard about his going to Chili, and then that he had gone.

"To speak my mind, I thought that he had gone away, and never meant to come back any more. I thought it not unlikely that matters were not going as well with him as he hoped they would, that he was sick of it, and that going to Chili was an excuse for getting away altogether. I don't put that as an excuse for doing what I did, but I do say that thinking so made it seem not so much harm in me going over to the other side. I had not received any money for some time, though I was so hard up that the brokers were in my house to seize my goods, which was the fact, and may be remembered in my favour as showing that in spite of the bargain that was made between us, that he would find me in money enough to live on, I was left to get to such a state of destitution.

"I wrote, and told him about the brokers being in my place - two letters - and begged him to send me something. Then I heard that he had really started for Chili, and I wrote to his wife- they had gone to live at Alresford then-writing in the name of Brand, and asking if Sir Roger had left any message or letter for a person of that name. But I got no kind of answer to my letter. I waited awhile, and then I went to see my old partner at Hermitage Street, and we talked it over, and I at last agreed to put myself in communication with the other side. I did so, and shortly afterwards made an affidavit telling the whole truth. A little time after this the plaintiff's solicitor came to see me, and to inquire if what he heard was true, and I told him it was, and he went away. Before this, though, I had a visit from Mrs. Tredgett, and she told me that she had heard it rumoured that I had turned traitor. After I had made the affidavit I wrote to Mrs. Tredgett begging her to consider the matter, and make a clean breast of it, as I had done; but all the answer she sent back was that I was a cowardly cur, and that was the last I heard of her.

"And this, as far as I am concerned, is the real truth and nothing else.
"CHARLES ORTON.
"*March* 6, 1874."

IT is a fact not generally known that within the last four or five years a foreign horde has penetrated to the very heart of London, and successfully besieged and ousted the inhabitants, dispossessing them of their houses and tenements, and settling themselves in their place without further contention or remonstrance on the part of the ejected.

To be sure, it is a somewhat shady quarter of the metropolis which has thus been subjugated; nor is it very extensive. Possibly it does not occupy more than three acres of land, and the brick-and-mortar growths thereon have, as a rule, long ago attained even to dead ripeness and decay, so as fairly to entitle them to condemnation and demolition. Nevertheless, they are still crowded with lodgers from garret to kitchen. The occupants of the dilapidated houses are Italians chiefly, and the colony in question is situated within gunshot of the Holborn Viaduct, and still nearer the Farringdon Street Station of the Metropolitan Railway. When it is further revealed that the slice of the city which has fallen into the hands of the Italian enemy is bounded on one side by Leather Lane and on another by Saffron Hill, the reader may feel disposed to smile at the so-called discovery, and regard it as of the mare's-nest order. There always was an Italian colony in the neighbourhood indicated, from a time so remote as to be beyond the memory even of the oldest inhabitant. Saffron Hill, with the adjacent squalid little thoroughfares and blind alleys, including Back Hill, Eyre Street Hill, and Summer Street, have been known, at least to the police, as the haunts and nightly abiding places of the majority of the organ grinders, as well as of the bagpipe and hurdy-gurdy players, and the whole host of musical tatterdemalions. The reader is possibly likewise aware that from time out of mind the invariable system pursued by the whole race of peripatetic instrumentalists was to quit their sunny clime unattended by their wives and families, and sojourn amongst us only for so long as sufficed for the scraping together of a certain sum, and then to make their way home again, thus giving place to new adventurers, their kith and kin, who were eagerly anxious to try their luck in the same direction.

Of late, however, this system appears to have been abandoned - our foreign friends seem to have reconsidered the entire question from an economic as well as a domestic point of view, and to have arrived at the conclusion that in the long run it would be cheaper and decidedly more comfortable to induce their spouses to embark with the children, and while the nest of the future was in process of feathering to be content with a home in foggy England. Thus is accounted for the bewildering spectacle which greets the eyes of the daring explorer or of the unaccustomed wanderer who finds himself lost in the mazes which exist west of Liquorpond Street. At two minutes to ten in the morning, say, he may be threading his way through the unmistakably English crowd that throngs the Leather Lane market. He progresses but a hundred yards or so, and before the clocks chime ten, he has altogether lost sight of his native land, and is stranded on a foreign shore. It is in vain that, seeking a solution of the sudden mystery, he looks up the Street and down the street, and at the windows of the houses to the left and right of him. The thoroughfares are narrow here, and the houses tall, and the amazed stranger gazes upwards to see a pair of strangely draped and becowled old women briskly gesticulating, and chattering to each other from opposite sides of the way in outlandish lingo; while lolling negligently from neighbouring casements are other women - olive-visaged, big-eyed beauties of more recent years, whose magnificent locks are half concealed beneath brilliant silken head-gear, and who wear in their ears great earrings of gold, coral, and amber, and about their necks, and depending over their quaintly-laced stomachers, necklaces of carved beads, cumbered with twinkling charms, weird-looking, and suggestive of fetish.

Half reclining on the door-steps on Eyre-street-hill, and lounging against the door-posts, are bearded fellows of brigandish attire, with slouched hats adorned with a bright bit of feather, while at the street-corners and at the mouths of the numerous alleys are younger men, gay-hearted Italian youths, who innocently disport with lively damsels of their own nation; and besides these there are becloaked and scowling old men who puff at their cigarettes vehemently, as though they were trying to make them flame as well as smoke, and who stand in groups of twos and threes in whispered counsel, and looking as though they were bent on business, at the bottom of which were poniards at the very least.

That they are harmless creatures enough there can be no doubt; indeed, while the stranger wonderingly regards them, there occurs an incident which, while it totally destroys the romance, serves to exculpate at least one of the cloaked, moustache-twirling patriarchs from all suspicion of being anything but an honest handicraftsman. A ragged young native of sunny Italy emerges from an alley, staggering under a head-load of chalk images and monuments, calls out to one of the seeming conspirators, evidently his master, and engages with him in brief converse, the subject of which, seemingly, is the victualling for the day of the image vendor, for the former enters a baker's shop close at hand, and presently emerges with part of a loaf of the half-quartern size. But then comes the question, how is the lad to carry it? His old jacket is buttoned to his chin, and it is plain that an overture on the part of the aged man to break the bread in two pieces, and thrust one in each of the youth's trousers-pockets, is not favourably regarded. At last the difficulty is overcome by the ingenuity of the master. He detaches an effigy of St. Paul's Cathedral from the board on the lad's head, squeezes the bread into the interior of the sacred edifice, first compressing it between his hands to make it fit, and St. Paul's being then replaced, the boy goes on his way contented.

The shops of this odd bit of Italy in London are exactly in keeping with all the rest. The stocks exposed therein consist almost entirely of maccaroni, half-yard lengths of crusty bread, all manner of beans in bowls, common sausages in their vulgar brown skins, sausages of genteeler mould smartly coated in tinfoil, and green, yellow, and purple liquids in clumsy glass bottles heavily stoppled with coarse wax; but most un-English of all are the children in the streets. The boy of British blood - albeit of ragamuffin extraction - is invariably an active lad. He is all for running and jumping, and is incessantly on the move. If he is off his feet for a few moments it is merely that he may enjoy the luxury of walking on his hands, or in order that he may indulge in one of those somersault or other acrobatic performances in which his soul delights. But the Italian boy, even when transplanted to English soil, loses nothing of his innate love of lounging and taking his ease in a recumbent position. His playground is the pavement, and the only amusements he takes kindly to are those which are not inconsistent with his lying on the flat of his ragged back, or curled up dogwise in sunny nooks and corners. His games are those in which the fingers and tongue play the chief parts, his most favourite pastime appearing to be a sort of easy adaptation of the English game of "Buck, buck, how many horns do I hold up?" but without the fatigue of laying a back or leaping thereon. It is pleasant, however, to find that be is happy and content with English gutters and the manufacture of mud-pies, and that, cut off from the grapes and melons of his native clime, he finds consolation at the sweetstuff shop and at the stall at the corner where damaged plums are sold at the rate of a half-penny the saucerful.

Speaking of these last, the luxuries of the children of the poor, reminds one of another very prominent feature of this picturesque Italia in the slums. It is not many years since the youth of London were amazed by the appearance of the first perambulating ice-cream vendor. Hitherto the dainty in question was as foreign to the street-boy as the taste of mangoes or green figs, and it appeared about as unlikely that he would be induced to take kindly to the one as to the other. The probability of the British working boy, with his natural appetite for solids, accepting a spoonful of sweetened congealed water for his hard-earned penny seemed distant indeed.

But the boy of the period has advanced with the age, and his taste has grown refined. Such prodigious success attended the first penny ice-cream seller that hundreds of others scented the feast afar off, and at the present time ice-cream stalls are as common almost as fruit-stalls. It seems, however, that an Englishman can no more manufacture the dainty than he can turn the handle of a street-organ. The operator in both cases must be Italian, and to all appearance, the whole fraternity of ice-cream producers have pitched their tents by the side of those of the Back-hill organ folk. The extent of their prosperity may be judged from the fact that a smart public-house in the latter neighbourhood has thought it worth while to have conspicuously notified that that is the only house-of-call for ice-cream merchants and Italian musicians.

It seems a pity, since the former are doing such a profitable business, that they cannot be induced to remove to a less objectionable quarter of the town. How penny ice-creams are produced is a mystery, of course known only to the initiated. All that is certain concerning them is that they are devoured, to the extent of several hundred weight a day, by the children of the poor, and it would be a satisfaction to know, at least, that they were manufactured in cleanly places. This, unhappily, is not the case. It may be safely said that Summer-street, Back-hill, is about as nasty a street as any in London. The gutters stand stagnant, and the roadway and pavement are in an abominable condition. The houses, for the most part, are deplorably dirty and dilapidated, and a peep in the passage reveals backyards which are well worthy of the outer Street. And in this street and in these back-yards are scores of ice-cream barrows and ice-making machines, and one cannot feel quite comfortable over the reflection-what kind of places are those in which the dainty is made, and can the ingredients, under such unfavourable conditions, be particularly wholesome?

IT is now nearly twelve months since the Licensing Amendment Act became law, and the main feature of it - that which relates to the half-hour extension of the time until which public houses and beershops may remain open at night - was put to the test.

As the reader may possibly be aware, the last-mentioned indulgence was never demanded, never urged as necessary, never expected by a proportion of at least nine out of ten of those to whom it was granted. A mere hundred or so of tavern-keepers were at loggerheads with the authorities, as to the desirability of keeping open their houses a little later than twelve o'clock for the accommodation of people who chose to patronise places of amusement from which the audiences - were not dismissed until that hour, when the Home Secretary, by a device, as remarkable for its simplicity as for its boldness, solved the mighty difficulty.

The surest way of winning the affections of a people is to show respect for its homely, time-honoured traditions and maxims. The right hon. gentleman, who was doubtless aware of the popularity of the old English saying, "what is sauce for the goose should be sauce for the gander," shrewdly judged that he could not go far wrong if he cut the Gordian knot in which the publican's disagreement was bound, by declaring his conviction that what was good for the Crown and Cushion, in the Strand, was likewise good for the Three Jolly Tinkers, in Brick Lane; and that, to put an end to the vexed question, the shortest way would be to tar them all with the same brush.

The purpose of this paper is an attempt to make known the result of a personal inquiry into the working of the vast experiment in one of the worst and lowest neighbourhoods in London, where the public-houses outnumber the bakers' shops, and where gin by the "quarten" commands a sale of three to one as compared with quartern loaves.

It has always struck me as being not a little remarkable that those who regard it as their mission to preach against drunkenness and its attendant evils should pay so little attention to a rich and extensive field of material which lies all ready to hand - viz., the rieighbourhoods of Ratcliff and Shadwell, at the east end of London. Were I to enlist under the banner of Sir Wilfred Lawson, and be deemed capable and worthy of taking some sort of leadership in the praiseworthy crusade to which that inexorable opponent of the "demon Alcohol" is devoted, I would ask for a no more promising tract of battleground on which to display my prowess against the enemy than that discoverable between Breezers Hill, in St. George's Street, and King David Lane, in the same thoroughfare.

The distance between the spaces named is probably not more than eighty or ninety yards, but weeds in a neglected garden do not crop up in ranker luxuriance than the public-houses and beershops within the boundaries indicated. I am not certain, but roughly guessing, I should say that there are at least five and thirty of those places here. Genteel society may well be excused incredulity as to the existence of so many dens of vice and dissipation licensed by law in these days of school boards and public libraries. They might have been possible before gas and steam were enlisted to lighten the people and expedite their advancement to perfect civilization : there could be no question that such haunts were no rarity when Hogarth painted Gin Lane; but we are supposed to manage these matters very differently in modern times.

Well, those who think so should go and see for themselves; in no other way can they thoroughly comprehend how grave a mistake was made, when, as a short cut out of the difficulties which beset this particular branch of the Licensing Amendment Act, was resolved on the ingenious device of tarring the whole body of publicans with the same brush by making the extra half-hour universal.

It is generally agreed that the bane of drunkenness is never so hideous as when it is demonstrated in womankind, and no illustration of the disastrous effects of reckless indulgence in intoxicating liquors appeals to an audience with such telling force as that of the once sober and well-conducted female yielding by degrees to the terrible temptation until she at length sinks to the condition of a gin-soddened poor wretch, lost to every glimmer of self-respect, and capable even of starving herself and her children rather than forego her only remaining enjoyment in life. Such a story never fails to move to their inmost depths the commiseration and pity of those who hear it. It is no novel narrative.. Almost every day it is repeated in some shape or other in the newspapers; scarcely a morning passes but the "wretched woman" herself appears at the police-court to answer for her misbehaviour. But, after all, she is not by any means the extremest exemplification of the extent to which vice and strong drink may brutalize and change the nature of a human creature.

Were I in pursuit of the commission above hinted at, I would undertake with one cast of my net in the sea of infamy which flows between Ship Alley and Gravel Lane to bring to land fifty petticoated specimens, the least vicious of which, compared with the ordinary draggle-tail drunken woman of London streets, shall be of jet black, as it were, compared with mere grey. Not, however, as illustrating the prostrating effects both as regards mind and body, of inordinate indulgence in publicans' goods. The female of the locality in question is seldom seen dead drunk, as it is termed. Such a condition is almost impossible to her. She is far advanced beyond the weakness of succumbing easily to the influence of intoxicating fluids-if she was ever subject to it, which is doubtful-bred and suckled on gin, as she probably was, and weaned on gin and bitters. It requires a pen far more graphic than mine to adequately depict this modern Black-eyed Susan, whose prey mainly is men whose "follow the sea." It is marvellous that even spoony "Jack ashore" can discover anything in the least attractive in her. In language and manner she is as coarse as a coal-whipper, and the guiding principle of her shameful existence seems to be to make known her contempt and abhorrence of all that is modest and womanly.

It is no exaggeration to say that there are many hundreds of women of which she is a type, the daily and nightly business of whose lives it is to prowl about this delectable neighbourhood, seeking whom they may beguile and plunder, and it is equally true that it is chiefly at the public-houses and drinking-shops that they mature their plans for robbery. I do not mean to say that the publicans who keep these houses knowingly permit felony to take place on their premises; but it is absurd to suppose that they are not perfectly well aware that the women who swarm to their bars, and their concert rooms, and their dancing saloons, have no other object in view besides that of "picking up" and despoiling the weak-minded individuals who are so unfortunate as to fall into their clutches.

These women are the mainstay and support of half the public-houses hereabout. They go out in search of plunder of nights as systematically as did the foot-pads and the highwaymen of olden times. They do not resort to one tavern or dancing room and there spread their nets for chance corners; such a plan would be by far too slow, uncertain and unremunerative. It is as with every other kind of fishing, this "fishing for flats," - there is never any certainty as to the particular spot at which spoil may most plentifully abound. There may be an equal spread of it from the Pickled Herring to Paddy's Goose, or at may all have shoaled into one lucky corner; therefore it behoves all who would share in the take to be vigilant and on the alert. And vigilant they are. They pursue their investigations, these flashily bedizened and painted prowlers, with as cool an eye for business as do the night patrols in garrison towns, who look in at all the taverns in search of drunken and skulking soldiers. It might be imagined that such a proceeding would lead to quarrelling and contention, but it is not so. There really does seem to exist a certain sort of honour amongst these creatures which leads them to respect the laws of the chase, and should a pair of huntresses, - they usually go in couples, - succeed in snaring a victim, possession of the prey is never disputed even by the hungriest of the unlucky pack. No; twenty times an the course of as many minutes, the easily swinging doors of the dancing-room may be thrust open showing a head and shoulders, and a pair of eyes keen as those of a fox, but that is only to see how business is going. At these Ratcliff houses its fluctuations are rapid. There may be next to nothing doing in a dancing-room one hour and the next a gang of shipmates perambulating the highway may fall in with another gang, and they all turn in at the first tavern that comes in their way, offering instant employment to a greater number of wreckers that may happen to be on the spot. Should this be the case, the head and shoulders above mentioned are promptly followed by the full skirts, if not, if there appears to be no more than a fair proportion of plunderers to the to-be plundered, the head and shoulders vanish as suddenly as they appeared, and betake themselves elsewhere. They have no time to waste; every half-hour is precious, especially when the night grows late, and those to be beguiled become more and more helplessly drunk.

 An hour after ten is worth, to these man-catchers, more than two hours in the early evening, and it may be easily understood how inestimable is the half-hour after midnight, which is now vouchsafed them. And what amount of compensating advantage can be shown to balance the evils for which in Ratcliff Highway and its neighbourhood, "the extra half-hour" is responsible? There are no night factory hands, no railway travellers, no play-going folk in this quarter of the town to whom facilities for obtaining beer or spirits, after twelve o'clock, would be a convenience. Could it be tested, it would probably be found that out of every sovereign which passes over the bars of the hundred or so public-houses to be found between Cable Street and Limehouse Church after midnight, at least nineteen shillings is expended in drink for those who are already drunk at the instigation of the merciless shes, whose successful further attacks on their pockets and property mainly depends on the condition of helplessness to which their victims may be reduced.

 It is a marvel that, under the circumstances, the neighbourhood in question presents as a rule, and even up to the time when the public-houses and beer-shops close their portals, a comparatively orderly aspect. It is not unlikely, that if the various grievances which I have herein endeavoured to point out, were brought under the notice of the police authorities of the district, they would declare that they were exaggerated, and argue that if the place were the pandemonium it is said to be, to keep the peace there, as undoubtedly it is kept, would be impossible. But it must not be forgotten that, though undoubtedly a great deal is due to the excellent discipline and vigilance of the constabulary force, at least so much as regards avoidance of absolute outbreak and rioting, is attributable to the peculiar system of business adopted by the dancing-saloon and concert-room proprietors themselves.

 Never were truer words uttered than those constantly in the mouth of the publican, that a drunken man is his greatest detestation, and never did spoken sentiment so nakedly betray the debasing influence of the liquor traffic. The publican hates a drunkard as he hates the gout or any other inevitable result of excess; the man for him is he who is able and willing to sit or stand, and swig and swig until his last shilling is exhausted, comporting himself, meanwhile, as a jolly fellow should, and so setting a noble example to all who behold him, and finally walking off with his prodigious swallowings, as insensible to their influence as the beer barrel or the gin vat which originally contained them.

 The keepers of the dancing and singing rooms "down Ratcliff-way" share in the prevailing abhorrence of their class, for the objectionable persons who cannot drink like a pig without appearing as one, and take well-considered precautions against unpleasant results likely to arise therefrom. They employ their own police. By way of example, let us take the case of the Prussian Flag in Ship-alley. The Prussian Flag is probably as largely patronized as any public-house in the neighbourhood, to which is attached a free dancing-room. The nature of its business considered, it may claim to be regarded as a thoroughly well-conducted house, and it is evidently understood by those who frequent it that its managers are persons who will stand no nonsense. On the ground-floor there is a spacious and scrupuluously clean bar, and the bar space in front is partly occupied by a bagatelle-table for the innocent amusement of those who have neither taste nor talent for dancing. The dancing-room is upstairs.

On the occasion of my visit I was for a few moments in doubt as to the way to it. But while I was hesitating there came down a flight of stairs in the far corner two magnificent females, the one in a skirt of maroon-coloured velvet, and with a coronet of gold and pearls, and with a yellow "bandanna" temporarily covering the broad expanse of shoulders, &c., which the extremely "low" body of her dress left bare. The other lady either was, or affected to be a daughter of Scotland, and wore a plaid silk dress, with a broad scarf of similar material crossing her bosom and fastened with a brooch at her hip. They were both hot and perspiring from recent exertions and had evidently retired from the festive scene in quest of refreshment. They passed the bar, however.

"Going to have a drop of brandy, Beller?" remarked a hawk-eyed young fellow with a hook-nose and a meerschaum pipe, and who was drinking at the bar.

"It won't run to it just as yet," replied Beller, ruefully.

Seated on a corner of a table by the door was an old fellow with a basket containing something covered with a cloth, and approaching him one of the gorgeously attired females asked him for a "penn'orth," whereon he put aside the cloth and disclosed a tin pot full of peas boiled and still smoking hot. A "penn'orth" was a small saucerful, peppered, and well soused with vinegar.

"A penn'orth for you too, miss?" asked the old man to the syren in tartan.

"Ain't got the coin," as briefly she replied; "I'm goin' snacks with Poll," which she did, for Poll having devoured half the peas handed the saucer and the leaden spoon to Bella, who disposed of them in three mouthfuls, and after this economical refection the ladies made for the stairs again, I following in their wake.

The dancing-room, if not lofty, was spacious - sixty feet by thirty at least, with, at the far end of it, a refreshment bar resplendently painted, and gilt with looking-glass panels. At the end nearest the door was the space set apart for the musicians - a contrivance in shape and size closely resembling a corn bin perched up against the wall, and containing the performers, four in number, artistes of the street musician type, and who wore their caps and hats and took advantage of their short spells of rest to smoke short pipes and regale on beer from a quart pot. Above the heads of the musicians, dangling from nails in the wall, were four or five gorgeous hats and bonnets, the property of as many female frequenters of the room, and who with a praiseworthy regard for coolness as well as economy, preferred to disport themselves with their tresses unencumbered. Of the tender sex present, with a few exceptions, they were all of the Poll and Bella sisterhood, in flashing silks and satins, and with bare arms and shoulders; but one and all, and there must have been at least fifty of them, of exactly the stamp as regards manner and language as though they were cast in one mould. The same brutal, expressionless mouth, dead to everything but the intaking of brandy and gin and the outletting of foulest blasphemy, the same transparent mask of abandonment to the fun in progress, and through which unmistakably and invariably appeared a restless impatience of all frivolity that impeded business, and the cold, calculating sharp look-out for the main chance, and which was no more quenched or even tamed by the measures of strong drink, swallowed at the expense of the victims marked as fair prey, than fire may be quenched with oil.

As for the male dancers at the Prussian Flag, it s more difficult to describe them even than the women. In one respect only was there a striking family likeness amongst them, and that was that they were all drunk, or nearly-jolly and devil-may care drunk as the inebriated sailor as a rule is. A strangely mixed company, and presenting a picture well worth the attention of the clever artist daring enough to paint it; quite a theatrical scene. The painted and tricked out women as before mentioned, and the men of almost every country and climate under the sun. Lithe-like Italians, quick as cats and lively as kittens; bronze-complexioned fellows, with dull, jet black lank hair and bright red coral earrings, copper-coloured men, whose complexion was sickly yellow, and full black Africans grinning with delight, and perfect pinks of politeness as regards their behaviour to the ladies, and each one, although the heat of the room was stiflingly oppressive, wearing about his throat a bulky woollen wrapper of a gay colour for warmth sake; all there, and a dozen others beside, to say nothing of the "white folk," the spare-ribbed, hatchet-faced Yankee, the broad-beamed, heavy jowled German, and the true British mercantile tar, who, to do him justice, was rather more drunk than everybody else.

There was no attempt at ball-room attire as regarded the gentlemen. By far the greater part were dressed in that broad ship rig, and a few cases were to be seen of individuals who were so indifferent to, or defiant of ball-room proprieties as to appear in their great deck boots, but no one interfered or remonstrated with them. The "M.C's" certainly did not. Indeed, I am not quite sure that they were entitled to be so styled. "O. P.'s" would best apply to them, those initials standing for "officers of the peace."

There were four of them, long-backed, broad-shouldered young fellows, with their shirt sleeves rolled back above their elbows, and who acted as waiters, and who when not so engaged took each a seat at the corners of the room, and blandly smoked their pipes and looked on. But their business embraced something beyond looking out for and executing the orders of customers. A lady sitting in company with a huge Norwegian, whose shaggy hair, as he rested his tipsy head on the table, was dabbling in spilt rum and water, was seen while playfully patting his hand, to be endeavouring to relieve his little finger of the thick silver ring which adorned it.

"Stow it, Emma!" called out one of the vigilant waiters.

"It's on'y a lark," pleaded the young woman, coaxingly.

"Lark or linnet you stow it, or I shall have to show you down stairs," returned the waiter, civilly but firmly; and with a snarl and an oath the young woman desisted.

Shortly afterwards there were signs of a sudden row. A lady taking offence at her partner's-a black mm-stinginess, had forcibly expressed her indignation by punching him in the face and cutting his lip, whereon the other black men who witnessed the fracas hurried up to the rescue, and there was all at once a tremendous commotion and flourishing of fists. But before one might count twenty the four agile waiters were on the spot as well as two of the musicians out of the corn bin - the flute and the cornopean, and able-bodied men both, and in a jiffy all the coloured party were hustled down stairs and out of the house, and in less than five minutes the four waiters had resumed their corners, the flute and cornopean had returned to their duties, and the trifling interruption was forgotten in the delights of the mazy dance.

As the night advanced the dance grew mazier though, to the sober on-looker, possibly less delightful, for then it was that the hard-featured, keen-eyed women, who as before remarked, appear well-nigh invulnerable to the tipsying effect of wine and spirits, plied their victims with heavier and more frequent doses of potent liquor, so that they might render themselves utterly helpless into their Lands to be led captive to the infamous dens which abound in the neighbourhood, there to be plundered at leisure.

It may be said as regards the question of the extra half hour that in the case of the man who recklessly abandons himself to drinking all the evening and up to twelve o'clock at night, he is not likely to be much the worse for an extended indulgence of thirty minutes; and this may be so with men whose capacity for swallowing intoxicating fluids is reasonably limited; but as a rule the seafaring individual is not of this class. As long as he can stand he will go on drinking, and his "sea legs" remain faithful to him after his reason has gone by the board or very nearly. By twelve o'clock he may be drunk, but could if he were then left alone find his way home to his decent lodging house.

It is the broadsides of liquor, as it were, which are poured into him in his then crippled condition which undo him and lead to his becoming the stranded wreck we so frequently hear of: but not a tenth as often as if we heard all-invariably plundered and sometimes barbarously treated.

And how about the decoys - the cold-blooded pirates who, under false colours and in rich array, lure him to his ruin? Grateful, indeed, are these inexorable harpies for the "extension of time," which has been graciously conceded to them, in which to follow their abominable avocations; but, poor wretches, it is not them who reap the benefit. They are not birds of prey, tree to enjoy the spoil, which by hook and crook falls into their possession. They are as a rule no more their own mistresses than the silks and laces with which they are so gaily bedecked, are their own property. Their gay plumage is only lent to them to go a hunting in. It belongs to the odious male and female wretches who own the dens to which helpless drunken men are beguiled.

Let any one who doubts this pay a visit to Ratcliff or Shadwell any morning, say at noon. That is an "off-time" at the various sailors' drinking places and dancing saloons. The foolish Jacks who are ashore are still abed sleeping off the effects of the over-night's spree, or those that have beer, cleared out have skulked off somewhere penniless and ashamed; but the public-houses are not without customers. About the still dirty bars flock the splendid creatures I have endeavoured to describe, but bearing no trace of being the same, except for the paint with which their dirty faces are still smeared, and the burnt cork and pencilling which by daylight render more repulsive the expression of their bleary bloodshot eyes. Their gowns are draggletailed and tattered, their hair in greasy loops and ropes about their ears from which the tawdry earrings are still pendant. They meet to drink glasses of raw gin, by way, as they say, of a "freshener" after the ball-room fatigues of the previous evening, and to brag of the money and valuables it was their luck to "make" out of those who last night fell into their clutches. And when the day declines and the gas is ablaze again there they will be found, Bella and Poll, and their thousand wicked sisters, haunting the dancing saloons or prowling from public house and seeking whom they may devour, with no man seeking to hinder them, nay, cheered by the kindly dispositions of the rulers of the nation who have ordained that their hunting grounds shall remain open to them half an hour beyond the time their absurdly squeamish predecessors thought quite late enough.

DEVONSHIRE-PLACE, Old Nichol-street, Spitalfields, is a little court consisting of perhaps a dozen houses, six on either side, with a strip of broken pavement between. Precisely of the same type as those already described are these domiciles - mere hutches as regards size - a tiny room above and below, with broken floors and blackened walls and ceilings so shattered that every step overhead causes the rotten plaster to crumble and fall, further exposing the bare ribs of lath. In almost every case there are, upstairs as well as downstairs, lodgers, and the parlour, which is likewise the bedroom, opens on to a few square feet of space, where in one corner is a reeking heap of all manner of decaying vegetable matter and fireplace refuse, and in another corner the closet. In Devonshire-place I was made aware of a phase of the social economy of the Spitalfield slums which was new to me.

In one house I found the "parlour," as I first thought tenantless. There was a bedstead in the room, three-parts filling it, and a bed which I will not attempt to describe, with a heap of ragged female attire, by way of bedclothing. The terrible-looking old wooden bedstead was in such a shaky condition that it had been found necessary to tie it up with bits of rope, but even this could not induce it to stand upright on its four legs, and in the midst of the unsightly wreck was a baby of a few months old, peacefully asleep. Hearing me come in, the upstairs lodger came down, and informed me that the baby's mother was out at work.

"And what may be the rent of this little place?" I asked. "3s. 9d. a week."

"For the house, of course?"

"Oh, dear, no - for each room."

"3s. 9d. a week for this room?" I repeated in amazement.

"Well, you see, sir, it is let already furnished," explained the upstairs lodger.

"But where is the furniture?"

"There it is," said she, pointing to the dreadful bedstead and to the one wooden chair which, without the slightest reservation, formed the whole of the furniture of the carpetless, fenderless hovel.

"That's what's called a furnished room down here, sir, and the rent is 3s. 9d. a week, leastways, if you are weekly; if you are nightly, it's 9d. There's lots of the houses about here let like that. Some of them charge 9d. a night, though you go on stopping reg'ler, and come for the rent every day. If they trusted a whole week they wouldn't get it at all, p'raps, so they collects it daily."

Seven shillings a week for shelter in a tenement which at its pulling-down value would scarcely realise a five-pound note, and the use of two bedsteads and a few rags and flock to lie on! It seemed so preposterous that I could not believe it, but on referring the matter to a visiting clergyman of the district, he assured me that what the woman had told me was correct In every particular.

Immediately opposite is a narrow-mouthed alley known as Shepherd's-court, an irregular cluster of human habitations, the sight and smell of which are enough on an August afternoon to make one gasp for breath. There are houses behind houses, with no rearward yard or space for privacy or decency, and one and all are in a dilapidated state from cellar to roof and quite unfit to live in. There is no kind of arrangement as regards the buildings they are erected "higgledy-piggledy;" backs to fronts, anyhow, with narrow passages between.

Possibly the main reason why continually fever is not raging in every alley in Old Nichol-street may be found in the fact that the water supply is uninterrupted and unlimited. This, however, has only been so since some ingenious person invented an apparatus by means of which this essential to existence may be provided with certainty. Old Nichol-street is not a particularly honest neighbourhood. There may probably be found within its limits a greater number of thieves - petty and other - than a square mile of any other parish could produce. Metal taps and leaden water-pipes and ball-cocks used to vanish as soon almost as they were fixed, and even iron piping which would realise at the shop of the marine store dealer but a few halfpence was not safe from dishonest hands. Zinc and iron tanks, more than one man could lift, have before now in that light-fingered region disappeared between dark and daylight, as though they were mere portable articles that might be doubled up and stowed in a coat pocket. A remedy, however, has been found for this uncomfortable condition of affairs. An iron locker, about eighteen inches square, solid on all sides, and prodigiously heavy, is supported on a firm basis. There is a spout at the bottom of the receptacle, and at the side a massive iron knob, the turning of which sets the water flowing. One of these contrivances is to be found in almost every alley, and where it is not found one need only follow his nose to discover.

    The houses of Shepherd's-court are of a pattern with those of Devonshire-place - a room up and a room down, each affording refuge for a family, great and small, and at least three-fourths of the wretched tenants earn their bread at home. Match-box making seems to give employment to hundreds of hands in this squalid neighbourhood, every member of the family, down to the little child four or five years old, lending a hand as they squat in a ring on the filthy, uncarpeted floor. They receive twopence halfpenny for making twelve dozen boxes, and out of this have to provide paste. By working very hard and without reference to the clock, a woman and three or four children so employed may earn fifteenpence a day, and out of this the produce of two whole days' labour out of the six must go to pay the rent of the miserable one room, which is a heated and unwholesome factory from morning until night, and a bedchamber from night until morning.

    If nothing else is done it is high time that the same humane inspection that is vouchsafed to the common lodging-house occupant should be extended to these private abodes of squalor and wretchedness.

    There is an establishment of the kind alluded to in Old Nichol-street, not a nice place, certainly, but cleanliness is compulsory there, and any attempted evasion of the Common Lodging-house Act is very speedily exposed by the bull's-eye of Mr. Inspector, who has an artful way of making his dead-of-night visits as unexpected as possible. Though, however, the proceedings may be strictly in accordance with the requirements of the legislature they do not care to see strangers at these places. At the Old Nichol-street abode, for instance, there is a printed notice conspicuous to every one who enters at the door of the common kitchen, to the effect that, "Persons who don't lodge here are not welcome." They keep the best possible order at this refuge for the dissipated and poverty-stricken.

    Included in the notice above alluded to is an intimation that pelting each other with pillows and bolsters is strictly prohibited, and that individuals who insist on adopting such an outlet for their superabundant animal spirits will be at once expelled the premises. The rules and regulations conclude with a hint - as delicately conveyed as possible - as to the rashness of too implicitly confiding in the proverb that there is honour amongst all classes. " Beware of the cat who steals the meat; I wish that I could catch him," says rule the last, to which the proprietor significantly signs his name.

    Two in a bed, however, is an indecency which is not for a single hour tolerated in places where tramps and cadgers congregate, but in these "homes" of the people four times two may so sheep and no one interfere. I ventured into one house in Shepherd's-court and went upstairs. There was but one bedstead in the room-a mite of a place; I measured it with my walking-stick and found that it was three and a half one way and four sticks the other, and yet it was made to accommodate mother, father, and eight children; some of course would have to lie on the bare boards, the bedstead, which was barely of the ordinary size, could not have contained them all. The room was in a shocking condition, with holes in the rotten floor and damp patches on the walls and ceiling. For this the weekly rent was two-and-ninepence. But, bad as was this up. stairs room, I would rather, if doomed to the terrible alternative, have lived there than in the room below, and which comprised the remaining half of the habitation.

To be sure in this last-mentioned case there were but six children, but then their father was a cabinet-maker by trade and worked at home, and in addition to the apartment serving as a living and sleeping room for the eight individuals who contributed towards the unclean Shepherd's flock, it was made to do duty as a carpenter's shop as well. It was an uglier place than the rest, by reason of its floor being several feet below the outside mire, while the ceiling was so how that one might lay the flat of his hand against it, and like the upstairs room, it measured three-and-a-half walking-sticks by four. There were pieces of mahogany in course of shaping and others in the rough, and a large number of tools and a bench, and the floor was ankle-deep in shavings.

There was, as usual, but one bedstead, and the bench came so close upon it, helping to fill the narrow space, that it was difficult to conceive how the mother - who was a stoutish woman, and at present employed at the wash-tub in the open alley - contrived to get near the fireplace for domestic purposes without her husband first vacating the premises. She could not climb over the bedstead, because that was already occupied by several articles not pertaining to repose.

"It is warm work down here, sir," remarked the little old cabinet-maker cheerily, "but you see I'm 'bliged to keep up a good fire, howsomever hot the weather may be, cos of my glue."

Yes, reeking hot as it was, even out in the open court, there was a fire in the grate bright and brisk enough to roast a sucking pig, and the frowsy bedstead came to within a yard of it, and the intervening space was strewn ankle deep in mahogany chips and shavings as dry as tinder. Just image a smouldering ember igniting that combustible heap, just when the weary eight were deep in their first sleep. Eight! Eighteen in all, counting the general dealer and his wife and their eight children overhead, and with only a cracked ceiling and a touchwood floor between. But the little old cabinet-maker appeared to be not in the least alive to the possibility of such a catastrophe. He grumbled at having to pay so high a rent, but otherwise was evidently of opinion that Shepherd's-court was an eligible locality for a family residence, and one where a man might, if he tried, make himself very comfortable. The old cabinet-maker had tried, and with some show pf success. He had gone in for floriculture. There were garden-pots on his window-sill, and the presence of a small glass globe suspended amongst them betrayed that he had even aspired to gold fish as well; but the great fire which was so necessary for the glue had probably disagreed with them, and for the present, at all events, the globe was empty. But the garden was not so much on the window-sill as on the opposite side of the way. Facing the window- within a yard and a half of it, in fact-there was a blank wall, and to this the cabinet-maker had affixed two long narrow boxes, and given his attention to the cultivation of Indian corn and sunflowers in the one case, and "creeping Jennies," and, I think, a few balsams in the other. The latter, however, were in a state of health that occasioned him some apprehension and anxiety.

But there are plants seemingly as there are human creatures, which are exempt from what are called the laws of nature. In this close, pent-up place, where every respiration was an offence to the nostrils, the Indian corn was flourishing favourably, while the sun-flowers bloomed with a blowsy luxuriance as though their evil surroundings had quite corrupted their natural goodness, and they had acquired a taste for tainted air, and liked it. In the same foul alley, in an old butter tub, lashed to an upper window sill, there was a plant of rhubarb bristling with stout stems, and with leaves large nearly as dinner plates.

But these instances were quite exceptional, and as a rule the only green things visible were the verdant rime with which damp had blotched the rotten walls and the stagnant pools in the gutter. The alley-dwellers of this part are a terribly dirty race, and in the fastnesses of their slums seem to have deteriorated from civilisation, and gone a long way back on the road to savagery. It would, indeed, in one respect be rather an improvement if they would do so entirely and substitute a cheerful coating of woad or ochre for the grim dark grey that comes of long abstinence from soap and water. But how is it possible that cleanly habits can be cultivated in the midst of such foulness? A new comer who resolved to set a shining example and appear with a clean face and hands would soon grow discouraged. Nor would it be of the least use to endeavour to improve the inhabitants as they are at present domiciled.

Efforts have been made in this direction in one of the vilest parts of Spitalfields. It was conceived to be worth while to set up a public nursery for young children, where, instead of lying about in the alley gutters while their mothers were out at work or selling things in the street, they might he well cared for, and properly cleansed, and tended, and fed.

A home of this kind has been established in Quaker-street. A kind and capable nurse has been appointed; there is a nice playground for fine weather, and an admirably fitted play-room for wet weather; neat cots for the little ones to sleep in when they are unwell, toys, clean pinafores (on loan, of course), and warm boots; plenty of wholesome food, and all for the very small sum of fourpence per day. But the response on the part of working mothers is not hearty. Whether they resent the warm bath and its changeful effects on their progeny, or whether they find it cheaper to keep their children at home, I cannot say, but at present there have never at any time been more than seven small customers in one day at this admirable home, and the number when I visited it was only five.

If the Artisans' Dwellings Act prove efficacious in remedying the shameful state of things which exists in and about Old Nichol-street there is hope for every district in London. For many reasons one cannot but feel anxious to see what will result from the act in question in this neighbourhood. It is a fact, as I was informed on authority, that a very considerable portion of court and alley property of the kind I have endeavoured to describe belongs to gentlemen who, in some way or other, are included in the list of "local authorities." I was shown an awful place, consisting, I think, of eight tenements, in a secluded crevice between the front Street houses, and known as 4and 5 Half Nichol-street. The entrance is scarcely as wide as the passage of an ordinary house, and the residences in question have evidently been erected in what was once the back-yard of one of the large houses. The lower rooms of these delectable dwellings are so low down beneath the pavement that they are little better than cellars, with nothing tn prevent the rain pouring into them in times of storm. These are hovels of the worst kind, ruinous, ill-drained, and evil smelling, with a kennel of foul water in the yard-wide path which divides the double "row." It is a marvel how the tenants escape with their hives in such a noisome den; and yet this is the property of a vestryman, who derives a considerable income from the exorbitant rent exacted of the lodgers.

In Great Arthur Street, St. Luke's, there is a court called Thomas's Court, an old place, with an iron tablet at its entrance stating its age. The houses in Thomas's Court - which is a broad, stone-paved place, about twenty feet wide between the dwellings, and sixty yards from end to end-have during the last three months, been declared to be uninhabitable, and tenants turned out. We found two workmen in the court, and one of them had just prised up from the flagway in the middle a heavy wooden trap-door, which had been cemented down, and the opening disclosed a gulf of at least twelve feet deep, and extending, the men informed us, beneath the whole space and under the houses on either side, walled in and with this only outlet. In ancient times, it seems, the place was part of a brewery, and here beer barrels were stored; but, strangely enough, my guide, who had known the court and its inhabitants for fifteen years, had never heard of the existence of the vast vault, nor, to his knowledge, were the inhabitants aware of it. I looked down into it, and by all appearance it was an innocent place enough, but I could not help thinking to what strange purposes it might have been put in such a neighbourhood, had evil-disposed persons discovered it. I remarked as much to the bricklayer, but he laughed at the idea.

"God bless you, sir, said he; "if they'd known it they would not have ventured into it I They was a awful superstitious lot that lived down here. It has been always thought that the court was haunted."

"But why?"

"Well, there 'ave been suicides. A man hung himself from that lamp-iron, and another hung himself in the parlour at that end house -" and just at that moment, with a startling sort of "Jack-in-the-box" movement, a door was flung open within a yard or so, and opposite the ruined "parlour" in question, an old woman made her appearance, chuckling with glee at what she had overheard.

"Hallo!" exclaimed my missionary companion - they all know him in that region - "are you here still? I thought you cleared out with the rest?"

"Not me," replied the merry old soul, whose age must have been at least seventy; "hauntin' and ghosts don't frighten me, I don't mind 'em; let em come if they like, I shan't go until they turn me out," and she retired again to her snuggery, crowing triumphantly. And a brave old woman she must be, to be able to lay her head down unconcernedly of nights the only inhabitant of a ruined, out-of-the-way alley, mysteriously undermined, and with ample excuse for being haunted, if it is not.

Strange trades are carried on in these slums, and occupations are followed which in civilised parts are never dreamt of:, except it be in exceptionally bad dreams. One does not like even to hint at the way in which scores of poor wretches in the locality pick up a living, nor would I myself have believed it had I not been told it as a fact, by a gentleman whose veracity is unimpeachable. There is an awful little alley, for instance, in the neighbourhood of Hales's tallow factory, consisting of about twenty houses, inhabited almost entirely by folk who collect the ordure of dogs, which is used for tanning purposes. I say that the alley in question is occupied almost entirely by this class, and, repulsive as the trade is, it is preferable to that of the dreadful exceptions. There are but few left there now, I am informed, but not very long since the residents of this delectable spot consisted chiefly of "cat-flayers" - whose sole means of living was to go out at night with their sacks and sticks, hunting for cats to ha slaughtered for the sake of their skins. It is a business at which money may be made, since the furriers will give 12*s.* a dozen for big and little cat-skins, as many as may be brought them. It is unfortunate, however, that to be saleable the hide must be taken from the body of the animal while it is in existence, and still more so that the villainous cat-flayers are not deterred by this difficulty. I was further informed that the neighbourhood used to be scandalised by the presence of the flayed carcases of poor grimalkins lying about, but that now that indecency is avoided by an economical arrangement on the part of the flayer. He now puts his dead cats in the copper, and makes further capital of their bones and fat.

IT is not a little humiliating that such an insignificant creature as a puny squalling baby should occasionally present itself as an obstacle, not to say a downright stumbling-block, in the path of men whose mighty brains have conceived and matured gigantic schemes of reform, social and other.

That the absurdly small animals have this annoying propensity, however, might be proved by at least a score of well authenticated instances. Personally I can vouch for one, where a wretched human waif, too young to know the use of his feet, or indeed to have a single tooth in its head, had the audacity to set at open defiance, and on his own premises, the governor of one of the largest prisons in the kingdom - defied him, cried him down, and mocked his pride and vaunting to the level of the dust. It was at the time when the silent system as applied to criminals was regarded as a radical cure for every shade of iniquity brought under its influence. I walked over his model establishment with the worthy governor, and when we came to that part where the women - over two hundred of them - were bestowed, he beckoned me to tread softly, and come and stand by him on a mat. He was a big man, but he appeared several inches bigger, as, swelling with the pride of power, he whispered,

"Here, sir, I am happy to introduce you to the very perfection of our grand system. Within fifty yards all about you are more than two hundred prisoners, all women - mark that, if you please, - and not a sound!"

And he straightened the crooked finger with which he had been emphasising his remarks, and held it above his head as a signal for me to listen. Barely had he done so, however, when a lusty shout, a yell, a "yah!" burst from a neighbouring cell, and made the vaulted roof ring again. I never saw a man so visibly collapse in all my life. The lofty finger was ignominiously lowered, and he coughed and turned about that I might not see his troubled countenance,

"Ahem! that's one of the babies born here, sir; we can't, of course, be responsible for *their* noise."

In a manner almost as exasperating did the infantine rebels dare to challenge the triumphant onward march of the Metropolitan School Board. The inquisitor empowered by the Board went from house to house making inquiry, and got on swimmingly as regards the boys, but when he began to question concerning the girls of the family, and to insist that all who were under the age of thirteen must attend school forthwith, he found himself in troubled water. Mother shook her head. It was impossible that Eliza Jane, aged ten, should attend school. Who was to mind the baby?

"Mind it yourself," was the not unnatural suggestion of Mr. Inspector.

"How can I, when I've got to work and help my husband to get a living for our youngsters?"

"Then get one of your elder girls to mind it."

"How can they, when they are out at their daily work getting a living for themselves?"

It was the same story over and over again in whatever district the inspector pursued his investigations; and goodness only knows what might have been the consequence had it not occurred to the good-natured Board that, with a little contrivance, it might itself mind the baby. And so the difficulty was surmounted.

In this instance, however, our thanks are due to the tiny human encumbrance, since it has been the means of directing attention to a rapidly-increasing evil - the employment of girls of tender years at workshops and factories, and at such work as used to and would still be done by boys, only that the value of labour has of late years vastly increased, and it is found cheaper to engage female "hands" than male. Whether it is due entirely to the miserable and sometimes inhuman laws which regulate supply and demand, or whether it is in any degree owing to the endeavours of those strong-minded leading female spirits who are ready to wrestle with mankind for a share of the downright hard labour of life, need not here be discussed. This much is certain, however, that the tender regard for young folks of the female kind, of which in old-fashioned times no man felt ashamed, is fast vanishing from amongst us. Any one who doubts this may easily satisfy himself of its truth. Let him at early morning take his stand at the foot of London or Blackfriars Bridge, and make observation of the hurrying human throng on its way "to work." Ten years since, at such an early hour, the motley company would have been found to consist almost entirely of men and and lads and little boys, and rare indeed was it to see a little girl with them. But now it is altogether different. At least as many girls as boys may be seen, scores of them puny, delicate-looking little creatures, with their lean skirts and woefully ill-shod feet, but nine times out of ten, with their oily locks surmounted by a hat or bonnet gay enough for a May-day queen, in gangs of three or four, chattering like magpies as they scurry along quick march to their "daily work."

Or, should the incredulous reader be not one of the early rising family he may just as satisfactorily convince himself of the alarming change by visiting the neighbourhood of Holborn; or Westminster, or Bethnal-green, or Clerkenwell, at noon, when the hundreds of "girl hands" get the customary hour for rest and dinner.

Much may be learnt in that brief sixty minutes of the mischievous effects of substituting girl for boy labour. In the majority of cases the children - for many of them are little better - reside too far away from the factory to admit of their going home to the midday meal. They bring their food with them, the supply consisting generally of three or four slices of bread and butter and perhaps a penny or twopence to be expended in "something relishing" for dinner. The something relishing, however, seldom takes the shape of solid food, which perhaps is quite as well. Nothing bearing resemblance to animal sustenance, excepting such abominations as sausages and saveloys, is to be bought in these hard times for a penny or two- pence, and when the choice lies between semi-starvation and downright poisoning, it is commendable in the victim to adopt the latter.

As a rule, the insufficient bread-and-butter is munched up in a hurry, and then the troops of work-girls, poor, thoughtless little wretches! disperse through the streets, expending their halfpence in trash, and, as is the generous nature of the sex, bestowing it in part on factory boys who keep them company in their dinner-hour stroll, when the weather is fine, or join with them in frolic more or less innocent under market archways and such like shelter should it happen to rain or snow. There is seldom any help for this, even if the girls themselves desire it, for it is the rule at most of these factories for the "hands" to clear out at meal times.

Amid this is only one phase of the mischief. It is not the poorest and roughest class of girls that find employment at these places. The temptation to earn four or five shillings a week is, in hundreds of cases, more than can be withstood by girls delicately bred and hitherto kept carefully apart from all that is coarse and vicious; and, having once joined the working army, there is nothing for it, if existence is to be rendered at all tolerable, but to conform to "barrack rule" and make, at all events, a passable pretence of doing as other girls do. How difficult it is to avoid contamination under such conditions is but too well known.

Should the inquirer be anxious to discover what is the effect of this deprivation of home influences and freedom from wholesome paternal restraint on these young girls, let him listen to their conversation with the boys of their own age; let him observe their general behaviour at such times, and again when, come dark nights, boys and girls, are released from work alike, and troop hilariously home.

One reason, perhaps, why this growing grievance has not attracted more attention on the part of the general public, is to be found in the fact that these small female factory hands are employed in large numbers in manufactories situated not in the pent-up courts and alleys of the City, but almost "out in the country" - at Bow, Stratford, Victoria Park, Highgate, &c., &c. These suburban workshops are rapidly increasing. One of the heaviest drawbacks on a manufacturers' profits is the enormous rent he is compelled to pay for his City premises. He will be charged five hundred a year in the shadow of St. Paul's for no more accommodation than he can procure five miles away for one hundred. He need be under no apprehension as to the difficulty of hiring hands at such a distance from town. The hands will follow the work; they can by no means afford to do otherwise. He has but to beckon with his finger, or, in other words, to insert an advertisement in a newspaper, and in a few hours his gates will be besieged by eager applicants.

And it may, with some show of truth, be urged that, leaving charitable motives out of the question, the employer who uproots his manufacturing "plant" from the noise, and crowd, and dirt of town, and, transplanting it into the country, sets it down in company with hedgerows and daisies, confers a benefit on those who, by the sweat of their small brows, earn their bread of him. At least, the suburban factory-hand must be better off than her sister-toilers of the stifled and stenchful alley, inasmuch as the air she breathes is purer, and, from her healthful surroundings, she is less likely to be injuriously affected by her sedentary occupation.

There are, however, two views that may be taken of this picture, the effect depending very much on whether it is contemplated in the light and warmth of summer time, or whether it is approached amidst the murk and haze of winter. It is all very well, no doubt, when country roads are delightful, and it is worth an hour's journey to saunter beneath green trees. It will hurt no human creature to trudge two miles or so to work under such circumstances, and it will do the young "hand" good rather than harm after an afternoon spent in the crowded workroom, to exercise her limbs and refresh her lungs by a similar walk home in the balmy evening twilight; but it is a very different matter in the month of November. At such a time of the year, and under most favourable conditions, young girls whose poverty compels them to turn out to work at a tender age must suffer severely. And when I speak of "most favourable" conditions, I have in my memory a factory of the suburban sort, a few words concerning which will illustrate my meaning.

The establishment in question is to be found in the neighbourhood of Highgate. In its aspect there is nothing the least grim or repulsive, or suggestive of "Fee, faw, fum," or the grinding of small human bones for the manufacture of dainty bread for the ogre proprietor. Venerable trees surround the place, there is a big old-fashioned garden at the rear of it, and here are erected spacious and well-ventilated workrooms for the young folks employed. The work done at this factory is by no means of the "slop" character, such as that in which factory hands are commonly hired to assist. It is a branch of a great City business, the heads of which are persons of immense wealth, and not at all disposed to be ungenerous in their dealings with their *employées*.

The "hands" at the Highgate establishment include about two hundred girls from thirteen to sixteen years old. The Factory Act enjoins that no child whose age is below thirteen shall be taken from school and set to work. But contemplation of the petticoated flock that, when the dinner-bell rang, came pouring out at the gates, reveals how difficult it is to legislate in such a matter. It may be that at the age of thirteen a girl should have outgrown childhood, and attained strength of body and mind sufficient to fit her for the labour market, but very much depends on the conditions under which the child has been reared. Here, for instance, were girls, straight-limbed and sturdy as young colts, and yet with faces that bespoke them under rather than over the stipulated age, but these were decidedly the exception. Other "thirteens" were there that might well have passed for ten, nine, or even eight years old. Poor mites of things, hungry-eyed, sharp- shouldered, and with nothing ample in the matter of attire but their mud-bespattered cotton stockings, that hung in rucks and folds about their sticks of legs. Unhealthy-looking little creatures, with faces shrunken and shrewd as are the visages of women wrinkled with age, and of that complexion of greyish white that invariably denotes the child whose familiarity with butcher's meat is little more than a nodding acquaintance as it is displayed on the butcher's hooks, and who is bread-and-butter built from her weaning upwards.

It was a wretched day. The wind was keen, and a fine penetrating rain filtered through the chill fog that came rolling down the steep hill, at the foot of which Dick Whittington paused to listen to the suggestion of the friendly city church chimes. It seemed, legislative wisdom notwithstanding, a sin and a shame that such puny, ill-conditioned little children should be deemed fit for active service in the battle of life.

It wouldn't have mattered so much - nay, I will go so far, excluding for the moment the moral question-it would not have mattered at all, if these small "hands" had been warmly clad and plentifully fed; but in by far the majority of cases they were neither. Possibly they were bread-winners for the smaller fry at home, and there is no economy in sending them out to work at all if, in a vulgar manner of speaking, they consume all the grass they cut.

Perhaps some of them were the children of fathers who, never endowed with a violent affection for labour, were not so short-sighted as to be oblivious of its value when practised by their progeny. I saw three girls of the bread-and-butter built order, clean and neat-haired, but tattered and painfully poor- looking, and they came out at the factory gate, looking hungrily down the road. Presently exclaimed the youngest, "Here comes father!" and there hove in sight, through the rain and mist, a slouching, lazy-looking man, with a battered black hat and a black coat out at the elbows, and who, moreover, was smoking a dirty short pipe. Father had brought his children's dinner. It was not a bulky affair; indeed, it was comprised in a bundle, the dimensions of which were so small that he would never have been suspected of bearing it at all had he not opened a breast lappet of his greasy old coat and disclosed it.

"Catch hold, good luck to you," growled father; "a pretty day this is for me to come lugging up here! Make haste and eat it up, and cut away into work again."

They were glad enough to get it. I saw the small parcel unfolded, and that it contained three slices of bread and three morsels of fried fish, and, this being fairly divided, the three poor sisters turned their faces towards Highgate Hill, and went for a walk, dining as they went. Father turned back, and with his great hands thrust deep in his empty pockets, stretched his lanky legs to make haste home out of the disagreeable weather. Certainly he may have been a worthy but unfortunate mechanic, unavoidably out of work; if so, my instinct was much at fault. I hope that I was mistaken, and that the severe things at the moment I wished in his behalf not being his due, may never happen to him.

I met two other little girls of the Highgate factory. Under a sheltering wall, bonnetless, and their dirty faces streaked with the rain that trickled down from their untidy heads of hair; with nothing to cover their thin little shoulders, and with their feet but ill-protected by woefully dilapidated shoes, were these two mites of girls- hands, as could at once be judged by the gay smears of colour that lit up the dinginess of their attire.

"I understood," said I, addressing one of them, "that no girls were employed at the factory who were under thirteen?"

"And who ses *I* ain't thirteen?" retorted one of the little women, with a hard puckering of her lips, and a defiant glance that made her for the moment look thirty.

"I don't say so," I replied, "but you certainly appear younger."

"Then I just ain't," said she, "there's my teeth to prove it, and you can go and ask our doctor if you don't believe me."

After which she was good enough to explain that if there was any doubt as to the age of a child who applied for work at the factory she was referred to a medical gentleman retained by the firm, who by experience had learnt to rely on the evidence of dental witnesses within a child's mouth rather than on any oral testimony that might proceed from it.

The two poor little shivering wretches were in dire distress. They had not appeared at the factory gate at the exact minute when their dinner-hour expired, and, as a punishment for the offence, were shut out for half an hour and fined a penny as well. We grew quite confidential under the shelter of my umbrella. They were really not to blame for being late. Another girl - for a "lark," as my bonnetless friends now ruefully assumed - had told them of a certain cookshop in Camden Town where might be bought enormous penn'orths of pudding, left cold from yesterday. They couldn't go home to dinner on account of the long distance, but had been provided for the midday repast by their respective parents with a slice of bread and a halfpenny. The penny, therefore, with which the feed of cold pudding was to be purchased was a joint stock affair, and they had set out together to make the investment. They had a run for it - it is at least a mile and a half from the Holloway-road to Camden Town - but no pudding shop was there, and after a fruitless search for it they were driven by stress of weather to seek comfort in brandy-balls, the last remnants of which they were sadly sucking when I first addressed them. We had some discourse on the subject of work and wages. The diminutive "hands" informed me that they earned respectively sixpence and sevenpence a day, and that they got to work at eight in the morning, had an hour to dinner (from half-past eleven until half-past twelve), at three o'clock ten minutes for "luncheon," and left off at half-past five, excepting Saturday, when they worked no longer than one o'clock in the day.

Was three shillings or three-and-sixpence a week as much as any of the girls earned? I asked. Not by a long way, was the answer, some of 'em - the big 'uns - earned as much as eight or nine shillings, but that was piece-work. Were the girls compelled to turn out at dinner time, even though they lived so far away that they could not go home to that meal? Oh, no. There was a jolly fire for them that liked to stay in. She, my four-foot-high informant, meant to stay in dinner times when her father got some work. What had that to do with it? A precious sight; the girls that stopped in all brought something to cook at the fire, and it wasn't likely that the girl who had only bread for dinner would stay in to be looked down on.

So that you see, and as I before remarked, even in the best regulated of factories where poor little girls are employed it is impossible to avoid much that Christian-minded men and women must wish was far otherwise.

Of the two hundred girls, whose ages varied from thirteen to sixteen or seventeen, and who were hurrying out to the music of the bell, a considerable number were comfortably clad, and hurried away for home and a good dinner, it is to be hoped. But this was by no means the case. Dozens of them evidently had left the paternal abode in the morning with the intention of dining out, and they proceeded to do so literally, despite the mud under foot and the rain overhead - the younger hands, who are indifferent as to appearances, munching their slices of bread or bread-and-treacle undisguisedly, and the elder ones carrying their dinner in their pocket, its material being favourable to piecemeal demolition.

For amusement and to while away the dinner-hour, many of these last-mentioned girls - bright-looking, and by no means ill-favoured some of them - made a tour of the immediate neighbourhood, and, with their poor flimsy skirts bedraggled and clinging about their ankles, and their toes benumbing on the splashy pavement, feasted their eyes on the treasures revealed in the shop of the milliner, and on the gorgeous display of velvets, and silks, and sealskin on view at the drapery establishment. It was observable that they were not cast down or despondent while making their surveys, and that their conversation was not at all tinctured with melancholy or regret. They were free-spoken young persons, and it was not difficult to overhear what they said.

"That," remarked one of them, in reference to a modest woollen shawl, to which her attention had been called by another girl, "that! Pooh! All very well for a common servant gal, but it wouldn't suit *me*."

Bless you, these slipshod, half-starved factory hands affect the supremest contempt for domestic servitude, and would blush with shame to the crowns of their blowsy bonnets were it revealed that even a most distant female relative had so demeaned herself as to engage as a maid-of-all-work. A day or so previous to my visit to Highgate with the same business in hand, I sought to make myself acquainted with the habits and customs of a swarm of poor little female urchins, who work at a "frisette" factory in the neighbourhood of Wilderness-row, St. Luke's.

Again it was dinner time, and I watched a troop of them hurrying to a villanous-looking cheap cookshop to invest their precious halfpence in pease-pudding or some such hot and cheap though unsubstantial dainty; but there was one female, of fourteen possibly, with the rest, who stood wistfully beside the cookshop window regarding the stock and making up her mind before she took the step that was irretraceable. Finally they all came to a decision, excepting the damsel in question, and she, though jingling her halfpence in her hand, and with her very eyes as well as her mouth watering with hunger, somehow contrived to resist the temptation to cross the threshold. With a lingering look at the luscious display, she paused for a last sniff at the open door, and then, as though goaded by its maddening effect, rushed off at a half run towards the Goswell-road. Her speed was such that it was no easy matter, without exciting public curiosity, to keep up with her. "She is aware of another cookshop," I thought; "she is wiser than her factory mates, and will, doubtless, get more Pease-pudding for her penny."

But it was not at a cookshop that my heroine paused; it was at a "wardrobe" shop - an establishment where may be purchased second-hand apparel and finery. She did not hesitate, but at once entered the shop, and, after a few minutes, emerged with a somewhat faded but gorgeous bunch of artificial flowers, consisting of a rose, full blown, a poppy or two, and a fair sprinkling of wheat. With a glow of triumph on her wizen little face, she cast an eager glance to the right and to the left, and spying close at hand the secluded gateway of a timber yard, darted across the road, and, crouching in a corner, was soon high busy with her battered old hat on her knees, retrimming it.

I ventured to offer her a little friendly advice while she was so engaged. Did she not think it was foolish to waste her hard-earned money in such trash? To which she uncivilly replied, "that that was her business, and that it would p'raps be better for some people if they looked after theirs and let other people's alone."

How much a week did she earn at the factory?

"Four shillings, if I *must* know."

"That's very little. Why, a handy, likely-looking girl, as you appear to be, might earn twice as much at least, or the value of it, as nursemaid or under kitchenmaid in a respectable family. Such places are not difficult to obtain; why do you not make inquiries and better your condition?"

"Because," replied the juvenile maker of frisettes at the fee of eightpence a day - as she gave certain finishing touches to her off-hand millinery - "because I'm above that poor scum that mustn't wear a feather or a ribbin, and because I likes my liberty;" and, lifting her ragged flounces, she made me a curtsey and sailed out of the timber-yard exactly as became a young lady who wore such a resplendent headdress.

THE north wind is raging abroad, ferocious as a savage with his teeth newly filed, seeking whom he may devour, while the land lies benumbed under the heavy hand of frost, and it seems impossible that tender green wheat and fragile flower stems should ever again force their way through the floor of rock. Still, all the dull day, all the bleak night, one crop is growing, out of which poor men make their bread, and pile fire in the grate, and comfort their little children. A crop as important in its way as many a one grown and sown under the genial influence of soft rain and summer sunshine; a harvest, the fruit of which in the season of its consumption is regarded as a blessing, as a healthful luxury, and as grateful to the palate as rich ripe wine or strawberries newly plucked. It is the ice harvest.

It is a saying amongst the busy poor of the great city, that there "are always crumbs for the London sparrows," or, in other words, that a man in health, though never so poor, may always find a loaf by diligent seeking; and the reader who is sceptical on that point may, with a little trouble, discover an eloquent fact in support of it. Let him some frosty morning-well wrapped up, of course, and with his inner man fortified against cold by a hearty and substantial breakfast-let him rise two or three hours before his accustomed time, and while it is yet dark make his way to the North of London, and manfully trudge the country road that leads to Highgate, Hampstead, or Enfield. If he starts from home between five and six, he will probably reach one of the places mentioned about seven o'clock; but he will not have found the way lonely.

The roads are alive with ice-getters, who with eager eyes and their blue noses peeping over the ridge of ragged comforter in which their throats are enveloped, are hurrying to the ponds to see what sort of a crop King Frost has grown for them during the night. Yesterday they were there reaping the icy water-fields clean; and in their anxiety to make up a good load - one that might prove the last - with their drags, their hooks, and their poles, they gleaned in-shore even the small straggling lumps that floated here and there. As they lay abed the night before, these poor fellows, shivering may be under their thin coverlets, could hear the snow-flakes coming with a muffled thud against their chamber windows; and as they heard the keen wind spitefully spinning the creaking chimney cowl, they muttered, "There's comfort in that, although it's cold comfort. The ice is baking beautifully on the ponds up Hampstead way. I'll just try and have another hour's sleep, and then I'll be up and after it."

And here they are after it - in vehicles for the greater part; in carts and "half-carts," and "shallows" and barrows, tumble-down, paintless, and poverty-stricken, that nothing in the world could match except the gaunt and rib-bare horses and ponies and donkeys that are attached in the shafts. But they are not all owners of quadrupeds, these ice-getters; very many have nothing but a barrow, on which, all the way there, Jack gives Bill a ride, on condition that Bill takes the shafts on the homeward journey with the load. It is still freezing hard, and the stars are twinkling in the cold sky, when the ponds are reached; it is not yet seven o'clock, but the troop of ice carters are not the first in the field.

Other poor fellows, poorer than themselves, are there before them - men who have neither horse nor barrow. They have nothing in the world but a pole with a home-made iron hook at the end of it, and a pickaxe, but in desperately willing hands those tools are sufficient to win a loaf with. They brake up the ice, the poleman and his mates; they smash it into convenient pieces, and with icicles dangling from the fringe of their ragged trousers, turned up higher than their knees, they plash and dabble in the deadly cold water to bring the ice ashore, and they help to pack it into the carts at a charge of fourpence per load. It is well worth the ice-carter's while to pay for this assistance. The sooner he is loaded the sooner he may be off to where the great well is gaping its insatiable jaws for more and still more, and where the well owner is waiting with the "bit o ready money," so precious in frosty days to the poor man with a family. It is very important to be in time with the first load. Unless a man is tolerably early at the "well," he may have to abide his turn for an hour and more; and meanwhile. maybe, the youngsters at home, having turned out of their bed, are hungrily waiting round the bit of fire by which they made the kettle boil for father, who will bring in the bread and the coffee.

The ice trade of London and the suburbs is in the hands of half a dozen merchants; and the ice-wells or "Shades," as they are sometimes called, are few and far between. That one to which the northern ice-carters resort is situated in the Caledonian-road, just by the New Cattle Market. Its exterior on ordinary occasions is not very remarkable. It is simply a brick-built, windowless, "round house," with some sort of machinery that looks like a gigantic mouse-trap surmounting its roof. I have looked into that arctic gulf, and its aspect on a blightingly cold December day is almost enough to turn one's hair white; a terrible pit, seventy-two feet in depth- the height of a Belgravian mansion, measuring from the area to the attic-and forty-two feet in circumference. It was night when I looked down into it, and there were flickering lamps to light the men at the various "shoots" - flickering lamps down in the chasm, where, amid the shattered spiky ice, the levellers were at work with their shovels, and in awfully imminent peril did they look, poor fellows, down there, whence came up a breath as cold as the breath of death, struggling and slipping, pounding and shovelling while all the time load after load went shooting down, crashing and clattering, and making the glassy splinters fly about their purple ears. It was quite a relief to hear one of them whistle a tune lively enough to dance to, and to observe another wipe the perspiration from his brow ere he raised to his lips a beer measure, and took a swig long and hearty. The ice well at Islington contains, when packed from floor to ceiling, three thousand tons; to make up which seven thousand loads, little and big, are requisite. As I was informed, it was one of the best seasons that had happened for years. Every man to his trade; but I confess that the cheery tone in which the good ice merchant announced this last fact gave me no great amount of satisfaction.

I never could have supposed that ice-dealing was so moneymaking a business; and, considering the increasing summer demand for the highly useful article in question, it is a matter of no small surprise that many more adventurers do not embark in the speculation. The price at which the rough ice is bought ranges from 15d. the barrow-load to 8s. the pair-horse van load; which is, as was explained to me, an average of 2s. a load, "take them all round;" but the easiest way of reckoning will be to take the fact that the well of 3,000 ton capacity takes 7,000 loads to fill and that the average price is 2s. a load. So 3,000 tons of rough ice costs £700 carted and delivered. On the other hand, the contract price between the merchant and the fishmonger or the confectioner is 2s. per hundredweight, or £2 per ton; 3,000 tons of ice returning £6,000, or a gross profit of £5,300.

But the reader may exclaim, "There is the waste to be accounted for. It is all very well in the winter, but storing ice in the summer time, when the heat is at eighty in the shadiest of places, must be a ticklish operation." That certainly was my idea before I was better informed. The wasting of the stored ice is curiously small. I cannot exactly state it, but the reader with a mind for figures may easily reckon it for himself. The well, as before stated, is seventy-two feet deep and forty- two feet in circumference, and the ice is packed as closely as possible; but by-and-by it settles and becomes one dense mass, so solid that it has to be hacked to bits with axes; yet the shrinking from the wall on all sides of this dense block is only six inches. No artificial means are adopted to keep the temperature of the well low. It supplies itself with air cold enough to maintain freezing point. The ice trade begins in May; this great ice-holder is then broached, and by the end of July it is emptied. Indeed, it would be quite impossible to supply London with ice grown and garnered out of our suburban waters. We draw largely on Norway. Mr. Carlo Gatti, of the Islington well, is a mighty man of ice. At home he farms the New River and the Regent's Canal, and sends out his own carts and barges to get in the crops; and besides this he has ships on the sea constantly trading with regions which are almost perpetually icy, and which yield a pure block ice dearer than the rough by a shilling the hundredweight.

    And I wish that there were a dozen wells as broad and as deep as this one. There is a grim satisfaction in seeing poor fellows "taking a rise," as it were, out of their stern and implacable enemy; albeit it must be terribly hard and perishingly cold work, this picking the teeth of Death, of which frost and ice are symbolical, in order to win an honest loaf.

DURING the greater part of the journey, the two carpenters who sat to the left of the omnibus driver - I was seated on his right - talked of the strike among men of their craft; vehemently declaring that, but for the injudicious "caving in" of somebody or other, the contested nine hours a day at nine-pence an hour might have been won from the masters. More than once they appealed to the purple-visaged old person who held the reins, with a view to eliciting from him a confirmation of their opinion that nine hours a day was as much as any man should work; but his replies were brief and it was evident that he had no heart for the discussion. When the two carpenters at length got down, my old driver, with whom, as a frequent rider, I am on terms of considerable intimacy, delivered himself of a prolonged a-ah, and chirruped to his horses cheerfully as though now that the load which had oppressed his mind was removed they would find it easier going. As I was the only remaining "outside," he was at liberty to speak without restraint, and of this privilege he promptly proceeded to avail himself-indulging, however, in his sometimes embarrassing peculiarity of uttering aloud the terminanation of any mental reflection that might for the moment engage him.

"Silver spoons! oh dear, no! not in these days. What do *you* say, sir?"

I was about to reply, that for my part silver spoons were as welcome in these days as in any, when he interrupted me by remarking,

"Aye, aye; but in the mouth - being born with 'em there. Bless you, no; they're out of date. The lucky ones in these days are born with a handsaw or a trowel in their mouth - the *un*lucky ones, chaps of *my* breed, you understand, are born with a driver's badge in their mouths, and it would have been a mercy if it had choked 'em before they was weaned every man Jack of 'em."

"Why would it?"

"Why? because then there wouldn't have been four or five thousand slaves in the shape of bus-men toiling over London stones more hours a day, than niggers were ever expected to work on a sugar plantation. I don't envy 'em - Lord forbid - them carpenter chaps, with their nine hours a day; but it does make a man lose his temper when he hears his fellow-creatures not only laying down the law, but holding fast on to it, that nine hours shall be the length of a working day, when all the while he thinks himself jolly well off if he gets nine hours to himself out of the twenty-four, and that Sunday and week day.

"That's *my* case, sir, and the case of nine-tenths of the drivers and conductors. I don't call myself more ill-used than the rest, and yet it is as true as I've got this whip in my hand that for the last two months I've worked from a hundred and four to a hundred and ten hours a week - that's fourteen to fifteen hours a day - and out of that time not so long off my box as many a working man is allowed as his dinner-time. Why don't we strike? It's all very well to talk about striking, but it won't do any good unless you fust see your way, and we don't see our way at present. If you go a-plucking apples before they're ripe you'll only get a bellyache for your pains.

"Any body o' men can strike - they can have fust blow, as the sayin' is; but unless they're strong enough to floor the enemy, or at least to stagger him, so as to lead him to believe that it may be judicious to knuckle under before he gets further damaged, they had better think twice before they begin sparring. You may catch a man a stinger; the weakest fellow that ever put the gloves on may do that, especially if he picks *a* time when the other's off his guard, or has got his hands tied somehow; but if he's strong, maybe you hurt him only just enough to rile him, and he hits back, and hits hard. Still, comparing of it to a boxing match - and wulgarly speaking - where the enemy hits you heaviest is in the *bread-basket*; and that's the tenderest part to hit a man who has got a wife and half-a-dozen youngsters depending for their food on his daily earnings.

Besides, how *can* we strike? Ours isn't like a trade at which a man has to serve seven years before he is qualified. There are plenty of drivers of a sort hanging about the London yards, and if we were to throw down the reins to-morrow morning, there isn't a pair of 'em that wouldn't be snatched up before night."

"That possibly is because the wages are tempting," I ventured to remark.

He turned on me a look that was only redeemed from being witheringly scornful by the knowledge of our long-continued friendship.

"Yes; it looks pretty in print, doesn't it? to say that 'we pay our drivers two guineas a week, and at such wage we can command the best in London.' That's how the public are misled. If we were to strike for less hours the public would say that it was a shame to put 'em to inconvenience when we were taking such handsome salaries for our services. The public don't know how a poor driver's six shillings a day is nibbled at, and that in a way that he is quite unable to prevent. Every driver has his ostler at the yard, and unless he keeps 'well in' with him he'll suffer. This will cost him sixpence a day at least. The man looks for it regular, and expects it to make up his paltry wages. Then there is twopence a day for his accident club, and another twopence for the 'night man' at the stables for putting away his horses at the end of the last journey. That makes tenpence a day he is bound to pay out of his pocket; and then at the beginning and end of each journey there is the waterman, who will look black unless he gets his regular coppers. Then again a driver must find his own whip, and his own driving-gloves, and his own rug. Reckon, atop of all, that the man who is compelled to buy his dinner, tea, and supper away from home is put to an extra expense of ninepence - and if you come to calculate it all up, you will find that the driver's six shillings a day is brought down to four; and four shillings for fifteen hours' labour is something like threepence farthing an hour. Scorching in the sun, soaking in the rain, blown on by every variety of wind that keeps a weathercock spinning, from eight in the morning till eleven at night, and all for wages that a scavenger, or a hod-carrier, would laugh at you if you offered them to him!

"Nor is he even at this rate allowed to do his work quietly and peaceably. He is harassed by the police, and no driver can say at the end of a day's work that he can now go to bed on good terms with all men, including policemen. His name may have been booked that day for a summons. In unbuttoning and buttoning his coat he may without ever being aware of it, have for a few moments sinned against the law that says that he shall wear his badge conspicuously on his breast; he may not have pulled up to the near side as conveniently as in Mr. Policeman's judgment he should have done, to take up a passenger; the biting cold of a winter's night may have tempted him to risk the awful penalty attached to a bus-driver smoking a pipe or cigar - he is reported, and the Inspector summonses him, and he is lucky if he is no more out of pocket than the cost of the summons and six shillings, his day's work.

"Often enough he gets into trouble for 'squeezing' an odd bus that may venture to work his road. It is quite true, every driver is provided with a card, on which are printed the rules that are to regulate his conduct, and one of the said rules is that he shall not interfere with any other omnibus; but that's a rule he must shut his eyes to if he wishes to keep his situation. The road inspector will look pretty sharp after him, and make a note if he sees the opposition robbing his employers of a passenger when it can be avoided.

"Are there many road inspectors?"

"Rather - quite a little army of 'em, and they change their dresses as often as detective policemen, so that they may not be known. A driver expects his conductor to keep a good look-out for inspectors. Did you never see em telegraphing to one another? You'd think that they was larking or gone cranky sometimes, if you wasn't in the secret. For instance, one conductor going his way will whistle to a mate going the other, and then go through the pantomime of opening his mouth very wide, placing his hand about a foot above his cap, holding his badge up to his eye, and lastly motioning to the left or right, and raising his hand to his mouth in imitation of drinking. You would be puzzled to know what all this means, but to a conductor, it's as plain as A B C. It means That tall, bullying chap, who wears spectacles - he's just by the next public-house on the left; and then, in a word or two that none of the outsiders can understand, the conductor 'gives the office' to his driver, who sits the picter of good behaviour, you may depend, till the point of danger is passed."

"For your threepence farthing an hour you are expected to be a perfect model of a coachman, but a precious little do the company care for your comfort. Just see how we are left to shift for ourselves, and do the best we can in the way of getting a bit of food in the little time we have off during the day. It is a public-house we start from, and at a public-house we make our journey's end; and we are at the mercy of the publicans for a seat and a shelter, and the use of a plate and a knife and fork, to get the hasty bit of dinner we swallows. Generally the taproom is the best dining-room that is at your service, and you mustn't be particular if the place is full of tobacco smoke, or if horse-play and larking is going on all the while. Some publicans give you more decent quarters, but not many. But, lor! for that matter, when a man fumbles his way down off his box in the winter time with his feet like lumps of ice, and his face feeling as though it had been warnished and froze dry, he isn't very particular what place he puts his head into, so long as it is warm and snug. What I wonder most about is, that the public stand those public-house stations, without a bit of decent accommodation for ladies or children. Why can't they have waiting rooms, with p'raps some tidy parted-off place, with a fire, and a few tables and chairs in it, for their servants to rest and eat in? Talk about the advantage of being a bus driver! I'd rather be a - a -"

"A conductor?" I suggested, seeing that my venerable Jehu was at a. loss for a word. But he nudged me with the butt end of his whip and glanced warily over his shoulder in the direction of the monkey-board; then, bending his head bow he whispered,

"Have you ever seen that man who goes about in a black tarpaulin coat reachin' down to his heels, and a sou'wester, and he's writ all over in advertisements in jolly big white letters?"

I replied that I had not seen the interesting individual mentioned.

"I have, and a queer figure he cuts; well, I'd rather be that man than a conductor."

"And why?"

"Because I consider that, take it altogether, if I was that man I should have a better time of it. I don't say that I'd make more money - very likely not; but I should get better treatment. I've been eight-and-twenty years on the road, and I know conductors as well as drivers by the score; and it's my opinion that if the employers spent the thousands they now spend in spys and detectives in increasing the wages of their conductors, and making them understand that they treated them as honest men, and paid them fair pay, expecting fair treatment in return-why, many a decent chap would escape being tempted to picking and stealing, and the masters would be all the richer."

The old bus driver's terrible hints concerning the miserable condition of conductors led me to make some inquiries on the subject, the result of which is hereto appended.

They - the omnibus conductors of London - do not deny that it is a practice amongst them to make petty larcenous attacks on the money pouch of their employers; nay, they have no disposition to dispute that it is a very common practice But their bold argument amounts to this -

that perfect honesty is not expected of them, and that the wages arrangement between them and their masters is of such a nature as to make it impossible for them to render a fair account of their takings for the day; that the masters' standpoint in settling what their omnibus conductors' remuneration shall be, is, that all conductors are rogues, and that, since no amount of regular wages will induce them to abstain from picking and stealing, it behoves them, since a wages arrangement cannot well be done without, to fix the amount at the lowest possible figure. Finally, it is, rightly or wrongly, a common belief amongst omnibus conductors that so long as, to use a phrase of their own, they "draw it mild," and return reasonable "waybills," their known peculations are winked at and endured. It need not be said that the omnibus conductors' conclusions, however happily they may chime with the pleasant chinking of his increasing store, are undoubtedly erroneous. It is impossible to believe that the directors of a company dealing with hundreds of thousands of pounds every year would for a moment countenance such alleged pollutions and wasteful leakages at the very founts from which alone its income can flow, to say nothing of the grave responsibility of entrusting men of tainted character with the persons and property of those who patronise their vehicles.

It appears that the general pay of the class in question is, as the old driver had informed me, 4s. for what is called a day's work. The driver of the vehicle receives 6s. for the same time; and it is not improbable that it was while asking himself the reason why this wide difference should exist, that he first conceived the dangerous notion that his employers felt themselves compelled to provide against a weakness of human nature, which is as likely to develope in a conductor as any other mortal who has the handling of uncounted money, and who is inconstant in his prayers to be delivered from temptation. It is not easy to see to what other conclusion the man could arrive. As much skill at least is needful in civilly enticing customers, and in satisfactorily providing for them on the journey, as is required for driving a pair of horses; while, as for wearisomeness of work, there can be no question as to which side it is on. Anyhow, the conductor receives 4s. a day; or more properly, and, as above remarked, for what is called a day. As working men at the present period have a habit of computing time, it is nearly *two* days.

It seems almost incredible in these enlightened times that many of the omnibuses of London, which punctually appear at eight o'clock each morning, and remain visible and active from that time until midnight, and frequently beyond, are "worked" one driver and one conductor; that, under the blazing sun of by July and August, as well as in the teeth of the freezing winds of November and January, in fog, in rain, in snow, the unfortunate drudge of the monkey board, as well as he who occupies the driver's seat, is commonly kept hard at it for fourteen, fifteen, and even sixteen hours with only such brief spells of rest between as are necessary for breakfast, dinner, and supper. Now 4s. a day is less than is received by the bricklayer's hod-man - it used to be 4s., but at the last general rise amongst the building crafts the hodman was generally conceded another halfpenny an hour. But the bricklayer's humble attendant works only as many hours as his master, and at half-past five in the evening may be seen smoking his pipe at leisure. After that time the bus conductor has still six and a half or severs hours of hard work before his hurrying homeward steps may waken the echoes of the dark and deserted street he lives in.

That the poor fellow is desperately tried who can doubt? He is always on the alert, now in the bus, now in the road, now on the roof constantly climbing and stepping up and down, and never, excepting at his meals, enjoying the luxury of a seat for as long as five minutes. He works very hard and consequently, if he he a healthy man - as he needs must be to endure such a prodigious amount of labour - he has a keen appetite for food which must be satisfied. It is idle to talk of the regularly recognised three meals a day in the case of the omnibus conductor. Such an allowance may be all very well as regards a man who has but nine or ten hours' labour a day to perform, and that in most cases under cover and secure from blood-chilling and teeth-sharpening winds; but the individual who is exposed to the elements through fifteen hours out of the twenty-four requires much more liberal treatment. If the jog-trot ten hours a day man requires three meals, the busman should have at least five; or lacking the solid food, he must make up for it with liquid stimulant, and it is by no means difficult to see what an enormously great hole in his daily wage of forty-eight pence these natural cravings of his appetite must make. At the very least half-a-crown is expended in this manner, leaving just eighteenpence a day, or 9s. a week, wherewith to meet his own necessary expenses, including, probably, the maintenance of a house and a wife and a few children.

But he has many urgent demands on all that remains of his honest day's earnings before the last-mentioned responsibilities may be attended to. There are certain duties in the omnibus yard which he is compelled to engage to fulfil, but which at a cost of sixpence or so a day he performs by deputy. If he did not do this there would go another hour beyond the fifteen or sixteen which comprise his day's work. Then, if he would live in peace with his fellows and avoid making enemies, who have it in their power to make the situation too "hot" for him, he has this person, and that, and the other to fee and stand treat to, including the very policemen who are put on special duty to keep a sharp look-out that the much-harassed conductor is guilty of no kind of misbehaviour. He must, however, be decently attired; he must never appear in a threadbare coat or shabby boots, and for his life's sake he dare not be without a suit of serviceable "waterproofs." So that one way and another his 4s. a day are absolutely insufficient to pay his way from the time when he mounts his perch in the morning until he quits it at night, leaving home and its manifold obligations altogether out of the question.

Under such circumstances it must be admitted that it is a little too much to expect that every custodian of an omnibus shall be a model of rectitude. To be sure were he heroically devoted to his occupation and his employers, he might perhaps do better than he does with his four shillings. He might abstain from "nips" of spirituous liquor and glasses of ale, and there are many cheap and pocketable nutritious substances he might carry with him and covertly munch on the way, and so save the expense of regular dinners, teas, and suppers. Further, by a fearless declaration of his intention to do his conducting on strictly moral principles, craving only a fair field, and favour of no man, it is not impossible but that yard foremen, and time-keepers, and watchers-nay, even policemen, might in time cease to solicit him, and save him a shilling a day at least, and one way and another he might remain honest and yet be enabled to buy bread for his children, and keep the broker's man from pouncing on his household goods. Men, however, endowed with sufficient moral courage to act in this fashion are scarce, and if of the existing few any of them should turn conductors, they would speedily become scarcer still. Of course, there is no excuse for dishonesty in any shape or form. If omnibus conductors find that it is impossible to live on the wages at present paid them, they should quit their present employment and seek other. At the same time, it really would seem necessary that some move should be made towards amending the present state of things. No employer of servants can be blind to the fact that four shillings for fifteen hours of extremely fatiguing work night and day, and in every kind of weather, is hardly the sort of pay to attract upright and intelligent men.

WITH a knowledge of the powers vested in those to whom the working of the Metropolis Local Management Act has been entrusted, one might well feel justified in regarding all that has been said of "St. Giles's," the head-quarters of depravity and squalor, as a legend of the barbarous past. It must have startled innocent folk to learn that, but a year or so ago, no less than a hundred and seventy of the notorious St. Giles's cellars were still in use as human habitations, and that, after the manner of rats and other burrowing animals, as many families, consisting of mother, father, and a more or less numerous swarm of big and little children, passed their lives in these dismal holes under the houses, working, eating, dunking, and sleeping all in the damp and dirt and dark. Of course it was out of the question that such a disgusting and disgraceful condition of things should be permitted to exist for a single day after it was exposed. Indeed the Medical Officer of Health has been able to announce since, that the cellar-dwellers have been routed, and that, "to his knowledge, not a single underground room in the district is now illegally occupied."

Better late than never. To be sure, ignorance of such matters somewhat prevented one from understanding why it should take so long to unearth this colony of pestilence-breeders, but it was undeniably a comfort to hear that it had been accomplished at last. Was it quite certain, however, that they had been ousted for good and all? Had the entrances to the underground dens been bricked up, or what were the precautions that had been taken to guard against the possibility of these cave-dwellers making their way back to their old haunts as soon as the ill wind which had scattered them had blown over? It occurred to me that it might be worth while to go and see, and accordingly one evening recently I alighted from the omnibus that, on its westward route, takes a short cut through Seven Dials.

It was about seven o'clock, and the gas was alight - the gas and the oil and the paraffin and the naphtha. St. Giles's of 1873 is pretty much what it was a quarter of a century ago. A big brewery and three or four new streets have shorn its skirts somewhat, but it is heartwhole still, and as dirty and draggletailed as ever. The only "enlightenment" that modern customs and usages have brought it appears is in the increased brilliancy of its public houses, which are especially rich in plate-glass and gas glitter. There are the same ragged women, some with babies in their arms - some mere girls - and some with backs bent with age; and there are, as of old, the groups of lanky, ill-dressed youth, with a sharp look-out from under the peaks of their caps; the same knots of hulking men of mature age. too lazy even to support with their fingers the short pipe which hangs all aslant from their mouths, while their hands are plunged wrist-deep in the pockets of their trousers. The stalls are the same, so are the shops, the awful little dens - and there are scores of them - inside and out of which are exposed for sale scraps of household furniture, which, by a jocular fiction of the "trade," is termed "second-hand," although it must be twenty-second hand at the very least, and bedding, mattresses, and beds, and bolsters and pillows, the sickening complexion of which should be sufficient warrant for a sanitary inspector to seize them at once and consign them without delay to the flames.

I purposely fixed on the Dudley-street quarter of the St. Giles's district, because it was within my recollection that, in the disgraceful old times, the dwellers in cellars mustered very strong there. There used to be scarcely a house in the front of which there was not a hole in the pavement and a ladder by which the underground lodgers used to descend to their lairs. Used to! why there they were now! I could scarcely believe the evidence of my eyes. I had cut the comforting paragraph from the newspaper, and at that moment had it in my pocket. By the light of a street lamp I took it therefrom and once more perused it. No, there was no mistake-on my part, that is to say. There it stood in fair print. "The medical officer of health for the district of St.

Giles now reports that, to his knowledge, not a single underground room it in the district is now illegally occupied." And there, from where I stood, I glanced into Dudley-street, and left and right, within thirty yards, I could see the open mouths of several cellars luridly lit by the fire and candlelight below. As though to put the matter beyond a doubt, at that moment there slowly emerged from the jaws of the nearest gulf a male lodger with a pair of deplorably ragged trousers slouched about his legs, and wearing a shirt horribly dirty and so full of rents that his hairy chest and shoulders were almost bare. His face was dirty, too, and sickly white, and to prevent his lank black hair from falling ever his eyes - which blinked and winked as do those of a miner who comes up in the cage after many hours' labour in the gloomy pit - he had encircling his head a fillet of cobler's "waxed end." With his dangling shirt-sleeve he administered a refreshing wipe to his face and throat, and seated himself at the edge of his hole, with the evident intention of enjoying a few mouthfuls of the comparatively pure air of Dudley-street.

So emphatic a contradiction of my newspaper paragraph demanded further investigation. I crossed the road, and, as an excuse for lingering long enough at the mouth of the cellar to obtain a peep at the interior, made inquiry of the man as to the place of abode of an imaginary tailor.

"It can't be in Dudley-street, I should think," he replied, "there ain't no tailors here that I knows of; we are nearly all translators."

This was startling. Was it possible that individuals whose pursuits were literary could be brought so low as this?

"Are *you* a translator?" I asked him.

"Ah!" he replied, "anybody might know that with arf a hi in his head;" and as he spoke he jerked with his thumb in the direction of the cellar's depths. My eyes followed the movement, and presently in the steamy haze were enabled to make out a cobbler's seat in the midst of a heap - a couple of bushel, at least - of old boots and shoes, apparently in the last stages of mildew and decay.

"There's what I translates," explained the ragged cobbler, with a grin that showed how neatly the stem of his short clay pipe fitted into the hollow it had worn for itself in the side teeth of his upper and lower jaw; "I translates 'em into sound uns."

"Is it good pay?" I ventured.

"It's starvegut pay," growled the poor translator, most un-pleasantly scratching himself; "it ain't taturs and salt hardly for a cove's wife and kids."

"Especially with rents so high!" I remarked.

"Well you may say it, mister," he replied, ruefully; "fancy! four bob a week for that!" and once again, with a backward movement of his thumb, he indicated the underground den.

The excavations under the ancient houses of Dudley Street possess no windows at all, and the only way in which light and ventilation can be conveyed to the wretched inhabitants is through a hole in the pavement - a narrow opening, no larger than might be made by removing an ordinary paving-stone.

Leading down into the cellar is a ladder or a flight of wooden steps protected by a handrail. The roof of the cellar is level with the common roadway, and its floor must be several feet below the sewage and gas pipes. A wooden flap is hinged by the side of the gap at the head of the ladder, and is, I imagine closed at night time, and when the weather is unendurably inclement; though how, at such times, the benighted lodgers contrive to breathe is a mystery.

"D'ye hear?" exclaimed the translator, calling down to his wife; "there's the doctor goin' to see Mother Simmons's gal agin."

"Ah! poor thing," came up the hoarse though sympathetic response of the translator's wife; "she'll snuff it, you may depend."

By which I believe the good soul - a mother herself - meant that it was her belief that the existence of the girl Simmons would shortly be extinguished. But just imagine any one man, woman, or child lying ill abed in such a pestiferous, dingy den! Should the bedstead happen to stand at a far corner of the cellar, the doctor, even though it were noon in sultry summertime, would be compelled to examine his patient by candlelight. And the minister would have to read the dying words of blessed consolation by the flickering tallow flame, which would afterwards show a light for the undertaker with his measuring tape. But how about the coffin? It is not difficult to slide an empty box down a ladder. But a burdened box? To bring it to the surface as a shoulder-load in the ordinary way would, under the circumstances, be impossible; there could be nothing for it but to haul it up with a rope, tearful mourners clambering up in the wake and lending a steadying hand.

As I turned away from the hole in which the translator and his family resided, my impression was that the medical officer of health for the district of St. Giles had made a mistake, He had said that there was now not *one* of the ancient cellars improperly occupied. Here, without doubt, was one. Were there others? Were there! At every step I took in dark Dudley Street I grew more and more amazed. Surely the medical officer of health for the district of St. Giles must have been shamefully imposed on. Here was another inhabited cellar of precisely the same pattern as that already described, and next door another, and again next door still another, this time with half-a-dozen nearly nude and hideously dirty children wriggling up and down the ladder, and larking in and out of the cellar darkness below, like rabbits in a warren. More inhabited cellars on the right hand side, on the left hand side-sometimes two and three together, sometimes with half-a-dozen houses between. From one end to the other of Dudley Street, which be it borne in mind, is but a small portion of the district of St. Giles, I counted thirty of these underground dens, all alive with human life. Besides these there were eight others, which though inhabited, could scarcely be said to be lively. In these a solitary cobbler toiled, the flames of his tallow candle disclosing him deep down in the dingy hole, hammering and stitching with desperate energy in the midst of heaps of mildewed wreckage of souls and upper leathers. In these eight instances I could not see any one down in the cellars but the cobblers themselves though for that matter there was so little light that there may have been in each case a wife and a large family of children stowed away in the background. But, as regards the other thirty instances, they made no secret of their existence as human dwelling-places. There they were, with their mouths open, gaping on the highway, and there was nothing to prevent the passer-by from looking down their dingy throats. There were the fires in the places, and the pots and kettles on the fires, and there were the mothers, and there were the babies, the elder children hauling refractory youngsters down the ladder, at the same time threatening them in forcible language with what they would "ketch" if they didn't "come indoors and go to bed." It may perhaps be objected that the words used in the report were that no underground cellar was now "illegally" occupied, and that by illegal occupation was meant the using of the said cellars as sleeping rooms. I am bound to confess that I am not in a position to prove incontestably that the law is outraged to this extent. I can declare that in two cases I caught sight of the legs of a bedstead, festooned with a ragged bed-quilt; but, for all that I can show convincingly to the contrary, the bedstead might in each case have been the family dining-table, and the ragged quilt the tablecloth. At the same time it strikes me as being in the last degree improbable that these wretched ill-paid patchers of old boots rent other apartments besides that in which, all day long and far into the evening, they reside, and work, and take their meals, and that at a certain hour of the night they bundle up the ladder, and into the street, with their sleepy children, and proceed to a dormitory, the healthfulness of which is officially certified. Maybe it is taken for granted that because everything in the shape of sleeping convenience is absent from a cellar, the inhabitants by day do not pass the night there. This, however, is a view of the matter scarcely likely to be taken by the authorities of a district hundreds of the population of which sleep in their rags and on the bare boards as many nights in the year as they are not more decently lodged in prison or the casual ward of a workhouse. Besides, if it comes to that, what is gained to public decency and public health by drawing the line, as it would seem the officials of St. Giles's now draw it, and by which it is declared legal and unobjectionable for human beings to herd from early morning till late at night in dungeon damp and darkness, breathing foul air and breeding fever and all manner of disease, provided they turn out and go somewhere else to pass the hours between midnight and daybreak. It is no less marvellous than monstrous that such an appalling condition of things should have been permitted to exist so long, especially when, as is evident, the sanitary authorities have long had the matter in hand. I did not pursue my investigation beyond Dudley Street, but it is fair to assume that in the surrounding vile courts and alleys - Dudley Street is a broad and busy thoroughfare - the evil is just as prevalent. I must be permitted to say in conclusion that the picture here given is not a bit overdrawn or exaggerated. There, to-day as yesterday, are to be seen in Dudley Street, Seven Dials, the deep black cellars, reached through a gap in the pavement, and by means of a steep ladder, and in each, at a greater depth in the earth than the sewers and the nests of the sewer rats, families of human beings - fathers, mothers, and little children-live and eat and drink, and make themselves at home.

MUSEUMS, of the South Kensington and Bethnal-green order, are doubtless of great utility, and are without doubt highly appreciated by the thousands in whose behalf they were established and are maintained; but these and kindred social advantages do not entirely meet the requirements of what, without disparagement, may be called the commonality. A *bona fide* playground is required; a territory unbeadled and free, where on high days and holidays, such as Easter and Whitsun, holiday-makers may run reasonable riot, and indulge in fun loud and uproarious to their hearts' content.

Hampstead Heath furnishes the best possible proof of this. Hampstead is by no means a central spot for Londoners. As regards the inhabitants of the northern districts, the Heath may only be gained by an uphill walk of a mile or two, while those from the west and south of the metropolis can only reach it by rail or excursion van. Nevertheless, on a fine Easter or Whitsun Monday, it is no exaggeration to say that, somehow or other, at least two hundred thousand persons, working men chiefly, with their wives and children, find their way thither, and that from morning till night the grassy hillocks, from Gospel Oak to the limits of Hampstead village, resound with one unbroken hilarious roar, to which the shrill laughter of thousands of children contribute not a little. As full as any fair, the vast gathering is respectably distinguished from those bygone abominations, Greenwich and Bartle'my, inasmuch as it depends for its existence not on caravans of wild beast shows and sparring and drinking booths, but, for the greater part, on such amusements as the people make for themselves, bringing their own materials or finding them already provided on the ground. Curiously innocent are most of these pastimes. Skip-rope, for instance, appears to be one of the main staples of the day's enjoyment, with middle-aged as well as young - not skip-rope of the kind where the operator acts with a slender cord for his or her own amusement, but a thirty feet long, substantial scaffold cord, "turned" by able-bodied men, who provide skipping boards and invite any number to "jine in" it at a fee of a halfpenny each, and "keep the pot a bilin'."

The inhabitants of the metropolis should be thankful for the recurrence of Hampstead Heath jubilations, if for one reason only - the freedom from the plague of organ-grinders which for one day at least is secured them. The wondering observer might suppose that the Government, aiming at securing admiration and gratitude at one blow had effectually accomplished the arduous feat, by passing a law for the peremptory banishment of the whole Italian horde, who, to make their bread, worry the brains of Britons. If the lord of the manor of Hampstead has no licence for music and dancing, it would make the fortune of any informer who gave information against him, on the strength of being able to net half the enormous sum his lordship might be mulcted in the shape of penalties. Organ men, not simply in twos, but in gangs of at least half a dozen, may on such occasions be met from breakfast time until noon hurrying to the festive scene, made certain by previous experience of finding plenty of remunerative employment when they get there. They are busy from morning till night, or it may even be said from morning till morning,, since with a certain class of the carousers on the Heath, the curtain of night is lowered in vain. Throughout the afternoon, at fifty different parts, there are juvenile dancing parties, the grinning grinder acting the part of M.C. as well as musician, and proving himself the fount of such immeasurable delight that, for once in a lifetime, one's heart is inclined to soften towards the villain, who is kept in constant good humour by the ready inflow of halfpence, cheerfully contributed by the youngsters. He does not get on so well in the evening and night time, when his youthful audience has dispersed, and has been replaced by adults of the tag-rag and draggle-tail breed who have no taste for any tunes but those they can vigorously kick up their heels to, and who are apt to quarrel with him on account of his refusal to accept drinks out of their gin and beer bottles as payment in lieu of ready money, and who not unfrequently detain him - a hard-worked and unpaid captive - by the hour together by threats of sequestrating the handle of his instrument.

Nor were those mentioned the only active amusements to which the multitude that assemble on Hampstead heights devote themselves. There are swings, and in a dozen places at least rows of archery targets. But, at least as regards the youthful and juvenile throng, the Hampstead donkeys are the chief attraction. Quite a "Rotten-row" has been established on the heath, a gravel and railed-in space, with a handsome pump and stone water trough at one end for the refreshment of any thirsty and harassed quadruped who stands in need thereof, with a person in attendance to see that whenever a brute evinces a desire to drink he is not prevented. It is not, that I am aware, anywhere recorded that the donkeys of Hampstead-heath are a peculiarly artful race; but truth compels me to mention that the older animals, and those who, judging from the prominence of their ribs, are long experienced in the service, seem to take the fullest possible advantage of the humane arrangement alluded to. The agreement is, up the ride - a distance of perhaps fifty yards - and down again for a penny, the time occupied being so brief that the mouth of a donkey well wetted at starting can scarcely get dry in the time, yet there are animals there who at every turn will stop short in their gallop within a few feet of the trough, and at once simulate an appearance of extreme thirst, hanging their heads and gasping in a way that is well calculated to impose on the trough keeper, just for the sake of a short spell of idleness with their noses in the cool water.

To be sure there is great excuse for them. What becomes of the Hampstead donkeys during the winter months - there are several scores of them - is a mystery that will probably be solved when it comes to be settled beyond dispute by what means the same race of animals continues to vanish from off the face of the earth without leaving their carcases behind them as evidence of their demise. From their appearance when they are brought to light for the holiday season, it would seem not improbable that ever since the fall of last year they had been shut up somewhere in the dark, without benefit of currycomb or food, excepting such nutriment as might be derived from gnawing the flaps and hay stuffing of their saddles. If donkey driving was always as remunerative as it is on Hampstead-heath on an Easter Monday say, it would be as difficult to procure a license and a badge as a share in the New River Waterworks Company.

The fun of the great Hampstead Easter fair, of course, includes plenty in the shape of substantial eating and drinking as well as light refreshment. Amongst the latter must not be forgotten ice-creams, vended by an army of Italian stallkeepers. The successful advance which this unsubstantial foreign delicacy has made of late years amongst the juvenile population of Great Britain is not only amazing but almost enough to make one feel uncomfortable for England's future. The British boy of the last generation was a boy who, though free with his pocket money, invariably went in for solids - for cake and buns and savoury pies. Had a shallow mess of sweetened congealed water been offered to that boy for his penny he certainly would not have accepted it, or, at any rate, would have stipulated for a spoon.

Unfortunately, however, the well-behaved working man cannot have Hampstead-heath to himself at holiday time. That untamable and, from every point of view, objectionable animal, the London "rough," implacable in his animosity to the usages of decent society, must have his outing and enjoy himself. In doing so, however, he will consent to make no sacrifice of principle. He comes in his hob-nailed boots, with a hearty will to kick out of his path and trample on all weak and defenceless persons who for the moment, and however undesignedly, may stand in the way of his free and independent progress. In bygone times, Greenwich, Camberwell, Chalk Farm and Charlton fairs were the rough's Easter Monday delights, and these being abolished he has really nowhere to go at holiday season, if he wishes to kick up his heels with impunity, but to Hampstead-heath. He is drawn thither from all parts - from Shoreditch, from Lambeth, from St. Luke's, from Bethnal-green, and from his several haunts at Islington.

It is not his custom to "go in" for a long day. It is not until evening that he may be seen, with a choice set of half-a-dozen or so, accompanied by the females of their kind, with as few stoppages as there happen to be public-houses on the line of route, making his way Heathward. The attire of the London rough on festive occasions is worth describing. It is his pride and delight to wear a new pair of boots, of the kind known as ankle-jacks, and somehow he obtains them. He loves to wear them loosely laced, and it is accounted "the thing" to permit the "tongues" of the boots to lap out and wag freely, as though in dumb derision of tidiness. Similarly, and in accordance with his savage disposition to comport himself in all things in direct opposition to what the generality of mankind agree in regarding as proper, he wears the peak of his close-fitting cloth or hairy cap as a screen for his left ear instead of his eyes. As a rule he has no taste for neckerchiefs of flimsy texture or gaudy pattern; on the contrary he prefers to swathe his throat with almost surgical severity, in a bandaging of dirty white cloth, taking care that the knot which secures it is accurately adjusted under his right ear, by way, possibly, of balancing his cap peak overhanging his left. As his shabby coat or fustian jacket is usually buttoned up to his chin, nothing can be said of either his waistcoat or his linen.

What the rough ultimately develops into-whether having sown his wild oats, he reforms and cultivates the comparative respectability of costermongerdom, or whether it is his inevitable fate on approaching man's estate to give such grievous offence to the law that he is banished to Portland or Chatham, I am not in a position to say, but it is a singular fact that the London rough is invariably a young fellow with no more than down adorning his tremendous chin, while his ample breadth of cheek is as bare of hair as the shiny hillocks that seem placed behind his great ears to keep them constantly ajar. It is a curious fact that the rough has no heart for a holiday outing, unless he is accompanied by his ladylove, though whether this arises from affection on his part, or is merely a friendly and judicious domestic arrangement between them, is uncertain. Part of the programme of the evening, of course, is for the rough to get as drunk as gin and beer can make him; and it is understood that when in that state he has a habit of kicking or attacking with his fists the person who may happen to be nearest him. Ordinarily, it is his "young woman" that he so maltreats, and she having possibly grown too used to it to mind it much, would rather be at his elbow when his brutality sought vent at his knuckles and his iron-tipped boots than that he should practice it on a stranger, and fall into the hands of the police. And so it comes about that pedestrians happening to be in the neighbourhood of the heath or any of the main roads leading therefrom at a late hour on Easter Monday night, are apt, judging from the noisy, staggering crews they meet, to form an erroneous idea of the kind of company that as a rule is entertained on the great Northern playground at this holiday time.

MY knowledge of Old Tom is not of long standing. Indeed, for reasons which will presently appear, it may be as well for me at once to state that I have no desire that our acquaintance should ripen into friendship or even familiarity. Insinuating ways has ancient Thomas, and he is eagerly hailed and heartily welcomed as the boon companion and bosom comforter of an extraordinarily large circle of admirers, but, having obtained an insight into his manner of dealing with those who confide in him, I feel no scruples in declaring, that brief as was our intimacy, it was quite long enough for me, and further that I shall not hesitate to give him the cold shoulder should chance ever again bring us together.

For a considerable time I knew Tom only by name, though it was no secret to me that he was aged. Perhaps it was his candour in this respect which first induced me to feel an interest in him scarcely warranted by his ungenteel manner of existence. He resided at a public-house, not a quiet hotel or even a well-conducted tavern, but a gin-palace in one of the most squalid and densely populated parts of London, and doing a business aptly described by the "trade" term roaring. He appeared to take a vulgar delight in letting everybody know that he lived there. In each of the great plate-glass windows appeared a placard, on which, in foot long letters, was printed the words Old Tom. When the said placard grew fly-spotted and dirty, it was replaced by another spick and span new, so that it was evident that he was a permanent tenant. He was not the landlord of the "Jolly Sandboys" however. The proprietor of the roaring gin-palace was T. Whiffler. "T. Whiffler licensed to deal in beer and spirits to be drunk on the premises," was to be found for the seeking in the attenuated characters prescribed by the law over the principal doorway.

"T. Whiffler's noted stores," shone resplendently in green and gold, on each of the gorgeous pendant out-side lamps. Who then was Old Tom, and what was the nature of his connection with T. Whiffler of the "Jolly Sandboys," that he could claim to flaunt his name so obtrusively? I often wondered, and probably should have gone on wondering until this day, but for the following occurrence.

Happening just lately, to be in the neighbourhood of the "Sandboys," my eyes involuntarily sought Old Thomas's sign - but it had vanished. In place of it there appeared the elaborately coloured figure of a ferocious, sleek, and well-fed domestic grimalkin, mounted on a barrel, and spitting so spitefully that his rearmost grinders were plainly visible. The back of the animal was arched, its tail bushy, and one of its paws raised in the act of scratching, revealed a row of bare talons sharp as needle points. On the barrel on which puss was perched was inscribed "Whiffler's matchless Old Tom, the best gin in London." In an instant the scales fell from my eyes - the cat was out. Thomas the elder was not, as I had supposed, a fellow creature - he was not a human being at all. Old Tom was merely the cognomen of an animal, which on account of its fiery nature and the sharp and lasting effects of its teeth and claws on all who dared to venture on a bout with it, had been selected as being aptly emblematic of the potent liquid called gin. The fact, however, of Old Tom existing not in the flesh, but only in the spirit, was evidently " all as one" with its host of admirers. Even while I stood for a few moments contemplating the savage creature on the tub, and marvelling at the boldness of distillers and publicans who could venture so frankly to declare the nature of the wares in which they dealt, there approached the portals of the "Jolly Sandboys," two women, each with a marketing basket on her arm.

"Well, what do you say?" one remarked, "shall we wet t'other eye?"

"Right you are," returned her companion, "but, good luck to ye; Annie, let it be Old Tom; don't let us mix it," and straight-way in they went.

There came along within half-a-minute two other women and a man, the dirtiness of whose attire betokened the drudgery to which they were doomed that they might earn a living.

"Old Tom, of course," said the man pausing at the threshold.

"Yes, that's the ticket," replied one of the women, and the three customers, like the two that preceded them vanished from sight.

It was on a Saturday, and as the doors or jaws of the "Sandboys," kept ajar by a spring and a strap, oscillated waggishly, after having swallowed the last catch, there occurred to me the following arithmetical riddle - if at noon five customers enter a public-house in the course of fifty seconds, how many will follow suit, in the same time, when the gas is ablaze and the regular evening tide of trade sets fairly in? Clearly it was a calculation from which Old Tom could not be excluded. So much would depend on the popularity of that subtle seducer. According to Mr. Whiffler, his Old Tom was a spirit possessing very uncommon and superior powers of attraction, and able on that account to draw the public much more effectually than a spirit of weaker capacity and influence. The only satisfactory way of arriving at anything like a correct solution of the problem would be to test it by the light of personal experience, so there and then I resolved that it should be done, that I would return to the "Jolly Sandboys" as soon after dark that Saturday night as might be convenient.

Five hours afterwards I was again an occupant of the "private compartment." Had Old Tom been a saint and martyr, and this his shrine, the motley crowd that clustered round the highly polished metal counter could not have exhibited more desperate anxiety and eagerness to do him honour. It was, however, evident at a glance, that the majority were not pilgrims from afar; indeed, as regards the female portion, the fact of their being, for the most part, without either bonnet or shawl, favoured the assumption that they were residents of the immediate locality. As for the men, they were, with few exceptions, of the labouring class, individuals whose attire was of the flannel or fustian order, and branded from boots to neckerchief with the various "trade marks which unmistakably denoted their occupation. The lime-splashed plasterer, the engineer smeared with lathe-oil and iron filings, the navvy with his clay smirched cap and smock, and almost enough of mother earth encumbering his mighty ankle-jacks to entitle him to a county vote as a landowner, the shoemaker with his blunt black finger nails, and his scrubby beard, and that roseate tinge of nose, popularly, though erroneously ascribed to an insatiable thirst for alchoholic pottage, and really, if the word of many doughty men of leather may be taken, the result of constant stooping over their work and consequent attacks of determination of blood to the head; these and a dozen others-not forgetting that most pitiable object of all the poor neighbourhoods, London journeyman baker.

I am not disposed to go the length of altogether denying the possibility, but certainly my opportunities of observation on the evening in question coupled with previous experience warrant me in gravely doubting whether it is in the nature of a journeyman baker - an old "night-hand" - to get drunk as do other men. He does not appear to be a creature of flesh and blood. He seems as though he was stuffed with flour, which silts through the pores of his skin as mankind in general exude perspiration-provoking the absurd fancy that if you were to hang up and beat a baker as a carpet is beaten the ultimate result, when the floury clouds had cleared away, would appear in the shape of a shrivelled epidermis, empty, save for a few bones, brittle and broken, and of the consistence of a Captain's biscuit. There were two of the unfortunate workmen in question drinking at the bar of the Jolly Sandboys. That they had but just left work was evident from the mealiness of their jackets and their slow, dull eyes, aching for want of sleep. They were elderly men both, and their faces were well lined with age, and having to earn their bread by the sweat of their brow in a floury atmosphere, had imparted to their countenances the strange appearance of being made up of irregular bits neatly fitted together like the pieces of a child's puzzle. The two melancholy old bakers did not drink in company with the other drinkers, but worshipped Old Tom with the haggard and almost hopeless aspect of men who were aware that it was as idle to expect a kindling of their depressed spirits by means of swallowing gin as to endeavour to ignite damp wood with a single lucifer match. All round about them the jolly tipplers lit up anew every time they added fresh fuel to the already brisk conflagration within them, but the pair of drouthy old bakers did not mellow in the least, even when, between them they had emptied three quartern measures. It was like throwing glasses of water on a sand heap the gin they swallowed, and there appeared not the least indication of their "clay" being a bit moister at the conclusion than at the commencement of their endeavours. Goodness knows what they were there at all for. Not for the sake of jolly companionship certainly, for to my knowledge not one glass of the dozen or so they shared was emptied with "A good health to you," or even the briefer and commoner "Here's luck." If they had a sorrow to drown their labour was evidently in vain. They might as well have tried to drown a taxable puppy by throwing cups of water over him. Their sorrow, if they had one, was not to be stifled in gin; it was rather as though every mouthful of the hot liquid swallowed down upon it scalded it and made it wriggle anew. The more they drank the more abject they looked. Of course I could not keep them in sight the whole time, still I can answer for it that they never once laughed or smiled even with any degree of heartiness. Had they done so I could scarcely have missed the fact. The dough plastering which filled up their wrinkles must inevitably have become fractured in the process, whereas, to the very last it remained intact. They were not even stimulated to animated conversation. All through the hour they remained there, they stood leaning over a beer barrel, and talking in husky whispers. But once they spoke aloud, and that was when the third measure had been drained dry.

Said one old baker to the other, "That's a bad kind of pimple you've got aside o' your nose,"

"Ha!" replied his friend, "he get's bigger, I think," and he chafed the affliction ruefully with the length of his floury forefinger.

"Erysipelas I shouldn't wonder," remarked the first speaker, whereon they both sighed heavily, and with a gloomy glance around them took their departure.

Not that the instances furnished by the two absorbent bakers were the only ones which, during that instructive evening with Old Tom, came under my notice of the individuals of the gin drinking order, who, with all the willingness in the world to drink, were denied the blissful consummation of drunkenness. This would appear to be an affliction peculiar to persistent imbibers of a distillation of the juniper berry. In all the indictments which have been laid against John Barleycorn, it has never yet been said of him, by his worst enemy, that he turned traitor against those who put their trust in him. Whatever his "colours" may be - brown, black, or golden, he is staunch to them - the same yesterday, to-day, to-morrow. As much certainly cannot be said for Old Tom. Like the creature from which he derives his name, he is treacherous, and apt, not unfrequently, to take a malicious delight in leaving his friends in the lurch when they are most in need of him, and one can scarcely imagine a more melancholy spectacle than is presented by the poor wretch who for years has been devoted body and soul to the quartern measure, and who before now has been known to make sacrifice to it even to the extent of pawning or selling the boots off his feet, and the shirt off his back - and who discovers that his favourite liquor will no longer yield him the wished-for solace, but turns as it were to water the instant it has passed his yearning gullet. It is as useless endeavouring to arrive at the desired end by the old means, as it is to spur a dead horse. He has cut himself adrift from all those ties by which mankind in general secure that happiness, and trusted to a gin-cask to keep him afloat on his sea of selfish and sensual enjoyment until life's voyage comes to an end, and all suddenly, he discovers that the sea is dead and stagnant on which his raft, rotten and rudderless, must abide, until by natural decay it falls to pieces and is engulfed with himself in the black depths.

Such instances may be rare but not extremely so, because, unless I am mistaken during the time I spent at Old Tom's palace, at least three or four looked in there. The members of the outcast tribe in question may be easily distinguished from bar frequenters of the sociable order, not on account of their rags or their general appearance of being poverty-stricken. On the contrary the miserable ones who are afflicted with this insatiable gin-hunger, seem as a rule to have been persons in a respectable condition of life, and still cling tenaciously to their shabby remnants of decent attire. If of the male sex the lank, shambling figure is tightly buttoned in the seedy black coat, as high as the throat, which is encircled by what was once a genteel "stock " and a frayed old shirt collar; the hat is of the tall kind and albeit bald of "nap," and battered, is sleek, and shining with an unnatural lustre. If a woman, a veil is invariably worn with the bonnet, and dilapidated kid gloves cover the hands which usually are encumbered with some sort of reticule and what was once a parasol, the object apparently being a daring attempt to impose on the credulous that she is a person whose sensitiveness suffers exceedingly from being compelled to the act of entering a vulgar common public-house, but who really had no choice between doing so and sinking in the street from sheer exhaustion. Male or female, however, the subterfuge is equally transparent, and the object the same - the stealthy, oft-repeated "dram" in the vain hope to quench the impotent thirst for gin which consumes them. It is not for such as these that the gas and glitter, the plate-glass and the flashy emblazonment of ceilings and panels has attractions. They know nothing of the delights of the "social glass." The only place where they would pledge "the cup of friendship" - if they owned such an article representing value - would be at the pawnbrokers. To linger over their libations is to them a tantalization - a weariness and a waste of time. If they could anyhow contrive it, they would get drunk at a leap as it were, and have done with it. They are shy as well as solitary drinkers, and would gladly eschew all such flaring and uproarious "publics" as the "Sandboys," but unfortunately if one wants Old Tom in all his fiery strength, it is here he must be sought. It is curious to watch the accomplished dram drinker's peculiar method of procedure. Urgent as is his want, of all drinkers who approach the metal counter he is least demonstrative. He will flit in, usually behind some other customer who has pushed open the door, and his quick eyes detecting the thinnest part of the crowd, there he edges his way. He has the money all ready in his hand, and catching the barmaid's eye he ejaculates as hurriedly as though he had not a moment to spare, "Glass of Old Tom." In seven seconds the liquor is drawn, the vessel raised to his pale lean jaws, and with a sudden gulp, such as ordinarily attends the swallowing of a pill, it is gone. Three pence disposed of as rapidly as a conjurer could twitch a halfpenny from his hand up into his sleeve, and with what profit to the investor? Mighty little to judge from his appearance. There is so little to feel grateful for that he does not even lick his dry lips, nor does the merest twinkle in his leaden eyes denote that he has obtained what he bargained for. He feels no thrilling of his nerves, no gush of warmth in his veins, - he is as horribly sober as ever, and mean, miserable, despairing wretch that he is, with one quick glance of malignant envy on the mirthful beer-drinking crew about him, he vanishes stealthily as he came, to make a "call" at the next of Old Tom's renowned abiding places, and the next, and still the next; as long as he has threepence left or the "houses" remain open. Then, his aim still unattained, he will slink home to that terrible bed, and troubled and dream-haunted, and filled with heat which yields no warmth to his shaking limbs, lay and quake until morning.

SAY the energetic and well-meaning gentlemen who would convert the whole country to be total abstainers - the lurking devil at the heart and core of the whole business, is not so much that pure spirit or a simple effusion of good hops and roasted barley hurts the man who drinks it: it is the sickening concoctions, the baneful ingredients, that the unscrupulous publican finds it to his profit to add to the various liquors he dispenses that works the main mischief. The "this" that destroys the liver, the "that" that benumbs the heart, the t'other that scorches up and withers the brain - the slow and insidious poisons that the publican sells in the guise of "good liquor." Without doubt, this is the most powerful weapon the total abstainers wield; and it is equally certain that they have availed themselves of the privilege to the fullest possible extent. It is on this spear that they are perpetually spitting the unlucky possessor of a licence to sell spirits and beer, and holding him up to public execration as a fiend in human shape-a sort of bloated vampire, squatted on the bodies of his million victims, whose blood and sustenance he has devoured. And though, of course, calmly reasoning people have felt it incumbent on them to make broad allowances for party-blind exaggeration, there exists a universal opinion, that the publican *does* doctor "his liquors." Doctor is the mild phrase used. Gentlemen of the House of Commons speak of it as an established fact. Ministers in the pulpit denounce it as a prevalent abomination, and no one contradicts them. Magistrates and judges proclaim in open court that, were it not for the pernicious and blood-inflaming concoctions that publicans sell in place of wholesome beverages, not one-tenth of the present number of criminals would be brought before them; and really the publicans' silence under such a formidable battery of accusations might well excuse those who opine that there must be "something in it."

How much? A penn'orth of proof is worth a shipload of surmise. There is no use in beating a bush with a straw, or in whispering our suspicions of these intentions to a company of crows blackening a corn-field. If the publicans really are mixing poisonous drugs with their liquors, let us see to what extent.

Acting on this resolve, I recently procured eight samples of gin - of common gin, such as is sold over the public-house counter at the rate of thousands of gallons every day. I thought it best to "sample" public-houses situated in the lowest neighbourhoods - *not* be it understood, because I wished to write a "sensational article," and artfully devised to obtain choice material to that end, but purely as a means of saving myself trouble. My idea was to take the very worst neighbourhoods; and then, if the result were very bad, to take neighbourhoods of a better class, in hopes of being able to show that it was only the hole-and-corner license-holder - the tradesman who accommodated the quality of his goods to the coarse and vitiated taste of his customer - that chiefly required looking after; and that the great majority of licensed victuallers are as honest in their dealings as could be desired, and entitled to the respect of their fellow-men. The most notorious neighbourhoods round London were visited for my gin collections - Saffron-hill, Leather-lane Shadwell; the New-cut, in Lambeth; Kent-street, in the Borough; Chapel-street, Westminster; Shoreditch, and Flower and Dean-street, in Spitalfields. A half-pint of gin was procured at each place, and tenpence was the price paid for it - except in the Shoreditch case, where, on the strength of a prominent announcement made by a publican that he had on tap the very finest Old Tom at fourpence halfpenny a quartern, I became his customer to the extent of ninepence. Eight pints of beer were bought at the same time and at the same houses, and the sixteen samples were sealed and placed in the hands of a thoroughly competent analytical chemist, who has made a most careful examination, and returned to me the following "report," which I have more pleasure than I can express in laying before the reader. It should be premised that pure gin, as it is sent out from the distillery, commonly contains forty per cent, of real spirit, or absolute alcohol, to sixty parts of water, and that the most notorious ingredients of gin adulteration consist, or rather are popularly supposed to consist, of tincture of capsicum, paradise grains, turpentine, sulphate of zinc, and salt of tartar.

Results of chemical analysis of eight samples of London gin:-

Sample marked "L." -This was procured from the unsalubrious neighbourhood of Saffron-hill, a place abounding in courts and alleys, and peopled by as ragged, brawling, tippling a population as London can produce. In this sample there were found thirty-three parts of real spirits, and *nothing besides* but water sweetened with sugar and a suspicion of cayenne pepper.

Sample marked " G." -This was from Leather-lane-from the very worst part of the lane - from a public-house in an alley of low repute; in fact, one frequently visited by the police. Real alcohol thirty-two per cent. No sulphate of zinc, no paradise grains, nothing besides the spirit, except sugar and water and some harmless aromatic flavourings.

Sample "H." -From Shadwell - from Ratcliff-highway, where, as soon as the gas is lighted in the evening, swarms of women of the most hideous type emerge from their loathsome dens, the sole business of whose life is to make sailors drunk and plunder them. In a neighbourhood such as this, if in any, there exists a temptation for the dishonest publican to "play tricks" with his gin. The lucrative pursuit of the vile trade that the women follow depends in great part on the accommodating disposition of the publican, and therefore the women dare not complain, and the sailors half their time are spoony drunk, and will swallow anything as long as gentle "Poll" of Wapping presses it on his acceptance. Well, what is the worst that can be said of the gin of Ratcliff-highway? Only that it contains thirty-one per cent. of spirit, with sugar and water. This sample, however, is prominent among the rest on account of one objectionable quality. "H" is very fiery from the presence of tincture of capsicum, says the chemist.

Sample marked "O." - This from the New-cut; from the roaring, rattling market-place that is literally crammed on Saturday night, road and pathway, by working men and their wives; whose belief in its being lucky to spend the "market penny" is as old-established as it is respected. It is the New-cut to which every teetotal lecturer in the country refers when he wishes to present to his hearers a soul-thrilling picture of what may be witnessed in certain parts of London on the Sabbath-day, as soon as the houses are opened after church time, and on the Sabbath evening; the New-cut, with its every tenth house a tavern, and its many legends of publicans who have "made their fortune" in ten - in seven years! How much of the enormous profit that goes to bring about this miraculous result is derived from the sale of poison? None at all, if the half-pint of gin marked "O" may be regarded as a fair sample of the whole. It is the old story repeated - thirty-two parts spirit, with sugar, water, and a flavouring of juniper.

Sample marked "M," from Chapel-street, Westminster. Another of poverty's market-places, and on Saturday night full as a fair; the costermongers with their barrows uproariously competing for trade with the shopkeeper. The house from which Sample M was procured stands in the midst of all this, and does a roaring trade as the attendant barmen, muscular of build, with their bare arms, attest. But the publicans of Chapel- street, Westminster, don't poison their customers. Their gin- brew is of the mildest description, yielding but twenty-six per cent. of spirit. It is stiffish cold gin and water moderately sweetened.

Sample marked "F " hails from Shoreditch, and yields better money's-worth (United Kingdom Alliance, forgive me!) than the last-mentioned. It shows thirty-two and a half of absolute alcohol, and all the rest is water and sugar, with a spice of aromatic flavouring.

Sample marked "I" is from the region of dirt and squalor, of lodging houses and drunkenness - Kent-street, in the borough. But even the publicans there have a conscience that preserves them innocent of the crime of hastening their customers' deaths beyond the speed at which simple alcohol is capable of carrying them. The gin of Kent-street is of fair average quality, registering thirty and a half - water, sugar, and "aromatic seasoning" being called in as substitutes for the amount of alcohol of which the original liquor has been plundered.

Sample marked "Q" was culled in the "worst Street in London -Flower and Dean-street, Spitalfields. There is no harm in it beyond those intoxicating qualities peculiar to gin; and even this "Q" landlord, no doubt with a laudable desire to keep at as low a temperature as possible the exciteable passions of the peculiar people who are his customers, keeps down his standard of alcohol at twenty-nine.

As to the rest, it is the same story hitherto seven times repeated - sugar, water, and aromatic flavouring, with a slight "fortifying" of cayenne pepper.

And this exhausts the Gin budget. I must repeat that what I have here stated is the result of deliberate and painstaking examination by men well experienced and trustworthy; and, as I need not remark, absolutely free from party feeling. Undoubtedly it may be taken that the examples here put forth fairly represent the sort of "gin" that is sold in all parts of London, including its very worst parts; and I respectfully submit that it sets the "hole-and-corner" publican, as he has been styled, in a much more respectable light than vague unfounded rumour has hitherto afforded him. He is not half so black as he has been painted - no, nor a twentieth part. Not that he is blameless. Tincture of capsicum is by no means a healthful ingredient in a drink that is consumed in such enormous quantities; and it cannot be denied that the publican resorts to it as a means of lending a semblance of strength and heat to his "Old Tom" that it could not otherwise lay claim to.

The gin disposed of, I next turned my attention to beer.

Originally there were eight pints; but the bottle that contained one of them by accident was broken, so seven were all that passed for analysis into the hands of the chemist.

Seven samples, each representing the popular English beverage, to "rob a poor man" of which is commonly accounted an offence deserving the severest punishment human ingenuity can inflict; and all collected from just that kind of public- house where beer worship is most devoutly observed. The seven pints have been put on their trial fairly - and without prejudice, excepting that slight degree of it which human nature is bound to harbour against anybody or anything brought up to be examined "on suspicion." It cannot be denied that my seven pints of beer were taken on suspicion. As I viewed the black row of bottles at the chemist's, each wearing a red cap of sealing-wax, I could scarcely forbear shaking my head in grave doubt, as I wished they might pass through the ordeal to which they were condemned, finally to be found "Not guilty," and acquitted without a stain on their character. I hoped that they might be so fortunate; but I was troubled with serious misgivings. They came professedly from the very lowest of the beer family - common, vulgar fourpenny; they had, one and all, been drawn without a moment's warning from the cellars in which their natures had been corrupted. Pure enough might be the liquid consigned by the jolly dray-men to those mysterious depths, the wide wooden jaws of which gaped in the pavement to receive it. But what happened afterwards? Where were the customers of that prosperous individual who unblushingly announced himself a "brewers' druggist?" What terrible hidden meaning lurked in the wording of that oft-repeated advertisement inserted in the publicans' own trade newspaper by out-of-work barmen, "clever at cellar work?" The mere screwing of a pipe into a bunghole, the tilting of a barrel, surely could not involve an amount of cleverness that was worthy to be vaunted? Besides, it seemed that there must be *some* truth in what everybody said, and what everybody almost was prepared to vouch for. It may be all very well as regards gin, I had been told. Gin is an article sold by the distiller to the retail-dealer at a price that enables the latter to clear a handsome profit, even though he sells it as pure as he receives it. It is altogether different with beer - with common beer, such as every publican in London keeps on draught at fourpence a quart. It costs, when bought of the most eminent brewers, within a shade of what it fetches; and the publican who would live and pay his way is bound to "extend" it. To do this, he must use something more than mere water. If he did not the extended stuff would be so threadbare that the most inexperienced would see through it. The beer-drinking public likes its liquor with a "body." It insists on an article that is "full in the mouth" - an article that, when swallowed, comforts the stomach as food comforts it. What can the beer-seller do? He has no fiendish desire to poison his fellow-creatures. If they would put up with the naked imposture it would be the same thing to him, and would save him a world of trouble; but since they insist on the disguise, all that he can do is to smother his conscience, and make it as pleasant tasting as possible. All this sounded terribly ominous for my seven pints.

Well, the trial is over, and what is the result? Hear it and be amazed, all ye that hitherto have regarded the shining pewter pint and quart pot but as whitened sepulchres, in which lurked corruption and death, none the less because he was disguised under the names of cocculus indicus and green copperas. Hear it and rejoice, all ye that throughout your manly lives have staunchly stuck to "brown beer," declaring your belief that some beer might be better than other, but that of bad beer there was none, and with eager lips saluting its creamy mantling in token of your undeviating loyalty, upon every convenient opportunity - rejoice ye, for here is proof that your affection has not been misplaced nor your confidence abused; your beer has been grievously maligned. To be sure, it is not so artless and innocent as might be desired; but it contains no poison; assuming, that is to say, that the seven samples that have undergone the severest tests it was possible to apply to them may be regarded as fairly representing the great bulk of fourpenny beer that in pints and "pots" crosses thousands of metal-topped counters every day throughout the year. As with the "quarterns of gin," they were collected from the lowest neighbour- hoods; and the following is the "report" returned:-

April 29, 1871.

RESULTS OF ANALYSIS OF SEVEN SAMPLES OF PORTER.

Percentage of real Alcohol by Weight. Cocculus Indicus Picric Acid or Copperas. Common Salt/ M. (Bermondsey) 5¼ Neither Yes T. (Shadwe]l) 4½ Neither Yes O. (Spitalfields) 5½ Neither Much H. (New-cut) 4½ Neither Very much Q. (Shoreditch) 4 Neither Yes F. (Whitechapel) 4½ Neither Very much I. (K-street, Boro') 4 Neither A little   Adulterated porter is commonly three parts or less porter and one part water, the resulting weakness in quality being masked by the addition of colouring matter, brown sugar, and bitter drugs, one of which produces lethargic stupor. I am of opinion that these samples have not been so adulterated.: (Signed)

JOHN BROAD,

Pharmaceutical and Practical Chemist, Hornsey Rise.

It may be as well to mention that the above-named gentleman, to make assurance doubly sure in a matter of such importance, submitted portions of each sample to Professor Attfield, of the Pharmaceutical College, whose return precisely agrees with Mr. Broad's.

It appears, then, as a rule, that the drunkenness which is said to peculiarly afflict the lower orders of humanity is, after all, real, unadulterated drunkenness, and that the coal heaver who swigs pots of beer until he is fairly floated off his herculean legs is as genuinely drunk as his affluent brother, whose means enable him to indulge in the genteel inebriation that champagne affords. It is all a question of alcohol, and the purchaser of an humble pint of porter may be tolerably sure of getting twopenn'orth of the spirit of tipsiness for his twopence. Still, the amount of satisfaction to be derived from a perusal of the "report" above falls far short of perfection. Undoubtedly, it should be an immense relief to learn that the chances are considerably against green copperas or cocculus indicus contributing their poisonous qualities to the social glass; but, this much admitted, the publican does not come off with flying colours by any means. The account of salt is seriously against him. Salt is an invaluable agent in the preparation of our food and drinks but it is very possible to abuse the use of it. There can be no question that this is what the publican of the present day is doing. Why does he dose his beer with "much," with "very much" salt? Is it out of a laudable regard for the taste of his customer that he flings the saline grains into the beer butt with so liberal a hand, or is it - and the suspicion will creep in - because he has discovered in salt as an adulteration of beer certain virtues that enable him to forego the use of the old-fashioned ingredients of sophistication? It is no more necessary to add salt to beer than it is to add sand to sugar or water to milk. It serves no honest purpose, except, perhaps, that it may help to "clear" the beer; but there are a score of other things that are more effective for the purpose. As a "mask" to the water with which the beer of the brewer is extended, it must be but flimsy and transparent. What benefit, then, does the publican derive from his use of "much salt?" With nothing to guide us to a conclusion, and treating the question as a riddle to be guessed, it at once occurs to the shrewd guesser - salt is a provocative of thirst Can this be the solution of the problem? Is the revolution that has taken place in the "preparation of beer for the public during the last few years the result of a discovery made by some keen, calculating member of the craft, who argued thus: "By the use of certain drugs that a fastidious public regard as more or less objectionable, I am enabled to produce, at a cheap rate, a beverage, the stupefying qualities of which shall exceed those of the genuine article. Jack Jones, who drinks as much beer as any man, likes it. Jack judges of the quality of beer by the quantity he is able to drink of it before he is made drunk. Jack finds that three pots of my mixture knock him clean off his legs, and then he reels home 'glorious.' So much for pernicious adulteration. Now, suppose I turn over a new leaf. Instead of using in my beer drugs that produce 'lethargic stupor,' I will dilute it with nothing beside burnt sugar and water, with the addition of a fair sprinkling of salt. With plenty of salt in his liquor, he will keep sober twice as long as formerly, and his drink making him thirsty, he will imbibe at least twice asmuch; and, while I bag as much again of his money as I used to do, it will go none the harder against my peace of mind to know that under the new system he gets drunk in a proper and legitimate manner." I by no means advance this as the correct answer to the riddle, Why does the publican use "much salt" in his beer? It is merely a guess. Beyond this If "give it up," and respectfully await the unriddling from some one in possession of the secret.

    On the whole, however, I think it must be granted that the publicans of London will lose nothing in public esteem by the revelations which my modest inquiries into the two staple articles of their trade have enabled me to make. To be sure, it is not much to prove that a large body of influential tradesmen are not stained with the guilt of enriching themselves at the cost of health-the life even-of the very people on whom they most rely for support; but it is a great deal to assist in dispersing the cloud of suspicion that undeservedly, and by virtue of vague rumour only, has been so long permitted to overshadow them. That the publicans of London are innocent of all "tricks of trade" cannot in truth be stated; *but* they never pretended that such was the case. Indeed, bearing in mind how easy they might have set themselves right with the public as regards the graver charges of adulteration that have for so long been openly asserted against them, it it hard to understand why they have remained silent.

IT is a fact generally known, that by far the greater part of the tens of thousands of tons of coal brought to London finds its way thither *via* the Great Northern, the North Western, and the Midland lines of railway, but it is questionable if one consumer in a score is aware of the vast and peculiar facilities that exist for the cheap and speedy discharge of the contents of the great trucks into the horse wagons which bear the valuable mineral to our coal-cellars. Any information that helps to put the "coal question" fairly and squarely before the public should be acceptable at the present time, and it was with this view that I recently paid a visit to the little known "coal bays" at St. Pancras.

To speak of a "bay" in connection with coal is to suggest the sea-borne article, but the bays of St. Pancras are not spaces of ocean hemmed in by land, but plots of land bounded by bricks and mortar. They are, in fact, railway arches, the feet of which are planted in the Queen's highway, while their respective crowns, for a length and breadth of scores and scores of acres, serve to support an intricate network of rails that, branching away from the various main lines, combine to form the most important of our metropolitan coal depots. At the spot in question, which is within a few minutes' walk of King's-cross Railway Station, there are hundreds of these arches, or bays, each inscribed with the name of the merchant who rents it - ten or a dozen in some cases, appearing as the property of one proprietor. The jetty combustible is not stored in the bays, however. It is true they are capacious, and would probably hold each a hundred tons or more; but such small peddling is quite beneath the notice of our modern princes of the coal trade, who not unfrequently send out two and three hundred tons a day. They must have a supply laid on direct and constantly from the main, or, what is the same thing, the mine; and by an ingenious contrivance, this is managed quite easily. It is a fact that speaks forcibly in favour of those who insist that there is no reason why coal at the present season should be at two guineas a ton, that the distance from the coal-field to the domestic coal-cellar is spanned by a single bridge, as it were. Under the existing system of transit it is quite possible that coal haled out of a pit two hundred miles away last night may, by noon to-day, be blazing in our fire grates.

The flow of coal to the London depot, and thence to the vessels prepared for its reception is as trustworthy and manageable as the water which is supplied to our domestic cisterns by means of the New River Company's underground conduits. As already stated, the so-called bays are the arches of the railway on the rails of which stand the coal trucks that have been shunted from the main lines. Penetrating the roof of each arch is a capacious "spout," the upper mouth of which is open at the tailboard of a coal truck. The lower mouth of the spout is below in the arch where the coal wagons draw in to get their loads, and is guarded by a lid that is easily managed by means of a lever. Immediately beneath this lid are the scales on which the coal is weighed. An empty sack is held upright on the scale, the lid which guards the fully charged spout is shifted aside and when the sack is filled, which is the work of not more than half a minute, the lid is thrust back and the stream shut off. All that remains to be Cone is to see to the exact balancing of the two hundredweight of coal, which is at once transferred to the wagon.

It is a very rapid operation, as, having timed it, I am able to vouch. An empty wagon drew into a "bay," and two tons of coal were deposited in it, and the vehicle drawn out to make room for another, in less than fifteen minutes. On either side of the thoroughfare, which is wider than and quite as long as Fleet-street, there are bays from one end to the other, and, business being at full blast, the downpour of coal from above must have been at the rate of several tons per minute; whilst, thanks to the admirable management above described, the waste of the precious mineral was scarcely worth mentioning. A fog of sparkling, gritty dust made each bay as gloomy as though it was already night, and set the horses in the wagons sneezing at an alarming rate. But the brimming over of coal bits of any size was rare. On the river and at the wharf where the coal is discharged from barges and carried ashore a sack at a time, so considerable is the spilling that the "mudlarks" who hover about Thames-bank with their bags and baskets make a livelihood by picking out of the ooze the lumps that have fallen there. In the neighbourhood of the St. Pancras bays, however, there was but one old woman, a privileged gleaner evidently, and during the hour I was there she had not more than half filled the small handbag she carried.

    Perhaps the custodians of the spout are less careful when coal is at a more reasonable price, and she then does better. It makes a difference to every one, their being so dear. The excessive cost of the article has, it is said, nearly ruined the dust contractors. Seven years ago, a successor of the renowned Adam Bell, whose celebrated cinder heap, as recorded in song, cumbered the soil of Maiden-lane, which is close at hand, paid to the parish of St. Pancras the handsome sum of £1,500 per annum for the privilege of carting away and appropriating the contents of the dust bins of the inhabitants. At present, however, and for some time past, he deems the job so unremunerative that he declines it under a less payment than £4,000 a year for his services. Coal at a guinea and a half the ton has taught the consumer to be economical, and to avail himself more industriously than of old of the saving "sifter." It is said by dust contractors that the amount of cinders committed with the dust to the "bin" is not more than a third of what it used to be, and that even these are of such a poor quality as to be worth next to nothing at all for brickmaking purposes.

    In justice it should be stated that in the general aspect of this, one of the chief strongholds of the London inland coal trade, I discovered nothing that was glaringly suggestive of those bandit propensities of which many concerned in the "black diamond" trade have recently been accused. There is nothing in the least piratical in the appearance of the sooty crews who man the coal spouts and generally manage the business of thie bays. On the contrary they are a subdued and meek-looking class of men. In the old times when nearly all coal was sea-borne and Bankside was famous as being the haunt and home of the British coalheaver, there was a lawlessness that distinguished "fillers" and "backers" on board the wharfside barges that is altogether foreign to the modern family of inland "coaleys." One can without difficulty imagine the kneebreeched, broad-backed, beer-swigging Banksider of ancient times taking a malicious delight in the increased value of coal, and his tripping along the shore plank, laden with a couple of hundredweight, with all the more pride and satisfaction for the knowledge that every sack he carried was worth a silver crown. But none of this sort of spirit is displayed at the St. Pancras bays. There is a degree of morality in the atmosphere that goes far towards counteracting the gloom of coal dust. With a feeling similar to that which was probably experienced by a certain man who once upon a time went down to Jericho, I entered on my exploration. Consequently I was the more amazed at the many evidences of a disposition towards probity that met me on every side. Over against many of the bays there were printed intimations to "dealers" to stand by the scales and see their coals weighed, and then - to make doubly sure - to see them weighed again on the weigh-bridge, before they were taken through the gates. Scores of coalheavers, off duty for the time, lounged about the bays, but they were neither brawling nor beer-drinking. Here, in one corner of a bay, might be seen half a dozen reclining picturesquely on coal sacks, and indulging in sober discourse were as many more, resting on their elbows and placidly puffing their pipes, as one Of the company read aloud from a weekly newspaper.

    But what was most noticeable and convincing, that the coal merchant, like other individuals that might be named, is not always as black as he is painted, was to be seen over against a coal bunk on which reposed a grey-haired heaver calmly enjoying his tobacco. The noticeable feature in question took the form of an inscription in chalk characters, very large and well written, and was a quotation from the Bible, "Be sure your sin will find you out." It was very extraordinary. To whom was the pious reminder addressed? Was it a modest and weak remonstrance having reference to the sin of slander indulged in during the past year or so by the general public against misjudged wholesale traffickers in coal? That could scarcely be, since it was improbable that half a dozen of the general public would pass that way in the course of a week. Was it intended as a warning hint to retail dealers who came there and, alter receiving fair weight and honest worth for their money, departed to play shabby tricks with their purchases, to bring discredit on the whole coal trading community? But it was idle to speculate, when possibly the individual reclining on the bunk beneath the inscription was placed there to answer the questions of the curious.

The man was civil, and not averse to conversation. The Scriptural quotation was the handiwork of a good street-preacher, who occasionally visited the bays and held forth to a numerous and appreciative audience of coal carmen. He was not aware that any particular sin was alluded to, nor did he think that it bore especial reference to certain malpractices of the trade, which had of late been exposed in the newspapers, though, of course, there was no objection to any one wearing the cap if his conscience suggested that it wouldn't be a bad fit for him. I asked him how he found the coal trade just now, and whether he was getting an extra slice out of its exceptional prosperity. He sighed, and sadly shook his head, and replied,

"Not a oat. I ain't gettin' a penny more wages than when Wallsends was at twenty-two. We don't get anything extra, not any of us carmen and carriers, I assure you, sir."

"Perhaps you already have what you regard as sufficient wages?" I suggested.

"Well, I could do with a bit more, sir," replied the civil heaver; "four-and-twenty bob a week don't go far where there's a family, even when it's eked out with ticklers."

"And do you eke out your family with - with ticklers?"

"Not the family; it's the wages that the ticklers ekes out. You know what I mean - the spiffs, the palm-oilers, what we has giv us when we deliver loads. And," continued my informant, with a sigh that sent quite a cloud of smoke out of his short black pipe, "they have come down miserable lately, 'pon my soul they have. 'Stead of bein' anything in by coals going up, it's all t'other way with us. You gets your nose bit off a'most every time you ask. 'Drop o' beer, mum,' ses you, after you've shot 'em and borrowed a broom and swept up all tidy - 'drop o' beer, please, mum!' 'What!' ses they, 'you ought to be ashamed to ask for such a thing with coals at two pound a ton.'"

"The coal merchants must be doing remarkably well," I ventured.

"Eggstryorniary," replied the coal carman - "so is the dealers."

"The retail trade, you mean - the shopkeepers who vend small quantities in poor neighbourhoods?"

"Well, they are doin' werry tidy, I should say, but nothing to what the nobblers are doing."

"The nobblers!"

"Ah - the advertising coves in the newspapers who offer to sell at about fifteen shillings a ton under the market price, and who make out a list as long as your arm of the different sorts they keep on their premises. *Their* premises, the wagabones! Why, it's only a back yard at best, with hardly room in it for marrying the few loads of low sorts they manage to lay in stock."

"I beg pardon. Hardly room in the back yard for doing what did you say?"

"For marrying the rubbish they sell the public. Anybody as knows anything about coals could tell that such a mixshur ain't natural. They'll buy a truck load of slate and another of screenings and another of decent coal, say, as coal goes now, at about twenty-four, and then they marry the three sorts together with quantities of each, according if it's best Wallsends you orders, or only seconds. They're poor beggars, all them nobblers, and never keep their own wagons."

"There you must be in error," said I, "it was only this morning that I saw a laden wagon bearing the name of one of the cheap advertising firms you speak of."

"Ah," bearing the name, returned the grey-haired coalheaver, with a wink, that contrasted oddly with the inscription in chalk over his head, "you saw a wagon wearing a 'dicky' you mean - a false front plate, with a name on it what slips on and off like them on the wans that the pianoforte makers borrow. Whenever you see one of these kinds of wehicles, sir, you may pretty well reckon on the sort o' coal that's in the sacks."

I should like to have pursued the interesting conversation a little further, but at that moment my informant was hailed to join his gang, and, with one last glance at the Scriptural quotation, I came away.

IT may not be generally known that at a certain time of the year an important movement takes place amongst certain people dwelling in our midst. Numerically they are not great, but, as is well known, on account of their peculiar habits and customs, and their means of obtaining a livelihood, they exercise considerable influence on a large section of the community.

The people in question are the gipsies, and just now, according to their invariable custom, they are engaged in preparing for their summer campaign, which lasts from April until the end of the following October. It is quite a mistake to imagine that they regard the "broad canopy of heaven" as such a mighty good thing that they cannot have too much of it. The "rollicking Romany," the hero of gaol bird vocalisation, the "child of the forest glade, roaming abroad like a bird or a bee," of more polite and romantic eulogy, is not so "green" as - just for the look of the thing and to uphold his theatrical reputation - to pass the frosty months by which Christmas is bounded camped out in the wintry wilderness. A pitch on a common, or in a snug lane, and by a country wayside, may be all very well when the yellow gorse is ripening under the sun to the complexion of a Maltese orange, and when the hedges are so amply cloaked in verdure, as to afford prime screening for a hen-roost robber, or a misappropriator of family linen; but when first frosts powder the short-nipped grass, and leaves fall thick, and the rook-nests are left naked aloft in the black boughs, the bold gipsy feels that his faith in mossy banks and bosky brakes is shaken, and that, after all, though haystacks may in their season be all that can be desired in the way of shelter, there is another season when chimney-stacks and their cosy associations are to be preferred.

Not that the gipsy will consent to do violence to the fine free spirit with which nature has invested him by becoming a house-dweller. No; as close as you please to the skirts of civilisation - indeed, if the said skirts are so immediately adjacent as to admit of his dipping his honest hands in the pockets thereof, he has no objection - but four walls and a roof are not to his fancy. It is the same with the women as the men. I recently overheard two middle-aged flowers of the forest discussing the matter in their encampment in the vicinity of Lock's Fields, Walworth. Both were sun-bronzed, and both wore coral earrings, and their straw bonnets hind side in front. Both were at ease, and comfortably disposed for leisurely chat. The one was seated in a barrow, for which her ample form was an easy fit, and the other was partaking of her midday meal, and was evidently actuated by a determination to adhere, as far as circumstances would permit, to those rural domestic rites and ceremonies to which her heart inclined. She was squatted on a wisp of haybands by the side of a recumbent donkey, whose four legs hedged her in, and she had utilised the flanks of the docile creature to serve as a table. There was bread-and-butter spread on it, and about a quarter of a peck of turnip radishes. There was a bald shiny patch on the donkey's hip set round with hair, and this served as a convenient salt cellar, and every time his mistress dipped a radish into this repository and proceeded to scrunch it up, there was an expression in the animal's half-closed eyes that betrayed his consciousness that now she was enjoying herself, and the satisfaction the reflection afforded him.

"And how's old Cooper a doin' since he give up the wan and took to the house?" inquired the female in the wheelbarrow.

"He's growing wus and wus," replied her friend with a grim serve-him-right-too expression in her beady eyes.

"He was right enough on wheels; why didn't he stay on 'em?"

"Ah, to be sure. I know what I should expect would shortly happen to me if once I trusted myself atween lath and plaster."

"But it ain't the laths, and it ain't the bricks, my dear," rejoined her friend; "its summat in the mortar that works its way into your cistern, and that's what'll bunnick up old Cooper, you mark my words."

I don't believe that she meant "cistern," though certainly she said it. If I might hazard a guess, I think she intended to convey her impression that there was something in the composition of mortar that was injurious to the human system, and that old Mr. Cooper was in danger of becoming a victim to rashly entrusting himself within its influence. If to be "bunnicked" means worse than this, the mortar is responsible.

As soon as the cold weather sets in the members of the various gipsy tribes whose headquarters are London and its suburbs, may be seen with their brown babies and their houses on wheels, the gay green and yellow paint with which their panels are bedecked, dulled and blistered by the sun of a long summer, leisurely making their way to the winter settlements. These are not few. There are two or three at Camberwell, and one at a place called Pollard's Gardens, near the Waterloo Road. Peckham boasts of several; they may be found at Homerton, in the back slums of Lambeth, and among the potteries between Notting Hill and Shepherd's Bush. Lock's Fields, Walworth, is a favourite spot with the fraternity, and has been since that remote time, when Lock himself, standing at the door of his farmhouse, was able to take an uninterrupted view of his cows browsing in the open meadows. Now, one might traverse the said "fields" from end to end and find nothing more suggestive of cows than the heels and paunches of the animals in question exposed for sale in the grimy little shops that plentifully dot the neighbourhood; while as for grass, not a solitary blade would meet the eye except in the form of those saucer-sized bits of turf retailed at a penny each, and which imprisoned larks speedily convert into the frowsiest of hay with their hot feet as they madly dance to their own pitiful piping. The gipsies are expected at these places, and the "bits o' waste" are reserved and kept vacant for their winter hiring. If the said bit o' waste includes a bit o' hedge, and anything of a ditch, no matter how inodorous or overgrown with green duck-weed, they are regarded as advantages. Nothing else except a stable for the one or two old horses and a donkey is needed. The house on wheels serves as kitchen, parlour, and all, including bedroom for the elders of the family. As for the younger fry, half a dozen or so maybe easily packed hammockwise in the haybag that is slung beneath the house to the fore and aft axle-trees; and should there be one or two still unprovided for, there is always a spare bed in the stable.

It is not so easy to understand how the numerous party is provided for by day. Should the question be asked how a livelihood is obtained, the short answer is, "Clothes-pegs." If they are produced at all, however, it must be by some necromantic process of manufacture, for no gipsy is ever seen engaged with such implements and materials as are ordinarily used. Perhaps, however, "clothes-peg" is merely a slang phrase of "Romany," and signifies living by one's wits, or by other folks' lack of them. This would appear the more probable since, when in town, papa Gipsy may invariably be found at the horse-market at Islington on Fridays, while mamma Gipsy is busy every day going her rounds and modestly concealing the light of divination and prophecy which possesses her under a simple handbasket, containing cottons and laces and hairpins. Readers of the daily newspaper may always know, on turning to the police reports, when the merry gipsy band have returned to town for the winter. Things do not appear to work smoothly with the fortune-tellers of the tribes at first starting. Perhaps exuberance of spirits at finding the "pastures new," as represented by silly housemaids and kitchen wenches, as green and promising as ever, causes them to be rash and recklessly grasping in their dealings; or, maybe, sufficient time has not yet elapsed for the weak-minded damsels to have forgotten the stories of barefaced swindle and extortion exposed and made public last season. At all events, it somehow happens that early winter is bad for the fortune-telling trade.

It was at Lock's-Fields that I recently scraped acquaintance with an interesting family of gipsies, thirty-three in number, including grandfather and grandmother and great-grandmother: and the old lady - eighty-nine last birthday, and with a face as hard looking and as wrinkled, though many shades darker, than a walnut - was as eager to "be off and get a sniff at the wholesome green leaves and the daisies" as the youngest of her tawny kindred. There was a tremendous bustle among them. There were houses on wheels and a cart; and, turning the corner to reach the "bit o' waste" where the vehicles found standing room, the wind came at me so powerfully impregnated with paint and turpentine as nearly to take my breath away. All the adults of the party were literally up to their eyes in brilliant colours - grinding and mixing and laying on first coats and second coats, and picking out wheel-spokes and panels; while the great-grandmother was the proud custodian of the three brass knockers, which she had splendidly polished, and which, as I was informed, she wrapped in a flannel petticoat, and took to bed with her of a night, to preserve them from marauding fingers.

As the whole family were, however, not engaged in the work of decoration previous to making a start, business as well as pleasure had to be thought of; and the nature of the approaching campaign was disclosed on every side. Here an industrious youth was high busy, stripped to his waist, but with the inevitable black short pipe between his lips, fashioning cockshy sticks out of hardy loppings of green elm; while his brother, and doubtless partner in the innocent pastime, was sorting and mending, with the aid of a glue-pot, a big bagfull of damaged cockshy toys, and which, as was in confidence confided to me, had been bought in the "ditch" (Houndsditch) that morning for two shillings. At a little distance off was another youth, whose simple implements of business were a little dab of clay, a bit of stick, and a threepenny-piece; and having stuck the stick in a hollow made in the clay, and balanced the coin atop of it, he went a little way off and practised knocking the three- pence off by throwing another bit of stick at it, his object being to hit the coin so that it should not fall into the hollow. As he did so he kept up in under tone a sort of incantation,

"Don't be afeard, gen'elmen's sons, hey a shy: try your luck and never say die. Every time you knocks off the little silver bit it is yourn, and on'y a penny a shy. In the hole's for me; outside the hole, which iver way, east, west, north or south, is for you - a penny a shy, and three to one in your favour."

He was a shock-headed, heavy-featured, lubberly youth of about fifteen, and, of course, smoked a short pipe; but it was plainly perceptible that his eyes were red with weeping, and that both his great ears, as though in sympathy, were red too. Every time he aimed at the little silver coin perched on top of the stick, it fell outside the hole; instead of exhibiting satisfaction, however, he scratched his head in despair, and growled, "Bust and beggar the jiggerin' thing, why the dl don't it fall into the hole?" and then he would put up the bit of stick again inclined a little more forward or backward, according to his fancy. It was evident that he was practising a "little game," in which, opportunity serving, the public were to be invited to join, the plan being that any one was to have as many "shys" at the threepenny-piece as he had a mind to, at the rate of a penny a shy, the winnings to be the said coin, provided it was so knocked off that it avoided the basin in which its support was stuck, and the manipulator's object was to adjust the stick at such an artful angle that "shy" how he would, the customer was bound to facilitate the descent of the threepenny into the hollow, and so lose his penny. It seemed to be a new branch of the cheating profession to the lad who was practising it, and that his progress towards perfection was not rapid; but what on earth did he find to cry about?

I discovered presently.

"Don't be afeared, gen'elmen's sons; hey another shy!" sighed the despairing youth, brushing a trickling tear from the side of his nose with the back of his dirty hand "Try yer luck, and never say die;" and this time he threw, and the coin fell into the hole. His eyes brightened as he stuck up the stick just as before, and threw again, and with the same result. Again, and still again, and every time the threepenny-piece was faithful. There was a middle-aged giant with great hairy arms engaged in sand-papering a newly-painted van-wheel a short distance off, and to him the lad presently cried,

"*Now* come and hey a try!"

And the hairy giant came, and, kneeling down, took wary aim. At the very first try he tipped off the threepenny-piece and sent it flying, whereupon he seized on the youth's large ears, and wrung them as though they had been two wet sponges, and his aim was to squeeze every atom of moisture out of them, after which, and never heeding the maddened bellowing of the tortured one, he returned to his wheel, and next instant was sandpapering away as though he were the father of the most contented family in the world.

"Bust and beggar and double bust the blessed threepenny!" roared the youth rebelliously; but at that instant he fortunately glanced in the direction of the sand-paperer, who had caught up a spoke-brush, and was poising it for a throw; so he judiciously altered his tune, and, once more adjuring imaginary gentlemen's sons not to be afeared, he gulped down his grief; again applied himself to learning his business.

But one of the oddest bits of information I picked up at the Lock's Fields encampment was, that, simmering in knavery as gipsies are, from the time when they are old enough to lisp lies to the gay company on a racecourse, until they arrive at the dead ripe age of the infatuated old lady who took the brass knockers to bed with her, they still believe, or seriously affect to believe, in the fortune-telling powers of their own women. Over a beer-can I put the question fairly to the herculean sand-paperer, and he replied that though she was his own grandmother, he should be very sorry to aggravate the old lady - who, at that moment, was breathing tenderly on the brazen nose of the dog's head that was part of one of the knockers, and rubbing it bright again with the corner of her shawl - to the extent of bringing on his head her malediction. "Do you think she really could tell you your fortune if she tried?"

"I'm sure of it," he replied, in a whisper.

"Then why don't you let her do so?" I suggested.

"Well, I'll tell you why," he replied, after reflecting on the matter for several seconds, with his face in the beer-can, "I'll tell you why. Every man, mister, has ups and downs in life afore him, as well as behind him; and though it might be werry pleasant to be put up to the hups aforehand, a man mightn't feel ekal to be put up to all the downs what's in store for him. Life's very much like bacon," continued the hairy-armed philosopher, intently regarding the ale in the can as though the revelation appeared in the liquor, "there's fat to it and there's lean to it, and him as tries to make a division makes a mess of it. It's best to put the two together and take it streaky. That's what I think about life, and that's why I don't see any pull in having my fortune told."

And this opinion was accepted as the correct one by the six or seven young men and old who were present, and they, one and all, expressed their implicit belief in the women of the tribe as fortune-tellers, "if they chose to give their mind to it."

"Then they don't always do so," I remarked.

"Taint likely," replied a young fellow, "it can't be expected that they'll go chucking away their talents for a tanner (6d.) or so a time. It would be a reg'lar insult to the stars to go to em and consult em at such a cag-mag price. They'd very likely chuck you over if you tried it on with 'em, and tell you all wrong, and serve you right too. But them as pays handsome and deals square, is dealt square by, and gets what they bargains for, as true as this here in my hand is a paint-brush."

I should like to have had another hour of the society of my interesting friends, but at that moment there came trooping a dozen or so of another tribe who had just broken up their encampment at Peckham, and so, wishing them a prosperous summer, I bade them good-bye, casting an encouraging glance, as I came away, on the youth who was still ruefully on his knees before the bit of stick and the hollowed clay, enjoining gentlemen's sons to try their hands, and never say die.

IT was quite a relief when the big hand of the clock at the Midland Railway Station pointed to half-past seven, and the guards in charge of the train called, "Right, here," and the engine-whistle peremptorily made known its intention to start immediately. To be sure, there was nothing to be sorry for presented by the spectacle of two hundred and thirty-six downtrodden and poverty-stricken ones, rescued by a single bold brave move from long-endured penury, and set fairly on the road to comfort and plenty.

It was all right when once they started; it was the seeing them start that was not enjoyable - it was such a woefully kindly starting. It was the prudent intention of the worthy promoters and conductors of the expedition to avoid as far as possible last moment adieux, and a barrier had been erected to keep from the platform every one who could not show a train ticket. But within the last ten minutes - just indeed when the majority of the emigrants had taken their seats with their little children and their babies in arms, and a couple of good Samaritans were going the length of the train doing a brisk trade as milkmen, filling bottles out of big pails full of new milk, for the benefit of the little ones who had a night ride all the way to Liverpool before them - somehow the barrier gave way (I should not be in the least surprised if the fatherly-looking policeman in charge of the wicket had a hand in the "accident") and the emigrants' friends and relatives made a sort of orderly stampede for the carriages, and immediately there ensued such a tremendous display of clasped hands between the platform and the doors and windows, accompanied by such a chorus of "God bless you," and "Keep your heart up, old boy," &c., &c., that one was compelled to fall back on the reflection, how immeasurably ample was the recompense that would reward this brief trial, in order to find courage enough to look on without blinking.

Two hundred and thirty-six this time rescued from that drear and hungry lane that seemed to have no turning, and placed on the highway to prosperity and independence, and all through the indefatigable efforts of the ladies and gentlemen who form the East London Emigration Committee. Their scheme is a very simple one, although its working involves infinite pains and discrimination. Its main principle is to assist to the healthy and remunerative labour fields of Canada, not those deplorably poverty-stricken ones who can no more exist without "help" in a new country than here, but those - and they may be counted by thousands in London - who, given a "wheel," will put their shoulder to it might and main, and never cease their endeavour till they have fairly lifted it out of the nick. They don't require much help; the worst of it is such a host of them require it. They come begging and praying to those who have the emigration scheme on hand; they send all manner o pitiful and imploring letters - manly, honest letters - promising to pay back faithfully all that is advanced to them, and all for the privilege of being "set on their legs again" and being allowed "another chance."

Lack of funds, however, prevented the sending a larger number than that already stated on the present occasion. The luggage had gone on before, and they were advised to be at the St. Pancras station of the Midland Railway at six o'clock, where their good friends and helpers would meet them. It was a strange sight to see them arrive. They were not like ordinary railway passengers of the third or any other particular class; they were not in the least like "excursionists." The fact of every party being distinguished by bearing a "bundle" slightly favoured the last-mentioned idea; but the said bundle, which at a cursory glance might have been mistaken for provisions, on closer inspection turned out to be something very different. The bundles contained something that was too precious to be entrusted to the dark and uncertain depth of a ship's hold, or something that would be wanted on the voyage. It would be difficult to imagine an assemblage so various in its component parts. There were women of every type -

little and big, old and young - and men to guess whose "calling," from their attire, would have been next to impossible. A few there were whose fustian nether garments still bore traces of their last job among oily machinery, bespeaking them out-o'-work millwrights and engineers; but the majority bore no trade mark at all.

They were one and all, however, stamped with what was much more to the purpose - an eager desire to get at some trade to make their mark on. There were big brawny men, with vast shoulders and fists of awful dimensions, loose about the throat, and clean cropped and smiling, who would insist that it was "Kennedy" they were going to, and who spoke of "Kennedy" as though it was an individual with whom they had been challenged to a friendly pugilistic encounter, and whom they already saw licked into submission after the first three rounds. There were tall men, who would have been big men had they not been half-starved, and who evidently had it in their minds to take it out of Canada as regarded that prime beef at two shillings a stone as soon as ever they found opportunity; but, little and big, they were all bright and cheerful, and confident of victory in the fight before them.

They had need be, were it only on account of the troop of children they took with them. I am sure that I am within the mark when I state that there were, without counting little babies in arms, at least fifty whose united ages would not equal that of a very old man; while the boys and girls of from five to twelve reckoned at least another fifty. And the little ones had not been forgotten. In many instances they had brought their dolls with them, neglecting them in their bewilderment, and carrying them by the hair, and head downwards by their heels; but good Countess de Grey had kindly provided for those who had no toys, and a big box was quite ready for unpacking when all were on board.

The tea went off quite as well as might have been expected; but, try as hard as we may, we shall never succeed in making of an emigrants' farewell party an occasion for genuine rejoicing, or a cheerful picture even. A deal of sunshine properly belongs to it; but, at present, it is too far away for its genial warmth to be felt to any very appreciable extent. It is all very well to be fortified by facts that have gone before and by argument that is sound and undeniable, but you will seldom or never succeed in persuading an Englishman when "good-bye" time comes that he should be downright glad to quit the old country. It is tolerably smooth sailing until the pinch comes. Five or six weeks since, in the midst of hopeless poverty and patient belief in better times to come, so thoroughly threadbare and worn out that it seemed a rotten stick indeed to trust to, when there dawned on the poor out-o'-work's family the blessed chance of presently taking ship and sailing away to a land of peace and plenty, there was joy enough. The only dread was lest this one should prove as delusive as the many other chances that had gone before it, and leave them in worse case than ever. When an incredulous mate asks poor Bill Jones does he really mean going if he can, Bill can find no other answer than a hearty guffaw at the possibility of the other's doubting it. "Will we go!" exclaims Bill. "Well, that's a rum question to ask a feller who hasn't handled a trowel since last November. Ask the missus whether we'll go or no." And Mrs. Bill, her motherly mind dwelling on the marvellous difference that meat every day at dinner, with milk plentiful as water, and flour dirt cheap, will be sure to make in her pale little brood of three boys and two girls, echoes her husband's sentiments right bravely. And when Bill, who has urged his suit with the "gentlemen of the committee," with the pertinacity of a Briton, returns home one fine day, the proud bearer of the document that entitles him and his family to a passage to Quebec on a certain day, fixed and settled, it is like nothing so much as merry Christmas with them.

But after that comes the sober time. The "perhaps they may go" has blossomed to a certainty that they are going, and with the dawning of this matter-of-fact realisation comes a reckoning up of who will be left behind. Nor is this all. It is imperative that they raise all the money they can towards assisting themselves, and to this end the home must be "broken up." The teeth of poverty have so long been nibbling at the said home that probably there is not very much left of it; but you may depend that the most cherished of the household goods are those that have stood out longest against sacrifice. But there is no help for it; they must go at last. To the unconcerned, the breaking up of a man's home is a very unpoetic performance. The broker lets fall no tear of sympathy as he surveys the shabby lot. He has nothing but a grunt of contempt for the cracked and odd china set, sacred to wedding days, christenings, and the like. He tears a rent in the treasured feather-bed, and plunges in his dirty fist to test the quality of the feathers, and is not a whit more favourably impressed with it when he is pridefully informed how many years it has been in the family. He has so little reverence for the mahogany tea-caddy that was poor mother's that he actually scrawls with a bit of chalk on the well-rubbed lid of it his meagre estimate of the worth of each item, and what the total is. It is nothing to him. He is used to the rooting up of homes, and thinks no more of the job than he would of rooting up parsnips.

It is a good thing when *that's* over. Now the cable is fairly slipped and they are launched, man and wife and children are drawn more closely together, and feel more than ever they did before how much depends on individual endeavour and a stanch resolution to stave off a faint heart. This is one of the chief secrets of the emigrant's doing in a strange land - one of the most valuable results of the emigration scheme. It is not so much the transplanting a human creature from a country where the only bread that can be spared for him is workhouse bread, to another country where butcher's meat may be bought at threepence a pound, and a wholesome, home-baked peck loaf is always assured him;-it is the lifting him out of the Slough of Despond, and planting his feet on ground whereon he may stand firm, and stand till the end of his days, if he will only try and steady himself. This is the grand object, and how seldom it fails of achievement let the thousands of letters from emigrants writing "home" attest The emigrant, provided always he is of the right sort, as soon as he lands in Canada feels like a man to whom a new lease of life has been granted. He is roused out of that apathy which surely comes of long grinding of his unfortunate nose against the grindstone of adversity, and the incessant repetition of that dolorous phrase. "Where's the use of trying?" And his wife catches his hopeful spirit, and he reads in the unwonted brightness of her eyes her reliance on him, and her steady determination to assist him heart and soul. So the battle is half won before the new land is invaded, and in every case, by this simple plan' of helping some poor willing fellow to help himself, a little more elbowroom is provided for the stay-at-homes of our own over-crowded labour market.

On another occasion I chanced to be down in Cambridgeshire when a batch of labourers belonging to a village there were on the threshold of being "off for Queensland." It had been resolved that there should be a turn out of the whole population, men and women, to accompany the bold adventurers to the railway station, and give them a hearty cheer by way of God-speed. I had never beheld anything like this. I had seen emigrants in plenty aboard ship in the docks, who were ready enough, nay, even eager to start on their voyage; but these were chiefly poor folks who had undergone all the weariness and worry and inconvenience which in such cases invariably attend every step of the way from the broken-up home to the shore-plank of the vessel that is to bear them away. It is something to have accomplished the tremendous undertaking so far, to say nothing of the comfort of companionship with a great many other people who are bound on the same journey; and it is no wonder if intending emigrants arrived at this stage show themselves cheerful enough to laugh and chat amongst themselves, and gather on the deck and wave their caps, and give out a lively hurrah as the ship steams out of harbour; but I was curious to see the sort of spirit in which our Suffolk son of the soil bade good-bye to the old spot and to friends and neighbours, and set out to seek his fortune.

I found, although it wanted yet two hours of the time when the train would be due, that the village was all astir. A Union delegate had come down to improve the occasion (the disagreement between Hodge and his master, the farmer, was then at its height) by holding forth to the locked-out brotherhood and sisterhood on the shining example the three married couples and the two single young fellows were setting them. It was an animated scene. It was on a green, close by the church and the white-dotted churchyard, that the gathering took place, and the spokesman, a thoroughly earnest advocate of emigration, had his appropriate stand on the great clumsy village-made box of one of the voyagers, inscribed with the owner's name and destination, together with the intimation that "this box will be wanted on the voyage. The men and women present must have numbered at least two hundred, and "blue" was as prevalent as at Hammersmith on a boat-race day. The women wore it in their caps and at their bosoms; the men wore bows and streamers of it in their billycocks; the babies in arms had the sleeves of their frocks looped up with the brave colour. The delegate had a choice rosette of blue, worn on the breast of his coat as a soldier wears his war medal. There was a great bundle like a bed in a canvas bag, labelled "Passenger for Queensland," and on this sat the three married women and their eight children all in a row in front of the speaker, all plentifully bedecked in blue, while their husbands and the single men were ranged on either side of him, and lustily led the cheering whenever the speaker made a point.

The women seated on the bundle were hardly as enthusiastic as their husbands. Of course, it was convenient to hold the meeting just by the church, for there everybody could see the time by the clock, and know to a minute when they ought to start to meet the train. The only drawback to this advantage was that the churchyard surrounded the church, and it might have been confidently wagered that of the three married couples and the single young fellows there was not one who had not kith and kin lying there, and to whom "Good-bye" must presently be said as to the rest. This, probably, was the reason why the three women all sat with their faces turned in that direction. It may likewise have accounted for the woman who had a baby in her arms hugging it and rocking it as though it was in pain, and she was trying to keep it from crying, though all the time the chubby little chap, with his dimpled arms decorated with the "stroikin' colour," was all alive, and crowing over her shoulder at the other youngsters.

He knew his business, that delegate, and, as the hands of the church clock moved on, his discourse grew more and more cheerful, and his pictures of the happy existence that awaited those who were immediately starting to enjoy it grew each minute more brilliant In his zeal for keeping up their spirits he made a little slip, which was convincing of the delicacy of the task he had undertaken. "It is no romance, my friends," said he; "it is a fact, as sure as that you now see the sun shining, that this other world of which I am speaking is, as compared with this place, a Paradise of plenty and contentment. There is no sorrow there, no tears, no heartache for the future, and the way to this glorious land, my friends, is that way;" and he pointed down straight to the grass at his feet. There was something in the gesture and the words that was so in unison with the thoughts of the women, whose gaze was directed towards where the grassy mounds and the white stones were, that two of them suddenly broke down and hid their faces in their handkerchiefs. The orator saw his error, and hastened to add that the glorious land he meant was Queensland, which was at the other side of the world, exactly beneath where they were then standing; but it required the telling of two or three amusing stories of English ploughmen who had become Queensland estate owners, and of old-country milkmaids, who ten years ago were expected to "bob" halfway to the ground when the squire's lady addressed them, and who were now the mistresses of farms ten times as large as any in Suffolk, before anything like the previous cheerfulness was restored.

It was not entirely restored when the delegate had spoken his speech, and wound up by hinting that, as it wanted but half an hour to the time when the London train might be expected they had, perhaps, better be moving. "Ay, ay! let's be moving!" everybody said, and proceeded to do so with such unanimous alacrity that it was clearly the one idea that anything was better than standing still and thinking of what was just about to happen. There was no lack of hands to carry the emigrants' luggage, or the emigrants' baby-in-arms, or even the two and three-year-olders who did not want carrying, and would rather have walked, but who nevertheless were shouldered by neighbours who had no other way at the moment of showing their kind regard for those they were on the point of losing. And so they went trooping up the street, the married couples arm-in-arm in front, with their friends about them, and the shouting, hooraying crowd bringing up the rear. As the station was approached, however, the hurrahs grew less boisterous and hearty, and occasionally there would elapse at least half a minute, when the whole company marched as silently as though they were at a funeral; then some one would cry out, "Keep it up, lads gi' em another - gi' em a rattler this time!" But when the rattler came there was a huskiness in the tone of the manly bass, and a dry shrillness in that of the womanly treble, that made anything but exhilarating music after all. I would have given a trifle willingly if at that moment the most tyrannical farmer in the county had passed that way. It would have done everybody an immense amount of good, I feel convinced.

In a few minutes the station was reached - such a little station that, though the station-master was willing to be as obliging as possible, he was compelled to shut the gate on half the ribbon-bedecked followers, who had to be content with looking through the palings. The pinch was coming now, and it was almost enough to make one laugh till the tears came to his eyes to witness the odd kind of hilarity that possessed the emigrants' old friends and neighbours, and by which they intended to make it appear what excellent spirits they were in, and how completely at their ease.

Then the station bell rang, and the London train came sliding in and stood still at the platform. Tides and trains wait for no man, and for a thoroughly unsentimental person commend me to a railway guard or porter. In a twinkling boxes and bundles, little and big, destined for Queensland, and addressed to that effect, are as unceremoniously hauled into the luggage van as though they were mere ordinary packages going no further than Shoreditch, and the three married couples and the children and the two single young men are hustled into the third-class carriage, which is of the cattle-truck order, and woefully suggestive of a hearse, and the two old women who are hanging on to the door handle, and whose puckered faces are now subject to singular spasmodic twitchings, are ordered to "stand away there," which they do, staggering to a seat where they are joined by other old women, and, turning their faces from the train, they rest their arms on each other's shoulders, and bow their grey heads, and all break down together. But this must not be; the men are not very blithe-looking just now, and blink and gulp as though this kind of thing were to them very distasteful physic, though taking their header's word for it, it was the very best for their complaint that could possibly be prescribed. "Stand afoor 'em!" "Stand afoor 'em!" the men whisper rapidly to each other as they range themselves in front of the weeping women. "Dang it! don't let 'em go away wi' such a last look as that!"

But the women are not to be baulked of a last look, and as suddenly as they were overcome they recover; and when the train moves, and there are handkerchiefs and faces white and wet at the window openings of that third-class carriage, there is a tremendous waving of "stroikin' colours" on the platform, and such a brave show of delight that, hard as it was to part, those who were left behind were, for their sakes, glad to see the others go, that one could but wish there was no make believe in it, but that it was entirely real.

"BUT don't you understand," remarked a farmer friend of mine, who like myself was present at the touching scene described in the preceding paper, "they wouldn't feel it as soon as other men?" They have not got any of those fine feelings and sentiments which those firebrands who are so constantly amongst them would persuade them they possess. They haven't got 'em, and they're better without 'em. Their fathers and their grandfathers were as good men as they are, and lived and died so, and they never troubled their heads about any sentimental rubbish. They knew their way to the fields on week days - that was enough for us - and they knew their way to the church on Sundays, and that was enough for them. That was all about it. It was the good old system, and they were satisfied with it, and they never would have rose against it of their own free will."

"But matters could not have arrived at their present pass without the free will of the men," I remarked.

"What I mean is," replied the farmer, "that they are naturally a dull folk, and that what these clever ones call 'progress' was until lately a foreign word to them, and that they'd fall to the ground again, like children in arms, if those who have taken 'em in hand were to slacken their grip on 'em. I don't ask you to take my word for it. Go amongst them yourself and hear them talk with one another, and you'll soon be convinced."

It was this last observation of the farmer that led to my finding myself a few evenings afterwards in the company of a little squad of agricultural labourers, who, as usual on Saturday night, had met at the ale-house of their village to indulge in the social glass and enjoy the pipe of pleasant companionship. When I first entered the room there were present but two persons, labourers both, and locked-out, as was denoted by the bit of "blue" twisted in the band of their caps. I was glad to make this discovery, as from their sitting apart and their apparent sulky demeanour towards each other, I at first imagined that they were not on speaking terms. There was nothing in their general appearance or the expression of their countenance that denoted them men "at play," or as having recently struck on a promising vein of good fortune, the yield of which at present was incalculable. They were dull-eyed and heavy-featured fellows, and sat with their broad backs bowed and their great fingers interlaced like men lost in profound meditation. I thought to myself: "That farmer did not know what he was talking about. These are men who may at one time have been stolid and stupefied by a long course of brutal treatment, but now they are awakening - slowly perhaps - to a sense of their position, and no doubt, when a few of them get together I shall hear much that is worth listening to." I was not kept long in suspense.

Presently one of the two elderly men took a pull at his beer, and remarked to his friend, "Summat haardish, beant it?"

On which his friend took a pull too, and gravely responded, "The waarm weather, I s'pose:" and both again interlaced their great fingers, and with downcast eyes puffed at their short pipes and said no more.

Then a third labourer made his appearance, likewise with a blue ribbon in his cap, and with a pint of beer he had got at the bar. As he entered he nodded and said, "Ee-yaar, then."

In response to that cabalistic salutation the other two responded, "Ee-yaar, then, Joe," and puffed a friendly whiff of tobacco smoke in his direction.

Now they'll begin to talk, thought I; but I was again mistaken. The third corner drank some beer, and, as he set the jug down, screwed up his eyes and whistled as he drew up one of his feet.

"Wut is it?" asked the man who had said that the beer was hard.

"Caarns - two on 'em, a saaft un and a haard un."

"Warnts cuttin', p'r'aps."

"Very loikely."

And then the third man lit his pipe, took a seat, heaved a deep sigh, interlaced his big fingers, and for at least five minutes nothing was heard but the ticking of the clock in the corner. It occurred to me that perhaps they were made shy of talking about what must be uppermost in their minds by my presence. For all that they could tell I might be one of the enemy; so, to set at rest any uneasiness that might exist in their minds, I remarked, "So you are making fair headway in these parts, I am told; you mean to win the day, it seems;" and as I spoke I touched the "striking colour" in the cap that was lying on the table.

"Ay, we're all union here, master," replied the man the cap belonged to.

"And union is strength," said the second man.

"That's what I say," added the third, and again the clock had it all to itself.

"The newspapers give famous accounts of the progress you are making," said I; "but I needn't tell you that; you have read all about it for yourselves, of course."

"Well, coorse we've heerd tell of it; we can't say ezactly that we've read of it, cos we caarnt read. We beant much o' scholars at newspaper print in these parts, master - at least I beant. I think that we three be all in dunce's class, hey, lads?" and at the joke there was a loud laugh, which brought in three other labourers who had been lounging at the door.

"What's goin' on?" one of them inquired.

"We was talkin' o' readin' and book larnin', Peter. We was born afoor the time when they coom in fashion, warn't we?"

"I loike they peapers that's got pictures in," remarked Peter, aged about 55; "they're a sight easier to understan' than readin'; no matter what it is, a murder or a accident, there it is all drawed out just loike as though you was there to see it."

"But," said I, "you couldn't have everything put in a picture like that; what is being said, for instance, all over the country at the present time about this lock-out, how could that be turned into a drawing?"

"It u'd make a rare loively picture, though," returned Peter, stirring his grey hair with a grin. "I'd bike to see a picture of they foamin' old varmers at Bury t'other day! Gushed if I wouldn't hey it framed and hung up over the foireplace."

Peter was evidently the recognized joker of the little community, and at this last utterance of his the others laughed till tears trickled in the furrows of their faces.

"But is it true," I presently inquired, "that there is no man amongst you" - there were eight by this time - "who is able to read?" To which question seven shook their heads, while the eighth modestly claimed to be able to spell out large print if time were allowed for the job.

"But we're not so much in the dark as our fathers and their fathers was, don't you think that, master!" one man remarked earnestly, and with something like a prideful twinkle lighting his dull eyes; "if we hed ha' been, p'r'aps we should never hey roused up to what we hev. We gets to know what they put in the newspapers, just as though we could read em with our own eyesight!"

"Indeed; how's that?"

"Why, through the youngsters, to be sure. They're got the pull o' we. They makes them barn and write and read, and them as can make out the print o' books can do likewise, by studyin' on it, wi' the print o' newspapers, and that's how *we* gets at it."

There was a dead silence after this, and the company regarded each other with something like consternation, and the speaker with reproach. It evidently was the general impression that he had let out a secret to a stranger which it would have been more prudent to have kept.

"And when we speak out that free, it isn't as though we wasn't talkin' wi' a gen'elman," one of them remarked.

"I am only too glad to hear that you are able to gain useful knowledge anyhow," said I; "the teaching your children get could not be put to a better purpose." Though at the same time I could not help marvelling how strange it was that spelling books in childish hands should have played so important a part in fanning into flame the smouldering discontent of generations. After this comparatively animated conversation we subsided once more to silence, and puffed at our pipes with a fixed regard each for his brown beer jug on the table. At last one old gentleman - a thatcher by trade, who sat in a corner by himself - startled the company by a strange noise he was making in his throat. It was at first supposed that he had been drinking and his beer had gone the wrong way, but alarm quickly gave way to amazement when it was discovered that the aged thatcher was chuckling with suppressed laughter.

"What's game amiss, Billy?" somebody asked.

"Oh, it's all right; don't mind me," said the thatcher. "On'y what you was jest now sayin' set me a thinkin' on what a wonderful thing book larnin' is. Why," continued the old man, suddenly growing grave, and bending forward over the table so as to get a better view of the company, "I heerd the other night, from the lips o' my young gran'darter, one of the most won'erful things as ever you heer tell on. She read it out of a book - not a true book, mind ye, but a book o' friction I think it was she called it; which makes all the difference. Well, theere was once a old woman as had a cow to sell, and likewise she had a lad what was name Jack. Well, Jack took cow to rnaarket to sell it, and goin' along, he met a old fellow who was - well, it was a long word, and Susy warn't quite sure about un - he was a negromuncher or summat o' that; anyhow he warn't no good."

By this time the seven grey heads at the other tables were all craned forward, while fourteen staring eyes were fixed on the thatcher.

"Mind ye," continued he, "it's on'y a story, mind ye; it ain't true, not a mite on it. Well, the old man, he sez to Jack, he sez, 'I'll gi' you these here beans for the cow;' and Jack, bein' a saaftish kind o' lad, took 'em for it, and away he goes home. Well, t'ould woman was in a bad way, as you may depend upon it; and fust she waarms Jack's jacket, and then she pitches beans out into back gaarden. Early next mornin', when Jack looked out of his window, there he sees a twinin' green ladder loike of green stalks a reachin' right out o' sight."

In short, what the old Thatcher had to tell, and what, with mouths agape and pipes grown cold in their nervous grasp, the seven middle-aged labourers for the first time in their lives listened to, was "Jack and the Beanstalk." Never did story-teller command a more attentive audience. They were with the thatcher every step of his way up the "ladder as high as the sky," and when Jack blew the horn that hung at the gate of the castle of the two-headed giant, every man wetted his lips with his tongue, as though in imagination he was taking a turn at it. When the giant's wife, after hospitably entertaining Jack, announced in a fright that her husband was coming; and the thatcher brought his fist down hard on the table, to imitate the giant's thundering knock at the door, the fourteen staring eyes winked again, and somebody said, "Stop jest haalf a minut," and everybody took a drink of ale to fortify themselves for what was to come. As the interest evinced by his friends became too painfully intense, the thatcher charitably paused to remind them that it was "on'y a story," and that they mustn't think that it really all happened. He found it necessary to repeat this caution more frequently as the story proceeded and its more sanguinary parts were reached, and with less effect, if one may judge by the fact that by the time

Jack, with the two-headed one in hot pursuit, stepped down the beanstalk into his mother's garden, and then, chopping away the root, brought the giant from the height of a mile or so, with a terrific smash to the ground, the hair of every man present was wet with perspiration.

    Nobody asked the thatcher any question when he had done. Every man relit his pipe and took a drink of beer, and composed himself to silent cogitation until the clock struck ten, when, with a nod for "good night, they took their departure; to dream, I have no doubt, of the redoubtable Jack, and wake in a sweat at the scratching of a mouse, exaggerated in the ghostly stillness to the noise of Giant Blunderbore coming head first down the chimney. Of course, I cannot say positively one way or the other. I may have hit on an exceptionally simple few, or it may be that those I have described are a fair sample of the agricultural labourer "at home" and left to himself. If the latter, one hardly knows whether to be glad or sorry at the prospect of his being admitted to the ranks of the intensely wide-awake and taught worldly wisdom.

I AM painfully conscious that, to all intents and purposes, I have "missed" a Derby. Not that I was absent from the great Epsom festival. I should much doubt if there were more than a very few individuals who passed a greater number of hours at the scene of the big race, or who, for that matter, were favoured with more excellent opportunities for enjoying the day's carnival thoroughly and completely. One of the treats I endeavour never to miss is on "Derby" morning to mount the hill which leads up to the breezy plain, while the earliest columns of smoke are lazily rising from above the roof of the Grand Stand, giving notice that the slaves of the kitchen which exists at the heart and foundation of the vast building in question have relit the fires, in order that they may renew their tremendous task of boiling, roasting, and stewing literally for the million; and while the fierce watch-dogs who keep watch and guard over the valuables contained within the colony of canvas houses on the hill are still tethered to the stakes beside the door, where they have all through the night been on duty; and while the footsore tramp as yet measures his dead length along the grass, with his old cap all twinkling with dew, as it lies just as it has slipped off his restless head, and with whole droves of little shiny backed ground-beetles curiously exploring his tattered exterior, and losing themselves in his tangled forest of hair.

Soon after five, I was astir and abroad, and it was not until after the great event of the day had been decided that I for the last time descended the hill, and, seeking my peaceful abode, vacated my walking boots in favour of more comfortable slippers; and yet I again repeat that, as regards the programme as set forth on the "card," I know but little more than the individual who did not stir out of his house at Pimlico or Peckham-Rye from morning until night. If I endeavour to recall any particular feature of the day's proceedings, or try to bring to mind any remarkable or peculiar circumstance connected with the sports, there rises before my mind's eyes a figure blotting out everything else. Neither an enormous nor a formidable figure, nor, excepting for its ghastly pallor, one very shocking to contemplate.

It is the figure of a baker - unmistakably a baker, though he appears abroad at an hour when all well-advised and business-minding bakers are hard at it in the depths of the bakehouse, and though his clothes have nothing of bakerish slovenliness about them and are quite free from dough stains. But he has the pale face of the maker of bread, and that spasmodic action of the nose as though he wanted to sneeze and couldn't, which I have no doubt is a habit contracted by the hard-worked operative in his constant endeavour to keep the fine flour-dust from entering his nostrils. Moreover, the baker is a tender-footed man, and walks with a bent knee and a half-shuffling gait, as though he were picking his steps over hot bricks. It was by these various signs that I recognised the person in question as being what he afterwards confessed to, before even I spoke to him. The way home for journeymen bakers who have been out at work all night is not commonly up Epsom-hill, however, and it was in this direction my baker was proceeding at the same time as myself. He was seemingly deeply engaged in the perusal of a sporting newspaper, as he walked, but when I came up with him he inquired of me, with startling abruptness, what time it was. I consulted my watch, and replied that it wanted a quarter to six.

"Nonsense," he said, with disagreeable sharpness; "you're too slow. I wouldn't carry a watch at all if it was of no use but to deceive people. You ought to know better."

His tone was so uncivil that I made no reply, but walked on. Before I had gone fifty yards, however, he keeping close behind me, Epsom Church chimed the hour I had told him. He muttered some inaudible words, and then, breaking into an odd kind of laugh, exclaimed,

"I beg your pardon; you were right, I find. It is not your watch that is slow; it is the morning. Infernally slow. It seems to me as though it was nearly a week since daybreak. How do you find it?"

It was evident that he was desirous of engaging in conversation, and, as we were going the same road and walking at the same pace, I had no objection.

"I hav'n't noticed that it is different from other mornings," I remarked; "besides, I was asleep at daybreak."

"I wasn't," he replied emphatically.

"Indeed; how was that?"

"Cursed if I know," said the baker (it will appear presently that he really was a person who followed this calling). "I'm hanged if I rightly know when I was asleep last - all sound and regularly asleep, I mean. Sometimes I think that *my* sleep has gone mad, it plays me such confounded tricks. I'm often afraid to shut my eyes and trust myself with it."

I noticed now more particularly how anxious and haggard he looked, and thought to myself "I should be sorry to be in your frame of mind, my friend."

Presently he abruptly asked, "what time is the race run?"

"The first race, do you mean?" I asked.

"The first race be hanged," was his impatient rejoinder; "the race, what time is that run?"

"About three o'clock, I believe."

He had his sporting newspaper rolled up in his hand like a truncheon, and he looked so vindictive that for a moment I thought he meant to make a blow at me with it.

"Upon my soul," said he, "you take it cool! About three o'clock! Something between five minutes past three and five minutes to four, I suppose. What do *you* care?"

"You've just hit it," said I. "I don't care a farthing. They may, for all the personal interest I feel in the matter, postpone the big race till five or six o'clock, if it suits them. I have no objection if they decide not to have it run until to-morrow, even."

He looked evilly at me, and laughed his brief ugly laugh again.

"You'll say next that you don't care which horse comes in first when the race is run," said he.

"It would be scarcely so true if I said that," I replied lightly, "for though I know nothing of racehorses or their merits, and never bet so much as a pound in all my life, I have a fancy that a certain horse will win the Derby this year, and though his doing so will not make a penny difference one way or the other to me, I should like to hear that it had won."

My companion's interest in the conversation instantly increased.

"How did you get your fancy?" said he, "somebody gave you the tip."

"No."

"Did you dream it - work it out in figures? Hang it, you know, there must be some groundwork for a man's fancying a thing!"

"There is none in my case, I assure you; it is absurd to say so, of course, when I cannot give any reason for it, but I think Atlantic will win."

That moment I would have given something considerable to have been able to recall my rash words, their effect on the man was so remarkable. His white haggard face became in an instant flushed and animated, and his dull eyes, that just now were expressive of nothing but aching for sleep, suddenly lit up brightly.

"Give me your hand!" he exclaimed, at the same time extending his own, with every finger of it twitching with excitement, "I'm as glad to have met you, 'pon my soul, I am, as though I had picked up a ten pun' note. Lord bless you, you are a trump, you are - have a drain of brandy on the strength of it."

And, still retaining my right hand in his, he made a plunge with his left at his coat-tail pocket, and withdrew therefrom a bottle half-filled with the liquor in question.

"Don't say no," said he, wringing my hand, and speaking with tears in his eyes, "take a pull at it, sir-a hearty pull, and I only wish it may do you as much good as your words have done me."

I was curious to learn more than I at present knew of my strange acquaintance, and, to humour him, took a sip at his brandy bottle; and no sooner were his hands released of it than, as though he were suddenly seized with the malady he had said afflicted his sleep, he burst into laughter loud and long, and, flinging his sporting newspaper down upon the grass, executed a diabolical dance upon it, and winding up by kicking it to the roadside and into the ditch, stamping his foot on it there with a vengeance that sent the black water squelching above the knees of his light-coloured trousers. I gave him back his brandy bottle, and, wishing long life to me he gulped down at least half-a-pint of its contents. Then he took my arm, and became confidential.

"You've told me something," said he, "or rather I might say you have prophesied something for me, and now I'll tell you something. *I* think that Atlantic will win the Derby. It isn't any what I may call supernatural fancy of mine, like it seems to be of yours, but I come at it weeks ago by plainly figuring it out. I was at Newmarket, and I saw the horse win the Two Thousand. I saw *how* he won it, and on the spot - leastways when I went to have a refresher at the Black Bear - I said to myself; 'Charley Watson' - that's my name, and I'm a master baker by trade" - I knew that he was a baker - "with a good business at Rotherhithe - 'Charley Watson,' I said to myself, now's your chance! Hit or miss, Charley, go in for that horse for the Derby, and you'll never be sorry.' 'It's the right string, Charley' -something seemed to whisper in my ear - 'pull it;' and I have pulled it," continued the sporting baker - bringing his hot, brandified breath within an inch of my ear to whisper it - "I have pulled that string to an extent that nobody dreams of, not even my wife, though she does keep the books, and in general settles with the miller herself. She don't know how I have been pulling the string, and she shan't know till I've landed my winnings, and then I'll astonish her. D'ye understand?"

I replied that I understood very well what a pleasant thing it was to win a lot of money, "But at the same time," said I, "on the other hand -"

But he impatiently interrupted me.

"There is no other hand," he exclaimed; "I was not quite certain of it before, and the fact is - this is quite between friends, of course - I had begun to get a little funky over it, and, on the extreme quiet, d'ye understand, raked up a bit more money - just a forty or fifty to hedge a little. I'm jolly glad that I didn't do it before I met you, and so I tell you, and here's jolly good luck to you," and the elated sporting baker took another taste out of the brandy bottle.

"But what difference will it make to you now that you have met with me?" I asked him - not, I confess, without a vague feeling of alarm.

"What difference!" he repeated, "why, this difference; I shall now put every shilling - every penny I have got - on Atlantic. Shouldn't I be a fool for flying in the face of my luck, if I did anything else? Why, man alive, it's all as plain to me as the pointing of a finger-post. Listen, now! I am not a knowing man as regards turf matters - not a very knowing man, perhaps I should have said. Indeed, somehow, Lord knows how, I got it into my head that there's nothing can beat this horse for the Derby. I've got the idea so firm in my mind that it don't matter to me what bad rumours there are about this horse. 'All right,' says I to myself, 'run him down as much as you like. I don't care; it will only make him come all the cheaper to me;' and I stick to him until the ugly stories that get put about begin to shake even my opinion, and I make up my mind, though loth to do it, to back water a little. Well, I come down here to do it, and then what happens? Why, just as though it was ordained, in a manner of speaking, that I shouldn't be spoilt of my chance, I fall in with you. Just at the nick of time I fall in with a gentleman I had no more idea of meeting than the Emperor of Turkey, and you reveal to me that something - you don't know what - tells you that Atlantic will win."

I attempted to say a word, but he would not hear it.

"Oh, it is a fact, you know," he continued, "you mightn't have meant to do it, but you did do it, and you'll excuse me if I keep you to it. I am not a superstitious man, but I am not such a fool as to miss a tip because it happens to come mysteriously."

It was in vain that I indignantly repudiated any capacity or intention of giving him a "tip;" the more I protested the more he exulted and rubbed his hands, evidently believing that I had inadvertently "let the cat out," and now was sorry for it. The least I could do was to make him promise that he would not put that fifty pounds he had with him, and which he confessed to having so much difficulty in scraping together, all in one lump on Atlantic.

"All right," said he, grinning, "I'll take your tip in that, too; I'll put it in small sums on all the races before the big one, and by that time, I feel sure of it, my fifty will be turned into two hundred at least, and I'll put all that on our fancy at ten to one, and there'll be another cool two thousand, out of which, mark me, I won't forget you, if you'll be good enough to look me up before the day is out."

I bade the desperate baker good morning when we arrived at the Downs, and was heartily glad to he rid of him. But, do all I could, I could not dismiss him from my mind. Maybe it was no fault of mine that in his infatuation for betting he had chosen to mistake me for a person possessing the gift of divination. Still, there was no getting over the fact that I had foolishly revealed to him what my fancy was, and I could have no doubt that it was his crack-brained intention to act up to the letter of his expressed determination. The reflection made me miserable till breakfast-time, and afterwards, as I rode up the hill again. One thing I had quite made up my mind to, however. I would have nothing more, under any circumstances, to do with the baker. It was very unlikely, in so great a crowd, that I should be able to find him, even if I tried, but of course I should not try, and, whatever the unhappy man's fate might be, I should be unaware of it.

But, alas! there were two to that bargain. The detestable baker was not to be denied. Despite my determination, I found myself on the heights of the Stand, furtively searching for a man with a light drab coat and hat, and with a gold horseshoe on a blue satin neck-scarf; in the crowd below, and was by-and-by successful. I don't know whether he was as diligently seeking me, but at all events our eyes met - the first race was over - and there he was, making the most extravagant demonstrations of delight, waving his hat, kissing his hand to me, and rapidly holding up and lowering and holding up again all his fingers and his thumbs three successive times, to make me understand, as I interpreted the movement, that he had already increased his store by thirty pounds. I nodded back with as indifferent an air as I could assume, and certainly experienced some relief of mind. But, do as I would, when my curious glance returned to the spot, there was the lucky baker, in such a perspiration of delight, that when he took off his hat to wave it to me I could see that his hair was dabbed close to his forehead and temples like sticking plaster. Again he made arithmetical signs with his digits, but I would not gratify him by looking. I almost began to wish that I was the baker, and to wonder if men ever really were racing prophets without knowing it.

And now the interval before the big race was nearly over, and once more I had the baker before me. His perspiration had evaporated, and he was in a dry white heat now; but that he considered he was about to be eminently successful in his speculations was unmistakable by the waving of his hat and the glitter of his eyes. This time he once more began to show me on his fingers what he had already won, but his patience failed him, and with a yelling laugh he commenced revolving his doubled fists rapidly over each other as the only way that occurred to him of adequately expressing the round sum he had netted. He did this, and then he gallantly waved his white hat once more, and made with his outstretched hands motions of swimming, and hurried away, by which I think he ingeniously intended to convey to me that he was now going in for the great Atlantic plunge.

    I believe that he made it. He had declared such to be his intention, and everything had favoured his intention. Nay, why should not I at once say that I know he made the plunge, for whose face was that but the wretched baker's, white as bleached flax, stark stricken, as with staring eyes and mouth agape, he makes out the numbers on the winning board, by which it appears that our mutual fancy was no better than third. I was afraid to catch his eye now, and peeped down at him from behind a corner pillar. This time he did not revolve his fists playfully. He carried them tight clenched and straight at his sides, and so he backed out of the crowd, still staring at the treacherous number board, and I saw him no more.

IT is now nearly six months since I first made the acquaintance of Master Jonathan Maxsey, and then under circumstances that were peculiarly unfavourable to that young person. It was inside one of the great prisons to be found at the outskirts of the metropolis, in which, for the crime of assaulting and robbing an errand-boy, Maxsey had been condemned to compulsory residence for the term of half a year. In company with the worthy Governor, I had been inspecting the gaol and its inmates, and it was not until our interesting tour had been brought, as I imagined, to a termination, that my friend remarked, "By-the-bye, there is one case you have not yet seen. Quite a boy he is, but a terrible fellow. I think it was never my misfortune to meet with such an instance of hopeless depravity. He has been here eight or nine times, and I don't know how often elsewhere. He is at present in the dark cell for insolence and throwing a plug of wet oakum in the face of a warder. You shall see him."

So saying, he led the way into a dismal corridor, at the extremity of which was a low-arched portal and a door. This the warder unlocked, and vanished from sight, and was presently heard to unfasten an inner door.

"Now, 99, turn out here; you're wanted;" and in a few seconds Jonathan Maxsey came shuffling out of the blackness behind him, and stood before us, blinking his eyes rapidly, as though, despite his over-hanging brows, the sudden light painfully affected them. He was not a prepossessing youth - squat-built and square-shouldered, with scarcely any neck, and an almost flat top to his otherwise bullet-shaped head, on which, although it was cropped as short as the gaol scissors could be made to bite it, the reddish brown hair lay as sleek as it does on the hide of dogs of a certain breed. He was said to be fifteen, but looked younger, and, in his tight-fitting suit of prison grey, his hands and feet appeared too large for his body. His legs were slightly bowed, as though in his tender years he had been used to horse-riding - an idea that was favoured by the stablish way in which he carried between his lips a bit of what at first sight looked like straw, but which turned out to be a splinter of wood torn from the hare unplaned "bunk" which in a dark cell is the sole article of furniture.

"This, I regret to say, sir," said the Governor, laying his hand with the keys in it on the sleek fiat head, "is really the most troublesome boy in the whole prison. I don't believe that he is fifteen years old yet, and to my knowledge he has been in this gaol eight times, and I shouldn't wonder if he is as well acquainted with other prisons. How many times have you been in trouble, 99?"

99 gave the splinter a reflective turn in his mouth, nibbled off a little bit, and spat it out ere he made answer.

"Oh, I d'n know; what's the good of keepin' count? - wo odds how many?"

"Twenty times at least, I'll be bound?"

99 drew the splinter into his mouth and chewed and swallowed it with a snort of sulky defiance.

"So you might be bound if you made it thirty times - five-and-thirty;" said he. "I ain't peritickler - wot's the odds?"

"Well, as I often tell you, 99, the way you seem bent on going can have but one ending. You'll think of what I tell you, and of the good advice you are now so wickedly deaf to, when it is too late."

At this 99 uttered a short laugh.

"All right, guv'nor; don't you bother. I'm good for the end, whatever it is. You won't funk me by talking about ends, so it's no use your tryin'."

"Get back to your cell, sir," said the Governor, sternly.

"Good evenin', gentlemen," remarked Jonathan Maxsey, with a grin and an easy nod; and next instant the double doors shut on him, and he was again buried alive in that vault of pitchy darkness. I saw the chaplain before I came away, and asked him to let me know how his unpromising patient, 99, progressed; but I heard nothing from him until a few days since, when I received a note, apprising me that no perceptible change had taken place in the young fellow in question, adding, however, that if I still felt any interest in him, he would be discharged from the gaol next morning at ten o'clock, and might be met at the gate.

Nothing could be more plain and simple than such directions, but a greater amount of moral courage was necessary in calmly following them than innocent folk may be aware of. The gaol in which Master Maxsey was confined is a mile or so out of town, and every "delivery day" the meetings at the "gate," or in its immediate vicinity, between discharged prisoners and their friends, are much more numerous than select. It is a queer sight. The rule appears to be not to let out the poor gaol-birds entitled to release all at one flight. The wicket gate swings ajar at intervals of three or four minutes, and they come scurrying forth in ones and twos. There is a broad space to be traversed between the prison portal and the main thoroughfare, and it is both curious and instructive to observe their demeanour on first stepping out again into the free world. In one respect only are they all alike, especially as regards the males. However old their clothes may be, they have in them that constrained and uneasy gait which commonly distinguishes wearers of bran-new suits, and they glance suspiciously at their coat-sleeves, and give their waistcoats a straightening pull, and look down on their trousers and boots as though not more than half satisfied that their moulting from prison plumage is perfect, and that a few of the old tell-tale feathers may not be still adhering here and there. Perhaps, as a rule, they are amazed that the dilapidated old things should turn out so fresh and smart-looking after their long rest in the gaol wardrobe; perhaps, on the other hand, having yearned for several months for this happy day, when they should, for the last time, strip from their bodies the hateful linsey-woolsey, and encase themselves in their own unconspicuous clothes of honest cut, they are a little disappointed at finding them so wofully seedy and unsuitable for a start in that amended and respectable life they have for so long been resolving to adopt.

One thing is certain, that if, as is asserted, cleanliness as a virtue ranks next to godliness, no body of men could appear as applicants for the renewed confidence of their fellow creatures with a fairer chance of success than these released prisoners. It must, I think, be some peculiar kind of soap with which the gaol-bird performs his final ablution before his emancipation. No common sort with which I am acquainted is capable of imparting such a peculiar chilblainish polish to the ears, or of making the entire countenance appear as though the outer skin had been delicately removed, leaving a surface so pink and tender-looking that the mere act of winking might cause it to crack like an over-ripe plum.

It must be a trying time that getting over the open space between the prison gates and the common street pathway, where, if a man have a mind to, he may speedily be lost in the crowd. In its way, the sensation must be something like that of "walking the plank" aboard ship - just a few steps, and then you go souse into that teeming sea from which you were stranded and left so dismally in the lurch six months ago. It is easy enough to separate the black sheep - the jet black animals, who no more than a blackamoor may be scrubbed white - and the misguided sheep who has strayed from the honest flock, perhaps only this once in all his life, and would give his ears to get back again. Their way of crossing the before-mentioned open space is entirely different. The sheep whose dye is ingrain and to the roots of its wool leaves the prison with pretty much the same air as a visitor from the country quits the train, and with easy confidence casts about him on the platform for those kind friends who he knows will be there to greet him and convey him straight to the refreshment room. He carries himself with a make-believe easy swagger, and generally with his hands in the pockets of his trousers, excepting when he releases one of them to wave a friendly salute to a faithful ally waiting in the distance. Just the opposite is it with the not utterly lost sheep. As soon as the grate opens to him he would like to take to his heels and run with all his might. He would do so if it were night time, but he don't know who may be looking, and so the next best thing is to endeavour to pass as some workman of honest occupation employed to do a little job within the spiked walls; and it is easy to understand with what delight this sort of man at that moment would exchange the painful cleanness of his face and hands for a whitewash-splashed visage, or a sprinkling of sawdust and a ladder to carry.

It must not be imagined, however, that while with the rest of the porters at the gate, or loitering about the lamp-post at the corner, or peeping over the inner shutter of the beer shop on the opposite side of the way, I am noting these interesting objects in forgetfulness of Master Jonathan Maxsey.

Here he comes at last.

As he quits the prison gate he raises his greasy old cloth cap and bows politely, but with a grin, to the warder on duty - who grins too, and says something which causes Master Maxsey to laugh outright - and then softly whistling, with a brisk step he crosses the open, and reaching the street pavement halts there and looks to the left and to the right, and across the road. There was no fear of my mistaking him, though he was so differently attired when last we had met. He was not conspicuously shabby or ragged. He wore a sort of cutaway black coat, with ample side pockets, and a gay coloured waistcoat, and a bright silk neckerchief of such bulky dimensions that the lobes of his great clean ears rested on it at the sides. His trousers were tight in the legs, and he wore light shoes. There, however, were the same quick, deep-set eyes, the same never-ceasing nibbling at his under and upper lip; and there, though very little was visible of, it outside the close-fitting cap, was the sleek foxy-brown hair close clipped to the skin. I war glad to perceive that he looked up and down the street in vain, though, judging from the scowl that gradually grew on his- bright face, it was evident that he had expected someone who was not there.

The business I had been deputed to negotiate with Master Maxsey was of a nature that might be best attempted without the presence of a third person - especially if that person happened to be one of Master Maxsey's own sort, anxious to welcome that young gentleman back to the lawless life from which, for six months, he had been estranged. After lingering yet a little longer, he turned his face in an easterly direction, and walked away so rapidly that we were nearly a quarter of a mile distant from the prison before I overtook him. He changed colour somewhat, and came to a dead halt as I pronounced his name. One swift glance, however, convinced him that his sudden terror was groundless, and he remarked savagely,

"What do you want a follerin' me for? What's your game?"

"To do you a good turn, if you have no objection. I suppose that you are not overwhelmed just now with friends who will take the trouble to run after you for that purpose?"

"Have you been a running after me?" inquired Master Maksey, in tones of disgust.

"I came after you as you left the prison," said I; "we have met before; do you recollect me?"

I could tell by the twinkle in his quick eyes that he did so as I spoke, but, folding his arms, he affected to scrutinize my features reflectively for at least half a minute, at the expiration of which, and with startling suddenness, he seized my hand and shook it warmly.

"To be sure I recollect you," he exclaimed, with all the heartiness of an old friend. "You come to see me that evenin' when I was in the coal-scuttle; you come along of Old Crabshells. 'Ow are yer?"

I was hardly prepared for this affectionate recognition, but though I strongly suspected its genuineness, I accepted it with the best grace at my command. At the same time, however, I informed him that he was mistaken as to the person who had accompanied me on the painful occasion alluded to - that it was the Governor himself.

"It's all the same; it's the same party," responded Master Maxsey, cheerfully; "we calls him Old Crabshells, because of the uncommon large size of his shoes. But about that there good turn you was speakin' about just now."

"First of all," said I, as we crossed to the quiet side of the road and walked along together, "let me ask you if you recollect the few remarks the Governor addressed to you - you know when - and the answers you made?"

"Let me see," murmured Master Maxsey, communing with himself; "what was it I'd been up to?" and then the pleasant recollection suddenly flashing to his memory, he broke into a fit of laughter loud and long. "Oh, I know now!" he exclaimed; "it was for shying a lump of wet oakum at the redraw" (back slang for warder) "Jolly lark it was! 'You're a quarter of a pound short,' he ses, when he come to weigh my day's dose what I'd been picking in my cell. 'Where is it, yer wagabone?' ses he. 'Find it hinstantly.' 'Oh, please, sir,' I ses, 'it was only a hard bit wot I put in my slop-bowl to soak; and here it is, sir. P'r'aps yer might tell me if it do well enough now, sir?' and turning round sharp, I slapped the whole lot in his blessed eye!"

Master Maxsey wriggled in mirthful convulsions, and laughed until tears ran down his cheeks. This was far from encouraging; but I was under a promise to a philanthropic friend, and I resolved to execute my mission.

"Now let us talk soberly and quietly for a few minutes. You are at liberty once more, Maxsey. What are you going to do?"

"How do you mean?" he asked, warily.

"Have you come to the sensible resolution of keeping at liberty should a fair chance offer itself to you?"

He appeared to consider the question for several seconds, and then replied,

"Oh yes; that's right enough. I mean to look arter all the fair chances that comes in my way, and I mean to keep my liberty as long as my luck lasts. No fear, I ain't so fond of the steel (prison) as all that."

"I should say not. You need not set your foot inside a prison again if you will take hold of and stick to the chance I bring you. You appear to be a strong lad, and you are not afraid of work, I suppose?"

"Course I can work when I'm put to it," returned Master Maxsey, hesitatingly "what kind of work was you thinkin' of guvner?"

"Well, to come to the point," said I, "there is a friend of mine who, knowing all about you, would be willing to take you, and feed you, and lodge you, and teach you a trade, and if you could but find courage to be industrious, and behave yourself, by the time you are one-and-twenty he would make a bright man of you. The trade you would have to learn is that of a tanner."

"Ah! how much a week did you say?" Master Maxsey remarked, after a pause.

"Well, at first some trifle of pocket-money, I dare say; but not very much."

"Ho. And how many hours a day?"

"I can't say exactly; ten perhaps."

"And that's what you call doin' a cove a good turn, is it?" and he turned up the tip of his plastic nose scornfully.

"As good a turn as any one in the world could do for you," said I.

"Then wot *I* got to say is this," returned Master Maxsey, signifying by the abrupt manner in which he came to a standstill that he wished the conference to be terminated then and there - "wot I got to say is this: You and that there tanner wots your friend can keep your jolly good turn, as you calls it, and tie yerselves together with it, and jump over London Bridge. I don't want it; not while I can prig enough in any a hour, p'r'aps, to keep me for a week. Ten hours a day at 'tannerin for a bit of grub, and a fourpenny lodgin'! Not if I knows it. Why, it 'ud be wus to me than a summery conwiction!"

And, too indignant even to bid me good day, the awful young thief turned abruptly into Church-street, Shoreditch, and was quickly lost to view.

MR. M'ROOSTER may feel slightly vexed with me for what he may regard as an unscrupulous advantage taken of information imparted to some extent in confidence. Mature reflection will, however - or, at least, I hope so - convince the enterprising tradesman in question that, so far from being injured by the publicity which is here given to his friendly communications, he may be greatly benefited thereby.

His object in advertising in the newspapers that his business was in the market could only have been to draw the attention of all whom it might concern to the fact. For obvious reasons, the terms of his notification were brief. Advertising is expensive. All that Mr. M'Rooster made known was that, for reasons which could be satisfactorily explained, he was desirous of disposing of the extremely profitable and rapidly-increasing credit drapery business of which for many years past he had been the proprietor. "The essential features of this snug concern," so read the advertisement, "are such that they need only be made known at once to secure a purchaser. To a man of moderate capital and of energetic and active habits the realization of a fortune in a few years is certain. There are at present over seven hundred customers on the books, many of ten and fifteen years' standing, and well secured by being employed in respectable firms. Weekly collections guaranteed to be over sixty pounds. Terms and full particulars can be obtained on application to -----," &c. Now, it is not unreasonable to assume that, could Mr. M'Rooster have done so without any additional expense, he would gladly have printed the said "full particulars" with the other matter, and so, without further trouble have secured that energetic and active customer he had in his mind's eye. It is to be hoped, if the "snug concern" is still in the market, that the following account of it - which shall cost Mr. M'Rooster not one shilling - may lead to its speedy disposal.

Doubtless to my peculiarly energetic aspect was due the frank and cordial reception accorded me by Mr. M'Rooster when I called on him to keep the appointment previously arranged. I was a few minutes late, and my friend was standing at the door of his abode, evidently looking out for me. I was glad of this. Had I seen Mr. M'Rooster's house, and not Mr. M'Rooster, it is not impossible that my first impressions would have done him injustice. A man who has more than seven hundred customers on his books, and whose takings exceed sixty pounds a week, usually makes more show of worldly prosperity than is compatible with an abode in a side street in the vicinity of Lambeth-walk, and bounded on either hand by a chandler's shop and a greengrocer's. No shop, no display of that enormous stock of stuffs and calicoes for which it was the delight of Mr. M'Rooster to give those who dealt with him credit - no sign, indeed, of his being engaged in a business of any description, excepting a wire blind in the parlour window, on which, in faded letters, appeared the words, "M'Rooster; Credit Draper."

But there was that in Mr. M'Rooster's appearance which was calculated to convince the most sceptical of the truth of his statements. It was evident at a glance that he was born to the credit business; if he had embarked in the ready-money drapery trade, he would probably have sunk in the course of a few months to a condition of commercial idiocy, and pined to death as men are said to starve who are confined for any length of time to a diet of plain bread. He was every inch a tallyman - tall and slim, with a genteel figure, but a keen-looking blade, with painfully sharp cheekbones and cold, quick eyes for calculation, and a nose which seemed to have enlarged under severe pressure of mental arithmetic, and to have morbidly assumed the shape of an unfinished number 6; but, withal, he was undoubtedly a man who, amongst a certain class of the more impressionable sex, would be voted a "fascinater." He seemed to have the power at pleasure of making that shrewd, pocket-picking expression retreat out of his eyes, just as a cat's claws retreat, leaving them simply nice eyes with an engaging twinkle in them. There was fascination, too, in the silken sheen of his scented but carefully combed sandy whiskers, in his wide mouthful of white teeth, and even in the curly brim of his glossy hat. But, of course, it was not his purpose to waste his wiles on me. It was understood that I should first glance at the "stock," and then accompany him on his round.

"Come in!" said my obliging friend briskly. "I drive round to-day, because I have got some heavyish things to deliver; besides, it will be more convenient for you, since you wish to see as much as possible in one turn."

"Is it an extensive round that you make to-day?"

"Pretty fair. I reckon to make nearly three hundred calls, which doesn't mean three hundred houses, bear in mind. It's where you get three or four customers in the same house that you do good and easy business. School business we call it, and it's the best of all, as you'll find if you mean to go into it."

"How is it the best of all?" I asked.

"In this way," returned Mr. M'Rooster, promptly - and as he did so making sixteen of his nose by laying his long forefinger close alongside it - "It's quite a family party, d'ye see, these first, second, and third floor lodgers; and the men very likely work all in the same shop. Well, they don't mind obliging each other; Joe and Bob will be security for your little account for Bill, and Bill and Bob will do the same for Joe, and so on all round. It don't seem that such a mutual give-and-take can affect them more than the giving of two sixpences for a shilling; but see where it lands you! It makes your money as right as the Bank. They look each other up on collecting days as sharply as though they were paid for it - not out of fear that you may be let in the hole, but that they may. But that's only one of a whole bagful of tricks I can put you up to if we come to terms.

I was by no means awe-stricken by the dimensions of Mr. M'Rooster's "warehouse." It was the front room upstairs, and though the shelves with which the walls were lined were closely stocked with calicoes and women's dress stuffs, and shawls and mantles, and boots and shoes, and with all manner of ready-made articles of wearing attire, while piles of carpets and rugs extended from the floor to the ceiling, still it appeared but a small stock on which to rely for the demands of seven hundred customers. I remarked on this to Mr. M'Rooster.

"That's one of the beauties of the business," replied he, cheerfully; "it's all in a nutshell. You don't require an extensive - that is to say, a various stock. When you've once got 'em they are glad to take what you offer 'em. I don't stand any nonsense with my customers about fashions, and colours, and patterns: 'There's the best I can do for you, take it or leave it;' and when, in a manner of speaking, they're standing still for a gown or a coat to put on, and they are depending on me for it, why they're bound to take what's offered to em. You see, it simplifies the whole business, and makes one's buyings, as well as one's sellings, so much easier."

"And as regards the quality of the goods?"

"Well, that's a question more easily asked than answered," returned Mr. M'Rooster, "though it comes as easy work as putting on an old glove when once you are fairly in the groove. It's this way, as a rule, however. Your small goods, such as stockings, and boots, and shoes, and stay, and stuff for men's shirts, and your calicoes, are bound to be of tidy quality. It's wise I think to stretch a point, and let them be of real good material, for it is this class of goods that have got to stand hard wear, and are, so to speak, in hand, and under the eye. Now, it's different with the large goods - the goods which run into money - silk, or expensive stuff for gowns and mantles and shawls. Black suits for men, again, you can stick it on in them things deep as you like almost."

"But are they not in hand and under the eye as well as goods of the other sort?"

"Certainly not," rejoined Mr. M'Rooster, smiling at my ignorance; "three-parts of the time they are lying at the pawnbroker's. You may rely on that. I should say now," continued Mr. M'Rooster, with the air of a man who had long studied the matter, and knew all about it, "that in nine cases out often those who get their best clothes on tally carry them to the pawn-shop. It stands to sense that they should do so. They're hand-to-mouth people, every one of them, and after a week or two they're sure to be hard up for the week's instalment: then what's more proper than that the article that has got 'em into the fix should be used to get 'em out of it; it comes as natural as basting a joint with its own fat."

"You being the joint," I remarked facetiously.

"And have an aversion to being done too brown," said Mr. M'Rooster; at which we winked at each other and laughed, like the two knowing dogs we were.

"But it's a fact, though," he presently resumed, gravely. "It is the commonest thing in the world to hear one say, 'Well, to be sure, M'Rooster does charge a high figure, but what he sells is of the very best, and lasts for ever almost;' and well it may, when the coat or the best gown, or whatever it may be, is lying in the pawnbroker's drawers from· Monday morning until Saturday night every week of the year. But it's a pleasant delusion, and hurts nobody."

Mr. M'Rooster'S "trap" was a sort of long-bodied phaeton, and as at this moment his boy looked in to say that it was at the door and all ready, we bestirred ourselves for starting.

"This South London beat is the heaviest I have," my friend remarked, as he took a stout memorandum-book and a portable ink-holder from a desk; "I've got over seventeen hundred pounds on it."

"And what do you calculate on collecting to-day out of that sum?"

"Well, according to Cocker, I ought to get a twentieth part of the whole," said Mr. M'Rooster, pleasantly. "The system is a shilling in the pound weekly payment; but, as I needn't tell you, it doesn't average sixpence. I shouldn't wish it to. If they were able to pay regular, you would lose your hold on 'em in a very short time."

The way we took, the boy driving, was towards Kennington, and our first halt was at the commencement of a long street, on either side of the way of which were decent-looking six-roomed houses.

"This isn't a bad bit," remarked Mr. M'Rooster. "They are nearly all -----'s men, the great engineers, who live in this street."

"But I should have thought that such men earned good wages?"

"So they do-first-class; seven and eight shillings a day, and never out of work. I've got customers amongst this lot who owe me as much as twenty pounds. They will dress, no matter what it costs; they don't mind."

We left the trap at the corner, and presently Mr. M'Rooster knocked at a door. Had he been the family doctor, he couldn't have walked up the passage and opened the parlour door with less ceremony.

"Mother in?"

"Mother's upstairs, sir," said the little girl.

"Then tell her to come downstairs," returned the tallymam with an air of severity; "she didn't pay last week."

The little girl went away, and soon returned with a dogs-eared receipt book and four shillings. The book was of the penny memorandum kind, and contained perhaps twelve leaves, and Mr. M'Rooster invited my attention to the fact that every leaf excepting the last one was filled with receipts for weekly payments, ranging from three shillings to seven.

"You tell your mother from me," said Mr. M'Rooster, "that I shall expect six shillings next week, and that I shan't take less." And he ungraciously signed for the four shillings, and we departed. The next four calls brought us in fourteen shillings, and then my companion beckoned the trap down the street to a house where there were some goods to deliver. It was the most slatternly abode we had yet called at, with half-dressed, untidy-haired children in the passage, and peeping down from between the banisters; there was also a powerful odour of rum when the parlour door was opened.

"Risky lot this," whispered Mr. M'Rooster - "four-year-old customers, but obliged to get your money as you can catch it. Stick it on according, of course."

And then in came the female head of the household, and, the balance of eleven shillings due on the last tally debt of ten pounds odd having been duly paid, the big brown paper parcel the boy had brought in was unstrung, and its contents discussed. No wonder that Mr. M'Rooster valued his business so highly. Had we been in the remotest colony in the Brazils, he could scarcely have demanded a higher price for what he had to dispose of. I do not lay claim to a profound knowledge of the value of drapery goods, but cannot think that I am wrong in deeming tenpence halfpenny a yard an exorbitant price for ordinary calico, and that five and ninepence a yard was not cheap for French merino, albeit it was of double width and war ranted a last colour, and that a pair of black cloth trousers and a waistcoat to match, fit for a working man's Sunday wear, might be obtained for a trifle less than two pounds eleven and sixpence. The gem of the purchase, however, was a black silk mantle, trimmed very elaborately, for which Mr. M'Rooster demanded the modest figure of three pounds seventeen. But it did not seem to matter much what the price of the article was; the customer's main desire appeared to be to renew an account that should be in amount at least equal to the last she had liquidated; and I was even yet more surprised when I presently discovered that the woman was perfectly aware that she was being scandalously overcharged. "I shall want you to make me out two bills as usual, Mr. M'Rooster," said she.

"Very good, ma'am," he replied, as though such matters were quite in the ordinary way of his business.

"You see," said the customer, turning to me as though she had remarked the surprise depicted on my countenance, "my husband is such a close-fisted man that if he was made aware that these few things cost nearly eleven pounds he would storm the house down, and it is only by making him believe that the tally goods are as cheap as may be bought for ready money, that he will let me run up a bill at all. Not that it makes any difference to him, for of course it all comes out of my housekeeping money. This silk mantle, now, he would think dear if he thought it cost more than a pound."

"Oh, come, come, ma'am," remarked Mr. M'Rooster, pleasantly, "you won't make us believe that he is such an ignoramus as that. I shall set down the mantle at twenty-five shillings, anyhow, in the bill that's for him."

And in "the bill" that was for the husband the account was. similarly falsified in every particular, the trousers and waistcoat appearing as having cost one pound twelve and sixpence, the French merino three-and-six a yard, &c. - the total, instead of eleven pounds, being a little over six. I could not help remarking to my ingenious companion when we had quitted the house that I thought the little game I had just seen played a somewhat dangerous one.

"For whom?" he asked, in some surprise.

"For you."

"For me! Why, it's as common a game as marbles," returned Mr. M'Rooster, with a laugh; "we couldn't do without it."

"But," said I, "supposing that the woman should turn round and declare that the bill for the lesser amount is the correct one, and decline to pay you any more."

"Well, of course, it can't be said to be impossible," he replied pleasantly, "but it's highly improbable. Lord help you, it's as good as a ten-pound security to go halves with her or any other woman in a secret that's hid from the husband. She dare not let the cat out of the bag, my dear sir. The men don't half like chaps like me" (and then he fondly caressed one of his whiskers) "calling at the house when they are away from it, and if it came out that there had been any mixing up between us and agreeing together to humbug the husband - whew! No, no, it wouldn't answer her purpose. It's a perfectly safe card to play, take my word for it. Besides, we all do it more or less. It don't do to be squeamish in these times."

I must confess that I had it in my mind to take leave of Mr. M'Rooster on the spot, but his last words fortified me, and I resolved, for the sake of the knowledge to be gained, to tolerate his edifying companionship a little longer. It was not long ere I made the discovery that his system of business comprehended a series of dodges quite as objectionable and as dirty as that which had caused my first qualms. His "instalments" he would have, by hook or by crook, wherever it was possible. I found that in many instances he had knowingly accepted, to the original agreement to pay so much a week, the wife's forged signature of her husband's name, and in more than one case, by bullying and threatening the terrified woman that he would send his lad to where the husband worked there and then, and tell him all about it, induced her to go and borrow the required money of a neighbour. But a much commoner dodge was for him, when the money was forthcomiug reluctantly, to say,- "Look here, now, I don't want to be hard on you. You can't spare the three shillings, I can see. Give me one for my trouble of calling, and see what you can do for me next week," and the temptation was often too great to be resisted, and Mr. M'Rooster walked off with the shilling, giving no receipt for it.

"Cheese-parings," the enterprising tallyman called these, and by the time his day's work was done he must have had quite a waistcoat-pocketful of them.

It was marvellous, considering how little of his business was of a simple, straightforward character, what a tremendous amount of it he contrived to get through between ten in the morning and four in the afternoon. To be sure, he had a few extra good customers, who paid him as much as ten and fifteen shillings by way of instalments, but I had no idea of what was the fact, that, cheeseparings included, Mr. M'Rooster had in the course of the day extracted from the three hundred and seventeen customers on his South London beat the considerable sum of thirty-three pounds.

THAT there is a "season" for oysters, for operas, for sea-bathing, for hopping, and a score of other of our social institutions, every one knows; but it was not until very recently that I made the discovery that there is a fixed time of the year when the "cadging" season commences, and when the hundreds who are addicted to that humble, though lucrative, branch of industry set out for the commencement of the winter campaign. It was quite by accident that I made the discovery. I need not trouble the reader with details of why and wherefore; but a few evenings since, happening to be in that shady locality known as the "Mint," Southwark, a public house, bearing the sign of the Black Boy, came in my way.

Now the Black Boy has a reputation of a sort, and having at all times a hankering for strange fish, the temptation to halt, to cast a line in its murky waters for a few minutes, was irresistible. There was no danger in doing so, the Black Boy being one of the most strictly conducted public-houses in the parish. Were it not so, it would not be permitted to exist for a single day. All manner of questionable characters resort thither, including many who rely for a livelihood on their dexterity as pickers and stealers. It must not be inferred from this, however, that the Black Boy is a den where congregate grim-muzzled ruffians, with close-fitting peaked caps pulled close down on their bullet heads, while their ample coats have cunning inner pockets, in which are stowed the life-preserver, the "jemmy," the skeleton keys, the matches, and the bit of candle, all so necessary to the successful prosecution of business.

It must not be supposed that the Black Boy is a house where villains of this breed meet and arrange their midnight maraudings, or that it is even a likely place for a desperado fleeing from the huntsmen of Scotland Yard to seek and find safe harbourage until the ill-wind has blown over, and the huntsmen are put off the scent. They are but a poor twopenny lot of robbers, lean, hard-worked and half-starved wretches, these Black Boy revellers, on whom the very beggars and cadgers, who are our landlord's best customers, look down with pity. They are the most meekly enduring mortals it is possible to imagine. There are men who are never worth their salt, as the saying is, whatever trade they may turn their hands to, and so, without doubt, it is in the profession of thieving. No matter though they serve the full term of apprenticeship, they turn out no better than cobblers, and all their industry is barely sufficient to provide them bread to eat and a shirt to wear. The marvel is that they are not driven back to honesty in sheer desperation. It was curious to observe the abject cringing with which these petty thieves, as they entered the Black Boy to make their way to the common room, saluted the young lady behind the bar, and the haughty and disdainful nod of the head with which she acknowledged the act of homage. The very potboy tyrannises over them, and, I have no doubt, conveys to them in the tap-room, instead of the sixpenny they have ordered and paid for, common fourpenny, and pockets the twopence.

Hawkers, as well as cadgers and beggars, swarm in the vile courts and alleys of this delightful neighbourhood, and, like them, "drop in" of evenings to partake of the social glass and discuss the state of trade. At the time I entered the doors of the Black Boy several customers of ungenteel aspect were crowding about the dingy narrow bar, and amongst them two individuals who, judging from the baskets by their sides, were of the hawking class. At first sight the said baskets appeared as though filled with huge crimson sausages, but a closer inspection showed that they were what are known as "window-bags," a sort of long pocket, made of red cloth and stuffed with sand, used as draft excluders for ricketty casements. The men were engaged, as they partook of rum out of one measure, in discoursing on the slackness of trade. "It's owing to the back'ardness of the season, I s'pose," one remarked; "it's the most back'ard season, bust it, as ever I knowed. It was always understood that when the leaves fell off the trees sandbags would sell, but, bust 'em, it ain't so this ear. A man might as well hawk horniments-for-yer-fire-stove or ketch-'em-live-oh's, and think to sell 'em."

"Oh, it'll be all right by-and-by," returned his more hopeful comrade; "it's the wind what's agin us. What *we* want is a out-and-out cuttin' east wind-a regler marrow freezer. Lord send that one would spring up to-night, and last a whole month. I'd give 'arf-a-crown to see it. Here's t'-ords it;" and so saying, he finished his rum at a draught.

I was standing within two yards of the man, and while as yet unrecovered from my amazement that a native of a country where neuralgia and rheumatism are so well known could find it in his heart to utter so diabolical a wish, a lanky cadaverous-looking individual at my elbow remarked to another with whom he was drinking, "There you are! Now you hear it from somebody else p'r'aps you'll believe it."

"Yes; but his 'lay' ain't like jours. You ain't got nothing to sell."

"It don't make no difference," urged the cadaverous man, who was a dirty, lazy-looking wretch, "it all hangs on the same hook. I'll turn out sharp enough when the weather breaks, no fear; and so'll the missus."

"Well, weather break or not, you don't lodge at my place after to-night," returned the other, who was more decently dressed than the dirty man. "You know very well that I've trusted you for grub as well as lodging all along on the strength of your turnin' out at the reglar time, and here's nearly the end of the third week in October, and you ain't turned out yet - you, who can turn your eight and nine bob a day, too! I feel regular ashamed of yer."

"And so I can earn it, if you give me the right sort of weather," said the dirty man, sulkily, but with some pride in his tone, too; "but what can a feller in my line do while it keeps so thunderin' fine?"

"Well, I've had my say," remarked the lodging-house keeper, "and I'll keep my word."

The dirty man pondered the matter for a few moments, with his elbows on the counter, and his ragged sleeves dabbling in the spilt liquor. Suddenly he seemed to make up his mind.

"Look here," said he; "stand another quartern, and lend me a shillin' for a startin' drain, and me and the old woman'll start in the mornin', rain or shine."

"That's a bargain," replied the man who let lodgings. And a shilling changed hands, and the gin measure was promptly refilled.

"And what does all that mean?" I whispered my unobtrusive but terribly knowing companion.

"Simply this," he replied, laughing; "it means that that rascal and his wife are street singers and cadgers of the sort known as 'mud-plungers.' Fine weather don't suit 'em; they can't come out strong enough. Give em a soaking wet day, with the mud over their naked toes, or a freezing cold one, with a good breeze to set their rags flying, and I'll be bound that they make as much in a day as the sum you heard mentioned, and more, too. This 'second summer' that we've had since the middle of September has played the deuce with chaps of his breed. Put 'em back a fortnight, at least."

"Is there a regular time of year, then, for street-singers and cadgers to commence business?"

"Yes; the middle of October is the time."

"And you think that this fellow will keep his word, and make a start with his wife to-morrow morning?"

"I have very little doubt about it. He's in debt at the place where he lodges, as you heard him say. That's his landlord he was talking with. Oh, yes; if you were coming this way about ten in the morning you'd see the precious pair going to work."

I at once resolved that I would be coming that way in the morning, and, if I was so fortunate as to catch my mud-plunging friends going to work, to do my best to keep them in sight for a while, with a view to ascertaining how they set about it, and how, as a business speculation, it was made to answer.

To my great satisfaction, the following morning proved to be as wretched as the most inveterate "mud-plunger" could desire. It was cold, it was windy - the clouds were leaden, and a fine rain was falling with sullen persistency. Warmly buttoned in my unremarkable old coat of many winters, and with a change of caps in a pocket thereof, by half-past nine I was in Lant-street, in the Borough, that being, as my friend assured me, the way the chanting cadgers would come if they came at all. As I anticipated, it was much too promising a morning to be neglected. Just as St. George's Church was chiming ten, a couple came along the street, and I had no difficulty in recognising the man as the individual who, on the previous night, had borrowed a shilling of his landlord, on the promise of "going to work, rain or shine." I was considerably disappointed at his appearance, however, as well as at the woman's. Had a night's reflection resolved him to abandon his cadging courses and seek honest employment? Moreover, the man had on a shirt that, compared with the rag I had seen him in yesterday, was a clean shirt, and his feet were encased in a comfortable pair of shoes. The woman carried a capacious handbasket, and she and the man, who was cheerfully puffing at his morning pipe, stepped along briskly, looking so little like beggars that, meeting them promiscuously, I should have no more thought of bestowing a penny on them for charity's sake than of asking them for one.

The drizzling rain still continuing, the pair made their way, at so nimble a pace that it was not the easiest thing in the world to keep up with them, down the Borough, towards Newington-causeway, and up the Kennington-road. Suddenly turning a corner at Kennington-cross, I missed them. There was a public-house at the corner, with a convenient side door, and the sight of it, coupled with their disappearance, recalled to my mind the words the man had used the night before as to the purpose to which the borrowed shilling was to be applied. There was another side-entrance at the other side of the corner public-house, and this I availed myself of, calling for a glass of ale. The morning's newspaper lay on the counter, and, taking it up, I had the pleasure of making out in the opposite compartment my friends of the Mint, partaking of two fourpenn'orths of hot rum-and-water and an Abernethy biscuit. I. read at least half a column, and when I ventured a glance in the direction of the opposite compartment it was empty! Somehow they had stealthily slipped out, and I had again lost them!

In three seconds I was in the street looking to the left and right; but no-they were clean gone, and I had had my three- quarters of an hour's tramp through the rain and mire for nothing. But hark! was not that the sound of plaintive singing? At a distance of fifty yards or so, and opening out of the main street, there was a square or crescent and hurrying thither, lo! there I beheld my friends, but how miraculously altered! How had the metamorphosis been accomplished? Ten minutes ago the man in the patched jacket might well have passed, as I have remarked, as some honest poor fellow in quest of a job; but he had moulted since then, and become what I now beheld him - a scarecrow; a shoeless, shivering outcast, gingerly progressing with his naked toes through the squelching mud, as though constitutionally he had as great an aversion for it as a cat has; a much-to-be-pitied, consumptive wretch, judging from the frequency with which he was compelled to pause in the middle of the top notes of the touching hymn he was chanting to give utterance to a hollow cough, and press against his aching side the crochet nightcaps he was offering for sale. The woman, too, was amazingly transformed. But hungry, benumbed with cold, and wet as she was, she was not idle. No! as she walked, clinging close to his side, her shaking hands grasped the crochet needles, and with all her might she spun another nightcap from the ball of cotton concealed at her bosom. It was very astonishing - but stay, there was the capacious basket!

It was then ten minutes to eleven, and still raining, though not so fast. After all, there were beyond denial the naked feet dabbling in the cold kennel; there were the naked limbs exposed to the chilly blast - limbs that, of course, were not proof against rheumatic pains and penalties. These and other drawbacks considered, I must say that it did not strike me as being ample and handsome compensation that during that ten minutes of hymn-singing and shivering three compassionate persons were moved to bestow relief on the afflicted pair. I cannot, of course, say what in each case was the sum given, but submit that it is not unreasonable to set down the total at twopence-two halfpennies and one penny. This is not much. One would hardly care to do it at the price. But then it is not only for one ten minutes that these professional cadgers are so employed, but for hours together. As before remarked, although I continued to keep my Mint-street friends well in sight, it was impossible to tell the amounts they received.

There was nothing but their number to go by, and from ten minutes past eleven until a quarter past twelve the number of times the woman - she was the money-taker-found occasion to dart out of the middle of the road to the pavement, with her shaking hand extended to receive alms, and fervently ejaculate, "May-Gord-bless-and-thank-yer-mum," was twenty-three, included amongst the contributions being two gifts of bread and meat. The latter consisted of the bone of a ham, an angular and awkward joint, which was not without difficulty, and, I am afraid - notwithstanding that he still kept singing "a day's march nearer 'ome " - several maledictions, thrust into the basket by the "starving hoperative," as in the course of the neat little speech, at stated times delivered, the man announced himself to be. The ham-bone appeared to be a difficulty. Its meaty knuckle *would* protrude between the lid and the body of the basket, and threw suspicion on the statement that the famished pair had divided their last "kerrust" with their starving "horfspring" ere they quitted the wreck of their broker-demolished home at an early hour that morning. Possibly it was the aggravating bone that decided the mud-plungers to retire for luncheon at an earlier hour than was contemplated. Anyhow they did retire. Entering a chandler's shop the woman purchased a small quantity of the best old Cheshire cheese and a small crusty loaf (they had several thick slices of bread in the basket, but possibly it was stale), and so provided they adjourned to a public-house.

It was past one o'clock ere they emerged therefrom, and a glance at the basket convinced me at once that the objectionable ham-bone had somehow been disposed of. The man was smoking his pipe, and, from the cheerful tone of his discourse with the woman as they came up the street, it was evident that he had not stinted himself of ale. Merry as he might be, however, he was not unwise. With his poor wife, who "had been delekit and hailing since her last kon-fine-ment," he made his way back to the mews, where there were several barrows and carts, and disappearing amongst them for a few moments, the pair once more came forth to view, the same deplorable-looking objects they were before luncheon.

They did not, however, recommence business immediately. They hurried still Kennington-ward for fully a quarter of a mile, and then diverging into a quiet street again took to the mud. In one street-a long one, certainly, and composed of houses of a superior kind - I took note, and estimated that the outcast pair received no less than nineteen donations, and this in the space of twenty-five minutes! It was not, however, in these instances of almsgiving that the cruelty of the imposition appealed most strongly to one's feelings of indignation. The occasion on which I felt most inclined to interfere was when some poor soul, who, judging from the two peculiar-shaped loaves she was carrying half concealed under her shawl, had just come from Lambeth workhouse with her weekly dole, compassionately stopped and bestowed more than one coin - for I heard the jingling - on the villanous cadgers. "I'm poor enough, God knows," said the widow woman, "but *you*!" "May-Gord-bless-and-thank-yer-mum," croaked the female bird of prey with a bob that dipped her draggletail in the gutter, and the widow's mite was dropped into the capacious pocket, already gorged with copper money.

It was after one o'clock when my friends of the Mint began their second turn, and I kept them in sight until nearly four. I cannot, of course, be quite sure, but to the best of my knowledge, the number of times their pathetic appeals exacted charitable responses was *one hundred and eight*. This, with the twenty-three contributions received before luncheon, brought the total to one hundred and thirty one. It is perhaps scarcely fair to the calculation to put it that half this number of gifts was in halfpennies and the remainder in pennies. Probably three-fourths were pennies; but taking the first computation, it will be seen that the day's work of the two cadgers amounted to over eight shillings, exclusive of bread and meat. It was not very surprising, therefore, that come four o'clock-ten to four are the cadger's business hours, I presume - they should, after having availed themselves of the dinginess of a gateway to resume their boots, &c., think themselves entitled to a stiff glass of rum and water each before they returned to a nice hot dinner at their lodgings in the Mint.

MY friend's house is on the Surrey side of the river, and is one of a long row in a wide thoroughfare extending from the Blackfriars Road to the foot of the bridge at Westminster. Although somewhat faded, it is still a very respectable thoroughfare, but the neighbourhood behind the tall houses on either side of the way is about as wretched a one as may well be imagined. It consists for the most part of low streets, and narrow courts and alleys, which, though not absolutely "blind," might almost as well be so for all the intelligence of the outer world that is obtainable by means of the scowling little arched entrances that are to be found in the locality.

It is a grubby neighbourhood, and in summer time not particularly sweet smelling. In one respect, however, its "drainage" may be said to be perfect - the respect which applies to the flushing and clearing out of the pockets of such of the inhabitants, by far the majority, who give their minds to the imbibition of gin and beer. The handsome pumping stations at Barking Creek are scarcely less imposing than the magnificent ginshops to be found between Windmill-street and Body's Bridge, nor are the inflow (of profit) and the outflow (of intoxicating liquor) less brisk because the business done is strictly confined to the "low level." My friend's house has broad steps leading up to it, with an old-fashioned portico before the door, and, it having somehow become known that he is an easy going kind of householder, the said steps are not unfrequently resorted to in foul weather by the poor little slipshod, ragged-frocked children of the back settlements, whose parents are out at work, or engaged at something or other by which a little money may be made, and who, knowing how prone little children are to get into mischief when left in a house by themselves, provide against the danger by turning them all into the street and taking the key of the street-door with them.

A year ago and a day over, three of these poor things sat on my friend's doorstep, or, rather, on his very doorsill; for it was growing dark, and they were glad of the friendly shelter of the portico, out of the way of the wintry wind and the spiteful sleet that in the open highway was driving everything before it. There were two small girls and a still smaller boy, a mite of seven years or so old, more ragged than a Shetland colt, and with his small blue toes unprotected, save by a substantial casing of mud - a sickly big-headed little boy with a white face, as was shown here and there at spots from which the dirt had by accident been brushed away.

"Don't go to sleep, Billy," remarked one of the girls - they had Billy between them for the sake of warmth - "Mother'll be home in about an hour, and then I reckon we'll get some tea and a warm;" and then, turning to her female companion, she continued,-

"It'll be an hour and more before your old woman comes home from cheering; let's play at something to keep up our sperits - let's play at 'On'y suppose.'"

"Ah! let's play at that," exclaimed Billy of the big head; suddenly rising - my friend was no further off than the keyhole on the other side of the door, so he heard all that was said quite distinctly- "I can play at that. I'll tell you about a 'On'y suppose.' I've been a thinkin' about it when Sal thought I was agoin' to sleep."

But his sister, which was Sal, took him up with cruel abruptness.

"Oh, we don't want to hear your on'y supposins," said she. "Your'n is all about wittles."

And then, in a mollifying tone, she continued, evidently conscious that she had hurt Billy's feelings,

"Arter tea we'll have your 'On'y supposin',' Bill. You tell 'em very beautiful, Billy dear, but the joyment of 'em is spilte when they are told on a empty stomach. Blest if I can stand 'em at them times, and that's the truth. *You* tell us one, Emma. Tell us one about queens and dimons, and lords and ladies goin' to be married in golden carriages; that'll be best."

But Billy turned sulky, and maliciously threatened that unless they agreed to listen to his

"On'y supposin'," he would forthwith kick up a row on my friend's steps, and get them all turned off; on which they at once came to terms with him.

"Then 'on'y suppose,'" began Billy, firing away at once, "on'y suppose that it's to-morrer, which it's Christmas Day. And on'y suppose that me and you, Emm, and Sal is playin' out in the street, jolly miserable cos we ain't got no dinner, and we agree to go and have a smell at the areas" - "There, I knowed it would be wittles," remarked his sister Sal, experiencing her empty stomach's first twinges - "to go and have a smell at the areas," continued Billy, with an aggravating smack of his lips, "at the houses where the people live what are always baking and biling such lovely grub. Well, and we went; well, and on'y suppose that as we was a-standin' at the railin's and a-sniffin' and a-sniffin', and getting the smell of the stuffin' and the cracklin' on the legs of pork and the sossages just abustin' in the fryin' pan (Sal relieved her agonised feelings by a suppressed groan), just when we was gettin' these lovely smells well up our noses, on'y suppose that the door opens - the street door - and there's a servant a-standin', and she says, 'You're got to come in here, all three of you;' and she looks so jolly kind that we knows she ain't making game, so in we goes - me and you, Sal, and Emm - and we goes into the parlour, where there's oh! such a toastin' fire, and where the table has got a table cloth on it and ever so many dishes - little 'uns and big 'uns" - under pretence of adjusting her bonnet, Sal stuffs a bit of hair into the ear that is next to the torturer - "and all of the dishes has got kivers on em, like what you see in the winder of the cook-shop in the Cut. And then on'y suppose that there are cheers - three of 'em - to sit on, and the lady comes in, and she says, 'You're all three of you going to have as much as ever you can tuck into.'"

"Draw it mild, come, Billy; I can't stand too much of it," in a warning voice from Sal; but Billy was reckless.

"'You're going to have as much as ever you know how to tuck into,' she ses, and then she lifts off the kivers; and first there's baked beef, all smoking hot, fat roast beef, with a bit of holly stuck in it because it's Christmas, and a regler high tide of gravy in the dish" - Billy's waterside experiences must have furnished this simile - "rich gravy, with a spoon in it, and bits of brown. And in another dish all hot, and, some broke and some not, and all crisp and mealy, there was the taters what the beef was baked over. And on'y suppose that we got a helpin' of that-a regler piled-up plateful swimmin' in gravy, and -"

"And then we come away, Billy," observed Sal, persuasively; "that's a good boy, and then we come away."

"No we don't," returned Billy, doggedly; "on'y suppose that when we had as much beef as ever we could eat, we saw another kiver lifted off, and there was puddin' - a whackin' all. hot Christmas pudding, as big - ah! pretty nigh as big as that woman's umbreller, and we all had as much as we could eat of that. And then another kiver was took off and there was goose, roast goose, stuffed full of sage and onions, and on'y suppose -"

But the endurance of his afflicted sister was not equal to roast goose following on as much as she could eat of plum pudding. Starting up, she gave her brother a vicious shake, and exclaiming, "On'y suppose you come along home and let's have no more of it," without further parley walked off with the young romancer in custody.

Our scheme for a Christmas party of a perfectly new and novel kind was founded on my friend's narration of the fate of luckless Billy and his "On'y supposing." It was agreed that on Christmas morning we should set forth and select each three juvenile guests, and bring them home and set them down with a hearty invitation to partake of the good things spread before them to the extreme of their ability. "We won't," said my cunning friend - he is a terribly artful fellow when he likes - "we won't say a word about the story telling after dinner, but that, of course, is to be the prime part of the business." I hoped that it might so turn out, but having had already some experience of such matters, in my secret mind I doubted it. There could, however, be no doubt as to the primeness of one feature of the programme, in the ordering of which, when Christmas-eve came, we both took great interest. Ten pounds of sirloin of beef, ingredients for a plum pudding-not so large as an umbrella, but at least approaching the dimensions of a lady's modern sunshade - mince pies, nuts and oranges, and a liberal allowance of elder wine, were confided to my friend's housekeeper, with an intimation that on the morrow we dined at one o'clock sharp.

At twelve o'clock on Christmas morning, having seen the beef and pudding in the cook's hands, we parted at my friend's doorsteps, and went our separate ways, each pledged to return in less than an hour with three eligible guests. I observed that, with his accustomed artfulness, my friend chose the way which he had seen that renowned story-teller Billy take, in company with his sister, with the vague hope, I have no doubt, of securing that accomplished young gentleman, and thus, single-handed as it were, throwing completely into the shade any trio of youthful romancers I might chance to fall in with.

My way lay in the direction of the New Cut and the streets which tended Lambeth-walkward. In such a locality it was by no means a difficult matter, at such a time, to discover ragged little boys - many more than enough - who were in want of a dinner. Had I but made my purpose publicly known, I should, in a very few minutes, have found myself surrounded by as many small folk as flocked together at the seductive strains of the Pied Piper of Hamlin; but I wished my selections to do me credit, and cast about me cautiously.

My first catch was a girl - not a beggar-girl, or an idle little gutter-prowler - but a mite of a child with the anxious and careworn face of a middle-aged woman, who was desperately bent on turning an honest penny by the sale of hard-working cobblers. At ordinary times the hard-working cobbler is a toy much in favour with the children of the lower order, on account, it may be assumed, of its being a plaything which, while it affords amusement, inculcates habits of industry. It is a jointed toy, and represents a mender of old shoes, who, when a string concealed at the back of his body is sharply pulled, commences to work his arms to and fro in the act of sewing on a shoe-sole with such hearty will and with such praiseworthy determination to accomplish his job in a manner to give satisfaction to his customer, that every time he tugs a stitch tight the strain on his physical powers is such as to cause his movable eyes to squint in the most frightful way. The girl had, as far as one might judge, about two dozen cobblers in the little rush basket slung on her arm; but though she pulled at the string of the one she carried in her hand with such desperate jerks that the hardworking cobbler's eyes were set squinting at the rate at least of sixty times a minute, and at the same time kept up the cry, "Here's the 'ard-workin' cobbler for a a penny; who'll have two 'ard-working cobblers for a penny?" no one was tempted to become a purchaser. The crowd was a holiday crowd, and had - thank Heaven! - something more pleasant to give their minds to than hard-working cobblers. As I paused to observe her, her delight at the prospect of having a customer at last caused her to skip out of the gutter and on to the pavement with such a sudden and spasmodic action of her limbs that I should not have been surprised if her eyes had squinted as did the industrious cordwainer's.

"On'y a ha'penny, sir! I ain't took on'y threeha'pence, and I've been here since ten."

"I wonder that you have taken so much," I replied. "Could'nt you have managed to bring out something to sell that was a little more seasonable?"

"Yes,! said she; "but father can't make nothin' else. You can't make what you likes, - don't you know? - when you are layin' on your back in bed - nobody can't."

"But is your father compelled to lie on his back in bed?"

"He ain't got no legs to getup with," replied the mite, dolefully; "leastways, not reg'ler legs."

"Wooden ones?" I suggested.

"No, sir, pair-o'-lysed 'uns," she responded, in all sincerity; "his back's agoin' too, the doctor ses; and when it creeps right up to the top of his back he won't live no longer."

Her small voice quivered with emotion, and, as some relief to her feelings, she gave a tug at the cobbler's string that bade fair to make his squinting eyes start out of his wooden head.

"Now," said I, "supposing - only supposing that somebody was to offer to take all your stock of cobblers off your hands at the full price? - and, besides that," I continued, checking midway her gasp of joyful amazement, "that the same somebody should take you home with him and give you a beautiful dinner of roast beef and plum pudding?"

But this latter part of the supposition seemed to her to be so monstrously improbable that she lost all faith in the first part; and her heart, a moment before in her mouth, as the saying is, sank within her as heavy as lead.

"Ah," she remarked, in an altered voice, as she stepped back into the gutter, "and s'pose pigs was able to fly? Won't you buy a penny cobbler after all?"

So I cut the matter short by telling her to come along with me; and, having seen her safely housed at my friend's abode, I had to hurry off to find two other Christmas guests, for I had no more than a quarter of an hour left to do it in.

My next catch was not so satisfactory as my first - a crossing sweeping boy, with nothing remarkable about him except that he had festooned his muddy old broom with holly, and earnestly pleaded for a copper, "for the sake of Merry Christmas." But whatever of poetry there may have been in his appeal to those who availed themselves of his industry, he proved to be an alarmingly matter-of-fact boy when I began to reveal my intentions to him. My proposition that he should come home with me and dine he received as coolly as though we were intimate friends, and had known each other for years. All right; he'd come-what was up? In a tone that was intended to convey some amount of rebuke, I briefly explained, but he was not in the least impressed, though rendered for the moment suspicious.

"Do it mean 'ims and trying to convert a feller?" he inquired; "or is it only a lark? Not that I care, mind yer," he hastened to add; "I'd as lief go in for one as the other. I can make myself comfortable anywheres. Just stay a minute while I goes and plants my broom - I dessay you won't care about me taking it with me - and then we'll make a start."

I was so conscious that I had made a mistake that I really believe, if it had not been Christmas morning, I should have been guilty of the meanness of retreating as soon as my free-and-easy young friend had turned his back, and so avoided his further acquaintance. I was glad, however, that I did not; for after being absent for five or six minutes, he made his appearance accompanied by another boy - a lanky boy, ragged, wan-faced, and hungry-eyed, who had one leg shorter than the other, and walked, or rather hopped, with a crutch. The friendly young crossing-sweeper left the other boy, and by a wink bespoke my private ear.

"Talk about boys wantin' a dinner, now," he whispered; "here's one, if you like. I don't believe that Joe - that's what his name is, Joe the Whistler - I don't believe that Joe has had any dinner worth speaking of since he came out of the 'orspidal."

"And how long since is that? and what took him to the hospital?" I asked.

"How long ago? Six months and more. What took him there? Bein' run over took him there. Got his leg broke - wuss, too, got his woice broke - his whistling woice, I mean. That's how Joe used to get his livin', whistling tunes about the streets, and naturally when he come out of the 'orspidal with his crutch he went at it agin. But he couldn't do it. Summnat had gone wrong with his bellus. I s'pose he tries at it still, cos he's got nothing else to fall back on, but things is bad with him - drefful bad."

Poor Joe the Whistler stood leaning on his crutch at a respectful distance while, with rapid utterance, his friend (of whom I began to form a better opinion) urged his claims on my charitable consideration. I need not say that I readily admitted them, and the next minute I was steering for my friend's abode with my prizes in tow.

He was home before I was - had been home, he triumphantly informed me, twenty minutes and more, which was easily accounted for. With his usual impulsiveness and lack of discrimination he had (but not, as he afterwards confessed, until he had wasted nearly half an hour in a vain search for the redoubtable Billy) fixed on the first three likely-looking objects that presented themselves. His catch consisted of two juvenile carol-singers, ragged and deplorable looking enough, in all conscience, if that was to be regarded as a recommendation, and one other boy, concerning whom I had misgivings as soon as I was made acquainted with the particulars of his capture. My friend had detected him gazing longingly in at the window of a cook-shop, and after apparently painful deliberation, the boy was seen to hurry into the shop, and presently emerge with a penn'orth of baked pudding on a cabbage leaf.

"Poor little chap!" remarked my tender-hearted acquaintance; "just imagine a boy - a hearty boy, such as he evidently is - being reduced to such straits as that on a Christmas morning."

"Did you experience much difficulty in persuading him to accompany you?" I asked.

"Not the least; he came along as cheerful and thankful as possible."

But scarcely had my friend uttered the word when there came a banging knock at the outer door, a gruff voice was heard inquiring if there was a boy there, and the young gentleman of whom we were discoursing was observed to turn pale. We found the owner of the gruff voice on the mat in the hall, a muscular man, and evidently in the navigating line of business, red and wrathful, and fierce in his demand to be informed what we meant by kidnapping his son. My friend soothingly explained the facts of the case. I could not help thinking that the indignation with which the lad's father listened to the explanation was not unmixed with admiration.

"The hungry young warmint," said he, "why, he knows that there's as fine a stuffed bullock's heart as ever was baked over a dish of taters as'll be ready at ha'-past one o'clock. But I never see such a buster of a boy to eat. If he hadn't been bowled out, he would have finished his feed here, and then come home and polished off his share of heart and taters as though he hadn't tasted a bit since his breakfast. I knows him."

And after further pacification by an offering of rum, the father took his departure, having a tight hold of the greedy boy's collar.

So it came about that our dinner party was reduced to five, and I must say for it that, as a dinner party, it was an unqualifled success. Thanks in no small degree to Master Piper, the crossing-sweeper. Piper's self-possession never for a moment forsook him; while poor Joe the Whistler was in an agony of bashfulness, and could only be persuaded to take a chair at the table when it had been clearly demonstrated to him how impossible it would be for him to enjoy his food with a crutch under one arm, a knife and fork in his hands, and standing on one leg all the time. The small retailer of hard-working cobblers - who had washed her face and made her hair tidy since I last saw her - was amazed and speechless before the glories of the table, and even the two carol-singing boys (who, as will presently appear, were a sad disappointment) were as yet pale and nervous. Piper made himself as much at home as though he was at least a younger brother of the host. I believe that he would have carved the beef had he met with the slightest encouragement in that direction. He did volunteer to pour out the beer, and more than once gallantly assisted the only lady at table to gravy. Piper freely criticised the quality of the beef, and inquired how much a pound we might have given for it, and when he was informed whistled incredulously, and expressed his opinion that if we had gone over to the dead meat market we might have saved at least fifteen pence on the joint. His example, after the first serving or so, gave courage to the others, and by the pudding time we were all as jolly as sand-boys. I don't believe that ever a pudding was so severely punished by five small assailants. As for Joe the Whistle; kept in countenance by the encouraging winks of Piper, it was quite delightful to see him "come up smiling" for a fourth slice, and at present none the worse for the contest.

The two carol-boys were quiet munchers, and, as they emptied their repeatedly-filled plates, nudged each other, and whispered under their breath, and grinned as though they could see in the whole business a joke that was not apparent to anyone else present. They proved themselves ungrateful rascals, for no sooner had they partaken of everything that was to be had, including a large-sized glass of hot elder wine, than they rose and said that they must be going.

"But we are not going to break up just yet," said our host; "we are going now to sit round the fire and have a song or two - you are just the fellows to sing a song, you know - and some of us, I dare say, can tell a story."

But the carol-singing boys rejected the genial proposal with rude contempt. It wasn't likely, the older one said, with a laugh; they had something better to do with their time. They had been asked to dinner, and they had had their dinner, and that was enough. It was all very well for them that could afford it to waste their time, but they couldn't, and so they didn't mean to stop any longer. Of course, there was no use in arguing the matter with two such mean rascals, and so my friend, with a severe though somewhat chapfallen countenance, handed them their bundle of carols, which for security had been taken downstairs, and let them out. They went laughing down the steps, and added insult to injury by at once making for the road, and, almost under our very windows, struck up "God bless you, merry gentlemen," their voices quavering and their teeth chattering as though they had not tasted food since the day before.

Now our party was reduced to three, and we brewed a little more hot elder wine, and stirred the fire, and drew our chairs closer, while my friend directed at me a glance that expressed, "We shall be all right after all, you will find." But I regret to state that his expectations were hardly realised. Would somebody sing a song? Yes; the hard-working cobbler girl would. But she was unfortunate in her selection. With her shrill small voice she began the melancholy ballad known as "Dear father, come home;" but she had scarcely got through the second verse when, as it seemed, the repetition of the words "dear father" called to her imagination (heightened, probably, by the elder wine), such a picture of the hapless cripple, her own parent, lying abed with a pair of legs that were of no use to him, that she broke down and sobbed so dismally that even Piper was affected, and it appeared nothing short of gross cruelty to urge her to continue.

To enliven the spirits of the company generally, Piper volunteered to give us "something lively;" but here we were again unfortunate, Mr. Piper having a particularly loud voice, and his ideas of "liveliness" being such as might provoke adverse criticism on the part of the neighbours. He was cut as short as politeness would permit, and Joe the Whistler was appealed to. Joe declared that he couldn't sing.

"Then tell us a story," suggested my friend eagerly, hope reviving in his bosom.

Joe evidently had been thinking about it, for without the least hesitation he made a launch: "There was once upon a time a plum puddin';" but then he came to as dead a stop as though a piece of the subject of his narrative had stuck in his throat.

"Well, go on," said my friend, encouragingly.

"There was once a plum puddin'; -" and Joe mused for several minutes, and then, taking the cue, continued: "And it was a reg'ler whacker - another pause - "One of the whackingest plum-puddin's it was that ever was biled in a sarsepan, and -"

"Get on, Joe."

"And one of the most reg'ler--"

Here Joe made another halt, and of such long duration that my friend once more exclaimed, "Get on, Joe."

On which Joe gave such a sudden start that there could be no doubt that he had been disturbed from the commencement of a sweet sleep.

We all started up laughing, and shortly afterwards, presenting Mr. Piper and Joe the Whistler with a shilling each, and the little girl who dealt in hardworking cobblers with a new half crown, over and above the purchase-money of her stock, bad them good-bye at the door, and sent them away rejoicing.

THE unfortunate individual in humble circumstances who has no relative or private friend wealthy and willing enough to advance him the wherewithal to overcome his temporary pecuniary embarrassments, need not look far afield before he may discover signal lights of succour. It would really seem like an encouragement to thriftlessness, the abundance of cheerful beckonings from persons of means, who are above all such paltry considerations as interest for their vested capital, and who are at the expense of keeping offices and clerks, and advertising in the most expensive of newspapers, with the sole and single aim of assisting their downcast fellow-creatures. It is a satisfactory sign of the advancing philanthropy of the age that these benevolent lenders are increasing rather than diminishing in number - satisfactory both as bespeaking that the spirit of simple confidence of man in the integrity of his fellow keeps pace with the progress of civilisation, and that instances of abuse of the said confidence are rare. Of course, it is not to be expected that all who are blessed with wealth can afford to give it away. It may be all very well for such splendid fellows as "A. Z." and "R. B. D.," and one or two others who take a delight in occasionally astounding needy asylums of charity, whose directors are at their wits' ends how to meet the current expenses of their establishment, with an anonymous gift of a thousand pounds, included in a brief note to the effect that the donation might be acknowledged in the second column of the *Times*. One may picture the awful amazement of the corresponding secretary of some struggling home for cripples or asylum for sick children, almost on its last legs for want of funds, on receipt of such a startling enclosure. There are letters enough every day to open: business letters, letters from candidates for admission, letters in polite intimation of big accounts overdue, and letters with small post-office orders and with postage stamps sent in answer to the last pathetic appeal to the public for help. Then turns up out of the heap a letter that is registered, and the secretary in doubt and fear breaks the seal. Some folks are so careful of their donations. that if they send five shillings they take the precaution of registering it; but it is more commonly done when the enclosure is a bank note. Perhaps this is a bank-note for five ten, maybe twenty pounds! Such plums as the last-mentioned are by no means common, but they *have* been known to find their way into the asylum's letter-basket. And then the letter is opened, and there appears the cheque, and the bewildering words "Pay to A. B., secretary of the Neglected Babies' Home, the sum of One Thousand Pounds." It would be worth double the money to noble-hearted "A. Z." could he see that secretary's face as he reads and re-reads the miraculous scrap of paper. He folds it up, and takes a turn up and down the office with it held tight in his fist, and then carries it to the window and opens it again - as people do, who, in dreams, pick up purses stuffed with bank-notes and diamonds, slowly and with bated breath, and thinking that despite that first peep surely it *must* be a delusion. No! it's all right. "One thousand pounds" are the words, plain and unmistakable. Acknowledge it in the *Times*! Why, if he were permitted to do so, the grateful secretary would sit down there and then, and in the thankfulness of his heart pen an acknowledgment that would fill a couple of columns at least, exclusive of the double row of signatures of the helpless little ones whom the money of happy "A. Z." had made glad.

But, as before mentioned, we cannot be all "A. Z.s," and the best that we can do is to be charitable according to our means. Such, according to their own showing, are the amiable men of money who advertise their willingness to assist their fellow-mortals in distress. They are even at the pains to invent ingenious "catch-lines" to head their advertisements, each one trying to outvie his fellow-philanthropists in this respect, in order that he may gather to himself the greater number of subjects for the exercise of his sovereign healing. Every morning, all the year round, do these charitable ones call aloud from the newspapers; and there are so many of them all of a row, that if each had a sounding voice instead of a typo-graphed one, there would ensue a din that there would be no such thing as paying proper attention to the police reports or the parliamentary debates. "MONEY! MONEY! MONEY!" one calls out, in letters so large and distinct that they seem almost to chink like sovereigns in the pocket. "To all in want of money - apply immediately at the Houndsditch Financial Discount Office. Interest, five per cent. per annum. Payable by instalments to suit the convenience of the borrower." And the next: "To THE EMBARRASSED. If you wish to obtain a loan of from five to five hundred pounds, all that you have to do is to cut out this advertisement and send it to our office, stating sum required, etc., and four stamps for reply." Why four stamps? Why? He must indeed be a stupid person who cannot divine the reason at a glance. Does not the registration of a letter cost just fourpence? and would it be safe to send a money enclosure, especially to a stranger, without taking *some* precaution? All that you have to do is to state the amount of money you require, "etc.," and you may rely on a crisp little parcel of bank-notes by return of post. To be sure it is somewhat difficult to define the requirements of that brief "*et cetera*," but for that matter one's necessities must be pressing indeed if he cannot wait the space of two posts for the wherewithal to relieve him of his anxieties; and there can be no doubt that the obliging clerk of the office will be but too happy, on receipt of an extra stamp, to enlighten him as to what "etc." in loan-office parlance means.

It can scarcely be that the philanthropist who so frankly appeals to the "Embarrassed" intends by his indefinite promise to subject those who apply to him to the trouble and inconvenience of looking up anything in the shape of tangible security he may happen to be possessed of, and which the lender might like to hold, or that he will be expected to procure a signed bond for the amount from two or more substantial householders. It cannot possibly be so, or the "Friend to the Embarrassed" would do no business at all. The good Samaritan who figures next on the list would cut him out as neatly ever an intending borrower cut out the advertisement as invited to.

Here is proposition number four, copied just as it stands in the newspaper. This is an explicit announcement if you like. There can be no concealed meaning here. No doubtful phrase that can make a borrower half resolved still further hesitate. "Do you WANT TO BORROW MONEY? If so, apply at once to Mr. -----, at the office, Kingsland. Any amount under fifty pounds granted next day, after application, on borrower's own note of hand. Repayments may be made monthly, quarterly, anyhow that is suitable to our clients, and by post-office order to save the trouble of attending at the office. No inquiry! No office fees! No security required!"

In the name of all that is generous, what can a man who wishes his fellow-creatures to enjoy a little of that which he has in such superabundance say more to induce the needy to apply at the office in Kingsland? - an office, bear in mind, that the advertiser himself provides without fee or reward; for he particularly mentions that though you are welcome to its use you are not called on to pay as much as a penny towards gas, coal, or clerk's wages. As for inquiry fees, he is scarcely the man to impose them, since his nature is so confiding that he never makes inquiry at all. He prefers *not* to make inquiry; if he did so he might have his eyes opened to the fact that there are in this wicked world a certain class of persons so utterly heartless and depraved as to design to abuse the childlike trust of a loan-office keeper. If there is a plan to cheat him, he would rather be in ignorance of it, even until after the base purpose is consummated, so that he may enjoy the sweet consolation of reflecting that possibly the borrower meant well, but that circumstances over which he had no control prevented him from acting up to the terms of the agreement. Anything, anything, rather than that the loan-office keeper should be rudely shocked to wide-awakeness as regards the world's iniquity, and should feel compelled, however regretfully, to give up business altogether, or do violence to his nature by making inquiries as to the solvency of those who seek his aid.

Another kind of public benefactor who proclaims his disinterested desire to benefit his species, is a person who, having money to lend, is by no means disposed to be confounded with professional financial Samaritans. This person heads his advertisement in an amateurish, unbusinesslike manner, that one would think would expose him to the machinations of those unscrupulous ones who are perpetually roaming about seeking what in the shape of guilelessness they may devour:-

"A PRIVATE GENTLEMAN, with a few thousands at his command, is desirous of negotiating loans of small amounts, - say from five pounds to twenty-five, - with persons of integrity who are temporarily embarrassed. Tradesmen, clerks, and others must be prepared to furnish credentials as to their respectability, as the system of inquiry adopted by the principals of ordinary loan-offices is dispensed with. The gentleman has no connection with professional money-lenders, and makes the offer as a *bona fide* boon to the public, on a New and Improved System, whereby all respectable persons can have immediate cash accommodation. The rate at present charged, and until the alteration is publicly announced will so remain, is five per cent. Prospectus free. No office fees. No preliminary charge of any kind."

And yet poor folks talk about the difficulty they at times experience in tiding over their temporary troubles, and of how hard they find it to make both ends meet! Likewise they are not unfrequently heard to grumble about the proneness of the rich to grind and oppress their brethren in distress, and of the monstrous difference there is in the rate of interest exacted from the humble compared to that which is cheerfully accepted from the well-to-do. Why, here is an individual who expresses his willingness to lose by every monetary transaction he engages in. With the bank rate at seven per cent. he comes forward, with his cheque-book in his hand, and invites "all respectable persons" to come and borrow of him at five per cent. All that an unfortunate tradesman has to do is to look up a few evidences of his respectability, - a copy of the registration of his legitimate birth, a duplicate of his marriage certificate, and any old receipts for the payment of pew-rents or income-tax he may happen to have by him. These, it may be presumed, will suffice, - these and the tradesmen's note of hand, to the effect that, as soon as it may be convenient, he will refund the amount of the loan advanced, and the Private Gentleman will forward the money at once.

The most wonderful part of the business is, that despite the vast number of "embarrassed ones" who must be constantly on the look-out for a friendlily-disposed person, such as the "Private Gentleman," and the certainty that thousands must ere this have found him out and profited by his munificence, he has not tired of his good-natured task. He still advertises in the newspapers, - nay, it is a fact, that whereas a year since he modestly confined himself to one or two of the cheap and popular "weeklies," he now appears every morning of the week and every week of the year in the dailies as well. Surely he must be ruining himself-unless, indeed, s business is like that of the Cheap Jack, who lost by every separate article he sold, and whose only hope of making any profit was in the enormous extent of his dealings. Either this, or the majority of the "respectable public to whom he so candidly appeals, must have discovered that the Private Gentleman is an arrant humbug, the most objectionable humbug of the whole loan-office fraternity, who, as a rule, are merely wolves in sheep's clothing, while Mr. "Private Gentleman" appears as a lamb - innocent and tender, and with a blue ribbon round his neck. His great card is this affectation of simplicity, and he deliberately lays himself out as a noodle, who has money and don't know what to do with it. This answers a double purpose. He catches the timid borrower, - the really respectable, bashful, poor fellow, who never in his life borrowed money before, and who would sooner die almost than reveal his temporary destitution to his friends. This is the individual who is shy of the ordinary loan-office. He has heard that there is a bond of brotherhood amongst the whole gang of loan-office harpies, and that the ledgers of each are open for inspection for the mutual protection of all. This being so, it is possible, despite all he may be able to do to the contrary, that his secret may leak out and become known.

But the Private Gentleman who fearlessly tells the company of loan-mongers that he has not, nor desires, any connection with them, that he eschews their method of business altogether, and has one of his own that better agrees with his conscience - there can be no harm in applying to such a one. No one need ever know it. As the advertisement says, the utmost secrecy will be observed, and repayments may be made by post-office order. This is the sort of customer the Private Gentleman prefers to any other, as affording fatter and more tender picking. But he relies as well for a goodly share of his profits on the many who come to bite, and find themselves bitten, - on persons of the Micawber breed, who, in order that the steed may not starve while the grass is "turning up," will borrow at every available opportunity-men who have dabbled in "loans" obtained at the regular offices until their names are no longer good for anything at those establishments. True, there is not very much got by bagging this kind of game, but with the Private Gentleman it is merely a question of powder and shot expended in bringing such birds down, compared with the value of their carcases. He lures them to him, these old birds, and they come to his call meek as pigeons. It must be an instructive spectacle to witness a passage of business between the two, - the Private Gentleman protesting against the abominable ways of the vulgar professional loan negociator, and the other agreeing with every word, and asserting that *he* never could have been induced to apply for assistance to such a ravenous horde, and that it was only because of his implicit faith in the Private Gentleman, &c, &c. But the Private Gentleman gains something by the interview. The wolf peeps out of the lamb-like eyes, and discovers in the applicant a fellow-creature of prey, though of meaner capacity than himself, and from that moment there is as much hope of his obtaining a loan from the Private Gentleman, as of that individual turning honest. Still, the latter cannot have his time wasted completely. "Oh, yes, he has no doubt that what is desired may be done. He cannot say off-hand, of course. He must submit the proposition to his lawyer, without whose advice he never acts, and his lawyer's fee is ten shillings - a mere trifle only, in fact, ninepence in the pound, but it must be paid in advance. It is not for the Private Gentleman's benefit. He is prepared to act strictly in accordance with the terms of his advertisements, and to charge not one farthing for his personal expenses or for inquiry, but these legal men, my dear sir -"

And twice out of three times the would-be borrower, wide awake and experienced as he is, is taken off his guard by this eccentric and decidedly un-loan-office-like way of doing business, and parts with the ten shillings, and there is an end to the transaction.

But it is the *bona fide*, willing-to-pay borrower who is best worth fishing for. The loan-office shark has invented a beautiful and perfect system of late years. So safe! There is not a loan-office in London and for twelve miles round that is not perfectly well acquainted with the transactions of every other similar establishment. Every night of his life the Private Gentleman doubtless receives from the other offices a list of all applicants on the preceding day, together with the results of inquiry into their past lives and future prospects. Were it not for this, the same individual, the borrower and his surety or sureties, might make successful application at every establishment in the metropolis, and so do an immense stroke of swindling business. He must be, however, an extremely clever person who can "raise the wind" at anyone's expense but his own, if he ventures to take the owners of a loan-office in hand as his bellows for the purpose. He is a very lucky person if, having meddled with the limed twigs that the rapacious villains hold out so temptingly, his wings are not so utterly crippled and clogged as to be useless for free flight for many a year afterwards.

    The newspapers have of late revealed many instances of the heartless behaviour of money-lenders towards their victims, but where one of the latter finds courage enough to go to a magistrate and explain the wrong he has endured, there are fifty who are so completely crushed and ruined, alike in spirit and worldly estate, that they sink and are passed over and heard of no more. It is appalling the amount of mischief these petty loan-office people work. It is a fact within the writer's knowledge that there is a broker and auctioneer in only one district, a district at the east of London, who is kept constantly going, and has as much as he can do to sell by auction at his "rooms" the seizures made on bills of sale, and which are provided him by only *three* loan offices. The "bill of sale" is the weapon that the modern lender of small sums at an interest at from forty to seventy per cent. wields with such deadly effect. It did not used to be so. If a loan-office borrower failed in the payment of the agreed-on instalments, his creditor sought no other remedy than the county court, but it is different now. The security insisted on is much more substantial than a promissory note with two or three names appended; the moneylender will have, by hook or by crook, or by both - for his daring in this respect is very remarkable - a document that shall enable him, in the event of the terms of the contract being in the least disregarded, to swoop down on the household goods of the defaulter, and cart them away without a moment's notice; and right and left the whole tribe of extortionists are making hay until such time as the sun of knowledge shines and disperses the haze of ignorance that at present envelops the minds of men of humble station as to what a terrible scourge in the hands of an inexorable enemy a bill of sale is. The amount of ignorance prevailing on this subject is astonishing. It may be safely said that in no one case brought before a police court has it been shown that the victim was aware of the power that the loan-office proprietor held over him. In the majority of cases, by some sort of sleight of hand and bamboozling the borrower and his unlucky surety have been induced to sign a document improperly filled in; and, incredible as it may appear, in four cases out of five, what the dupe signs is merely a blank stamped paper. It has been said so many times that it is scarcely worth while repeating here, that men who do such rash things are unworthy the sympathy and condolence of men of sense; at the same time, it should not be forgotten that it comes fairly within the functions of the law to protect fools from the machinations of rogues. It is common for a magistrate to remark to a poor fellow who comes to him to declare that the loan-office vultures have pounced on his house and cleaned it out, from attic or kitchen, that if he has been guilty of the monstrous absurdity of allowing another man to rob him with his eyes open he must bear the consequences; but it may be said that the victim does *not* so commit himself with his eyes open. A man's faculties are not generally at their keenest and coolest at the moment when he is about to receive the amount he has experienced so much difficulty in borrowing, and for the use of which his dire necessity makes him in such red-hot haste; and then again, it should be borne in mind that loan-offices as a rule are little dingy, ill-lighted dens, and when a borrower is requested "just to pop his name down here-for the mere form of the thing, he has no reason to assume that he is dealing with rogues and rascals. And, after all, a man who attaches his signature to a paper he has not first carefully perused, or one that is folded over so that part is invisible, is certainly no greater simpleton than the one who is led by a skittle sharper to stake all his money, and then to go and pawn his watch to raise more with the certainty of losing it; but although the magistrate is apt to tell a greenhorn of this class that he has no pity for him, he sentences the skittle sharper to a few months at the treadmill. It makes no difference what are the implements of "hocus-pocus" used: a rogue will naturally apply himself to such tools as he can exercise with most dexterity, and it seems quite clear that the man who by conjuration, peculiar to the line of business he has adopted, makes it appear that another man has signed away goods of the value of thirty pounds, when at the time of signing he was led to believe that he was pledging himself only to ten or fifteen pounds, is as crafty a swindler as he who inveigles you to trust him to take a short walk away from you with your purse in his possession, as a test of your faith in his honesty, and who walks off with it altogether.

 It is quite time the law stepped in to enforce the better regulation of petty loan-offices. It interferes with sufficient stringency as regards other of the poor man's facilities for borrowing. No one may carry on a pawnbroker's business without first obtaining a licence, and giving very substantial guarantee for his respectability. He is not at liberty to make the best terms he can with his client. He may do business on only one system, and according to certain rules fixed by the legislature. What is sufficient interest for the capital he invests in the pawning department is arranged for him, and he must abide by the said arrangement or suffer the consequences. Should he overcharge so little as a penny on a pledge, the aggrieved may rely on having prompt justice at the nearest police court. He is debarred the exercise of his free will to be honest, and is compelled to be so by Act of Parliament. The petty loan-monger, however, is hampered by no such restrictions. He may charge what interest he pleases, and make his own terms as to repayment. For a loan of ten pounds it is his common practice to obtain as security, in addition to a note of hand, a bill of sale for at least twenty-five, that not only the amount still unpaid of the advanced money, but also the "attendant expenses" may be covered; and attendant expenses means just anything that the rapacious creditor may please to name. Besides, it is impossible to hold a more potent screw over a poor fellow than authority to break up and destroy his home. The old law that enabled a creditor to lay hands on a small debtor and carry him away to prison was stigmatised as barbarous, and repealed accordingly, but to wreck and desolate his home is even more cruel. At all events, and although a prisoner, he was only so until such time as his family could raise money for his ransom, and with his ransom his domestic affairs resumed their peaceful and comfortable course; but the breaking-up of a home is very often irrevocable. In the first place there is the enormous loss the debtor sustains by the sale of his goods by auction. Such sales are invariably "Without reserve," and anyone at all conversant with the subject is aware of what *that* means. Nothing more nor less than the banding together of half-a-dozen unprincipled brokers, who take care not to bid against the one who is deputed to secure at his own price every lot that is put up, the whole gang dividing the spoil afterwards. By means of this arrangement it is not at all uncommon for house furniture worth, say, forty pounds, to realise not more than seven or eight pounds; and if the auctioneer is "in the swim," of course the matter is much simplified. There can be no doubt that the misery arising from this source is wide-spread and increasing. As already has been mentioned in this paper, the patronage of three loan offices is enough to occupy the time and attention of one auctioneer who has extensive warehouse room. The ordinary rate of business at this last-mentioned establishment is four hundred "lots per week. This from three loan-offices It may be safely assumed that in and about London there are at least a hundred of these petty money-mongers; and if they are all equally active with the bill-of-sale dodge, it requires but an easy exercise of calculation to discover the amount of domestic devastation worked by them every week of their lives.

I HAVE been at Barnet Fair on the great day of all - the ~ Costermongers' Carnival; I have talked to many of those participating in the festivities, but as any narrative of the events must greatly depend on colour and phraseology, I think it better that the story should be told to you in the terms and answers given to the friendly inquiries I made of one in particular among the confraternity.

"Barnet Fair comes on a Wednesday, and, of all the days that are in the year, there is not one that can come up to it; leastways, I mean with the thousands wot move in that spear of life the same as your humble servant. Christmas isn't nothin' to it. There's nothin' stirrin' at Christmas. There isn't nothin' in season but ice cartin' and holly and mistletoe; and, though the last mentioned as a pictur looks very well piled up in a barrer, it isn't werry festive servin' it.,. out in pennorths, and everybody so stronary awaracious arter the bits wots got lots of berries on to 'em. No; Christmas time ain't a jolly time for the costermonger it's a starvin' time. It's a time when, symbolikle speakin', the wolf scratches the door open and walks off with anything wot he can stick his hungry teeth into. Easter and Witsun is a little better; but then a man is glad to make the most of his yearnins to make up for what h'is gone back. I got back, and I ain't ashamed to own it. The wolf wot I was speaking of, after eating up mine and the missus's Sunday togs, to say nothing of a green and brass fender and our American clock, ackshurly entered the stable and seized on the pony for rears of rent; and, if it hadn't been for my brother Joe, wots in the coal way, and consequently doing werry tidy in the winter time - but I'm diwergin' from my subjeck.

"I'm in the fish way myself, consequently Wednesday suits me to a tick. Wednesday ain't a fish day among our customers. It's a rum thing, but poor people don't take kind to fish - not naturally kind, I mean. They'll hold off from it as long as they've got ha'pence enough to get a scrag of meat at the butcher's; and so, d'ye see, as the Saturday night's wages generally hold out till the middle of the week, it ain't no use inwestin' heavy in fish, till Thursday or Friday, when my customers is down to the knuckle-bone, as the wulgar saying is; so, as I said before, Wednesday couldn't suit me better if it was made to measure for me. Not that I should stop away from Barnet, even if the day didn't fit me. No fear. It's only once a year, and even Guy Foxes have their day once per annum. It's uniwersal, from the New Cut, Lambeth, to Dog-row, at Mile-end. It would be good for weak eyesight to find a stall or a barrer that day from one end of Brick-lane to the other.

"There's two ways of going to Barnet, like there's two ways of doing everything. You may take the rail for it - but that's not my way. I ain't a proud cove, but, cert'ny I *should* look down on any one that I knowed as was capable of keeping up the anniwersary in that shabby kind o' way. Mind you, I don't hold with extrawagance; and though it was all right havin' them four new spokes put in the barrer wheels (Joe Simmon s wife being a hounce or two heavier than a hinfant, and my old gal rapidly growin' cut o' that silf-like figger she had when we was courtin'), there's no denying, as it was werry much like pomp and wanity, havin' the wehicle painted yeller with a picking out of green. But her mind was bent on havin' every thing to match her shawl and bonnet, and, as she tenderly remarked, bless her hard workin' 'art: 'We don't kill a pig every day, Samuel:' wich so touched me that I went the whole annimal, and had it warnished as well.

"It was a neat turn-out, cheerful without being owdacious. The sun was shinin' brightly, and we wasn't squeezed for room, being only four in a barrer, which is better than being so crowded that you are obliged to sit on the prowisions, to say nothing of the temtation to get the two-gallon bottle empty, and chucked out as an encumbrants before you're five miles on the road. It's a longish trot between Mile-end and Barnet, but long before we got to Whitechapel

Church there was wisible signs of the horsspishus occasion. There was carts and wans, and regler four-horse drags, loaded and looking as 'ansome as many a time I've seen my barrer when there was a glut of collyflowers, and they was goin' reasonable, and all in the highest of spirits, as might be seen from the way in which many of em had already got their paper garlands round their hats, and horsehair mustaches and jolly noses. I likes to see it. There is a lively sarsiness about it that aggrawates the perlice without givin' 'em sufficient excuse to be down on yer, which is very comfortin' to be'old; but I beg it to be understood that it isn't what in superior langwidge might be called 'nobby.' It's a hindication of a mind not much above pennywinkles or creases, or any of them lower branches of the purfession what's hawked in baskets. No reglar pony-and-barrer coster would behave as sich. Him and his missus, if he's got one, should on such an ewentful occasion be a pair of patterns and examples to the uncultiwated, and let em see, without cheeking 'em or appearing to be toffs, what is the spectable thing to do. It's better to have a drain at home, if it's only half a pint a rum amongst four, before you start, and then you can blow your bacca and enjoy the lively chaff you meets with in the crowded parts of the roads like a gen'leman. We only made five halts on the road; the last one being more for the sake of getting a bit of raw steak for Simmon's eye that he got in the heat of argyment with a cat's meat man wot threw a turnip at his missus, just the t'other side of Whetstone.

"We didn't drive right into Barnet, being otherwise purvided. We drew up under a hedge a yard or two out of the traffik, and got out the meat-pie and that, with the new dawg's-paw horsecloth for a table-cover, and picknicked in a manner that I wager made 'em wot stood round a'most bust with envy. A werry comfortable hour that was. We was not alone under the hedge. There was several other parties wot I had met at the markets wet had brought their wittles; and, bein' friendly and open to deal, it was a chunk o' pie for a bit o' cold pickled pork, or a cold baked tater for a cold biled 'un, or a ingun for the worth of it in cheese, as fair and friendly as possible. After which, and the rest of the' beer wot was in the bottle, we was in a proper frame of mind to get towards the fair. There was only one thing that clouded my cup of 'appiness goin' along, and that was the sight of them Manor of Barnet fellows outside of the Queen's Arms. Three of 'em - two with p'liceman's staffs, and one - him wot had the toes peepin' out of his boots and was smoking a dirty short pipe - that carried a sort of little barber's pole, striped blue arid white, with 'M. B.' lettered on it. I knew 'em again direckly, having had wot was werry nigh a row with 'em on the Monday, when I bought the werry pony wot I'm driving now, and was bringin' him home. It was all about payin' a penny toll, and all who had bought a horse had to pay it, and everybody kicked at it. No pike - no giving you a ticket - no nothing; only him with the dirty short pipe that looked like a drover out o' work, and the other two chaps in their shirts and trousers, and with their sleeves tucked up and flourishing them staffs as though goadin' of you not to pay the penny, so that they might get an excuse to have a shy at you. I don't object to tolls when it's all reglar and there's a pike to show for it - and I spose it *is* reglar since the perlice allowed it; but swelp me goodness! if I was a lord of a manor, and I wanted to screw a penny out of a poor cove wot couldn't afford it, I would contrive to put by enough out of the profits to alter the cut of them toll takers."

"I never approaches Barnet Fair but I feels proud of the purfession I belongs to, and grateful to my country. I believe it does me a jolly lot a good, and kinder clears off the bile that twelvemonths at wariance with the perlice nataraly afflicts a cove with. I ain't always proud of my country and them as governs it, and anybody that has been fined twice - once five, and once fifteen shillings - because his honest barrer was called a 'obstruckshon,' can enter into my feelings; but when I comes in sight of Barnet Fair I feels my werry neckhankesher growing too tight for me, because of what Simmons ses is the emoshuns swellin' in my throat. Here, I ses to myself, is a trybute to the wirtue of the British Costermonger! Bartlemy had its fair, but it was 'bolished. Camberwell had its fair, and quite a 'spectable class went to it, mecanicks and their families, but somehow it grew ugly, and it was 'bolished too. Then there was Greenwich. Gents went to Greenwich with tall hats and collars and cuffs, and females dressed in the wery height of fashion, but Greenwich was 'bolished. The townpeople complained of the orful goings on, and the perlice was down on it. But *our* fair, the fair wot's kep going by the London costermonger, is as flourishing and rosy as ever. A proper sort of fair Barnet is. It's snug, in the fust place. It's so down in a hole that you might clap a lid on the top, of it and shut it all in. Then there's nothing stuck up about it; no doing the grand and playing the lady and gen'leman; a good solid cut-and-come-agin kind o' fair; a pleasant mixshure of the comforts of home with the amoosements one has got a happytite for. It's a hexcellent place for grub. You can buy a cooked bloater all hot and a chunk of bread for threeha'pence, or you can go as high as eighteen-pence for a feed off the joints and unlimited wedgatables. We had had our peck; but really, comin' on a booth where there was werry tidy-sized thumb-bits of bread and bacon and a pint o' beer for fourpence, it looked so nice that Simmons and I went in and had a snack just out of hadmiration of the thing, while Mrs. S. and my old lady took a turn on a roundabout which was worked by steam, and played a organ.

"It isn't a fancy fair by a long ways, that wot is here at Barnet. It's all as real as two 'apence for a penny. It wouldn't do if it was. The eddication and sperience of the costermonger is of a kind that spiles the play of his 'magination. Therefore there's no gipsies telling fortunes. Ha, ha! Just picter my old girl being got over by an old guy with a pack o cards, and chisselled out of sixpence, to have her 'tivity cast. She'd find summat harder than a 'tivity cast at *her* if she was to try it on. Just imagine one of that old lady's male relations trying the three-card trick, or prick in the garter, or the one little pea' on one of us! They know better than to try it. They may hang about the outside of the fair and try to catch a Johnny Wopstraw or two, but they never try it on the lads of our school. You might walk through and through the fair and not meet one of the gang in question if you looked for him. There's hardly one of us lads that couldn't give any on 'em a chalk and then beat 'em at the game he was sweetest on. It is that as keeps Barnet Fair so wirtuous. I did see one lark of this pattern. One of them sleight-of-hand young men that work the purse and money trick. He was up on his stool with that pouch wot's got such a awful lot of 'arf-crowns in by his side, and his cuffs tucked up and his decoy in his hand, patterin away like a steam-engine, and trying to conwince them wot was listenin' how werry foolish they was not to grab at the chance of buyin' seven-and-sixpence, placed in the purse before their werry eyes, for the ridiculous sum of 'arf-a-crown. Simmons and I stood by, and Simmons jogs me, and ses, 'Blest if there isn't Long Ned Spankers' boy a listenin' with his mouth open,' and the willain will nail him sure as eggs ain't chickens!' And sure enuf there was young Ned - he's as long a'most as his father, and stiffish built for a lad of seventeen, but a awful fool at business. I was sorry to see it, for his father's sake, but I ses, 'Let him bite if he's green enough; p'raps it'll do him good.' So the young man with the purse kept the game up; of course he had spotted young Ned, and talked at him till he'd almost talked him off the little 'ead he's got. At last the lad pulled out his 'arfcrown. 'Look here,' ses he, 'let's have no mistake about this ere; the seven and sixpence *is* in the purse?' 'Listen for yourself; can't you hear it jinkin'?' ses the chap. 'It ain't a swindle. Mind yer, it won't be good for you if it's a swindle,' said young Ned. 'It won't be good for *you*, you mean,' grinned the young man; 'catch hold.' And young Ned did catch hold, and parted with his two-and-six. When he opened the purse there was three pennypieces in it. 'Where's the three 'arfcrowns? he asked savage-like. 'Ah, that's the trick,' grinned the young man with the purses. 'Oh, is that the end of it?' asked young Ned, with a twist of his wisage that made me hope some good of him. 'That's the end of it - unless you'd like to have another shy,' returned the aggrawatin' fellow, laughing with the rest. It's the neatest trick you ever see, I'll wager.' 'I'll back the one I'm goin' to show you for twice the money,' said the young barrer-man; and makin' a spring at the chap on a stool, he had him down and with his head in chancery afore you could count six. 'The sitiwation was embarrassin,' as they say in the newspapers; and swearin' that it was all a joke, the purse dodger gave him back the 'arfcrown and sneaked off rapid. I hope his father won't read this, for on condition of young Ned spendin' a shillin' in a couple of pots of beer we promised not to tell him.

"Then there's the shows. Barnet Fair sets a example in that line sich as other places of public amoosement might get a wrinkle out of. Women's tastes ain't like men's; their ideas of enjoyment being naterally more delikit. At Barnet they manages to suit all parties, and gives em a opportunity of pairin' off so as to suit their tastes. For instance, while the missus went to the wax work, me and Simmons was in the next tent having a game at skittles; then we took a turn in Sluggers' sparrin'-booth, while the ladies passed a pleasant 'arf-hour in the Star Ghost carawan and got their blood froze for a penny, which, considerin the 'eat of the afternoon, wasn't dear. After that, by way of restorin' their sperits, they went to see the four-legged duck and the big-headed child and the livin' skellington; Bill and me meanwhile enjoyin' ourselves in a wan where there was a Kaffir eating live rats; by which time we was ready for tea and a relish with it.

"After that, findin' ourselves in cheerful company, and a fiddle comin' in, we had a song and then a dance. Lots of dancers, and werry glad we were that beer was sold on the premises, and I believe we should have kep' it up later than we did, had not that confounded cat's-meat man that Simmons fell foul of in the morning poked his ugly 'ead in, on which Simmons, who had got the liquor aboard, wanted satisfackshun for his black eye. That was only fair; so while the women found their shawls they settled their little difference outside, after which we ordered the barrer, and by means of steddy drivin' and stoppin' to breathe the pony at every place that had a sign-board hanging out, we managed to get back to Mile-end just in time to get a partin' drain before the houses closed."

SUNDAY outings are, by a large number of highly respectable and worthy people, denounced as having a direct tendency to demoralise the nation and encourage all that is low, vulgar, and objectionable. The sight of the great placards of the railway companies, which at the spring time of year so plentifully bedeck the walls, announcing that on next and every succeeding Sunday excursion trains will run at the rate of something like a farthing a mile, while they are so welcome to thousands who have been anxiously waiting for the cheap season to commence, are, to the more soberly disposed, lamentable indications of the increasing disregard of the people for the sanctity of the seventh day, which in their opinion should be a day of rest and religious exercise for everybody.

It is their honest belief that it would be better if every railway engine-driver, guard, porter, and signalman were released from duty on the Sabbath day, and that the pleasure vans that at present convey light-hearted folk to Hampton or High Beech should be compelled to stay at home, and that the steamboats on the river, stokerless, all their crews, from the captain to the call boy, having Sunday's rest secured to them, should float idly at their moorings from Saturday night until Monday morning. That those who urge this reformed state of things do so out of their sincere conviction that it would be for the general good, there can be no doubt; but there is also no gainsaying the fact that so sweeping a change would occasion consternation and dismay, if not rebellion, amongst the thousands who cannot be made to understand that it is impossible for them to have respect for Sunday because they use it for their recreation.

Sunday outing is a treasured institution amongst the working classes, and one that is in favour particularly with the female portion of the community. Not the gay and giddy of the sex, but the staid and steady hard-working mothers and sisters who really have no other opportunity for the enjoyment of a few hours in the green fields or a blow on the river. It is the last-mentioned who more strenuously, because with most cause, would oppose any interference with their Sunday. Their husbands have their evenings' leisure, their half-day on Saturday, and their amusements at the clubs and lodge houses, but it is only on Sunday afternoon that the working man's wife may, in accordance with her sense of duty to her family, snatch a few hours of relaxation, and no one can deny that she is justly entitled to it. It is not to excursionising on an extensive scale that the worthy soul in question is chiefly addicted.

To go to Brighton and back in a day entails an amount of real hard work that, to her thinking, outweighs the advantages. What she and her steady husband most admire is a quiet jog-trot jaunt by water or otherwise, just a few miles away from home, where a change of air and a change of scene may be quietly enjoyed at so small an expense that the trip may be repeated half-a-dozen times, say, in the course of the summer, without any severe strain on the domestic exchequer.

To Kew Gardens by steamboat is a favourite outing on a Sunday with these good people. From London Bridge, Blackfriars, Westminster, or Chelsea, the boats start at convenient times, and at fares that enable them to compete with the railways. But it is not a matter of a penny or so that would divert the patronage of this kind of excursionist from the river to the rail.

It must be borne in mind that the Thames is not as it used to be. There are now but few filthy and unsightly mudbanks to offend the organs of sight and smell; and nowadays steamboat accommodation - even for the very humblest penny customers - is such as might satisfy the most fastidious. To be sure, the Sunday steamboats to Kew are crowded, and it is not always that the luxury of a seat on deck may be depended on throughout the whole journey, but that rather adds than otherwise to the pleasure.

If the steady-going excursionist of the class in question found the steamboat but scantily freighted, he would be at once troubled with qualms lest he were guilty of the extravagance of indulging in a treat that but few of his class thought fit to venture on, and he would have gloomy forebodings probably of his good lady and himself having Kew Gardens all to themselves.

There is no fear on this score, however. From the time - and it is not so many years since - that the magnificent gardens at Kew were thrown open to the public, the privilege has been thoroughly appreciated, and fortunately by exactly that class of persons whom the authorities make most welcome. The regulations designed for the guidance and control of visitors, conspicuously posted at the various entrances to the gardens and pleasure grounds, are as liberal as could be desired; indeed, one or two of the clauses are vested in a good-natured vagueness of language which must cause the gatekeepers, who are the only responsible interpreters, some amount of difficulty.

It is well-known to be a characteristic of the London holiday-seeker of a certain class to be jealously on the alert against the machinations of publicans and other refreshment vendors who spread their nets for the unwary in the immediate neighbourhood of places of popular resort. It is all very well for the youthful and thoughtless - for free-handed sweethearting young Jacks who would scorn to be particular to a crown or so in matters that affect the pleasure and comfort of the dear little Jills, their companions, and who, on their part, have no desire to thwart such generous sentiments - it is all very well for them to patronise the half-crown ordinary at the Crown and Cushion, and even after that to accept a card from the insinuating young lady who "touts" at the flowery gate of Honeysuckle Cottage, and discourses of tea with watercresses and unlimited shrimps for the small charge of eightpence a head; but it does not do for steady-going Darby and Joan, who have outlived such heydey vanities, and who, while they like as well as anyone to take their pleasure, would have no relish for it at all were it not thoroughly well-seasoned with the salt of economy.

It is for Darby and Joan, worthy souls, who come to Kew Gardens on a Sunday, accompanied by their small flock of heavy-feeding youngsters, that "Clause E" of the "Regulations was specially invented. It says: "Packages and parcels and bags and baskets above a certain size are not allowed to be carried within the grounds." It is the indefinite phrase "of a certain size" that is the occasion of expostulation and argument, more or less mild, between the gatekeeper and his customers. A market-basket of the ordinary domestic pattern and capacity would, for example, be regarded by the officer as being inadmissible, nor would he feel at liberty to "pass" a half-gallon stone bottle artfully concealed by the creole skirt of baby's innocent robe, or a bundle handkerchief extended to its extreme dimensions with crusty loaves and boiled beef in the "round" and the inevitable knuckle of ham. It would be altogether against the rules to admit such wholesale victualling; but the keeper is too polite to turn away such visitors absolutely. He blandly, though firmly, suggests that the questionable luggage shall be left in his care at the lodge while its owners take their pleasure by making a tour of the gardens.

It is not with such as these, however, that any difficulty arises. The idea of abandoning at the very outset the mainstay of the day's enjoyment is not for a moment to be entertained, and the disgusted bearers of the bottles and baskets seek more congenial quarters in the village of Kew, returning in the afternoon eligible for admission, and casting, as they enter the guarded portals, glances of defiance at the beadle, whose objections to the provender under its amended form of stowage are no longer tenable. But the gate-keepers are by no means tyrannical, and make no objection to a bag large enough to contain all that moderation can require.

The people are left to find out themselves the countless marvels and beauties which the Pleasure and Botanical Gardens at Kew offer to the sensible seeker. If the charge for admission was "one shilling," and every day there appeared in the columns of the daily newspapers glowing advertisements of the various attractions; if prodigious posters on the walls told of whole acres of splendid rhododendrons all in the glory of full bloom - of great plantations of the rarest azaleas, literally blazing like burning bushes, so dazzling is their wealth of crimson and amber and scarlet flowers, and all most delicately scented - of the great palm-house, with its matchless exotic treasures - of the tank where the marvellous Victoria Regia may be seen, of the water-lily house, and the Cape-house, and the tropical stove, and the house where there is on view such a display of orchids as no other gardens in Europe can boast of; if all these, which are but a few of the treasures of Kew, were paraded and announced with as much pains as are taken to make known the glories of the People's Tea Gardens at Peckham-rye, the great pleasure-grounds at Kew would be crowded Sunday as well as weekday. Not that there would be any great advantage in this. As the matter is now managed, those who find their way thither may make sure of enjoyment unalloyed; it would not be so if the authorities were to be at the pains of parading the attractions of Kew. If they did so, it would be a pity; for that plague of parks and of all public places where decent folks seek recreation - the "rough" - would surely respond to the invitation, and come, as is his wont, with his roaring, and his ravaging, and his rags, and his insolent defiance of all law and all order. There are no "roughs" at Kew Park at present. There is no printed law against their passing through the gates, but there seems to be something in their severe respectability, in the chaste gravelled way by which they are approached, and in the emblems of royalty with which they are conspicuously emblazoned, that is sufficient to warn off the tag-rag of humanity. Only respectable people - which, of course, includes the great body of working men and their families - visit the costly gardens, and that only respectable people are expected is proved by the singularly small staff of servants provided to take care of so great an amount of valuable property. There can be no question that half-a-dozen of the terrible gentry above hinted at, actuated by their usual inclination for wanton mischief might unperceived, and in an hour or so, do more damage in some of the choice places at Kew than many hundreds of pounds could repair. There are flowers that grow in profusion in solitary and unguarded nooks, to which the public have unchecked access, every bloom of which is worth, say, a shilling, and half-a-dozen of which might be snapped off by larcenous fingers and concealed in a hat or parasol, and very probably brought safely away; but it is gratifying to be able to state that anything so disgraceful is rarely attempted.

"We, of course, should find it out afterwards, if not at the time," said a garden-keeper to me, "the plants are too carefully watched by the gardeners for there to be any mistake on that score, and it is a fact that, to the best of our knowledge, we do not lose a dozen blooms in a week."

"Of course, there is no merit in abstaining from flower-stealing, any more than in refusing to yield to the temptation offered by unprotected goods displayed at a draper's door; but as regards the security of the flowers at Kew, it means something more than an observance of common honesty by the people; it shows that every adult visitor has a personal care for the safety of the floral treasures. Every day of the week, including Sunday, are hundreds of children admitted to the gardens, including boys and girls of just that lawless age when they can no more resist flower-picking than dipping their ravenous fingers in an unwatched pot of jam. If the grown persons did not look after these idle hands, for which, according to Dr. Watts, it is the especial pleasure of Satan to find employment, it would go hard, indeed, with the azaleas.

And it is not to any very heavy penalty threatened in the Garden Regulations that this vigilance on the part of parents and guardians is due. All that the printed rule applying to the safety of the flowers has to say on the matter is to the mild effect that, "It is hoped that visitors will abstain from touching the plants and flowers. A contrary practice can only lead to the suspicion, perhaps unfounded, that their object is to abstract a flower or cutting, which, when detected, must be followed by expulsion."

My observations on the particular Sunday when I was there did not warrant me in asserting that this polite suggestion was observed in its strict integrity. The visitors *did* touch the flowers when they came on a handsome lot of them, and opportunity favoured the infringement. They touched them - holding them tenderly by the stems, mind - and took ecstatic sniffs at them; and in the case of one old lady, who carried a reticule of ample capacity, and who stood for fully half a minute drinking in the intoxicating scents, with her venerable nose fairly hidden among the flowering petals, I confess that I felt some alarm. She was an old woman, meanly dressed, and of that complexion which invariably distinguishes the dweller in close and pent-up places, where flowers refuse to grow - common flowers, such as the balsam and the wall-flower, let alone a blazing glory like that she was now fondling over. It was very rash of her to get so close to it. She should have been content to admire it at a distance, instead of deliberately walking into such a hotbed of temptation.

"Ah!" she exclaimed to her old husband, who was with her, and who evidently trembled for her honesty even more than I did; "lovely ain't a good enough word for it. I've smelt roses before now, Joe, but never like this. This must be the otter of 'em, I'm sure."

"Yes, and you'll find that you'll get it hotter than you expects if they ketches you a-clutching hold of it like that," returned the grimly jocular Joseph. "You come away, that's a good old gal."

But I was afraid that the good old gal evinced symptoms of being anything but good. She took another powerful sniff, and uttered a prolonged "A-a-h!"-and then I heard a sharp click, and lo! the mouth of her reticule yawned wide open. Wishing her no harm, but all the good in the world, I should have felt rejoiced if at that moment a bee had started out of the flower and stung her to a sense of her perilous position. Should I warn her? Should I utter some admonitory sound from the sheltered bank on which I was reclining and all the time watching her? But I might have spared myself my alarms. In unclasping her bag, the worthy old soul had no more intention of committing a robbery than I had. She merely withdrew her pocket-handkerchief and, clapping it to her nose, exclaimed, "I'll keep the beautiful smell of it in as long as I can, anyhow," and so passed on innocently with her old man.

the end

Printed in Great Britain
by Amazon